I0748581

FRACTURE

RD BAKER

Cover design by RD Baker

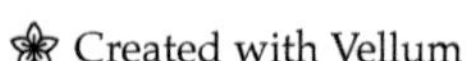
Created with Vellum

ALSO BY RD BAKER

Afflicted

The Lost Heirs Series

A Realm of Dark Fury

The Shadow Drawn Series

The Shadow and The Draw

The Earth and The Flame

Publishing as Rihannon Baker

No One Else Ever

Clearwater

Endlessly

CONTENT NOTE

Fracture is a dark taboo romance that contains themes and situations some readers may find distressing. These include:

Explicit sexual situations

Graphic violence, torture, mutilation and murder

Taboo relationship between step-siblings

Explicit descriptions of childhood sexual abuse involving a parent (historical)

Rape, molestation and sexual assault (not involving the MMCs)

Child abuse (historical)

Themes of incarceration

Loss of loved ones

Parental neglect and abandonment

Alcoholism

Drugging and sedation, involuntary (not involving the MMCs)

Homophobic slurs, and reclamation of those slurs by the victims

Mild drug use (cigarettes and marijuana)

Revenge Porn (not involving the MMCs)

Abortion (historical, off-page)

Discussions of PTSD, trauma and panic attacks

Discussions of poor mental health and therapy
Mention of stroke and resulting death
Mentions of car and motorcycle crashes

Please be kind to yourself, and put your mental health first, always x

For the Survivors

You are loved
You are valued
You are important

I see you

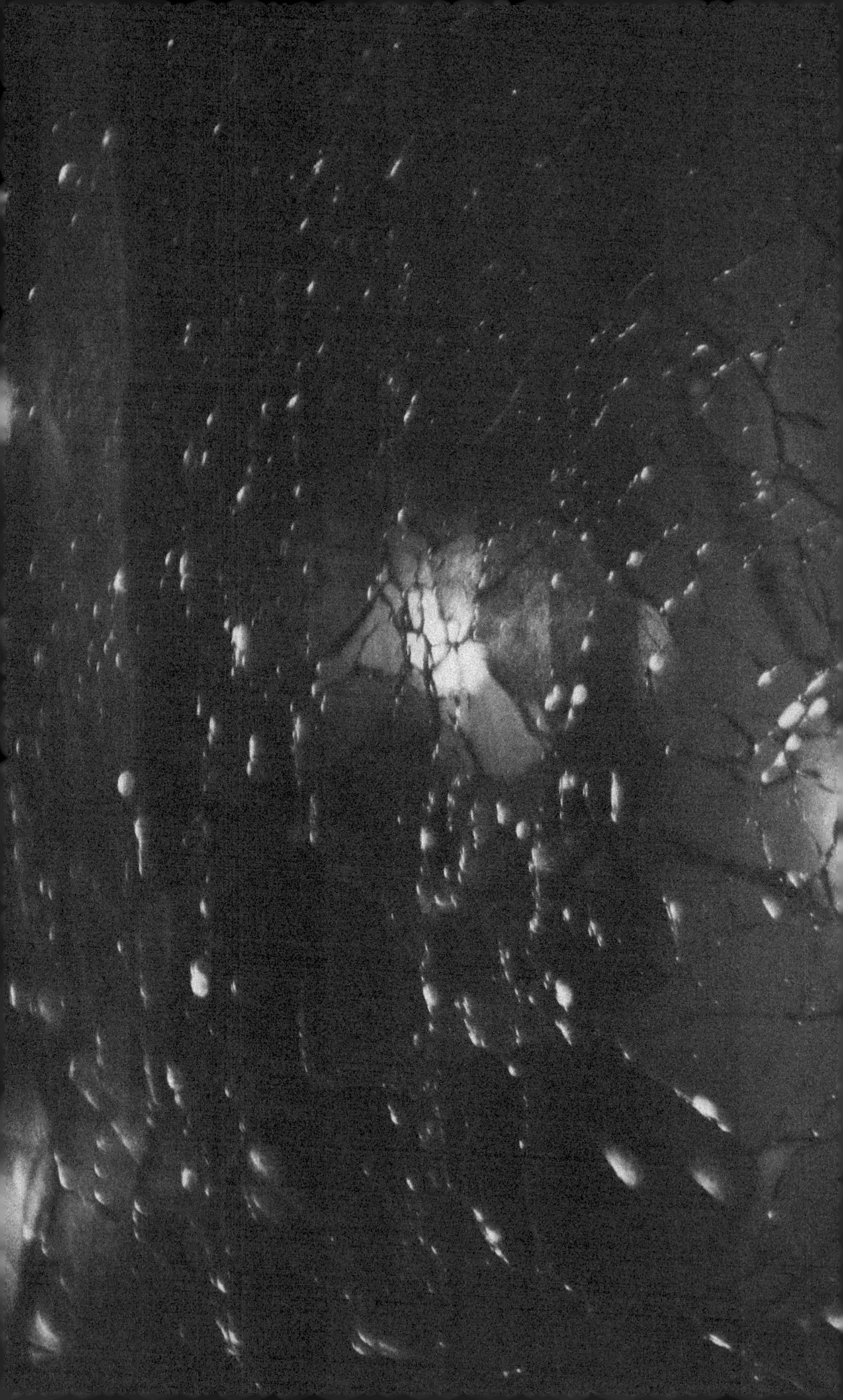

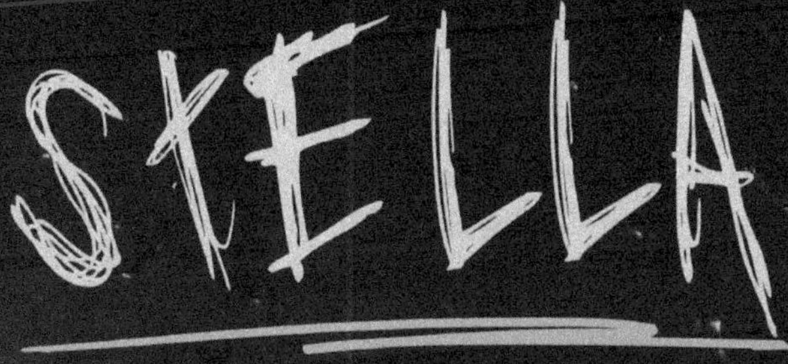

CHAPTER ONE

STOP PULLING *on your damn dress. The guards are gonna think you're doped up or something.*

With a deep breath, I clasp my arms across my chest to stop my restless fingers tugging at the waistline of my dress. The dress I spent three damn hours picking out. I try not to think about the state of my bedroom right now, clothes strewn across the floor and my bed, like the ladies' department at Nordstrom's after being torn apart on Black Friday.

Why did it even matter what I wore today?

I don't even know. But every single outfit I put on was wrong. One dress was too short, another made me look like a Mormon preschool teacher (that one ended up in the Goodwill bag). I wanted to look the part - what part that was, I still don't know.

I was trying to prove something, that I was sophisticated and trustworthy. I'm a lawyer after all, the responsible little sister who's letting her stepbrother and his best friend stay with her while they get their lives together.

But the thought of Levi and Dylan seeing me in my silk blouses and pencil skirts after 10 years apart made my cheeks burn. I wanted them to see me, *me*, not a lawyer, not jumped-up trust fund baby Stella Langford.

I just wanted them to see me.

So the silk blouses ended up on the floor with the rest of my wardrobe. I'm standing outside the prison on Governor's Day in a black and white knee-length dress and ballerina flats, my hair loose, because Dylan always liked it that way.

I hate that I hope he still does.

I pace back and forth, past all the other groups of anxious folks, waiting for their loved ones to pass through those gates. It's a mass release, celebrating 15 years since the prison opened. It's been all over the news, the governor crowing about how these men are all rehabilitated now thanks to the prison's stellar programs. Even the two murderers who killed Harold Langford are being released.

And moving in with his daughter.

My eyes dart to the perimeter of the parking lot. I'm sure a van followed me here, and I wait for the reporters to jump out and start taking pictures. It's been several years since they stopped hounding me, but I have a sick feeling they'll be here just to get an exclusive scoop on this day.

I release one of my trembling hands to run it through my hair. That's why I'm nervous. It's the reporters, not the fact that I'm about to see these two men again after 10 years. 10 years of nothing but letters that were never answered.

But it's still us, right?

My stomach drops as I consider that they'll be disappointed, and mad. That they'll demand to know why I never visited, why my letters were so bland, telling them nothing about me or my life, nothing meaningful at least. Maybe they'll lay their eyes on me and hate what I've become. They'll see my pretty little Cape Cod house on the good side of Bellford Heights, and laugh at me.

But their bikes are in the garage. I made sure to take those from the old house when I sold it. They're in there with a pool table and their pock-marked dartboard, and the bar I had built especially for them. I stocked it with beer and whiskey, all in preparation for them. For us to start our lives again.

Surely they're going to be happy about that, right?

I give myself a mental slap. *Goddammit, Stella. You're a grown-ass woman and you're acting like you want to impress two little teenage boys. Get a fucking grip.*

There's movement behind the gates, and the guards start shouting commands. The families around me all seem as tense as I am, watching and waiting for the men we love to emerge from behind that endless razor wire.

My throat goes dry as I wonder if I'll even recognize them? Will Levi still have that floppy blond hair I used to tease him about? Will Dylan still have that lip ring that was warm against my mouth whenever he kissed me? They were barely men when I last saw them, all those years ago, that last moment when their eyes met mine in the courtroom.

And now…?

The gate rolls back, and a woman in a tight red dress and sky-high heels races past me and into the arms of the first man to walk through. He scoops her up and she wraps her arms around his neck, kissing him like no one else is around. *Good for them.*

A young man walks out hesitantly, he can't be older than 22. He pushes his dark curls from his forehead, his eyes darting around at the people gathered outside the gate, when suddenly someone screams, and a group of people rush at him. He bursts into tears as the people encircle him, crying and cradling his face in their hands, all of them caught somewhere between sorrow and joy.

One prisoner after another emerges, and I count them all out, *five, six, nine, fourteen.* Twenty prisoners are being released today.

My throat becomes tight. Shit. Did they rescind their parole? Did I get the date wrong? Maybe not everyone is getting released today? I pull out my phone and check my emails. No, it's definitely today.

Where are they?

My hands begin to tremble again, just as two figures emerge from the gray building and start walking towards the gate. Both are dressed in dark wash jeans and tight black t-shirts, duffle bags slung over their shoulders.

One has messy dark blond hair, both arms and hands heavily tattooed. The other has a close-shaved head, shadowed with dark stubble, his brown skin glowing in the warm summer sun. They stop at the guards' house, shaking the guard's hands and laughing heartily, before turning back to the gate and walking towards me.

My heart stops.

It's them.

I'm frozen to the spot, just watching them approach. Should I walk towards them? Should I run into Dylan's arms like the lady in the red dress did with her man? Do I scream and throw my arms around Levi, caught between sorrow and joy just like that family was? That would be weird, right? If someone sees me tearfully run into the arms of the two men who murdered my father, people will think there's something wrong with me, even more than they already do.

My heart restarts, and sinks into my feet. No, these two aren't my men.

It's not like that. Not anymore.

Dylan's full lips - now minus the piercing - quirk into a smile as his dark eyes lock on me. He's so much taller than I remember. He always towered over me, but now he's a sheer wall of muscle. Tattoos snake up his neck, emerging from the neckline of the black t-shirt that's straining around his body. When he raises a hand to his head, saluting me, I see his hands are tattooed as well.

My gaze shifts to Levi, and my heart does a weird flip. He looks so different. The boy who used to argue with me over bathroom rights, who let me borrow his car to sneak out and meet up with my friends, is now a broad-shouldered man. His ice-blue eyes are startling in his tanned face, the black t-shirt he's wearing straining across his chest, and while he's shorter than Dylan, he's no less intimidating when he's standing right in front of me.

Oh god, they're right in front of me and I'm just staring at them.

"Stella Langford," Dylan says, shifting the bag on his shoulder. "You look beautiful."

I don't say anything. I just stare at them, my gaze shifting from one to the other, hoping and praying this is real. They exchange a glance, and when Levi looks back at me, his lips raise into a smile. He steps forward, and slips his arm around my shoulders.

"Hey, baby girl," he murmurs against my temple, pressing a kiss to my hair.

Something inside me cracks a little as I lean against him. I put my hands on his chest, tears burning my eyes as I let out a small laugh.

"Hey."

Levi pulls back and notches his fingers under my chin, angling my head so I'm looking up at him. "No tears now. We're here."

"You smell good," I blurt out, and Levi laughs, making him look even more beautiful.

"Well, lucky for us it's a good prison. They even let us shower."

I sniffle and brush my tears away from my face before turning to Dylan.

His big dark eyes burn into mine, and he drops the bag from his shoulder. He moves towards me, then hesitates, looking around us.

"I'm not going to get gunned down by a husband if I hug you right now, am I?"

I shake my head emphatically. "No, it's just - it's just me."

His expression is totally unreadable as he closes the distance between us and crushes me against his chest.

"Fuck," he mutters, burying his face in the crook of my neck. "I missed you."

I wish now I'd run across the yard towards them, like the woman in the red dress, and launched myself into the arms of this man. It still feels like him, like Dylan, *my* Dylan. I let out a breath that carries 10 years of sadness and longing with it, and clench my eyes shut, fresh tears running down my face.

"I can't believe you're here." I reach out for Levi and pull him against us, so we're all touching, all breathing together, and for the first time in 10 years, something like peace washes through me.

But it doesn't last. Calls of *Stella! Stella!* shatter the moment instantly, echoing across the parking lot as cameras start to flash.

Dylan growls out a curse, leaning down to scoop up his bag before shielding me with his body. "Which car is yours, sweetheart?"

I raise a shaky hand and point to my shiny black Volvo. "That one."

"Fucking reporters," Levi spits out behind us. "They do this a lot?"

"No. But they knew you were getting out, so…" I trail off, feeling cold despite the hot sun that's beating down on us. That peace I felt mere seconds ago is gone, and replaced with the knowledge that the past will never stop snapping at my heels. Even Dylan's hand on my waist as he guides me back to my car feels wrong.

I was a fool. It can never be what it was, what it was meant to be. Not when the past was right here, staring me in the face, never to leave me alone.

"Hey girl, how're the jailbirds?" Zee's voice is bright and in stark contrast to how I'm feeling right now.

I turn to look out the kitchen window towards the garage. The lights are on, and bass thumps faintly through the evening breeze. "They're good. I think?"

"You think?"

"They've been out in the garage since they got back." I scrunch up my nose. "That's bad, right?"

"Why would it be bad?"

"That they… I don't know." I twirl my hair around my fingers, tapping my foot against the ground. "I keep thinking I should go out there, but maybe they don't want me there? Do you think? Was it wrong to bring them here?"

Zee lets out an exasperated sigh that whispers across the line. "Will you *stop* overthinking things? They're probably trying to just reclaim some space while not stepping on your toes, y'know?"

"Yeah, I guess."

"Stop chewing your lip."

I instantly release my lip from between my anxiously gnawing teeth. "How the fuck do you know these things?"

They laugh lightly, and I can practically hear them flipping their hair. "Girl, I told you, I'm psychic."

"Yeah, or a stalker. Bet you got cameras in my damn kitchen."

"Nah, only in your bedroom."

I huff out a laugh, gazing back out at the garage as the bass stops for a moment, then starts up again with the next song. "You're probably right. They just need time."

"You *all* need time, girl. It's been 10 years, you need to get to know each other again." Zee waits for my response, but when I simply keep staring out the window at the fairy lights dangling in the trees, they sigh heavily. "OK, listen. I want you to order some takeout, and go crash that bachelor pad. They've had their boy time, let them have some family time now."

I cringe a little at the word *family*. "Reporters were at the prison, waiting for us."

Zee's disgusted retch sounds over the line. "Those absolute pigs."

"I can see it now, all over the National Enquirer tomorrow - *Daughter of Murdered Politician Embraces Father's Murderers*."

"Well, no one reads that trash, so don't you worry about that. Sorry, wait, hold on." Zee's muffled voice barks out commands, probably to one of the stylists at the salon they own downtown.

I pivot the phone away from my mouth, taking a few ambling steps across the kitchen to the open back door. I lean in the door frame, taking a deep breath of honeysuckle-scented air as a sliver of moon rises into the sky.

"OK, sorry, I'm back." Zee's harried voice sounds back over the line.

"You're busy, I don't want to keep you."

"I'm sorry, girl, I got a whole crew of bridesmaids in here for trial styles, and this bride needs her own goddamn TV show."

"They have one, it's called Bridezillas," I say with a chuckle.

"Oh, this one needs her *own show*." Zee groans. "If you need me, I can stop by after I close up."

"No, no, it's OK really. We'll do coffee this weekend."

"We sure will. Tell Dylan I said hi. Love you!" They hang up before I can respond, and I take the phone from my ear.

A message from my cousin Lily appears on the screen, but I swipe it away without reading it. I'm not ready to talk about what's happened or what I'm doing with my family yet.

Family. There's that word again.

I roll my shoulders, using the breathing technique my yoga teacher taught me to calm my system, and feel my spine fall into alignment. *It's OK. You're all together. They wanted to be here. Just order some dinner and go on out there, and have a beer with them.*

By the time I've submitted the order and the little orange scooter icon appears on my screen, I've calmed down enough to head across the yard to the garage. Music meets me as I step through the door.

"Hey!" Thankfully my raised voice doesn't crack, and is heard over the music that's almost loud enough to have the floor vibrating. Both men look up from where they're crouched next to their bikes. I hold up my phone and give it a wave, instantly feeling like an idiot. "I ordered dinner!"

Dylan rises to his feet and goes over to the speaker, swiping his finger across the screen to turn the music down. The sudden silence is almost startling, and we all just stare at each other for a moment before I remember why I came in here.

"Sorry to bother you, but I ordered some food." I am feeling totally out of my depth for absolutely no reason.

Dylan smiles warmly, and retrieves a beer from the fridge. "You're not bothering us, sweetheart. This is your house, we're just guests."

"Oh no, come on, this is your house. I want you to be comfortable here." I gesture around the garage. "That's why I did this. For you. Both of you." I swallow hard. "You do like it, right?" I want to slap myself, standing here begging for approval from these two.

Levi grunts from where he's crouched next to his bike, not looking up from the wrench he has jammed into the engine. "You kidding? This place is great." He runs the back of his hand across his forehead. "But I wouldn't expect anything less from you."

My cheeks burn at the praise and my eyes drop to the floor. "Well, thanks."

"Gotta say, I nearly died when I heard you were a lawyer," Dylan says, taking a swig of his beer.

I give him a blank stare. "Why would that shock you?"

He shrugs, putting the beer bottle on the bar and twirling it back and forth between his fingers. "I don't know. Guess everything I know about you now is a shock. You know, since you never told us anything."

"Or came to see us," Levi mutters from the floor, and my head snaps to look over at him.

"I heard that."

Levi rises to his feet, wiping his hands on a rag. "I kind of meant you to."

I try to swallow down any unpleasant words I want to hurl in his direction. I'm determined to be nice Stella tonight, not Overthinking Stella, not Paranoid Stella. But his words leave behind a sting so sharp they make my throat turn sour.

"And where are all my letters, huh?" I put my hands on my hips. "Or did you forget how to write as soon as you were inside?"

"Stella." Dylan approaches me with his hands raised, like I'm a bomb ready to go off. "Come on, things were weird and-"

"Weird?" I laugh cynically. "*Weird,* Dylan? Weird doesn't even begin to fucking cover it. That still doesn't explain why neither of you ever once replied to a single letter of mine until it came to you through my fucking *lawyer*."

"We needed a place to stay," Levi interjects, crossing his tattooed arms over his chest.

"So, that's all I am to you, huh? A place to crash?" I stalk towards him so we're almost chest to chest. "That's it? After all your fucking 'oh baby girl' this and 'don't cry' that?"

"Hey, I'm happy to see you, but-"

"But *what*?" I shove him in the shoulder with my open palm. "But what, huh?"

He leans down, his eyes narrowing. "But I guess I'm not surprised to see that you fell into line."

My mouth gapes, and I suppress the urge to slap him. "I fell into line?"

"Sure you did, look at you. Pretty little Stella Langford. Perfect as ever, doing exactly what everyone ever expected of her."

Dylan is beside us, looking back and forth between us. "Hey, come on now, it's been a crazy day for everyone. Let's not ruin it with fighting."

Levi laughs out loud, and turns to him. "Don't you even pretend you're here for anything more than a piece of ass."

Dylan's jaw ticks, and he puts his hands against his hips. "That was fucking uncalled for, man."

"Oh, but is it true?" I round on Dylan, and hurt flashes through his eyes. "Because the first thing you asked about is a husband."

He tries to move closer to me, and I take a step back, which just has more pain etching across his face.

"Sweetheart, listen to me-"

"Food delivery!" A cheerful voice rings across the garage, and a young woman stands at the door with two paper bags in her hands. "How y'all doing tonight?"

The three of us must be looking at her with enough rage and tension to make her very uncomfortable, because the smile wavers and she eyes us nervously.

"I have the right house, don't I? It said 1247, just let me-" She anxiously looks down at the bag, and I quickly paste a smile on my face and hurry across the room.

"Yes of course you do, this is the house, thank you so much." I fish the fifty dollar bill out of my pocket and hand it over, taking the bags from her. "You have a good night. Be safe!"

The poor woman hurries down the drive, away from the house, and I turn back to face the two men in my garage. The two men I was so happy to see this morning, and who I now don't even recognize. It all just changed in an instant.

"I got us dinner." I swallow hard, biting back tears.

Dylan takes a few steps towards me, but before he reaches me, I drop the bags and spin on my heel, hurrying back into the house alone.

CHAPTER TWO

I HAVE A THING FOR NAILS, and hands. When a woman has real pretty hands, and her nails are all done, it just fucking does something to me. The thought of those nails scratching down my back, leaving behind long, red marks in my skin…

That, and I haven't seen a woman all done up and looking good in years, especially not one as beautiful as Stella Langford. And right now, Stella is tapping her pretty white-tipped nails against her wooden countertops, her hair hanging loose around her shoulders.

God fucking *dammit*, she looks good.

She gathers her honey-colored hair up in a hand, twirling it and tossing it over her shoulder, turning slightly so I can see her profile. Her white tank top barely covers her stomach, and I can't think too much about the fact she's not wearing a bra, because her breasts are fucking perfect.

Her tiny pink and white striped shorts barely cover her ass, sitting low on her hips. She's definitely not a girl anymore. When I left her, she was still a teenager, but now she's a woman with a figure to fucking die for.

Shit.

I made a promise to myself when her offer came to us via our lawyer, when Stella said that we could stay with her when we got out - I wouldn't make any assumptions. I wouldn't be possessive and weird about it all, because we couldn't just pick up where we'd left off. For all I knew she was married, or at least had a boyfriend. The thought kept me up at night, but I didn't have a right to her, not anymore. I had to leave all of that behind, because I didn't know a thing about the woman she was now.

But as I watch her from the shadows, pacing her kitchen because she can't sleep, I know I was an idiot. There's never been anyone else for me. She's so beautiful it fucking hurts to look at her, just the same as the first time I ever saw her.

She bends down to put some glasses in the dishwasher, her tiny shorts riding up to reveal the curve of her round ass, and I have to stifle a breath. But my hand flexes on the door frame, and she hears the whisper of my fingers against the wood. She jerks upright and snaps her head over her shoulder to find me standing there, watching her. Like a fucking creep.

"Can't sleep?" Her tone is cold, and after what happened in the garage a few hours ago, I can't blame her. I should have defended her, I should have sent Levi packing for how he spoke to her. But that throws up a whole new complicated layer of emotion, my chest tensing, and I have to push that away and focus on Stella instead.

I step into the kitchen, illuminated only by the light over the range and a candle Stella lit by the window.

"Nah, the bed's too comfortable."

"You can always throw a blanket on the floor." She gives me a flash of a cynical smile, before her face drops back into the classic Langford Mask, tossing her hair again and turning her back to me. "Dogs like sleeping on the floor, right?"

I can't help but laugh a little. "I guess I deserve that."

"To be called a dog? Yeah, you do." She fills a glass with water and gulps it down, turning back to me with narrowed eyes. "You think the same as Levi, huh? That I'm a sell-out?"

I shake my head emphatically, raising my hands. "It's not like that, I-"

"Because if it's offensive to you both that I am what I am, you can leave." She lifts an eyebrow, looking me up and down. "I was just trying to be nice. But nice has never gotten me very far. You know where the door is if you need it."

I try to close the distance between us, but she takes a step back, arms crossed over her chest.

"Baby, that's not-"

"Do *not* call me baby, Dylan. Or sweetheart, or anything else. Those days are long gone." She notices the dip in my gaze, and presses her tits together even more firmly. "Listen, I know you just got out of jail, and I know they're amazing, but you can keep your eyes fucking *up*."

I laugh and run a hand over my head. "Jesus, Stella, you sure know how to make things hard for a guy."

"Oh, you have no idea." Her lips curl into a grin. "And in fact, you will never know. Now, I need to get some sleep." She shuts off the range hood light.

"Stella, I'm sorry. I am. He shouldn't have spoken to you like that. And I should have told him as much. But I do not think you're a sell-out. I would never think that. You're doing great, and I'm so grateful you're giving us a chance here."

She pauses in the candlelight, body bent slightly over the counter as she prepares to blow out the flame. She exhales heavily, the flame dancing lightly. "Great. Thanks." She blows out the candle, and the kitchen is illuminated only by the faint flow of the streetlight through the window. She goes to move past me, and my hand shoots out to grab her arm.

"Stella-"

She wrenches her arm out of my grasp. "Don't."

"*Stella.*" I put my hands either side of her and cage her against the door frame. "Please, talk to me."

"Dylan, let me go right now." Her eyes are dark, her full lips almost red in this light.

"I just want to talk to you."

"I tried that, remember? I tried to talk to you and my stupid stepbrother, tonight, in my fucking garage." She shoves me in the chest lightly. "I'm not in the mood to talk anymore." She turns to shove against my arm, but I drop it and put it around her waist, pulling her close to me.

"Don't walk away from me, please."

"*Stop.*" She fights me, nails scratching at my bare skin.

"So that's it?" I ask, not letting her go, keeping her rage-flamed body pressed to mine. "No second chances?"

She writhes in my grasp, wriggling her hips as she pushes against my chest. "Dylan, fucking *stop*."

"I went to prison for you, and you can't even fucking talk to me?"

Her mouth drops open and she gasps. "Fuck you!" She hisses at me in the dark, her teeth flashing in the cold light. "How fucking dare you."

I know I shouldn't go down this road. It's not fair. It's not her fault. But all the hurt and the fear, all that fucking injustice bubble up inside me and I can't help it.

"I went to prison for you, and you couldn't even be bothered visiting me? For ten. Fucking. Years."

Her eyes widen, and she goes still in my arms. "You have no idea what I went through in those years.

"What are you talking about?" I grip her arms tighter, trying to pull her closer and maybe even shake the truth out of her, something, anything, to let me feel connected to this woman again.

"You weren't the only one locked up." She shoves against me, hard enough to unbalance me and make it very clear I'm going to get my eyes clawed out by those pretty nails if I don't ease off. She braces one hand against the wall, her head dropping, shoulders heaving as one breath after another skitters across her full lips. "You have no idea about me. None."

"Then let me in." I take a step forward, met instantly by the thud of her outstretched palm against my stomach.

"No. Not again. Not anymore."

"Baby, it was meant to be us."

"You thought you'd get out and we'd just pick up where we left off?" She lifts her head to meet my eyes, and even in the darkness I can see the pain etched in that pretty face. I can feel it permeating her amber eyes. It rolls off her whole body. "Is that what you thought?"

"No, it's what I hoped."

She laughs bitterly, running a hand through her hair. "Hope is for kids, Dylan. Reality is for the rest of us."

"Come on." I try to take her hand again, but she clutches it tight against her body. "I just want to hold you."

"I'm not the girl you loved anymore, I haven't been for a very long time."

I huff out a breath, desperate to take her in my arms and smell the sweet scent of her skin. "Well, maybe I don't want her. I want you, as you are, right now."

"You don't even know me."

"Yes I do."

Suddenly she's pushed off the wall and headed down the hall. "Get some sleep, Dylan. Even if it's on the floor."

A door closes softly in the dark house, and I'm left alone with nothing but my memories, and a scratch mark down my bicep.

That night, I dream of a party, long ago, when Stella was young and sweet, and I was a teenage boy with a crush. When she'd touched my hand under the table, her pinky curling around mine as she smiled at me, and it had felt like coming home. When she'd let me pull her down the side of the house and push her against the wall, and I'd kissed those full lips for the first time. When I'd whispered, "You're mine, aren't you?" against her mouth, and she'd nodded.

I'm yours, papi. I'm yours.

The salon is busy when I push through the door, my arrival heralded by the ringing of a bell above me.

"Can I help you?" The young woman at the counter eyes me with a crooked smirk, brushing her copper red hair over her shoulder and tilting her hips.

I spot Zee working on a client in the corner, and gesture to them vaguely. "I'm actually here to see Zee."

Her eyebrows shoot up, and with a quick nod she looks over her shoulder. "Oh well, they're busy right now." Her gaze turns back to me, and that suggestive smile is back. "Since you don't look like you need a haircut, maybe I can get you a coffee while you wait?"

I shove my hands into my pockets, giving her a polite nod. "That'd be great, thanks."

"How do you like it?" She lifts an eyebrow as she says it, her gaze wandering up and down my body in a brief flicker that has me suppressing a cringe.

"Just black."

She purses her lips, her eyes widening. "I read somewhere that only psychopaths take their coffee that way." She leans on the counter, squeezing her tits together in her low-cut black shirt.

I roll my shoulders and look her square in the eye. "Well I did just get out of prison for murder, so…"

Her eyes bug out, her body instantly straightening and her hands curling protectively against her chest. "Are you joking?"

Zee's light laughter sounds across the salon, and they approach me with raised hands. "Homo!" They call affectionately, and the girl at the counter looks like she wants to melt into a grease spot on the floor.

"Hey, Freak." I can't help but smile as Zee wraps their long arms around me and hugs me tight. "Nice place you got here."

"Oh, you're too kind." Zee draws back from me, looking me up and down, shaking their head. "I see prison gave you around 100 pounds of muscle and 200 of ink." They run a finger along the snake tattoo that encircles my neck. "But this work is gorgeous. Was it done with a plastic spoon and a biro?"

I laugh out loud. "Hate to disappoint you, but it was just a plain old tattoo gun."

Zee's eyebrows quirk almost comically. "Since when do they let you have those in prison?"

"Since I went into San Verenas where Yolanda Crosby's son is incarcerated and she wants to make sure we're all very comfortable."

Zee rolls their eyes. "Oh god, I forgot about the governor's son." Zee looks over their shoulder at the redhead who's still regarding us with a look of wild confusion. "Amy, honey, my friend is taking me out for lunch."

"OK, no problems, I got everything under control." She eyes me apologetically. "I hope I didn't… I mean, I didn't realize you were gay."

"He's not!" Zee waves breezily, pushing me out the door and onto the busy main street of Bellford Heights. They link their arm through mine and click their tongue. "Amy's sweet, but simple."

I chuckle, falling into step with Zee's energetic strides as they drag me down the street. "Poor kid looked like her heart stopped when you called me Homo."

Zee tosses their purple locs over their shoulder and smiles up at me, their smiley piercing glinting in the sun. "Her parents are good bible folk, and you're probably the first bisexual man that's ever crossed her path." They lean their head against my shoulder. "Freak and Homo, together again." Suddenly, they shove me away and stop in front of a florist, glowering at me. "Wait a second, I forgot. I'm mad at you."

I run a hand over my head, my eyes dropping to the pavement. "I was wondering why you were being so nice to me. I was ready for you to tear my ear off."

"Stella told me you expected to get laid the second you got

out, you animal." They tap their foot against the ground. "And something about blaming her for going to prison?"

The well-dressed people passing us by look a little shocked by Zee's outburst, taking in their colorful clothing and even more colorful hair with a sneer. Zee's head snaps around to them, their face bursting instantly into a bright smile.

"Hey folks, gorgeous weather, amirite? Y'all have a blessed day!"

The people return Zee's enthusiastic smiles with slightly more awkward ones, and hurry along the footpath. Zee watches them go, the smile not dropping til they turn back to face me, one hand perched on their hip.

"OK asshole, explain."

"Can we go sit down for this lunch I'm buying you first, so we don't put this lovely flower store out of business?"

Zee huffs, and grabs my arm again. "Fine. I'm starving and I need sushi. Let's go."

It's not until Zee has a plate of spicy tuna rolls in front of them and I've downed half a red enamel cup of miso that they tilt their head and snap their chopsticks in my direction.

"OK, Kovac, speak."

"Pointing your chopsticks at people is considered rude, you know."

Zee jabs the chopsticks in my direction with renewed gusto. "I said, speak."

I sigh and throw up my hands. "I was an asshole. It wasn't like that though, I didn't expect to get laid, I really didn't. And the other stuff, I was… I was hurt."

"Over?"

I watch Zee dunk their tuna roll in a bowl of soy sauce lashed liberally with wasabi. "Her not coming to visit us."

Zee nods, chewing their food thoughtfully. "Mmm. Did she tell you why?"

My stomach does a deeply unpleasant flip, and my mouth runs dry. "She just said we weren't the only ones locked up."

"Mmm."

"Mmm? Is that all you're gonna say?"

Zee finishes chewing and takes a sip of their diet coke, eyeing me critically over the edge of the can. "You're hurt, I get it. I would be too. But it's not that she didn't love you."

The word love makes my chest ache in the worst fucking way, all the memories that kept me from sleeping the night before welling up at the backs of my fucking eyeballs. She loved me. Stella *loved* me. She loved us. And she stayed away from us for ten fucking years.

"If it wasn't that, then what was it?"

Zee leans back in their chair, crossing their lithe arms over their chest. "Has she told you anything? About where she went, who she lived with? What her life was like?"

I can't help but frown at the questions Zee is throwing my way. "Who she lived with? Well, her mom of course."

Zee laughs out loud, a sound that overshadows the other conversations going on in the cozy sushi restaurant. "Her mom? The bohemian alcoholic with 17 husbands to her name? You really think she came swooping in when her daughter needed somebody?"

My blood runs cold, and my mouth is the fucking Sahara. "Where did she stay? Her mom really didn't come back?"

Zee shakes their head emphatically, picking up another tuna roll and inspecting it carefully. "Did y'all ever write to her? Like, did either of you ever sit down, and write her a letter, and ask what was happening?"

I swallow down my shame. "No. Her letters, they… They made us angry. They were… They were nothing. Just bland, like it wasn't even her writing them." I lift my gaze sheepishly to meet Zee's. "It made me think she didn't care anymore."

"So there's some truth to what you said the other night then?" Zee's eyes bore into mine. "You and Levi felt she owed you, and when she didn't perform the way you wanted, you dropped her like a fucking stone."

I rub the back of my neck, laughing awkwardly. "Now, Zee, come on."

"After everything that poor girl went through, you had the audacity to sit there and wait for her to come to you? To write you in a way that made *you* feel special?" Zee throws their chopsticks on to the table and shakes their head. "Unbelievable."

"I love Stella. I went to prison *for her*."

"You went to prison for killing her dad." Zee's indignation is cutting, slicing straight through my confidence and the surety that I did the right thing. The look in their eyes tells me in no uncertain terms that they're judging me, hard. "You and Levi, what happened that night, if either of you had thought about Stella for even one second, neither of you would have pulled that trigger."

"I was thinking about her."

"You don't get it." Zee thumps two fingers against their temple. "You just do not comprehend what the fuck you left her in."

"So tell me!" A few heads jerk in our direction at my outburst, and I take a deep breath. "Zee, we've always been friends. You and me, Homo and Freak, right? You have to know, you have to believe me, I did it for her. I did it because I love her. I did it because that asshole deserved to rot in hell for what he did to her."

Zee crosses their lithe arms loosely over their chest again, tilting their head and tonguing their piercing as they regard me thoughtfully. "I've never doubted that you love her, Kovac. But she does. And if you want that back, get those knees ready for a whole lot of groveling."

"I'll do anything. Anything. Please just tell me what happened after we went inside."

Zee shrugs lightly, unfurling their arms and reaching for their diet coke. "Gloria happened."

I blink, and shake my head slowly. "What do you mean?"

Zee runs their tongue along their teeth, eyes widening over a sigh. "Gloria kept that poor girl right where she wanted her."

The words make bile rise in my throat. "But why would Gloria take guardianship of Stella? By what right?"

"By Rich White Lady Right. By Widow of a Politician Right. By Nearly First Goddamn Lady Right." Zee's voice slows to an emphatic drawl, their eyes filling with pain with every word they speak. "Gloria had the sympathy of the entire fucking country, and she played that role perfectly. She even wore black for a full six months after Harold died. And then she had Stella to take out all her anger and resentment on, behind closed doors of course. Levi knows his mother is a straight up sociopath. So do you."

Gloria Fenton-Langford. My hands curl into fists on my thighs as I remember the last time I saw those ice-cold blue eyes, that blonde hair pulled back so not a strand was out of place. The Demon Bitch of Bellford Heights was what everyone called her. A woman so consumed with hate she'd put the gas to the floor if she saw a dog wandering across the street.

And Stella had been left in her care.

"Levi and I fucked up."

"You did." Zee's face shifts suddenly, into softness and understanding. They take my hand, wrapping their fingers adorned with silver rings around mine. "Hey. You were young. You were stupid and young and you found out someone hurt the girl you loved. I get it. What happened to Stella is not your fault, just like what happened to you and Levi wasn't hers."

"I don't know how to make this right."

"You could try apologizing, just as a first idea."

"I tried that." I run my hands along my thighs, staring out at the brilliant sunshine and the passers-by. "She wouldn't listen to me."

"Did you apologize or did you try to make it about you?"

I whip my head back to look at Zee. "What do you mean?"

"Do not look at me all Shocked Face." Zee draws a

haphazard zigzag in the air in the direction of my face. "Stop that. If you want Stella to actually know you're sorry, it needs to be about more than 'I missed you and want you back'."

How do they know these things? I want to protest, to tell them it wasn't like that, and I know damn well that makes me a liar. "So what do I do? Buy her flowers, take her out for dinner?"

Zee lifts an eyebrow, snapping up another tuna roll in their chopsticks. "Does Stella like flowers and dinner dates?"

"How should I kn..." I trail off instantly, and sigh heavily. "Right. You're right. Get to know her. Ask questions."

"Bingo, stud. There's hope for you yet!" Zee pops the tuna roll in their mouth with obvious delight, waving to someone who passes by the window. "So, what's next for you?"

I grimace, leaning back in my chair. "I have to go see my grandfather tomorrow."

"Oh Jesus." Zee rolls their eyes heavily, glaring at the table. "That old bastard's still alive?"

"Unfortunately. Probably going to try and talk me into joining the family business again. Since he doesn't have a son to pass it on to anymore." I swallow hard. I passed the cemetery on the way here, knowing my parents were lying in there somewhere. I haven't been to their graves since the day they were laid in them. I still can't face it. I blink hard, and suddenly Zee's reached across the table again and takes my hand.

"It's really good to see you, Dylan." They squeeze my hand, and give me a soft smile as I look up at them. "And I really hope you find some happiness out here."

"Yeah, once I figure out how this world works, I guess I might."

"Any ideas what you want to do?"

I shake my head, stretching my arms over my head. "I don't know. Might try and get back into bikes. Only thing I was ever good at."

"That and dancing."

An instant flush rises in my cheeks, and I cover my face as Zee begins to laugh loudly. "I danced at that bar for *one summer*."

"But what a summer it was." They shriek as I bunch up a napkin and throw it at them. "I'm serious, you got that Latino Spice, pretty boy."

"I say this with love, but fuck you. I am no dancer."

"Stella likes dancing." Zee's head bobs back and forth, their eyebrows raised as they look at me. "Just putting it out there, some info for, y'know, future reference. But that's all you're getting from me."

The idea of being in a dimly lit club with Stella and having her grind against me on the dancefloor is enough to have me huffing out a breath and scooping up my glass of water to try and calm down.

"Maybe I shouldn't be saying that to a guy that was just locked up for 10 years."

"You think I couldn't get laid in prison?" I can't help but laugh a little at Zee's shocked expression, and quickly wave my hands in front of me. "Nah, kidding, *kidding*. I didn't."

"Better blow off some of that steam before you scare the poor woman."

I don't even know how to tell Zee that being in a house alone with Stella and Levi is a certain kind of hell I wasn't ready for. Knowing they're a few feet away, barely dressed - it's enough to keep me awake and jerking off most of the night. I miss the feeling of another person, kissing and touching, the sounds and the heat, fuck it's torture.

I meet Zee's gaze and smile. "Don't worry about me. I'll figure something out."

"You always do, Kovac."

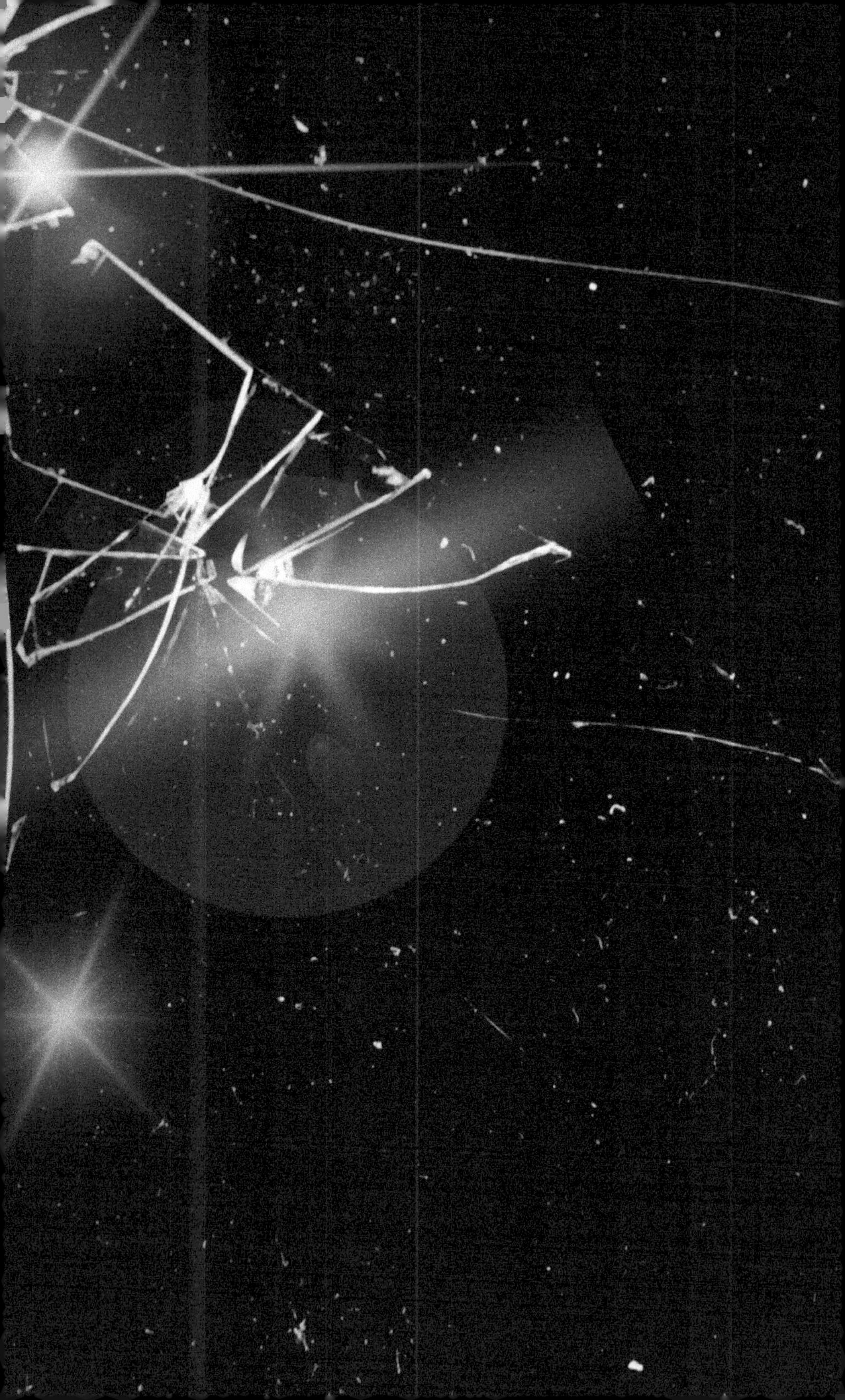

CHAPTER THREE

MY MOTHER'S house is just as fucking ridiculous as I remember it being. The gravel crunches under the tires of the bike as I make my way up the long drive, the rose bushes outside in full bloom, the rococo style gold detailing on the balconies and doorways glinting in the harsh summer sun.

It's so fucking ugly. I always hated this house.

I bring the bike to a stop and climb off, removing my helmet and placing it on the backseat. As I turn towards the front door, it flies open, and my mother bursts out, dressed in her signature blue skirt suit, hair pulled back into a blonde coiffe.

"My darling boy!" She flies at me, throwing her arms around me. "Oh my god, sweetheart."

"Hi Mom." I hug her back, trying to show some enthusiasm.

"Why am I only seeing you now?" She pulls back, and I'm surprised to see tears in her eyes. My mother has tear ducts, who knew? "I would have been there for your release, but I was out of town, I'm so sorry." She looks me up and down, hands on my shoulders. "You look… so grown up. More tattoos."

I can't help but laugh. "Not a fan?"

She waves her hand dismissively. "It's fine. Your father had tattoos too, I can live with those." She raises her eyes back to mine, the same shade of ice blue as mine. "Where are you staying?"

"With Stella."

My mother's face instantly drops. "With whom?"

"Mom, I came here to see you and I don't want a fight."

"Levi, you cannot mean that." She grips my shoulders. "I want you to tell me that you're joking."

"I'm not, and I'm not discussing that. I can leave if you prefer."

"No!" She seems to surprise herself with her outburst, quickly running a hand over her hair, smoothing the imaginary loose strands back into place. She clasps her hands together, and the paparazzi smile is in place. "Sweetheart, please, I'm just happy to see you. I just want us to spend time together. Please." She gestures to the house with a move clearly rehearsed for a Vogue Living special.

I finally nod. "OK." I follow her up the sandstone steps and into the marbled foyer. Everything still looks the same, smells the same. "So you sold the other place?"

"Stella did." Her tone is clipped. "Harold hadn't changed his will, so that house unfort- I mean, that house landed in Stella's hands."

Good for her. I smirk at my reflection as we pass a floor to ceiling gilded mirror. "Oh that's too bad."

"I suppose you've seen the house she lives in now.." My mother clicks her tongue. "On that side of town, living with teachers and… and…" My mother struggles to think of some other low class of worker that could afford to live in the slum that is west Bellford Heights, and I suppress a laugh.

"Mom, you are a class A snob, you know that?"

She glares over her shoulder at me, before turning right into the conservatory. It's cool in here, the glass walls mostly obscured by towering ferns and miniature palms. Bamboo blinds span the glass ceiling, and the air smells fresh. This is the only room in the house I could ever bear.

A lavish spread is laid out on a long wooden table, seafood and charcuterie boards, bowls of fruit overflowing on the table. The food my mother thinks rich people should eat. It's almost cartoonish.

"Jesus, Mom, you really outdid yourself." I take a seat, sprawling in the chair as my mother primly takes her place opposite me.

"Only the best for my son." She gives me a warm smile.

"Well, thanks. Beats prison food, that's for sure."

Her face instantly shifts with alarm, her eyebrows shooting up. "Was it very awful inside? Your grandfather tried to make sure you got the very best facility. If there were problems you should have told me."

"No, Mom, it was fine. As good as prison can be." I reach out and pluck a grape from a plate, popping it in my mouth, and meet my mother's critical gaze. "What?"

"Why do you have an obscenity tattooed on your hand?"

I raise my right hand and smile at the word Fuck tattooed across my knuckles. "I thought it was funny."

"That kind of language is not funny. How are you ever supposed to get a decent job looking like that?"

"Who says I want a decent job?" I can't help but grin at the mix of outrage and disbelief on her face. "Come on, did you really think I was going to be the next president?"

"You could have been," she mutters into a glass of sweet tea.

"No, Mom, I couldn't have been, and you never saw that."

She swallows her mouthful of tea and snorts. "Your father insisting on a name like Levi was probably the death knell of that dream anyway."

I laugh out loud. "That's what you get for disappointing Daddy and marrying a biker, I guess."

My mother sighs, reaching out to stroke her manicured hand along the leaf of a palm beside her. "Yes, well we all make mistakes when we're young and stupid." Her eyes move back to me. "So what are you thinking of doing with your days? Since you don't have aspirations of being president?"

I stretch out my legs, popping another grape in my mouth. "Dylan and I were thinking of opening a shop."

My mother's face darkens further at the mention of Dylan's name. "I suppose he's staying with Stella too?"

"He is."

My mother clicks her tongue, delicately placing a croissant on her plate. I know damn well she won't eat it.

"Are he and Stella still together?"

The question has my stomach in a knot. Of course they were together, long ago. Dylan had been down bad for Stella the second he'd met her. I'd been fine with it. Until... Until... I suddenly feel unsteady, and I can't explain why. Remembering that night, when Dylan had come to me in furious tears, telling me what he and Stella had been about to do. How she'd frozen in fear, and he'd immediately known something was very wrong. And then he came to me, and told me what she'd told him...

"Sweetheart?" My mother's voice draws me back into the moment.

"What was that?"

"This shop, what kind of shop is it?"

"Oh, uh, bikes."

My mother rolls her eyes. "Of course, what else? Just like your father."

"Hey, it's all I was ever good at." I shrug, pouring myself a glass of water. "That old fella downtown, Mario, he's going to retire. I figured I'd buy his shop from him, keep it going. I'm sure I still have my inheritance kicking around."

My mother's lashes flutter for just a split second, betraying the only weakness she has. "Of course, sweetheart, no one else has touched your father's money. That was there for you. He was... He was very clear on that."

"Well, great, that's my plan then." I give her a grin. "Following in my daddy's footsteps."

My mother nods, her throat bobbing lightly. "Yes, that's wonderful. I'm sure Dylan will be grateful for the opportunity. Immigrant kids have it so hard."

I can't help but laugh at yet another display of my mother's snobbery. "Mom, Dylan's family is probably richer than yours."

"They're Polacks." She stage whispers across the table, eyes darting around as though the FBI is hovering behind one of the palms. "Do you know *how* they make their money?"

"First off, they're not *Polacks,* Mom, his dad was *Polish* and his mom was Mexican. And they make their money in microchips and motherboards, for fuck's sake."

"Please watch your language." She folds her hands in her lap. "I'm not saying anything against his family, just that I think money-laundering is a thing that happens."

"Mom, I swear to god." I put my hands on the arms of the chair, making to rise to my feet.

"No! Please!" She reaches out, holding up a hand. "I'm sorry. I didn't mean that. I just want you to be happy, and safe, and to not violate your parole."

"I'm not going to violate my parole, and you need to start laying off of the people I care about."

"I'm sorry, I just worry about you. Stella has, well, she's caused so much pain for our family."

I push out of the chair and get to my feet. "I'm done."

She jumps out of her chair, eyes wide. "No, sweetheart, please-"

"Enough." I raise a finger and point it in her direction. "I am sick of you trash-talking Stella. It's disgusting. You should be ashamed."

I stride across the conservatory, ignoring my mother's protests and quick steps behind me. Her assistant, Valerie, appears from a side room as I head through the foyer, and raises a hand in greeting.

"Levi, good to see you!"

I ignore her, pushing through the double doors and out onto the steps. Within seconds I'm on my bike, roaring down the drive.

I always hated this house. And everyone who fucking lived in it.

When I get back to Stella's house, her black Volvo is just pulling into the drive. Stella still hasn't spoken a word to me since I gave her shit in the garage three nights ago, every time I try she just flips her hair over her shoulder and ignores me.

I can't blame her.

I kill the engine as she climbs out of her car, iced coffee in hand, a Barnes and Noble bag dangling from her arm. She's dressed in a pink jumpsuit that shows off her tan, and it sits tight around her ass. My chest tenses as I realize there's no way she's wearing panties.

Thoughts I should not be having about my stepsister.

"Hey, pretty girl," I call out, and she ignores me. I climb off the bike as she walks up the steps, and I rush to catch up with her. The door slams in my face. *Fuck she's really mad*. I push the door open, following her into the house. "Stella, come on, talk to me."

She spins on her heel, pushing her sunglasses up on top of her head. "Fine, I'll talk. You and Dylan have until the end of the week to get the fuck out of my house."

I stop short, caught off guard by the fury in her eyes. "Stella, come on-"

"*You* come on. You and Dylan made it very clear to me that you're so much better than me, that you're *real* men, and haven't sold out like me." She narrows her eyes, dumping her bag on the bench in the foyer. "So that means you're both more than capable of looking after yourselves."

"Stella-" I take a step closer, and I'm met with a pointy manicured nail in my chest.

"No."

I take her hand gently, wrapping it in both of mine. Her face doesn't change, still regarding me with fury and deep, simmering hurt. "Baby girl, listen to me. I am so sorry for what I said."

"I don't believe you," she snaps, trying to yank her hand away, but I don't let go. "And quit it with the *baby girl* all the time. I hate it."

"Do you really?" I lean over here, and her eyes flicker wide for a split second.

"Y-yes. It reminds me of things that are gone, and dead."

I take her hand and press it to my chest. "I'm not dead and gone, am I?"

Her amber eyes stay fixed on mine, the fury softening out of them ever so slightly. "Levi, don't."

"Stella, listen to me, just for a minute, please." I attempt to pull her a little closer, and when she resists I take a step towards her. "I know we hurt you. I said things to you, and to Dylan, that you didn't deserve. Not one little bit."

She grits out a harsh little laugh. "So Dylan wasn't just here for a piece of ass, huh?"

I smile down at her. "I mean, maybe the hope was there." I laugh when she rolls her eyes. "No, come on, he loves you. He missed you. I shouldn't have said that."

"Nice of you to recognise that." Her eyes drop from mine.

"Baby girl, I missed you too." I move even closer, so we're almost chest to chest. I raise one hand to her cheek, running the back of my finger down her soft golden skin. "I know words aren't going to help. I fucked up, and I hurt you. And I'm sorry I ruined this, all of this. Coming home to you."

"I was so happy to see you," she says, and the veneer cracks just a little, her eyes shining as she gazes up at me. "I missed you too. I was dreaming of that moment. God, I was so stupid. In my room, trying to find the right dress to wear."

"You looked beautiful, baby girl." I notch my fingers under her chin. "You hear me, you looked gorgeous. Perfect."

I can't tell her what I really thought when I saw her. That I called her baby girl, the nickname I gave her when we were kids, to try and stem the desire that flared in every cell in my body just at the sight of her.

That I let my anger and desire get the better of me in the garage, saying hurtful things just to push away that sweet scent of vanilla and that pretty smooth skin.

It wasn't just 10 years in prison - it was being back in the presence of the girl I'd been obsessed with since I was 16 years old, since I saw her holding those white flowers in her pretty pink dress at our parents' wedding.

I can't tell her any of this. She sees me as her big brother. So I smile down at her, and plant a kiss on her forehead. She sighs a little, and softens against me.

"Thank you." She leans against my chest, and lets me wrap my arms around her.

"I'm so, so fucking sorry."

"Yeah, yeah, OK." She pulls back and smiles up at me, rolling her eyes a little. "Good thing for you I'm a sucker for lost causes."

"Yeah Miss Lawyer Lady, that's kinda your forte, huh?"

"Hmmm. I guess I am." She quirks her mouth, then pushes out of my arms. "OK, you can stay."

"And Dylan?"

She turns and points a finger at me. "He can make his own case."

I hold my hands up. "You're right, he's a big boy, he can handle himself."

"Damn straight." She sweeps the Barnes and Noble bag up from the bench and heads into the kitchen. "So what did you do today?"

I follow her slowly, shoving my hands into my pockets. "I, uh, saw my mother."

Stella freezes, a book hovering half in and half out of the bag. I swear her jaw starts trembling.

"You… You saw her, huh?"

"Yeah, she told me you'd sold the old house." I shrug, leaning back against the wall. "I can't blame you, not like we had a lot of positive memories in that old shack."

"Did she… tell you anything?" She's still frozen, almost trembling.

"Tell me what?" I frown, and she seems to come out of her trance, slowly putting the book down on the kitchen counter. "Did something happen?"

"It doesn't matter." She shakes her hair out over her shoulder, and continues taking books from the bag. "But yes, I sold the house. Dad left it to me, and I didn't want it. I hated that place. Your mother was furious, but I didn't really care. I told her she could buy me out, but that didn't suit her either."

I grunt out a laugh. "She just felt entitled, if she'd wanted to buy it she could have."

"My thoughts exactly." She stacks the books up on the counter. "Anyhow, I sold the place, and bought this house. Suits me way better than some soulless mansion."

"You did good, kid."

She meets my eyes with a soft smile. "Thanks. Hardly a kid anymore, though."

Her words do not have the intended effect, and I hate myself for it. She's definitely not a kid. She's a woman with pretty blonde hair and big amber eyes. She's standing in front of me in a tight jumpsuit in no panties, and I shove myself off the wall before I do something stupid.

"I should go shower," I call over my shoulder, leaving her and her books alone in the kitchen. I head straight to the bathroom, turning the cold up all the way and dousing myself in the stream, chasing away all the fantasies of the things I want to do with my little stepsister.

I'm sick. Depraved. This isn't normal. Maybe I should have just let her kick me out after all. Because there's no way this is going to end well.

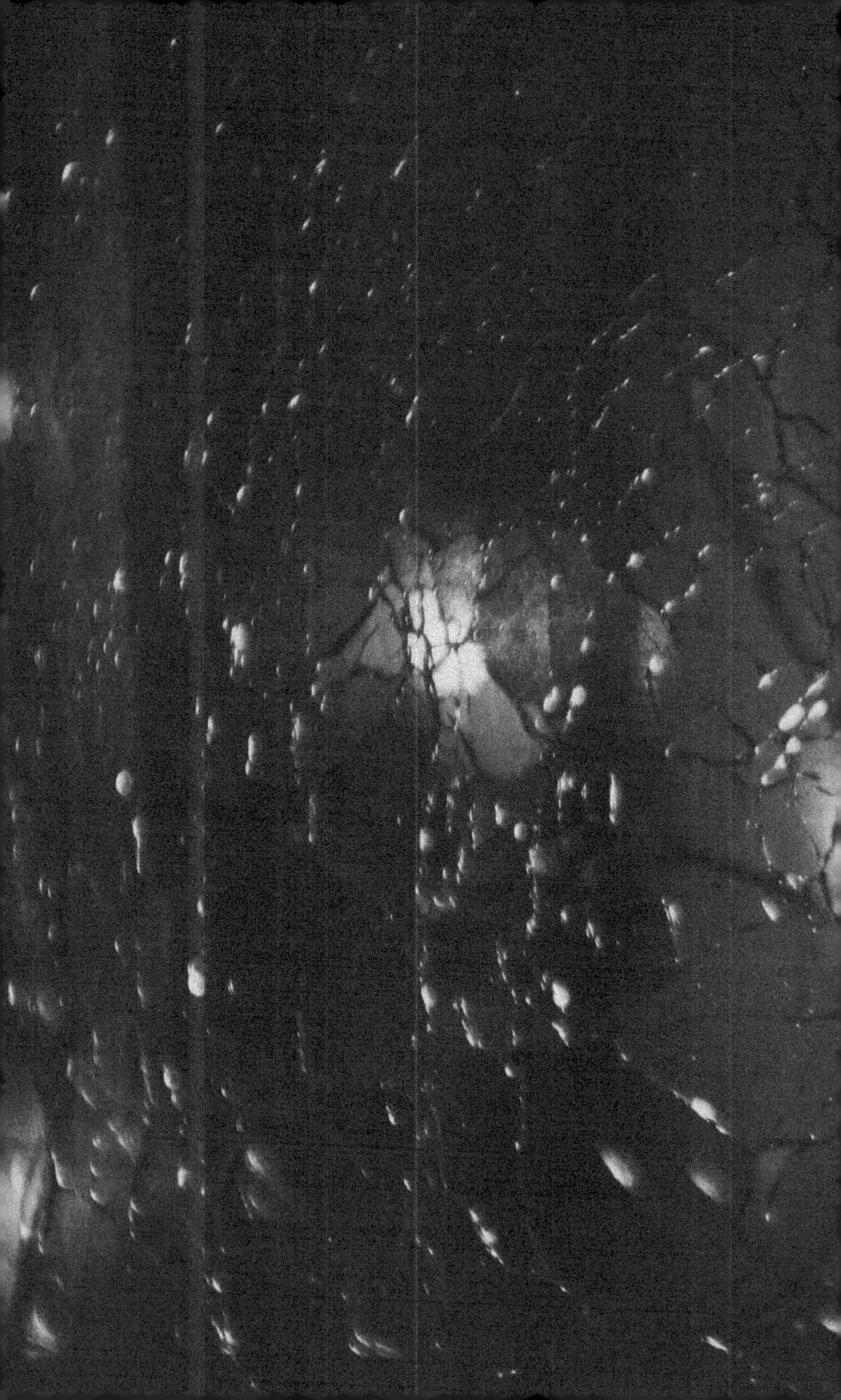

STELLA

CHAPTER FOUR

DYLAN WANDERS INTO THE KITCHEN, bleary-eyed, in nothing but black boxer briefs. I sit silently at the window and watch him stumble to the coffee machine. He pulls out the pot, then seems to remember he doesn't have a cup, and turns to find me watching him.

"Oh, shit. Uh, I mean, good morning."

"Morning."

He averts his eyes sheepishly. "Sorry, if I'd known you were here I would have gotten dressed. I thought you'd be at work."

I shrug lightly, looking out the window. "Stupid me took all my vacation days thinking I'd be catching up with you both." I take a sip of coffee. "More fool me, huh?"

Dylan is suddenly standing next to me, still holding the coffee pot. "I'm sorry. I don't know how many times I need to say it for you to believe me, but-"

"I don't need you to say it at all." I rise to my feet and fix him with my gaze. "I don't need words, Dylan. Words don't mean anything. You could stand here and say you're sorry til you're blue in the face, and all I'd think is that you wanted to get laid."

His dark eyes widen. "Stella, that's not what it is at all."

"No? Sure felt like that the other night when you got all handsy with me."

He runs a hand over his head, still clutching the goddamn coffee pot in the other, and he splutters as he tries to find the right words. "I-I fucking love you, OK? What do you want me to say? That I didn't come out of prison hoping to get you home and fuck you senseless? Yeah, I did."

A laugh lodges in my throat. "See? Nothing but a piece of ass." I move past him over to the sink, and then the coffee pot is on the counter next to me and I'm spun around in Dylan's arms. He stares down at me, his gaze a mixture of determination and deep pain.

"There has never been a single moment where I saw you as nothing but a piece of ass."

"Right. You love me." I don't know why I'm giving this beautiful man such a hard time. I don't know why I'm ignoring the sharp thud of my heart in my ribcage as he holds me close. I'm desperately tempering the need to pull his face down to mine, to kiss him till our lips hurt, to let him put me up on this counter and fuck away the longing and loneliness of the last ten years. I blink all that away, and stick out my chin. "I'm done being loved by people who hurt me, Dylan. I'm sick of it. If that's love, I don't want it."

"I've never wanted to hurt you, Stella." He lifts a hand and traces it down my neck, along the curve of my shoulder, and it makes me hurt even more. "And I know I have, because I was stupid and reckless. I know that. But you have to believe me, I never meant it."

I shrug, my eyes stinging so hard I have to blink to stop the flood of saltwater that's threatening to escape any second. "More words. More apologies. I can't do anything with that."

He takes a step back from me with a growl, his jaw feathering and his hands on his hips. "Stella, I don't know how to do this. OK? I spent my 20s in prison. I don't know what I'm doing here."

"So figure it out."

"How?" His voice is strained with frustration, his hands cupping the air in front of him hopelessly.

"Read a book. Go to Reddit. Fuck, I don't know, *talk* to somebody. Therapy is great, and after spending your 20s in prison, you probably need it."

He lunges at me, seizing my face in his huge, tattooed hands, his body flush with mine. "Listen to me. I'll do anything I need to do to win you back."

"I'm not a prize, Dylan."

"Yes, you are." He lowers his face to mine to nudge my nose with his, a small, sweet gesture that chips away at my anger, just a little. "No more words. I promise. But you got to tell me that I have a chance here."

His eyes gaze intently into mine. I want to tell him that I don't have to do anything. That I don't owe him anything. But with his warm hands against my face, and those dark eyes filled with hope, I don't have the heart to be a bitch and tell him no. Because I want him to have that chance. I want to give myself that chance. Which makes me a fool. I'll just get hurt again.

But the memories of how much I loved him are too strong.

"You have a chance. But I won't promise you more than that."

His face breaks into a devastating smile, and suddenly he's that 19 year old boy again, full of hope and joy whenever his eyes landed on me. He leans his forehead against mine, and laughs softly.

"I'm going to make you so happy, Stella."

I swallow down my bitterness, the words threatening to spill out. *No you won't. I'm broken. I'll hurt you. I'll make you miserable. I don't know what I want. I don't know who I want.* I clamp my eyes shut and push all my sick thoughts away.

Dylan can't know that about me. It'll disgust him. It disgusts me. Instead I just smile and nod, pulling on the mask I wear so well.

"I hope so," is all I say. And some small part of me, foolishly, does.

Dylan won't tell me where he's going when he leaves, but I guess he's headed to his grandfather's. I feel a pang as I watch him pull out of the drive on his bike, the engine roaring down the tree-lined street. His grandfather was always mean-spirited. He hated Dylan's mother, and by extension was horrid to Dylan after his parents died.

That time is bound with so much sadness but also love. That was when Dylan and Levi became close, and he spent so much time at our house. He was always there, lighting up every room he walked into. And, in time, Dylan and I became close, too.

With a sigh, I walk down the hallway and up the stairs. It's a beautiful day, and I consider going swimming. I pull my phone from my pocket, ready to text my cousin Lily and see if she's free, when I walk past Levi's open door.

I cast a glance into the dim room, light spilling across the bed from between a crack in the curtains. Straight over Levi's naked body sprawled out on the bed. He's lying on his back, one arm tucked behind his head. He's snoring lightly, obviously fast asleep. Thank god, because here I am staring at him while he's butt ass naked.

His body is beautiful, sleek muscles adorned with tattoos. I swallow, clutching my phone hard enough to crack the screen as my eyes land on his dick. It's difficult to make out a lot of detail in the half-light, but his girth and size are more than obvious. The throb I feel between my thighs at the sight is deeply unpleasant.

At that moment, my phone begins to ring.

Levi's head shoots up to look straight at me in the doorway, and I shriek out a *Sorry!* Before racing to my room and slamming the door behind me. I clutch my still-ringing phone to my chest, and try to compose myself. My step-brother just caught me staring at him naked. I clench my eyes shut. Oh my god, I'm disgusting. He's going to be packing his bags when I get back out of this room.

If I ever get up the nerve to leave this room again, that is.

The phone stops ringing and almost instantly starts again, and I look down to see Lilly's name flash up on the screen. I swipe my thumb across the screen and lift the phone to my ear.

"H-Hey!" I clear my throat when my voice squeaks. "I was just about to call you."

"Haha, twinsies!" She laughs. "I was just calling to see if you wanted to go for lunch?"

"Yes, yes, I would love that." I answer way too fast, but I need to get out of this house and as far away from Levi as possible. "Where are we going?"

"I was thinking DeLuca's, I *need* a cobb salad. Like, I medically require one."

I laugh awkwardly, shifting on my feet as I hear movement out in the hallway. A few seconds later the shower turns on. I breathe a sigh of relief. The perfect time to escape.

"That sounds great!" I shuffle off my pajama shorts and grab a sun dress from the closet. "I have a few errands to run downtown and then I'll meet you."

"Perfect! See you at 12!" Lily makes a loud kissing noise like she always does at the end of our talks and hangs up.

I throw my phone on the bed to peel off my shirt and pull the sundress on over my head. I decide to avoid putting on makeup because that might cost me time and I need to avoid seeing Levi. I don't know how I'll ever face him again.

With burning cheeks I run a brush through my hair and hurry out of my room and down the stairs. The shower keeps running, thank god.

By the time I park my car outside my favorite cafe, I've calmed down and the flush in my face has diminished. Maybe Levi didn't see me. Maybe he thinks nothing of it. We're basically brother and sister, it's normal to see each other naked, right? In some households that's normal. I know Lilly and her sister Donna get spray tanned together, and they're naked for that. It's no big deal.

Well, it wouldn't be if I wasn't squirming and clenching my thighs together thinking of Levi's dick in my mouth. With a groan, I pull out my phone and fire off a message to my therapist, asking if I can move my next appointment forward. I need to talk this shit out.

I push open my car door and head into the cafe. I need an iced coffee and I need it now.

Oh no.

"Hey girl!" Zee's wide smile greets me from where they stand at the counter, casually draped over the glass display as they talk to Jared, the owner of the Elephant Bean Cafe. "We were just talking about you!"

Oh great, I was just thinking about sucking my step-brother's cock.

"Hey! All good things I hope?"

Jared laughs, already setting about getting me my usual vanilla iced coffee order. "Of course good things!" His eyes move up to meet mine, and he flashes me a wide smile. "You look great, Stella."

Zee's eyebrows lift, their lips disappearing as though they're trying to keep some big secret, and my stomach drops. They really were talking about me.

"Oh, thanks." I run a hand through my hair. "I, uh, didn't have time to do my makeup today, I was thinking of going for a swim."

"Jared was just saying that, with all this heat, he'd like to go for a swim!" Zee's voice is filled with delight, and I try not to shoot daggers in their direction.

"Yeah well I'm meeting my cousin for lunch now, so..." I shrug lightly, fishing my purse out of my bag to pay for the iced coffee.

Zee throws up their hands. "That's OK, Jared doesn't close

up til 3 anyhow. Plenty of time to go see Lilly and then." They clap their hands to punctuate their sentence, and Jared's hopeful gaze lands on me.

I want to sink into the floor. It never occurred to me before that Jared likes me. He was friendly, sure. Good-looking in a sort of prep-school, peaked-in-college-football kind of way. He's from a good family and opened the cafe as a sort of passion project after living in Tanzania for a year and researching the best kinds of coffee.

As all this filters through my head, as I try to pinpoint the moment when he might have started to like me, it dawns on me - I know all this *because* he likes me. He shared his life and his dreams with me, and now he's looking at me with big brown puppy-dog eyes hoping I'll go on a date with him.

And Zee is playing wingperson. Fucking goddammit.

I take my iced coffee from Jared's hand with a light laugh and a toss of my hair. "I mean, yeah, sure. We can do that. The lake's usually crowded in the afternoon."

"Oh, I know a spot." Jared's triumph is written all over his face, in the cocky lift of his eyebrow.

Zee is practically chortling with glee, clutching their joined hands to their wide smile. "This is so cool."

"Zee, cut it out," I mutter through a forced smile.

"So I'll meet you here at 3?" Jared asks, leaning against the counter.

I nod, taking a long sip of my iced coffee to avoid answering, "Jared, this is so good."

"Thanks." Jared's head bobs on his shoulders, his arms crossed over his chest. "So, it's a date?"

I gotta get out of here. "Yeah, a date. For sure. See you at 3!" I spin on my heel and hurry for the door.

"The pink string bikini! The one you wore in Tulum! Bring that!" Zee calls after me, and I resist the urge to flip them off as I storm through the door and out onto the street.

The pink string bikini. Yeah sure, the tiniest item of clothing I own, and I'm going to parade on the local beach with Jared Marshall in it, tits and ass on full display. Great. Super. I take another long sip of the iced coffee and head down the street to the bookstore.

Why do you hate me, God?

Because who else would be standing right outside the bookstore, draped over his bike in baggy jeans and a tight black t-shirt, taking a drag of a cigarette?

"Hey sis," Levi drawls, stamping the cigarette out under his white sneaker. "Thought I might find you here."

I want to scream, or throw the iced coffee at him and run. I can't decide which would be more embarrassing. Especially since he just called me Sis and not 20 minutes ago my panties were soaked just thinking about him.

"Hey." I try to remain calm and not think too much about him catching me staring at his dick this morning, and decide with the friendly way he's looking at me now, that maybe I was, as always, overthinking things. "What're you doing here?"

"I thought I'd come find you and take you to lunch." He smiles down at me, a brief glance flickering up and down my body. "I'm going to Mario's with Dylan once he gets back, thought in the meantime you and me could hang out."

"Well, I'm due to meet Lily in a half hour, so..."

Levi raises his eyebrows and shrugs."No problem, I guess I can carry your books for you if you want?" He jerks his head in the direction of the bookstore. "That is, if you were headed in here with that mean look on your face?"

"I didn't have a mean look on my face." I push past him into the bookstore, the bell at the door tinkling lightly.

"You sure looked pissed." He follows me to the back of the store slowly, looking the shelves up and down as he goes.

"I actually just got asked on a date, so I doubt I looked that pissed."

There's no response from behind me, and after a beat I turn around to look at him standing square in the middle of the aisle, his arms crossed over his chest. Now *he* looks pissed. He lifts an eyebrow.

"A date, nice. Who asked you out on a date?"

"Jared Marshall, he's taking me swimming at the lake at 3," I reply lightly, flipping my hair over my shoulder and spinning back to the shelf of smutty romance novels. I run my finger along the spines pretending to be engrossed in the titles while deeply aware of Levi's stare against the back of my neck. "You remember him from high school, right? He owns the cafe around the corner now."

"A cafe?" Levi stands beside me, leaning against the shelf. "Cute. You like him?"

"I wouldn't go on a date with him if I didn't." I hope to god I'm not blushing, but my face feels like it's on fire.

Levi crosses his arms over his chest, nodding, looking the shelves up and down. "What do you like to read, Stella?"

"Romance, mainly." I pluck a book from the shelf and flick through the pages. "When you read heavy law books all day I like to have something fun to focus on."

"I can understand that. Fun is good." Levi takes a book I own from the shelf, flipping through it before he stops on a page, eyes traveling over the words. His mouth quirks into a crooked grin, and he chuckles to himself.

"Found something you like?" My head is going to explode. I know what that book's about. It's wall-to-wall fucking, and my cheeks flame knowing Levi is reading it right in front of me.

"Yeah, it's a good one." He looks at me, and I meet his gaze, knowing full-well I'm tomato red at this point. "She's got a guy's dick down her throat, and she likes it."

I swear to god I'm going to die. I can't breathe, and Levi's gaze drops to my breasts.

"Want me to read it to you?" He asks in a tone of voice that he should not be speaking to me in.

"No thanks," I snap, sounding way more breathless than I'd like. "I don't need my brother reading smut to me, that's gross."

"Your brother, huh?"

I narrow my eyes at him, grabbing the book from his hand and shoving it back onto the shelf. "You just called me sis, what, 3 minutes ago?"

He takes a step closer, bracing a hand against the shelf behind me so he's half-caged me in. "Did you like what you saw?"

My blood is replaced by ice water, and my stomach drops so violently into my feet I nearly stumble. "I don't know what you're talking about."

"This morning, baby girl." He lowers his mouth to my ear. "That's not how you look at your brother."

I push him away lightly so I don't cause a scene. "Fuck off, Levi. I barely glanced at you."

But he pushes straight back, and puts an arm around my waist. "I asked if you liked what you saw."

"I saw a man who can't close the door in someone else's house when he sleeps naked." I glare up at him, hoping he can't hear my heartbeat thundering through my ears. "Maybe next time, shut the damn door so you spare me a heart attack."

Levi grins, raising a hand to my cheek. "So, this date?" The back of his finger traces along my jawline. "You gonna fuck him?"

I shove him away from me and storm out of the bookstore amidst a confused farewell from the owner. I'm consumed with anger and shame, and a heaping dose of desire that won't fucking die down because every time I damn well blink, Levi's dick glows on the backs of my eyeballs.

His footsteps are right behind me, and I spin to meet him so fast he almost barrels over the top of me.

"You know what? Yeah, I am gonna fuck him. I'm gonna wear my tiniest bikini, and let him take it off with his teeth, and then I'm gonna fuck him."

Levi looks around us, and I realize I just yelled at him in the middle of downtown while people are around. People who are now staring at us. I could cry with embarrassment.

"Just leave me alone, Levi." I hurry back to my car, sending another text to my therapist to tell her it's urgent, before taking several deep breaths and heading off to my lunch date with Lilly.

CHAPTER FIVE

LEVI IS WAITING for me when I bring my bike to a stop outside Mario's shop.

"Hey." He gives me a warm smile as I take off my helmet. "How was it?"

"I don't want to talk about it." I can't voice what just happened with my grandfather, how mean and cold he was. "He gave me my trust fund, and that's all I cared about, so…" I shrug, and trail off.

"Fair enough." Levi claps an arm around my shoulders. "Sorry it went bad."

I swallow hard, resisting the urge to put my arms around him and bury my face in the crook of his neck. "Yeah, it always goes bad with him. But it's done now." I gesture to the shop, trying to ignore how good he smells. "So, what do you think?"

Levi releases me to tuck his hands into the pockets of his jeans, and gazes up at the front of the garage. "I think it's great. He has good staff, we both know what we're doing, and he trusts us to keep it going."

"So, we're in?"

Levi turns to me with a wide smile, holding his hand out. "Guess so, pretty boy."

The leap my heart does when he calls me pretty boy… It's

just a stupid nickname. But the way he looks at me when he says it, the warmth in the way he grabs my hand and pulls me in for a one-armed hug…

It wasn't always like this. He was my friend, my best friend, and my girlfriend's brother at that. He was there for me when my parents died. He was there for me those nights in prison when the bars became too much, coaching me through panic attacks, when I felt pathetic and small and like a stupid little boy who'd wanted to act the big man.

But now, we're out. We're free. Now I can say what I want, who I want, that these feelings I have are real…

I give myself an internal slap. *You want Stella. You love Stella, You're trying to win her back, and now you're here thinking about her goddamn brother. You're sick.*

My grandfather's stinging parting words pursued me out the door and straight into this moment, a moment which I'm meant to be celebrating. Instead I'm consumed with self-loathing for wanting to fuck my best friend and his sister, like some sadistic little home-wrecker.

Stella would never understand. She knows I'm bi, but she wants someone monogamous, who's faithful only to her. Not to her and her brother. Her brother who sure as fuck never looked at a man as anything more than a friend.

"Hey, where are you?" Levi regards me with a confused smile. "You just totally zoned out."

I step back from him with a shrug. "Sorry, it's just all of this, it's a lot." I wave a hand at the garage. "Life, you know? Possibilities. All the things we wanted to have, and now, we can have them. I guess I'm adjusting."

"Yeah, aren't we all?" Levi turns back to the garage and nods. "This is going to help, though. Give us purpose. A reason to get up in the morning."

"Stella suggested therapy," I blurt out, and Levi regards me with a sideways glance.

"Did she? I have a feeling our little Stella needs some of that herself." He rolls his shoulders, and a dark haze settles over his face. "Remember Jared Marshall, from high school?"

"How could I forget?" That asshole was responsible for most of my black eyes, slamming my head into my locker every chance he got until I was finally bigger than him. "Wasn't he a quarterback or some shit?"

"Something like that." Levi huffs out a laugh. "Stella's going on a date with him."

I clench my teeth so hard I'm sure I'm going to crack a molar. My hands curl into painful fists and I shove them into my pockets quickly so Levi doesn't see. "A date? Like, a *date*?"

Levi tilts his head and raises an eyebrow. "A date. 3pm at the lake. Said she'd let him take her bikini off with his teeth."

I shift on my feet, rage and jealousy so acute welling up in my chest that I swear my breath is green as I exhale. "Good for her."

Levi laughs out loud, his eyes glinting as he sizes me up. "Yeah, good for her. And him."

Mario picks that moment to come out, his hands lifted in greeting and a brilliant smile on his weathered face. "My boys! Come on in!"

I push all my negative thoughts and feelings to the back of my mind, and try to focus on the here and now. Mario takes us on a tour of the shop, which is completely unnecessary. We cut our teeth on bikes in this place. We learned everything we know from him. But Mario's proud of the shop his father opened all the way back in 1946, so we humor him and follow him, promising to keep everything just as it is.

"So, my boys," he says it again with paternal pride as he pours us both a honey-coloured liquor from a fancy gold-topped bottle. "Metaxa, from my home, and only for special occasions. And today is a very special occasion."

"Sure is." Levi agrees, taking one of the glasses and raising it in Mario's direction. "Cheers."

"Stin iyia mas!" Cheers. Mario smiles at us both, and takes a sip of the liquid.

When I raise it to my lips, it smells strong of berries, and the taste is sweet and cloying on my tongue. My eyes wander up to the clock on the wall, ticking away loudly, and I see it's just after 3pm. The image of Stella in her tiny bikini pops up in my head and, I wonder if she's already on her date with Jared fucking Marshall.

"So, we hand all the papers to the lawyers, and then the place is yours." Mario's joy-filled voice brings me back into the office and away from the lake where Stella is probably frolicking with one of the assholes who called me *homo* all the way back in high school. "I have to say, I couldn't be happier to see it go to you."

"We're more than happy to take it over and see you retire well, Mario." Levi places his glass on the table and leans back in the creaky leather office chair, his legs sprawled out in front of him. "It's the start we both need."

"And you'll keep all the men on?" Mario asks, his eyebrows raised. "It's not that I don't trust you, but these guys, they're all good men. They have families, kids, you know? Some of them are still so young, and I took a chance on them."

"No one is losing their job on our watch," I assure him. "I mean come on, fresh outta prison, we're not exactly in a position to judge."

Mario's expression becomes earnest, his fingers steepled over his soft belly. "I want you both to know, I always supported what you did. Harold Langford, he was no good. A bad man. If he'd attacked my best friend, I would have done the same."

Levi and I both dip our heads at the same time, and Levi gives me that side glance full of knowing. The silent agreement that's existed between us all these years, the one we signed our names to. *This is the story we tell. This is what the public knows. This is how we protect Stella.*

Levi quickly perks up. "Hey, so we were thinking of having a party at our place, well, the place we're staying."

"We were?" My head snaps to look at him with a frown. "I mean, will Stella be-"

Levi waves his hand. "Ah, she'll be fine, when we tell her it's to get to know all the fine fellas at this establishment, she won't mind."

Mario's face is beaming with pride. "You boys, you're good eggs. Bet Stella appreciates having you both around."

I down the rest of the honeyed liquid, which coats my tongue and throat in a layer of sweetness so thick I can't do anything else but simply nod. Levi grabs a piece of paper and a pen from Mario's desk, and scrawls down his number and Stella's address.

"Here, tell them to be there at 7pm tomorrow. Just some drinks, shoot some pool, let them get to know their new bosses."

"They'll be thrilled." Mario looks like he's about to burst into tears. He wags his finger at us both, and sighs happily. "You two, you two are going to look after this place."

"Sure will." Levi gets to his feet and leans across the table to shake Mario's hand. "Now, thank you for the drink, but we have some things to do."

Mario rises and shakes both our hands vigorously, thanking us again and again. We finally make it back out into the parking lot, and I turn to Levi with confusion.

"We have somewhere to be?"

"Sure." He straddles his bike and pulls his helmet on. "Kinda hot this afternoon. Maybe we should go cool off by the lake."

I'm on my bike and revving the engine before he has his helmet buckled.

The Fairview Lake parking lot is packed when we pull up. Loud music wafts up from the beach, and I know it's probably full of college kids home for the summer. We park our bikes under some trees at the edge of the lot, and the fresh breeze that hits me when I take off my helmet is more than welcome.

The lake looks much like it did when we were last here, all those summers ago. The trees are taller, and there's a new cafe on the edge of the clearing before the grass turns into sand. But everything else is the same - kids everywhere, teenagers playing music, families lying in the sun and plenty of folks swimming in the water.

Stella's here somewhere, maybe making out with Jared fucking Marshall. Maybe he's grabbing her ass while it's barely covered in a tiny bikini. I hate myself for the renewed surge of jealousy that has me balling my fists at my sides. Is it wrong for Stella to date? She told me she wouldn't make any promises. I read into it too much.When she said I had a chance, that wasn't a guarantee.

But it still doesn't do anything to temper the urge to find her and carry her off this beach like I'm a fucking caveman.

"Nice day, huh?" Levi peels off his shirt, tucking it into the back of his jeans.

"Yeah, real nice." The dark mood from before settles over me again, as I can't help but glance at Levi's abs, the tattoos that snake across his pecs. His jeans hang even lower now as we move through the crowd, and the deep V over his hips…

I tear my eyes away. What the fuck is wrong with me? Losing my mind over Stella and her date, and now ogling my best friend? Fuck. Maybe Zee was right. Maybe I do need to go and get laid, get this shit out of my system.

I force my attention back on to the beach, the people around us, trying to spot Stella's shiny blonde head of hair. Levi and I make it down to the water, to some rocks that line the beach, and he throws himself down, leaning back on his hands.

"Maybe she didn't come after all." He looks up at me, his gaze wandering down my body. "You look hot, pretty boy."

"Excuse me?"

Levi gestures to my black pants and shirt. "You, dressed like that. Strip off for god's sake, cool off a little."

"Oh, right." I grab a handful of shirt behind my head and pull it off. Just as I do, I hear Stella laughing. I look out over the water, and a flash of pink catches my eye.

It's Stella, thrown over Jared fucking Marshall's shoulder as he runs through the water with her. Her ass is right by his head, barely covered in a tiny triangle of pink.

"Jared!" She cries playfully. "Put me down!"

Levi lets out a low laugh from the ground beside me. "There's our girl."

"We gonna go get her?"

Levi raises a hand languidly. "Just wait."

I watch as Jared dumps Stella in the water, his face lit up in a brilliant smile. I can't help but judge the tribal tattoo across his shoulders. *Basic ass fucking bitch.* The closest Jared fucking Marshall has ever come to anything tribal is Spring Break in fucking Cancun. Every Spanish and Polish expletive I can think of bubbles up in my brain as I watch this milk toast fucking white boy prance around in the water with my girl.

Uncultured asshole dares to get himself a tribal tattoo. Fuck that.

"You should see your face," Levi says with a laugh, rising to his feet. "If looks could kill, that bitch would be fucking dead right now."

"Just looking at his ink." My face pulls into a sneer I can't even help. "Bet he cried like a fucking baby when he got it."

"He used the numbing cream." Levi chuckles, and bites his lip as he looks at me. "We should go say hi." He peels off his jeans, stripping down to his dark blue boxers, and dumps his clothes on the rock beside us. I follow suit, and we climb down off the rocks and into the cool water.

It laps at our calves as we make our way towards Stella and Jared.

"Hey sis," Levi drawls once he's at Jared's back.

Stella's face instantly drops into a scowl as she pushes wet tendrils of hair from her face. Jared turns around slowly, appraising us both with a somewhat surprised expression, before his stupid preppy face bursts into a wide smile.

"Levi!" He holds out a hand, which Levi takes. "Good to see you man." His gaze shifts to me, the friendly hand extended again. "Dylan, how are you?"

"Just fine." I cross my arms over my chest, ignoring the extended hand, and I can't help the twinge of satisfaction as Jared's smile falters a little.

"Good for you remembering his name," Levi says, his lips curving into a grin. "In high school it was, what was it again?" He turns to me. "I know Zee was Freak, but you? You were?"

I meet Jared's paling face. "I was Homo."

Levi wags his finger and turns back to Jared. "That's right, Homo."

Stella's face changes from a scowl to sheer fury, her brows pulled down as she gets to her feet.

Jared holds up his hands, and he shrugs. "Hey man, I'm sorry. I was an asshole kid who went to an asshole church. It was wrong of me to ever say anything like that."

"Yeah it was." Stella's voice is sharp as a whip, and all three of us turn to look at her. She crosses her arms over her chest, and fixes Jared with a look of pure poison. "How dare you."

"Stella, that was years ago."

She huffs out a breath and raises her eyebrows. "Oh, so ten years ago in the year of our lord *twenty-fucking-fourteen* you thought it was OK to call a bisexual man *homo*?"

Levi is suppressing a laugh behind his hand, one hand on his hip as he watches the scene play out in front of him. Jared looks from me back to Stella, and starts to stammer out an apology.

"Stella, look, hey, it was a long time ago, and kids do stupid things, and well, Dylan, I mean-" He turns to me helplessly. "I'm sorry, man. I really am."

"Not. Good. Enough." Stella starts to push past us, out of the water.

Jared lunges forward and seizes her hand, which she yanks away from him, spinning to face him, her amber eyes blazing.

"Do *not* touch me."

"Stella, honey, I'm sorry." He leans over her, and I can practically feel him trying to use those preppy good looks to win her over.

But it doesn't work at all, as Stella shoves him in the shoulder, a move he doesn't expect as he stumbles in the water.

"You should be ashamed of yourself. Zee is my best friend, and Dylan is my-" She catches herself, swallowing hard as her eyes land on me, and the air is charged for a second. But then she shakes her head, storming out of the water. "I'll find somewhere else to get my coffee in future!"

Levi's shit-eating grin lands back on Jared, and he shrugs. "Too bad, man. Enjoy the rest of your day."

Jared looks so lost I almost feel sorry for him.

Then I remember him slamming my head into my locker when I was fourteen, asking me what anal felt like, asking me if I had AIDS, and then telling everyone I did when I told him no. Maybe it's petty. Maybe I should let it go. Maybe he was just a misled asshole kid. But petty or not, I look down at him with nothing but pity and disgust.

"Dyan, I'm sorry, I really am." Jared stammers. "I was an asshole in high school, but I've changed. I have. I've worked on myself to be a better person."

I nod, looking out over the water. "Good for you." I turn and start to walk away, stopping to turn my head over my shoulder. *"Twój tatuaż wygląda jak tanie psie gówno,"* I spit at him. *Your tattoo looks like cheap dog shit.*

"What? Sorry, I don't speak Mexican."

I laugh as I walk out of the water, following Levi back to the rock to retrieve our clothes. I spot Stella hastily packing up her things, throwing her sun dress over her wet bikini, and Levi and I follow her back to her car.

"Got to work on that taste in men, baby girl!" Levi calls after her, and is met with Stella flipping him off over her shoulder. Levi laughs. "Oh, come on, you didn't know Jared Marshall was a raging homophobe?"

"No, I didn't." She gets to her car and presses a button to open the trunk. "I wouldn't have gone out with him if I'd known."

"Sorry to burst your bubble."

Her poisonous gaze is back as it lands on me, and she throws her bag into the trunk, slamming it shut and crossing her arms over her chest.

"I'm sorry he said those things to you in school, Dylan. I had no idea. It was wrong. But you two coming down here like a pair of fucking GI Joes to ruin my date? I don't think those two things are in any way connected."

"Sure they are." Levi gives her a brilliant smile. "We're just looking out for you."

She steps up to him and jabs a finger in his face. "You're pissing on my leg, that's all. Stop pulling the big brother act." She backs away from him, and shakes her head as she regards us both with a face of sheer fury. "You do not own me. Neither of you. So stop acting like it."

Before we can say anything else, she climbs into her car, gunning the engine and tearing out of the parking lot in a shower of dust.

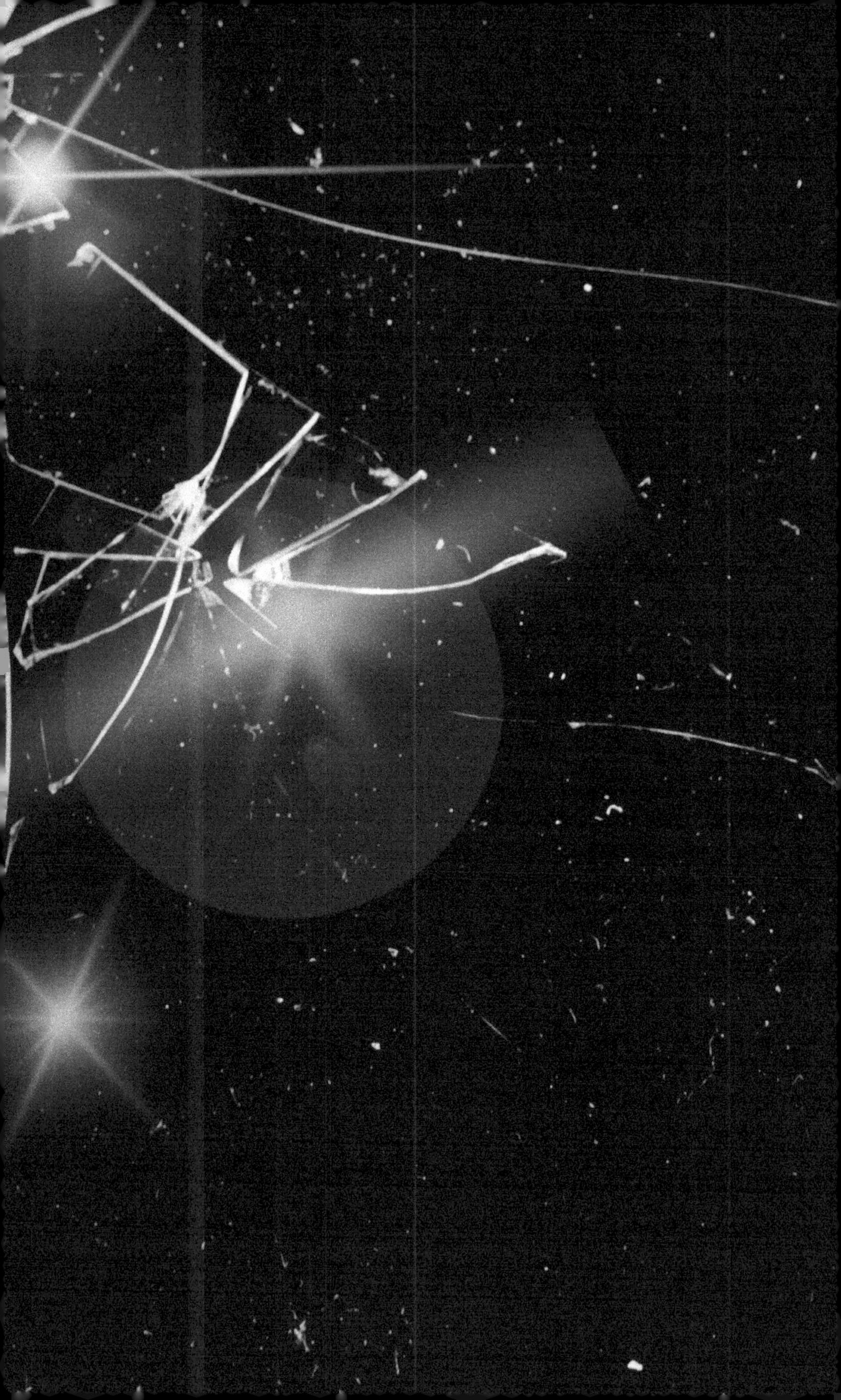

CHAPTER SIX

I'M NOT GAY. *I'm not gay. I'm really not.*

My fingers claw into the car door as I repeat the mantra over and over in my head. But it's pointless, because a man I just paid a hundred bucks to suck my cock has his head in my lap, bobbing up and down as his mouth works me hard. If I wasn't about to blow my fucking load right down his throat, I could almost believe the words I keep telling myself.

But here, in the dimly lit parking lot, I look down at this man, run my fingers through his thick dark hair, and I know I'm lying to myself.

I'd never been attracted to men before. I was popular with the girls in high school, and had a reputation, one I was proud of. The back seat of my Camaro was the scene of plenty of moaning and screaming, girls telling me they loved me, trying to tie down Levi Fenton because he was good in bed and loved eating pussy.

But then in prison, being close to Dylan every day, things started to shift. He grew into a man, bulging with muscle, and he was just so fucking beautiful. I'd never been intimidated by a man before. I'd never been intimidated by *anyone* before.

And then yesterday, watching Dylan walk out of the water, his brown skin glistening in the sun, his face triumphant after giving Jared fucking Marshall a piece of his mind - he looked so fucking good, and since that moment all my desire and longing was too much. I needed to do something to tamp all those feelings down. So this morning, I went downtown and bought a car, then spent too much time trying to find a quick hook-up.

But for some dumb reason, I didn't want a woman. I don't want any woman, but her.

I clench my eyes shut. No, I can't think about that either. Not my little sister. This is all messy enough as it is.

Instead, I surrender to fantasies of my best friend, his eyes that are so dark they're almost black, the way his mouth curves into that crooked grin. His abs, the snake tattoos around his neck. I clench my molars as my balls draw up tight, imagining bracing my hand around Dylan's neck, feeling him straining and moaning as I sink my cock into his ass.

Fuck, what the fuck is wrong with me?

The man's mouth sucks me harder, and my head slams into the headrest as I moan loudly, my cock pumping hot jets of cum down the man's throat. The man licks and sucks up every drop of me, and a sick feeling lands in my stomach. I run my hand over his head, but it's wrong. I'm seeking out a stubbled head, a scar over the right ear, the warm steel of his piercings.

A stranger just sucked my cock, and all I can think of is my best friend, and wishing it was him instead.

I run a hand over my heated face, and the man sits up, regarding me with a grin.

"Who's Dylan?" He asks.

My heart fucking leaps into my throat. "What?"

The man runs his fingers along his lips. "Dylan. You said that name when you came."

"I - what?" That sick feeling increases. "I mean, he's, he's just a friend."

"Just a friend, huh?" The man leans across and runs a finger along my jawline. "Listen, I get it. I see it all the time. Confused guys like you, experimenting with men like me." He kisses my cheek gently, and I like the feel of his lips way too much. "Trust me, handsome, whoever this Dylan is, you've got it bad."

"I'm not gay." Saying it out loud makes me feel even more foolish.

The man laughs lightly, and opens the car door. "Sure, honey. Tell Dylan that." He climbs out, closing the door behind him and disappears across the parking lot.

I sit with the heavy, sick feeling for a while, tucking my dick away and trying to get a handle on my breathing. Dylan is my best friend, and now my business partner. He's also madly in love with my sister. I can't come between that. I can't ruin this for them both.

My phone buzzes in the dash, and I pick it up to see a message from Stella.

> Next time you throw a party, maybe let me know first.

Shit, the party. I need to get back, right now. With a final deep breath, I gun the engine of my new bright blue Alfa Romeo, and head out of the parking lot into the fading evening light. I try to morph into some semblance of Responsible Adult. I have to present myself as the new boss to these guys, and the deep shame I feel over what I just did, and what I thought while I did it, just will not let me go.

Thankfully, in the fifteen minutes it takes me to cross town and pull into Stella's driveway, I calm down. I put on the cocky grin, the well-rehearsed mask. *I can do this.*

Until I see Dylan hauling a keg over his shoulder. With no shirt on.

Three more deep breaths, and I force myself out of the car.

"Hey!" Dylan calls, heading across the drive into the garage. "Where were you?"

"Sorry, I had some errands to run and lost track of time." I'm trying to be calm, but I'm sure there's a neon fucking sign over my head saying *I just said your name while I ejaculated in another man's mouth*. More deep breaths. I follow him into the garage, where music plays softly over the speakers.

"Stella's pissed," Dylan tells me, placing the keg behind the bar. "I feel like we're doing one thing wrong after another here."

"She'll be OK, it's not like we're 16 and the house is going to be trashed."

Dylan laughs, flashing me a broad smile. "No, so responsible now, right?"

I swallow so hard I swear my Adam's apple is going to bounce right out of my throat. "So responsible. Yeah."

Dylan cocks an eyebrow, crossing his muscular arms over his chest. "You OK?"

"Yeah, I'm fine." I gesture to the driveway, desperate for a change of subject. "See the new car?"

"I did, it's a real nice color." Dylan leans around the bar to get a better look. "I need to get one, too. At least try and act like an adult." He puffs out a breath. "Not that I think it'll make much difference."

The brief flash of sadness in his face and the heavy tone in his voice make my stomach twist, placing a strain on my lungs that makes me feel sick. I can't act on this. Not with Dylan. Not with Stella. He wants her so badly, he loves her and I need to support them. I have to swallow all that down.

They're not meant for me.

Thankfully, I don't have much more time to dwell on those thoughts, as a truck engine roars up the street and dies right outside the house. Dylan pulls his white shirt on and gives me that crooked smile that makes my heart stop.

"Ready, Mr Boss Man?"

"Ready as I'll ever be," I reply, and we turn to meet the first of our new employees.

Within an hour, the garage is buzzing with conversation, liquor flowing freely and friendly pool games being played.

"You two, you're alright." Eric, one of the older mechanics, clinks his glass against mine, and I answer him with a smile.

"We just want to do right by you all and by Mario."

"I appreciate that." Eric nods, looking out over the garage. "Nice place you got here."

"It's my sis-" The word dies on my tongue, and that sick feeling from this afternoon comes back like a freight train straight through my gut. Eric eyes me questioningly. "It's, uh, my step-sister's place. She let us stay after we, well, we got out."

"Oh yeah, I heard about that. You two, you, uh." His eyes dart around the room, and he lowers his head towards me. "I heard you two killed your step-father."

"It was an accident." The lie. The well-rehearsed lie. "He attacked Dylan, and well, shit got out of hand."

"Sorry about that man, that sucks." Eric sighs heavily, taking a swig of his drink, his eyes wandering over my shoulder. And they nearly drop out of his head. "Holy shit."

The garage goes strangely silent, only the low beat of music humming around us, and I turn to see what's caught every man in the room's attention.

Stella parades across the back porch in a scandalously small yellow bikini, martini glass in hand and a towel draped over her arm as she makes her way to the hot tub. Her hair is piled on top of her head and secured with a matching yellow scarf. She looks like she just wandered out of an old movie, or a high-class porno, I can't decide which.

"I guess that's your sister," Eric says with a low laugh, and I think I'm going to throw up.

My sister. Yeah, sure, my little sister who looks good enough to fucking eat right now. My sister with tits to die for and an ass I could spend an entire night leaving teeth marks in.

Stella doesn't look at us at all, merely sets her phone down in a dock on the small table beside the hot tub, and with a swipe of her fingers, music starts blaring, totally drowning out our own. A woman sings about *I don't need a man,* and it's so bratty and obvious I can't help but laugh, while also being overcome with the urge to run up onto the porch and fuck the brat right out of her.

You're not gay, and you're not into incest. Back the fuck up.

Stella lowers herself into the hot tub, still ignoring us, and takes a sip of her martini. The men around me gradually start to move again, finally broken of the trance of watching this bronzed goddess of a woman parade her body right in front of their fucking eyeballs.

I need a drink.

I excuse myself from Eric and head to the bar, where Dylan is already pouring himself a shot. His face is warring between frustration and admiration, his eyes flickering up to where Stella is languishing in the water.

"Drink?" He holds the bottle up, and I nod. "She's a fucking tease, man." He pours me a shot of whiskey, and we both down them without another word.

"She sure is." I cast a glance over my shoulder to see Stella's head bopping back and forth gently in time with the music against the edge of the tub. "She's just messing with us."

"What's that?"

I realize what I just said and turn back to Dylan with a smile. "I said she's messing with you. Trying to make you see what you're missing." I'm going to lose my fucking mind. I decide then and there to try and get my own place as soon as possible and get as much distance between me and Stella and Dylan as I can, before this whole situation goes south.

Suddenly, the men around us whoop and laugh, and a few whistles go up. Dylan's face is like fucking thunder.

"She just took her top off," he growls through gritted teeth.

I whip around to see Stella's naked back leaning over the edge of the tub as she selects another song on her phone. The yellow bikini top has been cast onto the porch beside the tub. Rage surges through me as I look at the men around me, ogling her as she's up there basically naked.

But I have to be professional. I can't fly into a fucking possessive rage on my new employees, not least of all because Stella would fucking love that. Getting a reaction like that out of me? She'd eat that up.

"OK, fellas, we get it." I raise my voice and hold up a hand. "Let's get back to pool, and stop eye-fucking my sister, please."

The word *sister* has the intended effect even though it makes my skin crawl. The men all respectfully lower their eyes with abashed chuckles. The conversations start up again, and I give Dylan a pointed look.

"I'll be right back," I tell him, before I cross the garage and go up the porch steps.

Stella watches me approach, swirling her hands through the water.

"Hey *bro*," she purrs, giving me a sly smile. "Good night?"

"Great night. You?"

"Oh, yeah, I'm having a great time. Enjoying the stars and my martini." She leans her head back, which lifts her chest so her breasts are bobbing just below the surface of the water, and I need to take those three steadying breaths again. "Next time you have a party, brother dearest, maybe give me some warning so I can reschedule my skinny dip."

"I'll keep that in mi-" Her bikini bottoms hit me in the face before I can finish my sentence, sending warm water straight down my front, and a chorus of cheers from the men in the garage. I brush the droplets from my eyes, and Stella smiles at me sweetly.

"Hand me my towel, would you?"

I lean over the edge of the tub, seething and soaked and fucking dying to slap that ass that I know is naked below the surface of the bubbling water. "If you think I'm going to let you get out of this tub buck-naked in front of all these men, you got another thing coming."

She pouts and holds up her hand. "But I'm starting to prune."

"Stella, I swear to god."

"What?" She moves through the water towards me until we're face to face. "What're you going to do, Levi? What would you do if I stood up right now?"

I'm barely containing my rage. This perfect face that won't stop grinning up at me is driving me fucking crazy, and all I can think about is forcing those pouty lips apart and shoving my cock down her throat to show her who's boss. And she'd love it. I'd make her love it.

Jesus, what the fuck is wrong with you, man?

"Come on, Levi." She rises a little, so the water bobs just below her nipples. "You going to preserve your little sister's innocence?"

Innocence, my ass. I know she's playing. I know she's doing this to punish me and get a rise out of me. She's not doing this to entice me. It's not like that. But then all I can think about is her standing at my doorway, watching me sleep naked, wondering what she was thinking, and suddenly it feels like she is fucking taunting me. Like she's trying to push me, *me,* not Dylan.

I want to push back. I want to play right into her game and see how devious the sparkle in those amber eyes can get. But I know Dylan is watching us right now, probably wondering why my step-sister is sitting right in front of me giving me half an eyeball of perfect, round tits.

Fuck, don't think about her tits that way.

Stella seems to sense her triumph, and with a loud swish she rises to her feet. Her slippery body is on full display, and I step back and gawp at her for a split second. She's fucking perfect. Huge tits and a round ass that's begging for the slap of my hand, a tiny waist against which is perched a manicured hand.

The whistles and cheers from the garage bring me to my senses, and I snatch up the towel and throw it around her before the men see too much of what I do not want to share with anyone. The men clap and laugh, and Stella waves haughtily.

Dylan is standing by the garage door, his face incandescent with rage.

"Stella, get inside now," I command in a low voice.

She steps out of the hot tub, clutching the towel around herself, and shrugs. "I thought I'd come join you all for a drink."

I grab her by the elbow and drag her towards the back door. "Get inside, dry off and get dressed."

"Or what?"

Fuck. That bratty, lilting fucking voice.

"Or nothing, just get dressed."

"It's so hot, maybe I don't feel like getting dressed right now."

Just inside the doorway, once we're out of view of the garage, I back her against the door frame. Her face is lit up with excitement as I cage her in with my hands, her body showing the tension of fear, but fuck it makes me want her even more.

"You get inside and get dressed now or I will spank the brat right out of you, you hear me?"

Her mouth twists into a grin, but her pupils blow out at my words. "Spank me, huh? Put me over your knee?"

"If that's what it takes." My hands are balled into fists against the wall either side of her, determined to hold on to my self-restraint.

"Would I be naked for this spanking?"

Fuck. "Stella, stop it."

She blinks, feigning innocence. "Oh, I'm sorry, yesterday you wanted to read me smut and now you're getting all uptight and antsy. That's so weird, *brother*."

"Stop calling me that."

"Why?" She puts a hand against my chest where my wet t-shirt clings to my skin. "It's true, isn't it?"

"Stella?" Dylan's voice rings across the yard, and Stella blinks and shakes her head, as though coming out of a sort of trance. She braces her hand against my chest and pushes me away, hard. "Next time you throw a party, ask me first," she spits out, before turning and pushing through the glass french door and disappearing down the hallway.

Dylan's footsteps thud up the porch steps, and he regards me with confusion as I emerge from the shadows. "What happened? Where's Stella?"

"She went in to get dressed." I lean a hand against the wall beside me, and inhale deeply. "That girl, she's... She's a fucking brat."

Dylan rubs his chin and nods. "Yeah, she sure is." He gestures to my wet clothes. "Maybe you should go change and come back and join us. Stella probably needs to cool off."

"Yeah, I'll be right back." I head inside, and I know it's a bad idea to follow Stella in here. For all I know she's walking around the house naked somewhere, downing another martini to give herself the confidence to sass me some more. I drag my hands through my hair, my skin inflamed and my cheeks burning. Fuck, the things I want to do to her.

I take the stairs two at a time and when I get to the landing, I breathe a sigh of relief to see Stella's door is closed. I head into my room and pull on dry jeans and a fresh blue t-shirt, and head back out. I walk quietly so Stella doesn't hear, pausing at the top of the stairs when I hear a strange sound.

A buzzing noise.

What is that?

I pat my pocket, and it's not my phone vibrating. Then I hear a moan, and turn to look at Stella's door. Like a moth to the fucking flame, I edge closer to the door, and realise - Stella's getting off mere feet from where I'm standing.

She was fucking taunting me. And now she's as turned on as I am.

I want to tear open that door and see what she's doing. I want to watch that pretty face as she comes. I take another step towards the door. I should turn around. This is wrong. Dylan's downstairs. Fuck, she's not mine. This is wrong.

Another soft moan. I'm going to go fucking insane.

Then there's a roar of a motorcycle engine, and loud cheers

downstairs, and I'm brought violently to my senses. *Fucking asshole. Get the fuck away from her.*

Shame coils around my throat as I head back down the stairs and outside to rejoin the party. The men crowd around our bikes, music plays loudly, and liquor continues to flow. Every now and then I cast a glance up at the house, to Stella's room, and by midnight, the light is out.

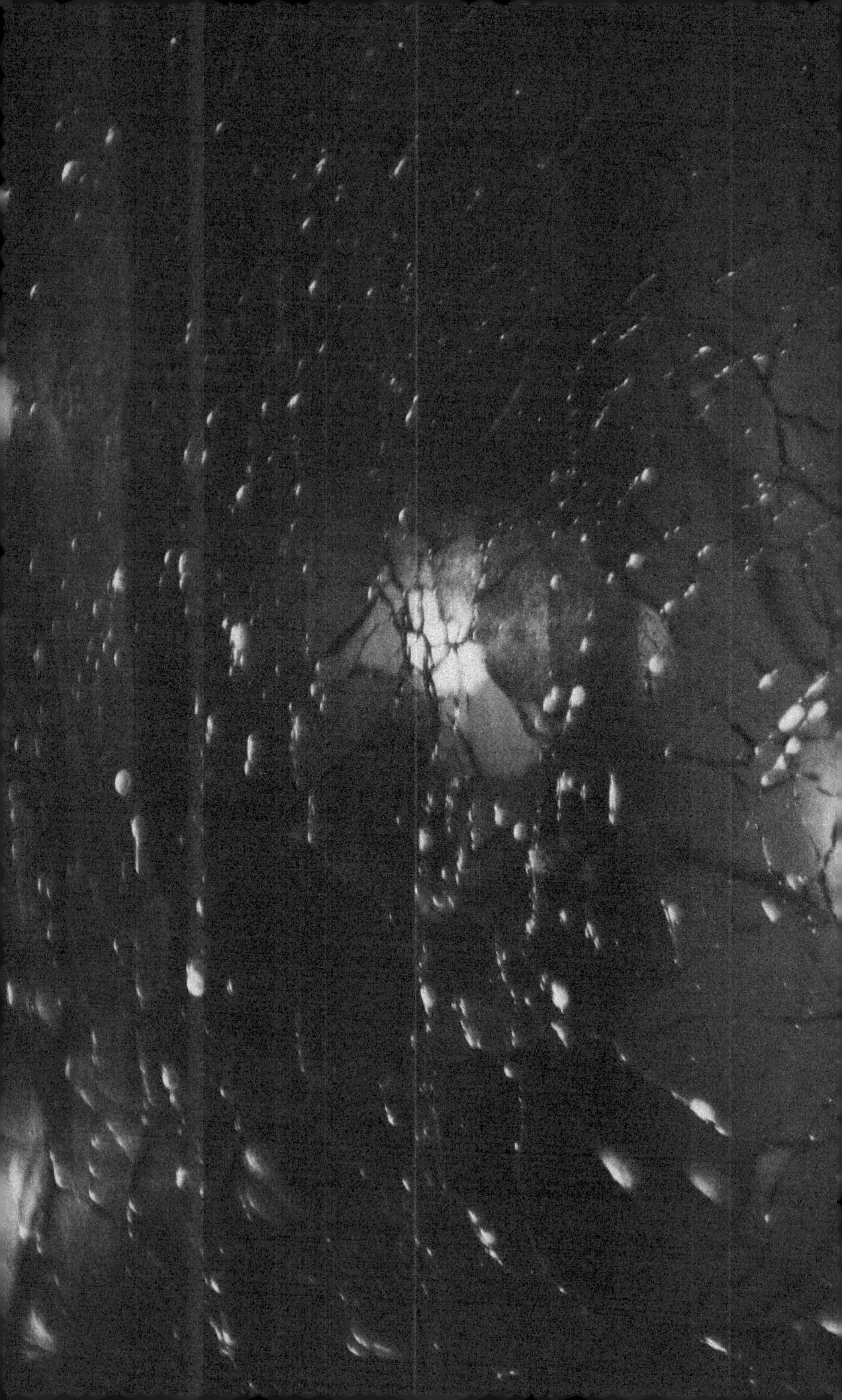

STELLA

CHAPTER SEVEN

"I THINK I want to fuck my stepbrother."

Bless Dr. Varden, because her face doesn't even betray the slightest hint of shock at my confession. "I see."

"And his best friend," I blurt out, before quickly raising my hands. "Who is also kind of my ex. I mean, I don't want to fuck them at the same time. I mean, maybe at the same time? I don't know, is that weird? I've never had a threesome before, and I mean, it sounds like it'd be fun, but that's weird, right? It's my brother and his best friend, why would they want to sleep with me at the same time, that's like them sleeping together and I don't think Levi is gay. I mean OK, not gay, Dylan isn't gay either, he's bi, but they're just friends and I'm Levi's sister for fuck's sake. I don't know what's happening to me, but ever since they got out, I've been all tangled up, and then I looked at my brother naked, and I-"

"Stella, I want you to take a deep breath," Dr. Varden interjects, raising her hand from her clipboard so her palm is flat and facing upwards. "In." She breathes in and raises her hand. "And out." She turns her hand over and lowers it as she exhales through pursed lips.

I copy her for a count of three, trying to calm the raging

thoughts in my head. I can't believe I just admitted to another person that I want to fuck Levi. This is gross. I'm sick. There's going to be some FBI suits on my doorstep tomorrow, revoking my entrance to the bar because incest prevents me from practicing law or something.

"This isn't normal, is it?" I ask once I've calmed down a little. "I mean, there's something wrong with me."

Dr Varden shakes her head, her blunt bob brushing against the shoulders of her artfully draped navy silk blouse. "Not at all. These feelings you describe are completely normal."

"*Normal*?"

Dr Varden nods, her face maintaining that neutral demeanor. "Familial attraction after an extended time apart is quite common in siblings, even biological ones. That's not to say that such relationships are advisable, much less appropriate, but it does happen."

"Is it different because Levi's my step-brother? Like, does that make it… OK?"

Dr Varden folds her hands in her lap, a picture of composure. "Do *you* think it's OK?"

I try to swallow down the lump in my throat. "No."

"And why is that?"

"Because… Because he's my brother. At least, that's how people see him, that's how people have always seen him."

Dr Varden mulls over my words for a few seconds, before raising her eyes to the ceiling for a moment. "Stella, when you say you want to have sex with your step-brother, what do you mean by that?"

"I-I mean, I want to… I'm sorry, I don't understand the question."

She clasps her hands on her knee. "Is it possible you're simply looking for closeness, and it's manifesting as a desire for sexual interactions?"

I stare at her for a moment, trying to find a way of telling this demure professional that I had a screaming orgasm while I imagined Levi spanking me and tying me to the bed so he could fuck me and punish me for being a brat. That I'd taunted my step-brother and pushed his buttons until I could see the thread of self-control come completely undone. That I'd spent an entire night with a vibrator buried inside me to try and alleviate the desire to have Levi and Dylan in my bed, to imagine all the ways they could both fuck me.

How do you tell someone all of that without sounding like a complete freak?

"I don't know." I finally reply, and shrug weakly. "It's all so twisted, and having them both so close, it makes me miss all that time we lost, and I want that back, if that makes sense?"

Dr Varden smiles warmly. "Of course it does. It's perfectly normal to have trouble compartmentalizing feelings of intimacy with your history."

Her words aren't meant to hurt me, but they may as well be a slap.

"Because I'm broken, you mean?" I swallow hard, that damn lump just growing and growing with every word. "I can't have a normal relationship with my own step-brother because I've never known what a normal, healthy, platonic relationship looks like?"

"You're not broken, Stella. We've gone over this." Dr Varden nudges the box of tissues closer to me, even though I'm not crying. "What happened to you hasn't broken you, it shifted how you view the world. Trauma does that. It just requires a little shift in your behavior so you don't engage in anything that could cause you harm." The word *again* hangs on the end of that sentence like a wailing ghost. She doesn't say it, but she doesn't have to.

"I don't do that anymore," I say, fighting the wavering in my voice. "I haven't done that in a really long time."

"I know, and you've done so well, Stella. And I don't want

you to feel shame over what happened. Engaging in risky sexual behaviours is very normal for victims of sexual assault, you know that."

Risky sexual behavior. It's such a sterile way to put it. It sounds almost harmless when she says it like that. It doesn't even begin to describe what I did to myself. What I allowed men to do to me, all in the name of wanting to feel something, anything, other than the shame and sorrow that threatened to pull me down into a black hole and snuff out any light that existed within me.

"I don't think this is like that," I say slowly. "I'm not trying to hurt myself. I don't want to hurt them either."

"Did you have thoughts like this of your step-brother while you were growing up?"

Another question I have no idea how to answer. Because I didn't. Not at first. He was just a stupid teenage boy whose mom happened to marry my dad. We fought and teased and stuck together, like friends do. I had no other siblings to compare the relationship to, so I didn't know what that felt like.

It wasn't until my 17th birthday, when he bought me a gold necklace, with a gold S charm, that something changed. His fingertips as they brushed against my collarbone, they didn't feel like a brother's hands. But I'd been involved with Dylan, and Levi was my brother, at least that's how our parents sold it to the world. And my father hated them both equally, which made everything complicated anyway.

"I-I masturbated to the thought of him the other night," I finally admit, expecting to feel sick but finding that the admission makes my shoulders feel a little lighter. "That's gross, right?"

"Stella, human emotions are complicated, and trauma makes them even more so." She moves the tissue box closer again, even though I'm still not crying. "Have you talked to your stepbrother about these feelings?"

"Oh my god, no." The thought has my cheeks burning.

"Is there any indication that he feels the same way?"

My head is going to spontaneously combust. I scrape my nails along my linen shorts, and bounce my foot against the ground. "God, I mean, I don't know." *Yes I do. I know what the look he gave me means, I know the way he's avoided me since that night tells me he wanted very much to spank me.* "He's been in prison a long time, so I think it's just..."

"He left behind a girl and has come out to find an accomplished, beautiful young woman?" Dr Varden smiles at me. "Again, totally normal. You've met each other again as a man and a woman, not as brother and sister. Perhaps that relationship just needs to be fostered again."

I don't know how to say that I don't think I want to go back to being Levi's sister.

"And what about Dylan?" Dr Varden asks.

"What about him?"

"Are you intending to rekindle your relationship with him?" She uncrosses and crosses her legs, grasping her shiny black pen in her hand.

"I mean, he's asked for a chance." Now my eyes start to sting. Because the love I feel for Dylan digs into my ribs, sharp and aching, and I don't know what to do with it.

"Are you going to give him that chance?" Dr Varden asks gently.

I shrug helplessly. "I don't know. I want to. But I don't know if I can forgive him."

"For what happened that night?"

I nod, biting my lip as my vision starts to swim. "I-I still blame him. I can't help but feel that if he'd just not done that, if we'd just gone to the police instead of them... I don't know. They ran off to play big heroes, and who stayed with me? No one." On the words *no one*, the dam breaks. Tears begin to roll over my lashes, and I snatch up a tissue, pressing it to my eyes. "I want to let him in. I do. Because with him, it's like... all the noise stops. All the chaos and the noise, it just *stops*."

"He's your calm." Dr Varden's voice remains soft and measured.

I nod. Dylan is my calm. Levi is my storm. And I need them both and want them both and can't have either of them because of that.

I cry my way through the rest of my session, at the injustice of it all, at everything that was taken from me, from all of us.

When I get outside, I dial Zee's number and ask if they have an appointment free for me. I start crying again when they say yes, and I can't even tell them why.

"Fucking love your hair, girl." Zee does the little zhoosh thing with their fingers so my freshly high-lighted hair bounces around my shoulders, and they sigh appreciatively. "So pretty."

"Thanks."

"And this tan, and the pink lip gloss? Damn girl." They snap their fingers. "Forget being a lawyer, get an OnlyFans."

I can't help but laugh. "You did always say my tits were camera worthy."

They throw their head back with a groan. "Girl, I dream of your tits and I am asexual."

"Gee, thanks." I chuckle, putting my gold hoop earrings back in. "Can I ask you something?"

"Of course."

"Did you know Jared Marshall was a homophobe?"

Zee purses their lips and shrugs lightly as they pack up their tools. "I mean, he wasn't especially nice to me in high school. Called me Freak, didn't leave me alone until Dylan got big enough to defend both of us."

"Why didn't you ever tell me?"

Zee smiles warmly at my reflection. "Girl, you were going through it, OK? We didn't want to burden you with anything else."

I dip my head. "I was a bad friend."

"No." Zee grasps my shoulders tightly. "You were a great friend, you *are* a great friend. But we all knew something wasn't right with you."

I sniffle, not wanting that dam to burst again. "So, when did you decide to forgive Jared for what he did?"

Zee rubs my shoulders, sighing lightly. "When he got back from Africa, he was kind of a new person. He came to me and told me that the church he'd grown up in had been a nightmare. His parents, too. I guess I forgave him because I know how badly brainwashed you can get when that's all you hear."

I feel a slight pang of shame. "Maybe I was too harsh on him."

Zee shakes their head, tossing their purple locs. "He's not owed forgiveness just because he's not an asshole anymore. And to be fair, Dylan didn't just get called names, he got black eyes."

I lift my eyes with a sigh. "So, why would you want me to go out with Jared?"

Zee suppresses a smirk, and shrugs. "I'm not ashamed to admit, I wanted to see what would happen."

"You were testing them, weren't you?"

Zee's brows knit together. "Them? I mean, Dylan, yeah." They look back down at their tools, winding the cord of a hairdryer around itself. "I think he needed a push to see that he needed to act to get you back."

My throat runs dry. Of course Zee wasn't pushing Levi because he's my damn stepbrother. I'm already letting the cat out of the bag. I need these men out of my house before I lose my mind.

"Well, I don't know if it did that. I kinda acted like a royal pain in the ass on Friday."

Zee raises their eyebrows and laughs lightly. "Yeah, I heard about that. My cousin works for Mario, and said his new boss's sister gave them quite a show at the staff party."

I sink into the chair with a groan, covering my face with my hands. "I don't even know what came over me. I made a martini with the vermouth you bought me, I'm going to blame you."

"Oh sure, blame me for morphing into Stripper Barbie, bitch." Zee huffs out a laugh as I sink further into the chair. "You know, you could just let Dylan take you out on a date rather than strip off in front of his employees."

"What is wrong with me?" I drop my hands to pout at Zee's reflection. "I'm being an ass and I don't even know why."

Zee grips my shoulders with their warm hands, and lowers their head next to mine, smiling warmly at me in the mirror. "My sweet girl, you have been through it. Stop overthinking, and just be with them. Stop thinking about who you were, and what was, and think about what could be. Think about how happy you could all be." They wrap their arms around my shoulders and hug me, and I grip onto them with everything I've got. "I love you so much."

"I love you, too."

"Give my man a chance, huh?" They kiss my cheek and tuck my hair behind my ear. "He's like a big wounded puppy dog when he's around you."

"I know. He's gorgeous." I swipe away the lone tear that manages to breach my lashes, and turn my head to smile at Zee. "Why do I go to therapy when I have you?"

"Comes with the territory." Zee holds up a hand and shrugs. "You become half-therapist, listening to everyone's problems here."

"I'll bet." We both glance over at the door as the bell tinkles and a woman with short blonde hair in black trousers and a neat cream blouse steps into the salon. Her heels clack on the marble floor, and Zee smiles warmly as they walk over to the counter.

"Hi there, what can I help you with today?"

"Hi, I'm actually looking for Stella Langford." As she says my name, her gaze lands on me where I'm still sitting in my chair. She raises a hand in greeting and starts to approach me. "Stella! Mallory Harris, Channel Four News. Can we have a-"

"Oh, no you don't." Zee rounds the counter and blocks Mallory's path, one lithe arm pointing at the door. "You get the hell out of my place, and stop harassing my client."

"I just want to talk to her."

I snatch up my purse and rise out of the chair. "I don't talk to reporters." I move across the salon, and nod at Zee. "Thanks, I'll talk to you later."

"Stella, have you heard about Gloria Fenton's interview?" Mallory asks as I pass her by, and I stop in my tracks. Her eyes fix on my face as I meet her gaze, and she smiles softly. "Hi Stella, I'm really sorry to ambush you like this, but I thought you deserved to know."

"Deserved to know what?"

She gestures to the door with a sweep of her hand. "Shall we go get a coffee and talk?"

"Oh hell no," Zee pipes up, crossing their arms over their chest. "You want to talk to her, you do it right here. I'm not leaving her alone with you vultures again."

Mallory's certainty slips a little, and she holds up her clasped hands. "Stella, I'm not here to hurt you or catch you out, I just wanted to talk."

"You can talk right here," Zee says with a jab of their finger in the direction of the plush armchairs by the door.

"We don't trust reporters." My voice is cooler than I intended, but I'm not going to feel bad about that. Instead, I stride over the armchair and dip my head in the direction of the other one. "Come. Sit. We can talk freely here."

Zee goes to the door and turns over the sign to the Closed side, latching the door and flipping off the lights in the window. Mallory nods, her corporate smile back in place as she clacks across the marble floor to sit down in the green velvet armchair opposite me.

"I trust this is all strictly off the record," I say as she opens her mouth to speak.

"Of course."

"I'm witness to that," Zee says from the counter.

"And you are aware I'm a lawyer." I fold my arms over my lap, regarding the woman opposite me with what I hope appears to be detached neutrality. Inside, I'm a tornado of butterflies as I wonder what the fuck Gloria is up to now.

Mallory smoothes her pants over her legs as she crosses one over the other. "Stella, I meant it. I'm not here to cause you any pain, or to dredge up the past."

"Go ahead then."

"Gloria Fenton has granted Channel Six a tell-all interview." Mallory looks genuinely apologetic as she says it. "She's apparently been working with some college students on her son's case, and this interview is being touted as a big reveal on information the public didn't know."

Zee's head snaps up to look over at me with alarm, and I dig my fingers into my palm to try and keep myself composed.

"I'm not sure why you're telling me all this. I haven't spoken to my stepmother in years."

Mallory leans forward, closing the distance between us a little. "I wanted to give you the chance to tell your side of the story."

"And there it is!" Zee storms over to us, eyes full of fury. "Get out of my place. You're not going to harass my friend after everything she went through."

"I just want to give her a chance to-"

"Chance nothing." Zee jabs a finger in the direction of the door. "Get the fuck out."

Mallory turns back to me helplessly, and I toss my hair over my shoulder. "I have no interest in talking to anyone or in rehashing what happened back then."

"But if people understood you, Stella-"

"People never understand." I cut her off as I rise to my feet. "And they won't understand now. Gloria can say whatever she wants, it doesn't even matter. That woman is less than nothing to me."

Mallory reaches into her pocket and withdraws a slim black business card. "This is my number. In case you change your mind. Call me any time, we can talk." When I don't take the card from her, she places it down on the low coffee table, and gives me a friendly smile. "I mean it, any time."

"Fine."

"I want to help you, Stella." She gives me a quick nod, before she heads to the door, which Zee is already holding open for her. Zee's venomous gaze pursues the reporter out into the late afternoon sunshine, and then they slam the door shut behind her.

"The fucking nerve of that woman," Zee mutters, shaking their head. "Coming in here like that. How the fuck did she even know you were here?"

I bend down to pick up the business card, running my thumb over the matte surface. "Yeah. Unbelievable."

Zee stops and regards me critically. "You're not thinking of actually doing it, are you?"

I shake my head, shoving the card into my bag. "No, I have no interest in talking to the press about all that. It's done."

"What do you think Gloria's up to?"

I shrug, putting my sunglasses on my head. "Who knows with her. I don't really care. What's she going to say that she hasn't already said?"

"Does she know the guys are living with you?"

"I don't know. I guess." With a sigh, I fish my purse out of my bag. "How much do I owe you for today?"

"Girl, that shit is on the house, as you damn well know." Zee walks up to me, their face twisted with concern, placing their hands on my upper arms and squeezing gently. "I know I talk shit, but if you did ever want to go public, tell everyone what happened, I'd be behind you. I promise. I want you to do it because you want to, not because you want to beat your evil stepmother to it."

"I know, honey. Thank you."

Zee wraps me in a hug, and they smell soothingly of rose and patchouli.

"I'm always here for you, you know that, right?"

"I know. I know you are." I pull back from them and smile. "If you won't let me pay, then promise you'll come for dinner this weekend. Maybe you can bring some calm into my chaotic household."

"It's a deal. I'll be there Saturday. No vermouth this time."

I can't help but laugh, and place a kiss on their cheek. "See you Saturday."

"Try not to kill my man before then!" They call after me as I head outside.

"I'll try!" I pull down my sunglasses against the harsh glare of the sun, the warm air brushing against my skin as I make my way back to the car. I pass a florist, and spy a display of peonies, and decide to buy myself a huge bunch before getting back into my Volvo.

The scent of the flowers fills my car, and I put music on as I cruise down the street back to my house. A figure is jogging down the road ahead of me, dressed in small black shorts, wearing no shirt so their tattoos are on display. I know instantly that it's Dylan.

I consider pulling over and seeing if he wants a ride home, but he's working out so I might be interrupting his mile. But maybe he's gotten hot and needs a ride? He doesn't look like he has water with him, and it's at least 90 today. Shit.

Before I can second-guess myself too much, I pull over ahead of him, and watch him approach in the rear view mirror. He's dripping with sweat when he stops by the car, shoulders heaving as he leans into the wound-down window.

"Hey *guera,*" he pants, running a hand over his sweat-soaked face.

"Hi." The nick-name *guera* - blondie - makes my insides do a little flip. "Did you want a ride? It's so hot today."

"I'll get your car all sweaty." Beads of sweat drip down his shoulders, and I hope to god he didn't just see me swallow hard.

"I don't care. I'd rather a sweaty car than have you get heat stroke."

"Ah, you're sweet." He opens the car door, retrieving the huge bouquet of peonies before flopping down into the seat. "These are pretty, gift from someone?"

I grunt as I pull back out onto the street. "A gift from me to me. I don't think anyone's ever bought me flowers in my life."

"I did."

I glance over at him, at this huge tattooed man clutching a bouquet of pretty pink flowers, and he smiles at me.

"Remember? For your birthday? When you turned 16, you said you wanted nothing but flowers, because no one had ever bought you flowers before."

My heart sinks. Because of course he had. He'd bought me seven bunches of roses in all different colors, and my room had smelled so good. I'd been so happy. But then that night, because it was my sixteenth, my father told me it was time to do something extra special.

I clench my eyes shut and suck in a breath.

"Stella?" Dylan's hand is on my shoulder as I force my eyes back onto the road. "Hey, you OK?"

"I'm fine." I brush the back of my hand over my eyes. "I'm fine, just tired. I haven't been sleeping well."

He reaches over and lays a hand on my thigh, and the touch is so warm and welcoming. Instantly, the sick feeling dissipates, and I just want to wrap him around me and dull all the noise in my head.

"Anything I can do?" He asks in a low voice.

I can't help but giggle. "Anything you can do? And what would that entail?"

"I don't know, a massage, a foot rub." He squeezes my thigh, running his hand to the edge of my shorts and back down to my knee. "I could join you in the hot tub."

I groan and put a hand to my forehead. "I blame the martinis, OK?"

"Hey, you want to strip off a bikini while I'm in there with you, I'm good with that." He leans over and brushes his lips against my shoulder. "That drove me crazy, just so you know."

Shivers erupt down my spine as his breath skates over my skin. "I was being an idiot. I can't believe I… Did that." I laugh lightly as he runs his fingers down my arm. "Keep doing that and I'll crash."

"Just get us home." His voice is full of desire, his meaning more than obvious. He squeezes my thigh again, his fingers straying just a little higher, under the hem of my shorts, and butterflies erupt in my bloodstream.

I want to tell him we shouldn't, but in that moment I can't find the words. Because I want him. I want to feel him and kiss him, I want to taste him and give him my body, finally, after all these years of waiting and wanting. I drive faster than I should to get us down my street, and the tires screech as I turn into the drive.

The peonies are forgotten as Dylan dives across at me, grabbing my face in his hands, his lips descending on my neck.

"Fuck, I need you," he murmurs against my ear. "Say yes. Please, say yes."

His body is still heated from his run and probably from being aroused as fuck now. I'm still strapped into my seatbelt and can barely move, though I'm trying to pull him down to me and turn towards him. He's pleading with me with everything he's got, and I want to give him everything. He just spent 10 years in prison, he deserves to be looked after, right?

"Dylan, just let me-" I reach down and try to free myself from the seatbelt as his hand moves over my breast. "Oh fuck. Dylan, wait, just let me-"

He unclips me and pulls me across and on top of him. His

hands rake up my back and into my hair, tensing and flexing as he pulls me against him.

"Jesus fuck, Stella."

"Dylan, wait." I push against his chest, and he slumps with an exasperated sigh, his forehead leaning against my chest.

"Do you not want this? Do you not want me?"

"I-I mean…" I don't know how to answer him. How do I tell him what I told Dr. Varden today? How do I admit to him what I want without hurting him, without losing him, without watching him walk away because of how sick I am? To him, I'm sweet Stella, the girl of his dreams. When really, I'm disgusting and depraved and broken.

He tips his head back and looks up at me, his beautiful dark eyes filled with pain. "I never expected you to wait for me." He lifts a hand to my cheek, cupping my face in his tattooed fingers. "Really. I never did. I hoped you'd still want me, and I understand if you don't."

"It's not that." I shake my head, clasping on to his hand and leaning into his touch. "I still love you, *papi*."

He sucks in a breath at my words, at the nickname I gave him all those years ago. I lift my eyes to his, feeling a tear fall down my cheek.

"I do. I still love you. But I need to take this slow. I'm sorry. But… I'm not *her* anymore. I'm broken, and I - I don't want to break you too."

He strokes my hair with his other hand as I continue to hold on to him for dear life. "I'll wait as long as I need to, *guera*."

"You know, I like *guera* better than baby, or sweetheart," I tell him shyly, kissing his thumb.

"Then you're my *guera*." He gathers me against his chest, wrapping his huge arms around me. "My girl. *Mi vida. Mi Ciela." My life. My heaven.*

I exhale heavily. I'm a horrible, selfish bitch. I'm keeping him here with me even though I know I can never give him what he wants because I can't bear the thought of him not being in my life. Sooner or later he'll find out, he'll realize, or I'll finally be big enough to admit to him that I can never be faithful to him, and he'll walk away from me. I'll lose the first man I ever loved. One of my best friends. The only person who makes all the noise in my head go quiet.

I wrap myself around him, hating myself for how broken I am. I can't even let myself be happy.

"I'm going to treat you so good, Stella." He kisses my collarbone, my neck, my shoulder. "Just you wait. All this pain, it'll be gone before you know it."

My heart leaps into my throat as the sound of a motorbike engine roars behind my car. Reality comes crashing down on me, and I just want to tell Dylan what's happening, what's going on in my head. Instead, I climb out of his lap, and pick the peonies and my bag up from the floor.

"We should go in," I say quietly.

"I mean it, Stella." Dylan reaches over and brushes a hand over my thigh. "As long as I have to wait, I'll wait."

"I know." I jump as someone knocks on the window, and I turn to meet Levi's grinning face. He eyes us through the window, taking in Dylan's half-naked body, and raises an eyebrow.

"Am I interrupting?" He yells.

With a roll of my eyes and a sigh, I push open the door. "We were just talking." I hope my flushed face doesn't betray me, and I hope to god Dylan's bulging erection has calmed down.

But the way Dylan hurries across the yard to the house and calls, "Going to shower!" Over his shoulder, I doubt it.

Levi eyes me questioningly. "*Did* I interrupt something?"

"No, we were just... We were just talking. He was out jogging and I picked him up."

Levi nods, then reaches out and strokes his fingers through my hair, pushing it back over my shoulder. "You look pretty. Did you get your hair done?"

"Yeah, I went to Zee's." I struggle to keep my breathing even as his fingers brush down my arm. "They always do a great job."

"It'd be pretty hard to make you look anything but perfect."

I clutch on to the bouquet of peonies like they're armor, and gaze into Levi's bright blue eyes, wondering what the fuck to do and who the fuck I am. Minutes ago, I was grinding on Dylan's lap and telling him I love him, and now I'm resisting the urge to wrap my arms around Levi's neck and devour his full lips with mine.

"I'm not perfect, and you all should stop acting like I am." I don't intend for my words to be so cutting or for my tone to be so cold, but the self-loathing leeches into every bone in my body, and before I look back into Levi's eyes, I turn on my heel and head into the house.

"Stella, wait up!" Levi is right on my tail, following me inside. He catches me in the kitchen and spins me around to face him. "What's going on? Did you and Dylan have a fight?"

"No, nothing like that."

"Then what?" He leans closer to me, his brow furrowed as he gazes down at me. "Baby girl, if you don't tell me what's going on-"

"What? You'll spank it out of me?"

His eyebrows shoot up for a second, and he exhales sharply. "I didn't mean to… Look, I know things are… Weird, but…" He breaks off, his eyes dropping to the floor and I can practically hear the cogs turning in his head. "We're all figuring shit out, and trying to find our way here."

"Things aren't weird, Levi. They're a fucking mess." Words I shouldn't say are threatening to bubble out of me. All the feelings I had when he had me cornered on the porch, the thrill I felt seeing him come undone and to know I was tearing all his restraint away from him. "You and me, we're damaged. And if we don't fucking stop, Dylan is going to get hurt."

Levi releases me instantly and takes a step back. He runs a hand over his head, and nods emphatically. "Yeah, you're right.

I'm sorry. I'll find my own place, OK? I'll be out of here within the week."

"Good."

He leaves the kitchen quickly, and I watch his retreating back with a heavy heart. I turn and watch the sun sitting on the horizon, casting orange light across the yard, and I wonder if this feeling will ever go away.

CHAPTER EIGHT

IT'S after midnight when I decide it's too fucking hot to sleep, and head downstairs. Stella went to bed a couple of hours ago, and Levi headed out on his bike to go god knows where. The sound of crickets singing wafts in through the open windows, and thunder rumbles gently in the distance.

I get myself a glass of water in the dark kitchen, and gulp it down. A gentle breeze starts to tug at the curtains, the gathering storm blowing in over the mountains.

I flip on the porch light and throw myself down into a deck chair. My cigarettes are still lying on the table where I'd discarded them before my run this afternoon, and I reach over to pull one out, lighting it with my silver lighter. I'm determined to quit after this pack is done. It was just a habit I picked up in prison, a way to cope and barter and have something to connect with the other guys inside over.

But I don't want to smoke anymore. I want to be healthy and have a long, long life outside.

I suck the smoke down into my lungs, leaning my head back and blowing it out into the dark sky. Lightning flashes in the distance, followed by the gentle growl of thunder. I turn my head to look up at Stella's window, and wonder if she's asleep or tossing and turning in this heat.

I don't know what I'm doing. This afternoon I was sure she wanted me, that she'd take me home and let me peel her clothes off and finally, finally have her. Maybe if I was a different kind of man, I'd have tried to convince her. I'd have pushed harder. But I'm not like that. Not with her.

She loves me, and that has to be enough for now.

It doesn't do much to lessen the burgeoning need for human contact.

I take a deep drag of the cigarette and decide I just need to fucking get laid. 10 years of no physical affection, of no kissing or touching or fucking, it's too much.

There's a crunch of gravel, and Levi appears down the side of the house, pushing his bike. He smiles up at me, nodding as he puts his bike under shelter.

"You're up late."

"Not really." I hold out the cigarette as he walks up the porch steps, shrugging off his leather jacket. "It's only midnight."

"Our girl asleep?"

I hate how much I love those words. If only it were true. I nod as he leans down to let me light the cigarette for him.

"I guess so. She went to bed a couple of hours ago."

Levi sinks into a chair, stretching his legs out in front of him. "Can I ask you something?"

"Of course."

"How did you know you're bi?"

I stare at him for a moment, the cigarette smoldering in my hand. "What do you mean?"

He takes another drag, shrugging, his eyes avoiding mine. "I mean, how do you know something like that?"

"How do you know you're straight?"

His eyes flash to mine with alarm. "What?"

"You're straight, so how do you know that? Because you just are." I can't help but laugh a little. "You're almost 30, man. Like, you gotta know this shit, right?"

He leans forward, elbows on his knees, and I can't believe it, but I think he's nervous. Levi Fenton is struggling to find the words to describe what he's feeling. And I hate myself for the sharp uptick in my heart rate, as I wonder if he's asking me this because of me.

"Where is this coming from?" I ask him slowly.

"I never told you, but there was a guy in prison, Conrad. Remember him?"

"Sure."

"He and I, we… I mean, I… I fucked him. Twice."

I am not prepared for the searing jealousy that runs through me at his confession. "Oh. Why didn't you ever tell me?"

"Because I told myself that it was just frustration and curiosity, you know, it didn't mean anything." He runs a hand over his mouth with a sigh. "And I told myself that it didn't count if you're not the one taking it, like it's somehow… less gay."

A laugh bursts from my lips, and Levi's dark gaze falls on my face. "Sorry, I'm sorry I didn't mean to laugh. But- less gay? Seriously?"

Levi leans back in his chair and runs a hand over his face. "I didn't grow up in a house where this stuff got talked about."

I grunt out a chuckle. "Me neither. You think my catholic grandfather ever took me to Pride?"

"So how did you *know*?" Levi asks, throwing his hands up.

"Because I can look at a man, and think he's hot. Because I can look at a woman, and think she's hot. How the fuck else do you think this works?"

"So you like having your cock sucked by a man?" Levi sounds almost incredulous.

"Sure."

"More than with a woman?"

I stamp out my cigarette and narrow my eyes at him. "No, not more than a woman. One is not better than the other, it just comes down to the person."

"I mean, have you… Have you done everything with a man? That you've done with a woman?"

"Yes."

He gets more flustered, his cheeks turning bright crimson. "So you've had anal sex with a man?"

"Yes."

He bites his lip, shaking his head. "Did you… Were you the one taking it or-"

"Both." I interject, narrowing my eyes. "Where is this sudden interest in what I've done with whom coming from?"

Rolling thunder punctuates my words, and Levi's gaze fixes on me under a flash of lightning.

"Come here." His voice drops to a timbre I've never heard from him before, not when he's spoken to me.

My heart threatens to beat straight out of my ribcage. His arms are draped over the chair, the cigarette glowing as it dangles between his fingers. His eyes darken, and he leans back further, body open and welcoming as he watches me.

"Why?"

"Come. Here." His voice is deep and gruff, and fuck, what that command does to me.

I get to my feet, rounding the table and taking the few steps towards him. I lean down over him, placing my hands against the frame of the chair, and our mouths are only inches apart. He smells faintly of whiskey, cutting through the scent of his cologne.

"Is this close enough for you, *guapo*?"

He shakes his head. "I don't know what I'm doing."

"I think we both know that's a lie."

We stare at each other for a few seconds, and then Levi's hand is on the back of my neck, pulling me down to him. My mouth crashes into his, his tongue licking at the seam of my lips, and I open up for him immediately. He tastes smoky and musky, whiskey and cigarettes mingling on my tongue, his stubble rubbing against my chin.

He's voracious, his tongue sparring with mine as he groans into my mouth.

I break the kiss and drop to my knees between his thighs. We're both breathing hard, and he watches as my hands move the waistband of his jeans.

"There's no taking this back," I tell him.

"I know."

I undo one button, then another. His eyes stay fixed on me.

"Where were you tonight?" I ask.

"I went out to get laid."

"And yet you're here, kissing me and wanting me to suck your cock." I palm him through his jeans, and he grits his teeth. "Was she no good?"

"I couldn't go through with it." He reaches out and cups my jaw with his hand. "I kept thinking about you."

"Really?" I push his t-shirt up, and run my lips over his abs, inhaling the woody scent of his cologne.

"Oh fuck." He runs a hand over my head. "I can't stop thinking about you."

"Got it bad, huh?" I gaze up his body as I trace my tongue over his stomach. "You been dreaming of this? Of me?"

He bites his lip and nods, head tipping back against his chair. "The way you looked this afternoon, when you got out of her car. Fuck, Dylan, you have no idea…"

When I got out of her car.

Guilt drops into my stomach like a fucking anvil, and I back away instantly. Levi's brows knit together as I rise to my feet.

"I can't do this."

"I'm sorry, did I say something wrong?" Levi reaches out for me, and I yank my hand out of his grasp.

"Don't." I take a step back. "I don't know what you have going on, but I'm not your little experiment in Being Gay."

Levi springs to his feet, shaking his head. "It's not like that."

"No?"

"No." He closes the distance between us, and cradles my face in his hands. "I can't stop thinking about you. I fucking need you. And I know that's fucked up, I know you love Stella, but-"

"But?" I push his hands away. "There is no But. I love her, and I want it to work with her."

"She wouldn't have to know."

"Fuck you." I shove him away from me. "So you just want me to be your dirty secret, huh?"

"No! I just meant… I just meant that we could… I don't know, just, just try it."

Thunder growls loudly, and rain begins to fall, landing on the porch in heavy drops.

"Try it?" I shake my head, laughing bitterly. "You know what, maybe Stella was right. Maybe we do need therapy."

Levi advances on me again, trying to put his hands on me, but I fight him off.

"Dylan, please, I care about you. I… I want you."

"I can't do this."

Levi doesn't try to stop me as I walk back into the house, and my head feels like it's going to explode. I lock myself in my bedroom, and throw myself down onto the bed, staring at the flashes of lightning as their reflections dance across the ceiling. After a while, the porch light clicks off and Levi's footsteps sound softly on the stairs.

Guilt and shame stop me from sleeping at all, and as the storm rages outside, as it gradually blows out and gives way to a brilliant orange dawn, I wonder if maybe the three of us are broken, and if that's exactly what draws us to each other.

Maybe it's what will end us all.

I sneak out of the house early, before Stella or Levi get out of bed. I don't want to risk encountering either of them, and I'm overcome with grief at the idea that I'm going to lose either of them because of this. If Stella knew I nearly blew her brother on her fucking porch, she'd never understand. And Levi crossed a line that can't be uncrossed, and the whole situation makes me sick and sad.

I don't want to lose him. I can't.

I gun the engine of my bike and tear down the street, welcoming the fresh breeze.

I decide to do something I've never done before, because right now I don't know where else to go. I need to talk to someone about this. Even if they can't answer me.

The cemetery is bathed in golden morning light, birds singing happily in the trees. I hesitate as I take off my helmet, but I take a deep breath and climb off my bike.

The last time I was in this cemetery, I was a fourteen year old boy, trying not to cry as I followed the matching coffins to their graves. The only comfort I ever took from their deaths was that they died together. My father had worshiped my mother, despite the fact his family hated her. She'd been beautiful, fiery and intelligent, and he'd fallen hard for her.

"See her?" He'd ask me whenever my mother did anything, whether it be go to work or cook a meal. "Find yourself a partner like that, son. One as extraordinary as your mama. You'll be happy for the rest of your life if you do that."

They'd been on their way home from her favorite opera when that truck had run a red light and snuffed out their lives. I often imagine that night, those moments before they died. My mother's animated speech about how the soprano had been perfect, about how the aria moved her to tears. My father's indulgent smiles, kissing her hand as she raved and wept beside him.

And then they'd been gone. They hadn't even seen it coming. My mother's hand was still in my father's in the wreckage.

I blink away tears as I navigate the wet path, my feet finding the way even though it's been fifteen years.

The graves look the same, slightly weathered. Their pictures smile out at me, and I shove my hands into my pockets on a heavy sigh.

"Sorry it took me so long," I tell them. "I don't have an excuse. Well I mean, I do. I was in prison for 10 years." I huff out a laugh. "Some son I ended up being, huh? But it was for a good reason. And you always told me, Mom, you said that sometimes the right thing is hard. I did it for someone I love."

I grind my foot into the ground, struggling to find the words even though I'm just talking to the air. But their smiling faces make me want to admit to everything, to seek some level of equilibrium in the fucking mess I find myself in.

"I've fallen in love with someone extraordinary, just like you always told me to, Dad." I laugh as tears burn my eyes. "The fucking problem is, that it's two someones, and they're brother and sister, well, stepbrother and stepsister, does that matter? And I'm here, loving them both and I feel like I can't have either of them. But the thought of not having them, I feel like I can't fucking breathe without them."

I drop to my knees, scrubbing my clawed fingers along my thighs.

"I wanted to be someone you'd be proud of. Someone who you'd look down on and be telling all the angels, yeah that's my son. And who am I? Some homewrecker who can't stay faithful to one person, who went to fucking prison for putting a bullet in a man's head. That's your legacy. I'm sorry. I'm so fucking sorry."

I hang my head, wishing the ground would swallow me up and take me down to them. I'm overwhelmed with the feeling of not wanting to be here, to be anywhere but here where everything is complicated, sharp and painful.

"I love them both." I lean on their graves, feeling the rough stone under my palm. "And I don't know what to do. I don't know how to lose one of them." I raise my face to look at my dad's picture. A face like mine. Paler, with blue eyes. But the same smile. The same dimple in his cheek. "I wish you were here, Dad. I wish you could tell me what to do."

My father simply smiles at me.

Footsteps sound on the path, along with the clacking of a cane. I turn to see a man in his Sunday best coming down the path, a golden pocket watch hanging from his vest, and black fedora perched on his thinning grey hair. He spots me where I'm kneeling on the ground, and his face twists into a scowl.

"Ah, *moj bezuzytecny wnuk.*" *My useless grandson.*

I hastily wipe my red face, and rise to my feet. *"Dziadek." Grandfather.* "Nice to see you too."

He grunts, shaking his head. "Surprised you even know where to find them, since you never bothered to come out here. Not even once."

"It's not easy, you know."

"Better for them." He retrieves a white handkerchief from his pocket, and leans over to wipe the glass over my father's picture. "They'd be so ashamed of you."

"They were never ashamed of me."

"Did they know you were an abomination in the eyes of our holy Father?" His crinkled eyes narrow as he takes me in. "Not that your poor excuse of a mother would care, *brudny.*" He spits on her grave, and rage so violent wells up in me that I have to stop myself from taking his cane and beating the old bastard to death.

"My father loved her, and that meant nothing to you." My fists are shaking at my sides. "You're the abomination, you hateful old fuck."

"Get out of this place!" He points over my shoulder, his face thunderous with rage. "Get out of this place, you are not welcome here!"

I get in his face, staring down at his tiny, frail form. "You're going to die soon, and you'll be all alone. And I will burn down your fucking house, and I will come here and spit on your grave, just like you spit on hers."

"Do it, I will be laughing at you from Heaven."A hacking laugh bursts from him.

"You'll be rotting in hell, and even that will be too good for you." I back away from him, placing a kiss on my fingers and placing them on each of the headstones. "Love you both."

"You are incapable of love." His words follow me down the path, just like every cutting remark he ever made in my direction.

I tear up the dirt in the parking lot as I gun the engine of my bike, gasping for air in my helmet. Pain and anguish well up inside me, and I speed all the way back to Stella's house. If a cop catches me, it's a parole violation. But I don't care. Right now, I don't fucking care about anything except erasing this feeling from my bones, from my heart, the sharp, howling ache of everything I was taught to hate about myself and just wanted someone to fucking love me for.

Homo. Faggot. Freak. All the horrible taunts and slurs thrown after me, the bruises on my face when yet another kid had slammed my head into my locker door, when I'd been cornered again in the school bathroom by the jocks who decided the gay guy needed a dressing down. It didn't matter how many girls I dated, how many I slept with, it didn't matter that I told them I was bisexual. I fucked men, and that meant I was disgusting. A freak. An abomination. Their pastors told them so. Their parents told them so. Everyone told them I was wrong, and therefore, I was.

Stella's car is gone when I pull up, and I storm upstairs. Her bedroom door is open. She's not here.

I turn to Levi's door, tearing it open, startling him as he's mid-stretch. He's on his back, head raised watching me with confusion, until I fist my shirt and yank it off over my head. His eyes move over my body with surprise and desire.

I know I'm doing something stupid, but I just need… him.

"One time." I undo the buttons on my jeans, letting them drop to the floor. "One time, and nothing changes between us. One time, and we get this out of our systems. Then it's done."

He sits up, and I see he's totally naked as the sheet slides down to his hips. "Nothing changes," he agrees. "Just one time."

"Good." I cross the room and climb onto the bed, and his eyes fill with lust. "I want you to tell me what you want. What you need from me, *guapo*."

He grabs my face, pulling me down onto the bed with him, kissing me, telling me just how bad he wants to be fucked by showing me with his tongue.

"I want to fuck you," he says, breathing heavily against my lips.

"You want my ass?" I chuckle, kissing my way down his jaw as he nods.

"Y-yes. There's lube, and condoms in the drawer."

I crawl across the bed, and reach into the drawer, pulling out the small bottle of lube and a condom. When I roll back to face him, Levi is breathing rapidly. I lean against him, kissing him hard.

"Just one time," I tell him again, and he nods. I wrap a hand around his cock, and he groans, his hips jerking almost involuntarily, to grind himself against my palm. "Is that good?"

He nods, his hand bracing around my neck to draw me in for another searing kiss, and he tries to take the condom packet from my hand.

"Let me." I tear it open with my teeth, and reach down to roll the condom over his thick length. He wraps his hand around my dick, and I hiss out a breath. He continues to stroke me gently, making it hard to focus on what I'm doing as desire blurs everything else.

"Fuck." I finish putting the condom on, and grip his jaw hard in my hand. "Do not be gentle."

He eyes me uncertainly. "I don't want to hurt you."

I nip at his jaw, and he gasps, arching against me. "Yes, you do, *guapo*," I breathe against his ear. "And I want you to. Now, do not be fucking gentle."

Something flares in his eyes, and I can see I've unlocked

something inside him, the confident Levi Fenton who knew he could have whoever he wanted with just a flash of a smile. His mouth curls in a lust-filled grin, and with rough hands he rolls me onto my stomach, hitching me up onto my knees.

"You want it to hurt, pretty boy?"

I groan as cool drops of lube run over my skin, and Levi works it up and down with the tip of his cock.

"Yes."

"Good." More cold lube, and then he slowly presses into me. He halts, and goosebumps break out over my back. He inches inside me, slowly, too fucking slowly for me. I buck my hips, trying to push back onto him, but he holds me steady.

"Slow down for me, and I'll fuck you like the good boy you are."

My head falls between my arms, and I press my cheek against my bicep as he inches inside me. It's pleasure and pain, all balled up together with the shame and delight of what we're doing. He's finally inside me, but I remind myself this is just once. One time, just to get us out of this funk.

He lets out a guttural moan as his hips finally sit against my ass, and he reaches around to stroke me with his slick hand. He's so big, filling and stretching me in a way that feels like punishment and salvation at the same time.

Just this once. Just one time.

He punches his hips forward, and I moan loudly.

"Jesus, Levi."

"Quiet, pretty boy." His fingers stroke down my spine as he starts to fuck me. "We wouldn't want the neighbors to hear us while I fuck this tight little hole of yours."

His words set my veins alight. Of course Levi is into dirty talk. Cocky Levi Fenton, talking dirty while he fucks his best friend's ass in his sister's perfect little house. I clench my eyes closed, pushing away the image of Stella walking in right now, the horror on her face.

No. She never has to know. I'm willing to be Levi's dirty

secret and for him to be mine if it means we can just go back to being us, if we can find our way back to a regular life.

"Fuck, pretty boy, you know how good you look right now?"

The praise draws me back into the moment, into savoring the strokes of Levi's cock inside me. His hands dig into my hips, hard and huge, holding me as he fucks me without mercy. I'm not going to last long. Not when it feels this good, not when I just need to fucking *feel*.

"Harder," I beg over a rasping breath. "Fuck, I need to come."

Levi obliges with a harsh grunt, rutting into me ruthlessly. My hands dig into the sheets, and I hiss and curse, my body taut with desire, my orgasm sending a white hot bolt to the base of my spine. With a choked moan, I explode, lashing the bed with one hot rope of cum after another, riding out the sensation as Levi continues the relentless rhythm of his hips.

I keep coming, and coming, the sounds coming from Levi now almost animalistic and desperate. With a sharp hiss and a tensing of his body against mine, he shudders, and he comes hard, dragging his fingers over my hips and down my ass to claw into my thighs.

"Fuck," he mutters. "Fuck. Fuck." He slumps onto my back, wrapping his arms around my waist. "Fuck."

"So good you can't say anything else, huh?" I laugh, trying to catch my breath, and Levi nods against my heated skin.

"You have no idea how long I've wanted to do that."

I don't tell him how long I've wanted to do it. That would violate the rule that this is a one time thing. He doesn't need to know I've been lusting after him. That won't help anyone.

He pulls out of me gently, and I tear the soiled sheet aside before I lower myself onto the bed. He flops down on his back, the condom still sheathing his mostly hard cock. He tucks a hand behind his back and looks over at me.

"What changed your mind?"

I shake my head, waving a hand. "It doesn't matter. I think

we both just needed to get it over and done with. Now it's not hanging over us anymore."

"You're right." He reaches over and strokes a hand over my head. "You feel better?"

"My first fuck in over 10 years, what do you think?" I roll onto my back and stretch my arms over my head. "I feel fucking unstoppable."

Levi rolls over, his hands over mine above my head, and he grins at me. "Your ass feels incredible."

"So I've been told."

"Makes me wonder what your mouth would feel like."

I lean up and nip at his lip. "My mouth has made people see right into Heaven, *guapo*."

"Is that right?" Levi chuckles. "You sure talk a big game."

"Unlike other men, I can actually deliver on that."

Levi lowers his face to the crook of my neck, kissing me delicately and in a way that makes my stomach twist. This feels too nice. I close my eyes, breathing him in, letting him kiss me like he's mine and I'm his.

But this was just once.

The sound of Stella's car pulling into the drive drifts through the open window, and Levi looks down at me with a look of defeat.

"Time's up, pretty boy." He climbs off me, and watches me scoop my clothes off the floor.

I expected to feel better, and for a split second, I did. But I expected this feeling to dissipate. I expected to head into my shower and wash off the longing for Levi and the shame of my grandfather's words.

But instead, I stare at my reflection as steam fills the bathroom, and I know I just made everything so much fucking worse.

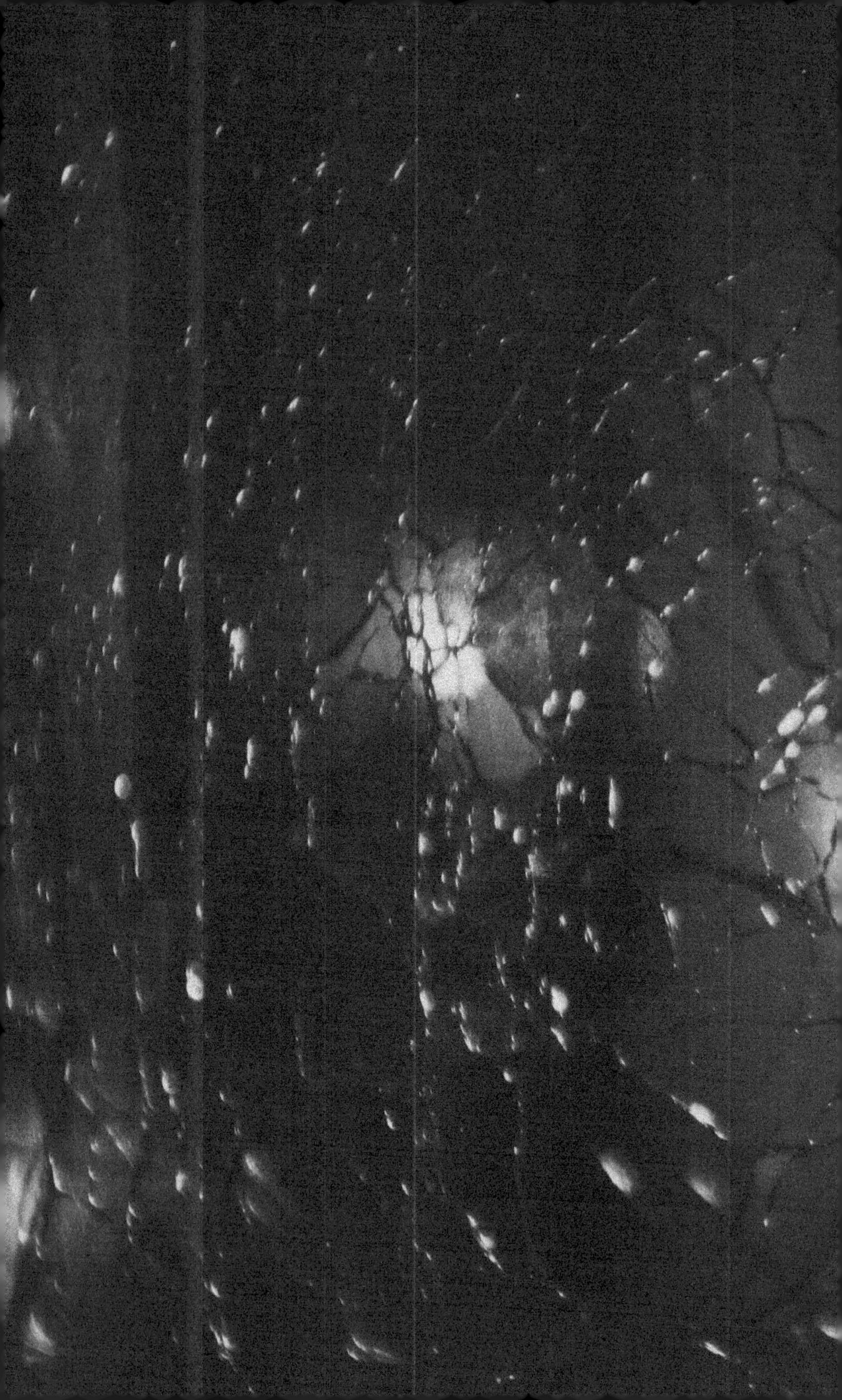

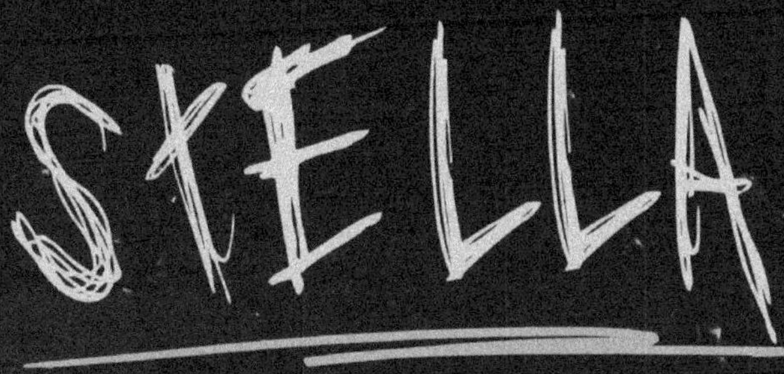

CHAPTER NINE

I STARE at Mallory's business card, the book I was reading forgotten on my stomach. A gentle summer breeze blows through my window to find me where I'm lying on my bed, and I turn the business card over and over in my hand.

I haven't spoken to anyone about the interview, and Levi hasn't mentioned anything. I don't know if he even knows. I don't know if there's any point telling him. I'd tried to push it to the back of my mind, but then I'd absently swiped something from my purse to use as a bookmark, and sure enough, it was Mallory's card.

And now I can't stop thinking about it.

Finally, I grab my phone from the nightstand, and dial Mallory's number. After three rings, I hang up. What the fuck am I doing? I don't talk to reporters. What for? There's no point.

I nearly drop my phone when it starts to ring, showing the number I just dialed. She's fucking calling me back. I swipe my finger across the screen and lift the phone to my ear.

"Hello, Stella Langford speaking."

"Oh, Stella, hi! Mallory here from Channel Four. I think I just missed your call?"

I cringe at myself, glad she can't see my flushed face. "Yeah, I was just, um… I wanted to ask you a few questions. Is this a good time?"

"Of course, go ahead."

I take a deep breath, trying to sort out the million questions in my head and trying to figure out which one is most important. "I wanted to know… Do you have any idea what this big reveal Gloria is making is about? Like, what brought this on?"

"Well, I'm sure you heard about Judge Gillman's trial."

I swallow hard, clenching my eyes shut. "I saw it on the news." I wish I hadn't, but I had.

"Well, as it turns out, when the FBI seized his computers, they found hundreds of files of child pornography. Even on his work computers. He had quite the collection, sick old bastard."

"I know," I choke out. *I know, because one of those kids was me.*

"Gloria Fenton was a witness in the case against him, did you know?"

My stomach threatens to empty its contents onto my feet, and sweat erupts on my brow. "I beg your pardon?"

"The testimony was delivered in closed court because it pertained to a minor."

Fucking bitch. Angry tears prick at my eyes. "Are we still off the record, Mallory?"

"Absolutely."

"The minor she talked about was me."

Mallory makes a sound like a gasp, professionally cut off as she takes a deep breath. "I'm so sorry, Stella."

"I mean, I can't say that with 100% certainty, obviously. But my stepmother, she… She knew what happened to me when I was a kid. She's denied it, for years. But she knew."

"I don't know what else to say other than I am more than sorry." Mallory's tone is slow and measured, and she continues to do a great job hiding any shock she may be feeling. "I hope you're surrounded by people who love and support you now, and that you know what happened to you was not your fault."

Her words are so unexpectedly kind, and I need to take a

shaky breath before I can respond. "Thank you. I am. I'm fine now."

"Stella, I have every reason to believe that Gloria Fenton is about to position herself as a victim of your father, and try to gain renewed sympathy for herself."

"And why would she do that?"

"She's entering into the gubernatorial race."

I laugh bitterly. "Gloria wants to be governor? Of course she does."

"Stella, if you give me an exclusive we can go on the record and stop her."

"I'm not doing that." I swing my legs over the edge of the bed, curling my hand into the blanket on my bed. "I can't revisit all of that."

"I understand this would be hell for you, but don't you want the people to know just what kind of person Gloria Fenton is?"

"No." I grip the phone hard, sure my knuckles are turning white. "This isn't about her, this is about me, and my peace. And her son, he just got out of prison. He doesn't need all this hanging over him either."

"Stella, I told you that some college students had been looking into Levi and Dylan's case, didn't I?"

My throat goes dry, and I try to swallow to wet my tongue. "You'd mentioned it, yes."

"Well, it seems they're questioning some discrepancies in their testimonies." Footsteps sound over the line, and the background noise dulls a little. When Mallory speaks again, her voice has dropped low. "I've looked into it myself, and there are locks and black-outs on their file I've never seen before."

"Mallory, strictly off the record - stay out of this."

"But-"

"I mean it." Urgency colors my words, the old panic and fear rising up in my chest. "There are things about this case that you need to stay out of."

"Like powerful men who pulled strings for a plea deal no murder suspect has ever received before?"

I suck in a breath, a tornado of anxiety unleashing in my stomach. "Goodbye, Mallory. Thanks for answering my questions." I hang up amid her protests, and throw my phone on to the bed as though it's suddenly made of hot coals.

I feel nauseous, the slanted roof of my ceiling suddenly a cave roof threatening to collapse on me. Anyone looking into those files is asking for trouble. They could get themselves killed.

I feel an anxiety attack building, and kneel on the bed, placing my palms flat on the comforter. "I'm OK. I'm here. I can feel the bed. I'm safe." I blink back tears, one shaky breath after another wavering past my lips. "I'm OK. I'm safe."

My heart stops thumping in my chest, and I run my hands over my face.

I need to get out of the house.

I slide my feet into a pair of black flip-flops, and grab my purse from the chair before heading down the stairs.

I stop short when I see Dylan in the kitchen, leaning back against the counter, book flipped open in his hands. He looks completely relaxed, shirtless in a pair of jeans that hang low to reveal the tattoos that adorn his hips. One foot is crossed over the other as his eyes travel across the page. He smirks, running a hand over his mouth, and I see he's reading one of my smutty Peter Pan retellings.

The knot in my stomach slowly unfurls as I watch him, as the smile on his face becomes wider. My shoulders start to relax. I move towards him slowly.

"Enjoying that?"

He looks over the book at me, and shrugs with a sly smile. "They just tied her to a tree, and well... She's having a good time."

"Didn't pick you for reading smut, *papi*."

"Where do you think I learned it all from?" His eyes stray back to the page. "I read."

"Dylan Kovac, Sex God trained by women, huh?"

He shifts on his feet, closing the book and putting it down on the counter. "Something like that." He tucks his hands into his pockets, looking me up and down. "You going somewhere?"

"I… I just had a weird phone call and I was thinking of heading downtown, maybe getting a coffee and buying more books."

"Want company?"

Yes, I do. I want you to stop all this chaos. I want you to make my head go quiet so I can breathe. Without thinking, I rush at him and wrap my arms around his waist.

"Hey, hey." He strokes my hair, cradling my jaw and tipping my head back to cast a searching look over my face. "*Guera*? What's going on?"

"I just… I need a hug."

He wraps his huge arms around me, holding my head against his chest so I can hear the soft thud-thud of his heartbeat. "Hugs I can do, any time." He kisses the top of my head.

It could all be so easy. Maybe Dylan doesn't even have to know…

I squeeze my eyes shut at the intrusive thoughts. "Why are you so good to me?"

Dylan inhales sharply, holding me tighter. His heart rate picks up, and I gaze at him to see his brow furrowed, as though my words have hurt him.

"Come on, *guera,* let's get you that iced coffee and some more smut." He smiles, though the pain remains in his eyes. He retrieves a shirt from the back of one of the kitchen chairs, and pulls on his sneakers. He eyes me thoughtfully as we get into my car.

"What?" I cast him a smile as I reverse the car out onto the street.

"That book, I mean… It's dog-eared to shit. You… You like that kind of thing?"

"It happens to be one of my favorites, yes." I toss my hair

over my shoulder and hope I'm not blushing. "Always gets me out of a reading slump."

"So the sharing and all that, it doesn't bother you?"

"No, why would it?"

"Have you ever…" He trails off, and I glance over at him.

"Have I ever what?"

"Had a threesome?"

The air in the car is suddenly charged, and I'm not sure if I'm still breathing. I panic for a second that somehow my dirty fantasies have been broadcast from my brain and straight on to a screen above my head. I laugh awkwardly, taking the corner a little faster than I intended.

"No, I haven't. Why? Have you?"

"Yes." His voice drops low. "It's fun."

"I bet it is." I knew Dylan had a lot of sexual experience. But this line of questioning feels leading, and my stomach does a pleasurable flip as Dylan reaches over to put his warm hand on my thigh. "So, two men and a woman, or what have you done?"

"Once with two men, and once with a woman and another man."

I want to clench my thighs together, because the rush of arousal between my legs has me puffing out a little breath. But I can't move, because Dylan will feel it, his hand still on me. The image of Dylan and Levi in bed with me makes my clit throb.

"Well I'm not a fan of anal, so I guess that wouldn't work for me," I say lightly.

"Lots of other things you can do besides that, you know." His hand squeezes harder, and I swear I'm going to combust.

We come to a stop at a red light, and when I look over at him, his jaw is set, his eyes filled with desire.

"There are things I want that are wrong, Dylan."

"Says who?" He leans closer to me.

"Everyone." Dr Varden's words echo in my head, and shame takes over again. "I'm trying to be better, I'm trying to get over it, but…"

"Stop worrying about what everyone else wants, what they say, and just do what feels good for you."

"That's how people get hurt."

His eyes drop, and he removes his hand from my leg. He falls back into his seat, and runs a hand over the darkening shadow of stubble on his head.

"Stella, I have to-"

A car horn blares behind us, and I turn to see the light is now green. We continue on our way downtown, but the mood has shifted. I wish I could tell him the truth, but it would hurt him. And Dylan's been hurt enough.

I bring the car to a stop on Main Street, and turn to him with a bright smile.

"Come on, let's have fun and not get weighed down, huh?"

He opens his mouth to speak, and stops to look down at his hands. "You have no idea just how good you are." He raises his eyes back to meet mine. "I mean it. I know you don't see it, but you're incredible. Do you have any idea how lucky I feel to know that you love me?"

I want to tell him that my love is sick and twisted, and will do nothing but hurt and poison him. But I once again just put my arms around him, and hold him close, knowing it won't last but I need it to for now.

"I don't deserve you, *papi*."

He kisses the top of my head. "Come on, books are on me today. Buy as many as you want."

I grin up at him. "You're gonna regret saying that."

"Not if you take me home and read me your favorite parts." He kisses the tip of my nose. "Come on. Let's go."

We walk down the street hand in hand, and it feels so blissfully normal and wholesome to have my fingers wrapped in his. I lean against his shoulder, and he chuckles.

"Coffee?" He asks as we pass the Elephant Bean cafe.

"Not from there." I wrinkle my nose. "I don't want to see him."

Dylan's eyes glint deviously. "Oh, but I do." He leans over me, stroking my cheek with his fingertips. "I'm just enough of an asshole to want to torture Jared fucking Marshall." His mouth quirks, and his dark eyes glint dangerously. "Just a little."

I lift my eyebrow. "Aren't we too old for childish high school games?"

Dylan narrows his eyes as he smirks, then shakes his head. "Nah. Come on, play along like a good girl." He drags me into the cafe, which is packed with the early afternoon crowd. Dylan wraps his arms around my waist, walking behind me to the counter.

Jared eyes me warily from the coffee machine, and I give him a dazzling smile. Dylan kisses my neck as we wait in line, his breath hot as he nibbles on my earlobe.

"Giving him quite a show," I murmur as goosebumps erupt down my arms.

Dylan's kisses wander along my jawline, and I know people are staring at us, trying to figure out what Stella Langford is doing being kissed and groped by a huge tattooed man in the middle of the busiest cafe in town. They probably think I've just gotten myself into another stupid mess, and the thought should make me uncomfortable, I half-expect it to wash away this beautiful feeling that's warming my veins. But with Dylan's hands on me, there's nothing in my head but all the thoughts of what I want him to do to me.

"Are you wearing panties today?" He asks against my neck, one of his hands wandering over my hip. "Sure doesn't feel like it."

I look over my shoulder at him, and kiss his chin. "I'm not, as a matter of fact."

A growl rumbles through his chest. "Bad girl. Might have to take you home and punish you."

"You sure are committing to this act."

I gasp as he shoves me harder against him, his growing erection pressing against me through his clothes. "Who said it was an act?"

"You did, outside, just now."

The line in front of us advances a little, and Dylan kisses my neck again as we take a few steps forward.

"I lied," he breathes against my ear, and I want to tear him out of here and drag him home right now. As though he can sense what I'm thinking, he chuckles in my ear, moving the strap of the tank top to kiss my bare shoulder. "I love knowing this is driving you crazy."

"You're so mean." I lean into him, turning my face to bury it in the crook of his neck. "Everyone's watching, you know?"

"Like that would stop me." Dylan kisses my forehead, his hand cupping my jaw. "I'd happily bend you over that counter right now, and I wouldn't give a fuck who saw us."

"Exhibitionist," I tease.

We reach the counter, and Dylan's arms stay around my waist as I smile sweetly at Jared.

"Hi!"

He gives me a withering look. "Hey. What can I get you?"

"Just a vanilla iced coffee, thanks. Anything for you?" I look at Dylan, and he shakes his head.

"Don't want to erase your taste, baby. That'd be a sin."

I suppress a laugh and I'm sure my face is bright red as I turn back to Jared. "Just the iced coffee, thanks so much."

He sets about preparing my order without looking at me again, and Dylan continues to kiss me, gentle enough to genuinely drive me crazy and make me want more, and more. Every brush of his fingertips along my skin makes me more determined to just forget about my coffee order and just drag him home. This was meant to be an act, but it's fast becoming much more than that.

"There you go, one vanilla iced coffee." Jared places the cup down for me, and I tap my card to pay. Jared looks at Dylan, then back at me, and gives me a weak smile. "I wish you all the best, Stella. I mean it. I hope you two are happy together."

"Thanks!" I take my cup, smiling brightly. "We're so happy."

"Take it easy, man." Dylan says, still not releasing me as we sidle out of the coffee shop. He chuckles against my ear once we're out on the street. "Now, was that too much?"

"That was way too much." I smile up at him, and nudge his jaw with my nose. "But it was also fun."

"Time for books, huh?" He releases my waist to take my free hand and walk beside me. "Then you can take me home and read to me. Without panties on."

"I thought we were taking it slow."

He gives me a sideways smirk. "There's many ways of taking it slow, you know."

"And those are?"

He rounds on me suddenly, backing me up against the wall of a small alley between two stores. I almost drop my coffee as he cages me in with his arms. His intense gaze stares me down, and he lowers his mouth so it's barely an inch from mine.

"You set the pace, *guera*. I mean it. We go as slow or as fast as you want." He brushes his lips against me, another soft touch that has need coursing through every inch of me. "But I'm just enough of a fucking animal for you that I'll push as far as you'll let me. So if you want to read me filthy books and toy with your pussy while you make me watch, I'll do that. If you want me to eat you out while you do it, I'll do that too. And if you let me tie you to the bed and fuck you til you forget your own name, I'll do that too. Because I know you want me just as bad as I want you, and whatever's holding you back, it doesn't matter. We're all that matters."

I've stopped breathing, I know I have. I look into his beautiful face and shake my head. "I'm not going slow to torture you."

"I know that. But you're torturing yourself, I can see it. Just let go, and be with me. Just be with me, for today. Pretend there's nothing else, but us."

I can do that. I can shut off for a day and just be with him. I can give myself that. I can give him that. I lean against him, tilting my face up to his.

"Do you like to watch, *papi*?"

He exhales through gritted teeth, and nods. "Yeah, I do."

"Maybe I'll show you my toys when we get home." I place a gentle kiss against his jaw, and his hand runs down my back. "Show you what I like."

"Mmm, I like the sound of that, *guera*." His fingers thread into my hair, and he pulls my head back. "Now, let's get my girl some more dirty books."

My whole body is pulled taut as we head to the bookstore, and I discard my coffee on the way in. I'm no longer interested in it because Dylan's hand is hot around mine and all I want is to have those hands all over me. We head to the back of the store, to the romance section, and Dylan stands behind me, his body pressed against mine as I pluck a few titles from the shelves.

"You smell so good," he says, brushing his nose along my neck. "Good enough to eat." He nips at my shoulder, and I tense against him, suppressing a squeak. "So edgy." He chuckles as his hands grip my hips.

"You sure know what you're doing," I say as I take another book down from the shelves.

"Oh you have no idea, *guera*." He lowers his mouth to my ear. "I'd make you see stars while I lick this pussy."

This does not feel like moving slow anymore. And I don't fucking care. Desire rages through me, and I want to run a fucking freight train straight through my certainty that I'd hold off on giving in. But with Dylan's hands on me and him whispering dirty words in my ear, I don't want to take it slow. I want to take it so fast I snap my goddamn neck on the way.

"How long has it been for you, hmm?"

My breathing is rapid now, and I just want to get the hell out of here. "About a year."

"A year? Shit. You really need to be looked after."

"Been a hell of a lot longer for you," I say with a laugh, leaning back against him, and suddenly he's tense, stepping away from me to take the books from my hands.

"Let's go." He won't meet my eyes, and all those happy, carefree feelings ebb away a little.

"Dylan? Did I say something wrong?"

"No, you didn't, I just want to get you out of here." He smiles but still won't look at me, not really. "Come on, let me spoil my girl."

He pays for my stack of romance books, and carries the bags back to the car. I try not to let my overthinking brain kick in, but when he still won't look at me back at the car, I reach over and take his hand.

"Did something happen?" I dip my head to try and catch his gaze. "Dylan, please look at me."

Before I know what's happened, he's grabbed my face, his mouth crashing into mine as he devours me hungrily. All my uncertainty melts away as his tongue swipes at mine, and I let myself get lost in kissing him.

"I slept with someone," he tells me, pulling back with a furrowed brow. "It didn't mean anything. It was just to blow off steam. I didn't want to push you, and I was just fucking dying for you, so I slept with someone else." He says it all so fast, like a hurried confessor admitting his sins, and I have to blink a few times to let the words sink in after the euphoria of him kissing me. "I'm so sorry, Stella."

I shake my head, cradling his neck in my hands. "No, no, don't be sorry. Really, I'm not mad. I understand."

His dark eyes bore into mine, filled with shame. "I love you. Not… anyone else."

"I know. I know. Please, don't feel guilty." I kiss him again, and he seems to sag with relief. "You needed it, I get it."

"I just want you," he tells me, his eyes boring into mine. "I promise."

Now it's my turn for my eyes to drop, because I can't say that back. I can't lie to him. I can't think about it. I kiss him again, and again, until we're both hot and frenzied, and he murmurs, "Get this fucking car home, right now" in a tone of voice that makes me shiver.

I navigate the streets at a speed that's barely legal, Dylan's hand on my leg, riding up higher and higher. Sweat prickles at my scalp despite the cool air I turn on to blast us, and I never realized how far I live from downtown until today. Every red light has me wanting to pound my fists against the wheel.

Finally, *finally,* we turn onto my street, and I bring the car to a stop in the drive. Dylan and I both clamber out of the car, the books forgotten on the floor. I fumble with the keys as Dylan kisses my neck hungrily, and as soon as we're inside the door and it slams shut behind us, Dylan has me on the floor, tearing at my clothes.

He yanks down my shirt, his mouth descending on my breast and sucking my nipple between his lips. My back arches off the floor as my fingers claw at his head.

"Oh my god." I grab at his shirt, yanking it off over his head and dragging him back up to me to kiss him deeply, grinding myself against him.

"Jodidamente hermosa." Fucking beautiful. The words are a breath against my lips, and he pushes my thighs apart with his hips.

"I love it when you speak Spanish."

"Te amo." I love you.

Tears prick at my eyes. This is how it was meant to be, that night. When he held me and peeled my clothes from my body, his eyes discovering me like no one else had before, his hands soft as they explored me. When he'd told me he loved me, and that he was going to be gentle with me.

I hold on to those moments, and push away what happened

after. I want to have that moment back, *that* moment that we should have had.

"I love you," I tell him, writhing under him as I try to shuffle my clothes off. "I missed you so much."

His mouth moves over my chest, along my collarbone, and just as his hand runs up my bare thigh, the porch door opens and heavy footsteps sound in the kitchen.

I clap a hand over my mouth, and Dylan grunts with frustration. He gets me to my feet, and drags me up the stairs.

"Hey, you guys home?" Levi's voice sounds from the kitchen, but we don't answer as we run for my bedroom.

No sooner is my bedroom door closed and locked, Dylan has me pressed against it and drops to his knees, taking my shorts down with him. His mouth is pressed to my pussy, and his tongue pushes me open, seeking out my clit. He groans as he tastes me, and I desperately roll my hips against his face.

"Dylan, oh my god."

His hand wanders up my stomach, pushing away my tank top to find one of my bunched nipples, and he pinches it hard. My legs go weak at the sensation, and I sag against the door with a moan. His tongue works me harder, and I know it won't take much for him to make me come like this. He puts one of my legs over his shoulder, and pushes one of his thick fingers inside me. So much for taking it slow.

Just as I'm about to come, he slows down, showering kisses over the lips of my pussy, and I swear I'm going to pass out.

"Dylan, please." I buck my hips again, desperate to have him back where I need him.

"Lie down on the floor, *guera,*" he says, taking off the remainder of his clothes as I lie down on my back, my legs practically buckling as I do. He kneels between my thighs, running a hand between my breasts, over my stomach, between my thighs. He sucks in a breath, and raises his eyes to mine. "Slow, right?"

I press a hand to my face and groan. "Oh my god, Dylan, *please.*"

He lowers his mouth between my legs, and takes his time, his tongue teasing around my clit, not giving me what I want immediately, not until I'm shivering and my legs are quaking on either side of his head. Only then does he press two fingers inside me as he drags his tongue over my clit. I almost scream, biting my lip to try and keep quiet as I hear Levi's footsteps come up the stairs. But I can't suppress my loud moan as Dylan sucks my clit between his lips, his tongue lashing me as heat grows and presses in my belly.

I know Levi isn't far away, I know that he can hear what's going on, and as I close my eyes and surrender to the orgasm that starts to crest, I imagine him in here as well. I can see his blue eyes as he gazes down at me, as he fucks my throat while Dylan's mouth continues to drive me closer to my climax. My fantasy roars through me, and I scream against my palm as I pulsate against Dylan's mouth and around his fingers.

He keeps licking and sucking gently as I ride out my climax on the sun-dappled floor of my bedroom. I'm a gasping, sweaty mess, and he kisses my thighs gently, moving over my hips, my stomach, and as he settles between my thighs, I dare to open my eyes.

Looking into his beautiful face douses me with shame, like an icy shower.

I push against his chest and wriggle out from under him, and the look he gives me makes me want to die.

"Stella?" He reaches for me, but I push his hand away. "*Guera*, what happened?"

"Please go." I turn away from him, pulling my legs against my chest. "Just go."

"*Guera-*"

"I said go!" I press my face to my knees, knowing I'm hurting him, knowing I'm hurting myself, but I can't look at him. "I need you to leave me alone."

He sits there for a few seconds, breathing heavy, before he gets to his feet, taking his clothes with him. He doesn't say a word as he leaves my room, closing the door softly behind him. I dig the heels of my hands into my eyes, willing away the stupid tears that threaten to fall. I'm awful. I'm a fucking horrible bitch, and I have to tell him the truth.

I have to let him go, even though it'll kill me.

Dylan deserves better than that.

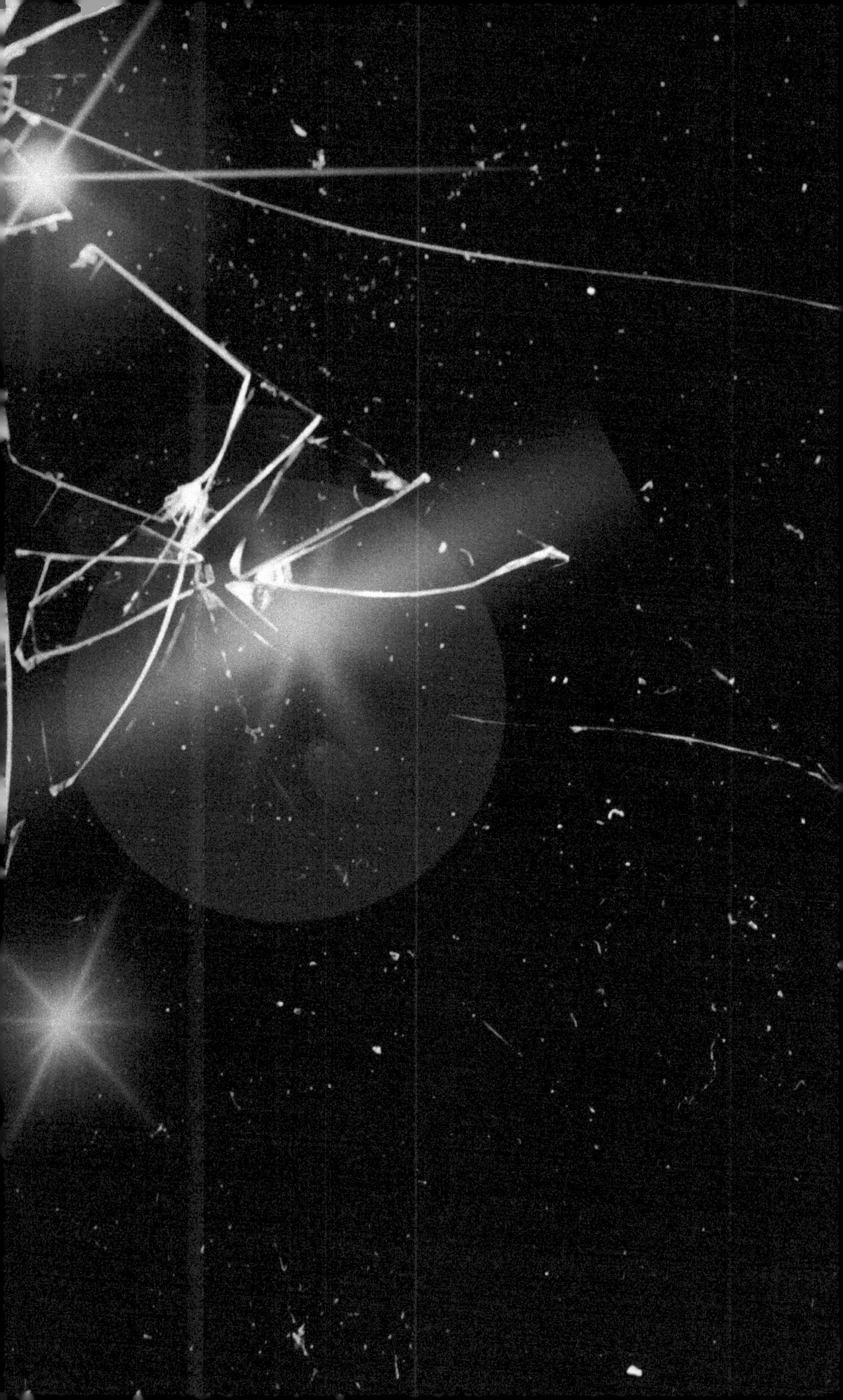

CHAPTER TEN

"FUCK!" The wrench falls from Dylan's hand for what feels like the fourteenth time since he started working on the red Harley, and he kicks the tool across the garage with a growl. "Fucking piece of fucking useless shit." His shoulders are heaving, and he runs a hand over his head. "God fucking dammit."

I lean on the seat of the bike I'm working on, and tilt my head as I look over at him. "You OK over there, pretty boy?"

He tears his shirt off and wipes his face with it, throwing it to the ground with a snarl. "I'm fine."

"You seem on edge."

"I said, I'm fine, Levi." He's louder this time, loud enough to be heard over the music playing, and a few of the other guys look over in our direction.

I wave them off with a reassuring smile, and round the bike to stand beside Dylan. "You're not fine, so stop lying to me. Let's go get a drink."

"I don't need a fucking drink."

I put my hand on his shoulder, expecting a slap but he sighs instead. "You can lie to everyone but me, Kovac. Now come on, I'm parched, it's hot as balls in here."

"Can you please stop trying to look after me?" He snaps.

"Nope." I grin at him as he scowls at me. "Watching pretty

boys torture themselves brings out my sweet side. Now get your ass up and let me buy my friend a drink. From our own personal bar, no less."

He rolls his eyes and brushes the dirt from his hands. "I'm fine, that engine is just being difficult."

"Yeah, it's the engine, sure." I chuckle over my shoulder at his dark look, and we head to the office at the back of the shop. I retrieve two beers from the fridge, clicking off the caps against the edge of the door before handing one to Dylan. "Cheers."

Dylan barely raises his bottle before downing a long swig. He clenches his eyes shut and throws himself down in one of the leather chairs. "Fuck," he mutters, before eyeing me apologetically. "Sorry for being an asshole, man. This isn't exactly professional of me."

"It's fine, the guys can handle the shop for a minute." I sit down opposite him, gulping down my cool beer, eyeing his tortured face. "You don't have to tell me anything, but you know I'm here if you need me."

He runs a hand across his chin, leaving behind a smudge of oil, and he sighs heavily. "I think I fucked things up with Stella."

"How so?"

"I pushed her too hard, I tried to move too fast." He laughs bitterly, shaking his head and raising the bottle to his lips. "She told me to take it easy, and I couldn't fucking listen, could I?"

"What happened?" I don't need to ask what happened, I know what happened. I heard it. I stood in my bedroom and listened to Stella moan and scream, furiously jacking myself off. I know what they did. But since then, they haven't been in a room together.

Dylan rolls his shoulders, avoiding my eyes. "We got all… I don't know, downtown, we played a game to taunt Jared Marshall, and then it turned into more than a game. We got home, and she… I mean, I thought she wanted… *Fuck.*" He hisses out a breath and leans heavily on his knees. "I… I went down on her, and she seemed to enjoy it, she told me she loved me, and she seemed to want me. But then she… Came, and then she just… She rolled away from me, wouldn't let me touch her, and told me to get out." He raises his eyes to my face, and he looks so hard it feels like my heart cracks a little. "It's like she regretted it, like she… She regretted doing that with me."

"I don't think she regrets it, she probably just needed a minute." I shrug, trying to remain casual and reassuring and not think too much about Dylan's face buried between Stella's thighs, because jesus fucking christ he's in pain and what the fuck is even wrong with me? "She just needed to get her head clear. Sex is probably a big deal to her, you know?"

Dylan's eyes widen, and he raises his hands almost defensively. "I didn't hurt her, I'd never do that."

"No, no, I don't mean it like that. I just mean… I don't know, man. I think Stella's struggling with a lot of things. Like we all are."

Dylan's eyes drop back to the floor, and his Adam's apple races up and down his throat. "Yeah, we all seem to be pretty good at nursing our demons, huh?"

"I wouldn't quite put it that way." My train of thought is cut off as my phone rings, and my mother's number appears on the screen. "Sorry man, give me a second." I suppress a groan, and pick the phone up. "Hello, Mother."

"Hello, sweetheart, how are you?" Her voice drips saccharine sweetness down the line. "How's the shop going?"

"It's going great, thanks for asking."

"I'll have to come down and see it some time."

I laugh at the image of my perfectly coiffed mother coming this far downtown to slum it in a dirty garage with burly mechanics. "I don't think this is exactly your scene, Mom. Might get some grease on those Louboutins."

"I'll have you know I spent a lot of time in that shop with your father." Her voice shifts, as it always does when my father comes up. "I used to be a very different woman before I became a mother."

"Yeah sure, Mom, blame me." I take a swig of my beer. "Anyway, did you need something or were you just calling to see how my job is going?"

"As a matter of fact, I'm calling to invite you to a party." Her voice brightens, the Miss America annunciation back. "I'm holding a big celebration for all our old friends."

"What's the occasion?"

"I don't know if you've heard, but I'm running for governor."

I nearly spit out my beer, and Dylan's brows knit together. "You're running for what?"

"Governor. I think I could do a lot of good for this state, get some order into it. I'm just what the people need."

"You don't know the first thing about politics, Mom. You think poor people should be outlawed and that God belongs in schools."

She takes a deep breath. "I will have you know that I'm much more progressive these days. I have many gay friends. Even the Blacks think I'm fantastic."

I clench my eyes shut, and roll my beer bottle along my forehead to try and soothe the headache that's threatening to erupt. "Mom, please tell me you're joking."

"I am not joking, Levi. I'd hoped you would support me and attend the party on the 16th. 7pm sharp."

"You sure you want your son who has obscenities tattooed on his knuckles there? Your friends might think less of me."

"No one will think less of you. You are my son, and the grandson of Oswald Perlman. That means something to these people."

"Great, well at least it means something to someone." I sigh heavily and roll my eyes as Dylan holds up a hand and mouths *what*. "I can't make any promises, Mom. I have a lot going on right now."

"But you just said-"

"I'll be in touch." I hang up and lean my head back against the chair with a groan. "Fucking families, man."

"You're telling me." Dylan watches me expectantly.

"My mother is running for governor." The words sound ridiculous as they come out of my mouth, and Dylan's eyebrows shoot up. "She's throwing a party to celebrate, and she wants me there."

"Why the fuck is your mother running for governor?"

"Because the *Blacks* love her apparently."

Dylan closes his eyes, and takes a deep breath, putting a hand to his head. "Jesus tits."

"You can say that again."

Dylan eyes me cautiously. "You gonna go?"

I shake my head, taking another swig of beer. "Hell no. My Mum just wants to play happy families and I am not into that."

"Fair enough." Dylan's phone dings, and he picks it up. His brow furrows, and his eyes fly over the screen as he reads. "Fuck," he mutters, and gets to his feet with a frustrated grunt. "My grandfather had a stroke, and he's in the hospital."

I spring to my feet. "Shit, do you need to go? Come on, I'll drive you."

He waves a hand, putting down his beer to go wash his hands in the sink. "No, it's fine. They just need me to sign off on the DNR, I'm his next of kin."

"Do they think he's going to die?"

"I have no idea, it was his neighbor texting me, I'll have to see."

I stop him and put my hands on his shoulders. "Hey, if you need me, let me know. I'll be right there."

He gives me a soft smile, and puts a hand over mine. "Thanks. I'll keep you posted."

I'm overcome with the desire to pull him close, to let him know I'm here, *here*. But I resist, and watch him leave the garage in a hurry. I feel bad for hoping that his grandfather dies quickly, so that Dylan can finally be free of him.

The rest of the afternoon passes uneventfully, and I keep checking my phone for a message from Dylan. Nothing comes.

The sun begins to send long shadows across the parking lot, and eventually it's time to close up. I check my phone again, and there's still nothing from Dylan.

I start to worry, then tell myself I'm being ridiculous. He's probably just caught up at the hospital in a mountain of paperwork.

I head home, wondering if Stella is there, and if I should take her out to dinner to get my mind off worrying about Dylan. When I pull into the drive, her car isn't there, so I send her a text, before heading inside to wash the grease and grime from the garage off me.

My phone is flashing when I get out of the shower, and I see a text from Stella.

I'm on my way home now. Picked up some dinner.

OK great, see you soon

Where's Dylan?

Tell you when you get home

OK

I dress and head down into the kitchen, pulling a beer from the fridge while I wait for Stella.

I should feel shame for what happened while she was with Dylan. But fuck, all I wanted was to go into that room and be with them, to watch him get her off. I wasn't even jealous, just aroused out of my fucking mind. I want them both to be mine, I want their pleasure and their bodies, I want all of them.

And I hate myself even more because now it's gone south for them. For some stupid reason I feel responsible, even though it has nothing to do with me.

Headlights appear in the drive, and a car door slams. After a minute, Stella appears on the back porch, two paper bags hooked over her arm. She gives me a shy smile as I open the porch door for her.

"Thanks. I got us some Thai, I wasn't sure what you'd like so I just kind of got a bit of everything."

"Sounds great to me." I take the bags from her and place them on the table as she takes off her high-heeled sandals. "What did you do today?"

"I went into work actually, just to catch up on some files, and to talk to HR about changing my leave. I took it all when you got out, and well… I guess things have gone a little different. So I moved the rest of it to the Fall." She goes to the cupboard to get out some plates. "So, I'll be back to work on Monday."

"I'm sorry."

Her eyes flash to my face. "What for?"

"That things haven't gone the way you'd hoped."

She shrugs, crossing the kitchen with plates in hand, and I can't help but notice how tight her black pencil skirt is, sitting around her curvy ass.

"I'm used to things not working out the way I'd hoped." She places the plates down on the table and starts unpacking the paper bags with a bitter laugh. "Jesus, that sounded so self-pitying."

"I really am sorry."

"Don't worry about it." She sits down and runs a hand through her hair, looking over the food laid out between us. "So, where's Dylan?"

"His grandfather had a stroke, and he's in the hospital."

Stella's eyes flash up to mine with alarm. "Oh my god. Does he want us there? Is he OK?"

"I don't know, I haven't heard from him."

"Shit." Stella snatches up her phone and calls Dylan. She waits as it rings, then exhales heavily. "Voicemail," she whispers to me. I hear the loud beep after Dylan's voice, and Stella turns the phone back to her mouth. "Dylan, it's me. Let me know if you're alright, please? We're worried about you." She hesitates for a moment. "I love you." She hangs up and dumps the phone on the table. "Goddammit."

"He's fine, we're worrying over nothing." Even so, neither of us can bring ourselves to eat much, picking at the food and eventually abandoning it on our plates, sending anxious glances at our phones constantly. I go and get another beer, and Stella pours herself a glass of white wine.

"So," I say as we settle back at the table. "How's everything with you?"

She shrugs, avoiding my gaze. "Everything's fine. Why?"

"Well, Dylan today, he was a little on edge. He seemed stressed."

She shifts in her chair, stretching her legs to put her feet up on the chair opposite her. "Things between us are… difficult."

"Difficult?"

She nods slowly, taking a sip of wine. "I mean, I guess that's putting it mildly. I… I fucked up."

"He seems to feel like he fucked up."

She lets out a small, sad laugh. "I tried to warn him. But he wouldn't listen."

"Warn him about what?"

"Me."

I sigh heavily, wanting to reach across the table and take her hand. "Baby girl, why would you need to warn him about you?"

"Because I'm not normal, Levi. And now he feels bad, like he did something wrong, and it's not even his fault."

"These things aren't anyone's fault, Stella."

Her amber eyes fix on me, like she's looking right into my soul. "Actually, it's your fault."

My stomach drops, and the room around me spins. Dylan told her. Why would he tell her? That makes no sense. He wouldn't do that, simply because he wouldn't want to fuck everything up with Stella. *Why the fuck would he tell her about us?*

"Mine?" I finally manage to say, grunting out an incredulous laugh. "And how is it my fault?"

"Well, maybe saying it's your fault is a little harsh. It's not like you can help it." Stella takes a large gulp of wine, and takes a deep breath. "I'm broken and Dylan deserves better than that."

"Stella, I still don't understand-"

"I thought about you while I came, and I hate you for it." Her eyes meet mine, and I swear to god my lungs have popped and there's no oxygen in my body. Stella's mouth twitches into a cynical smile, and she lifts her wine to her lips again. "So really, it's not your fault at all. It's mine."

"But you love Dylan," I stammer out. "Why would you think about me?"

"I don't *just* think about you. It's... It's both of you. And Dylan deserves better than to have a woman who can't be happy with him, who wants her fucking step-brother as well as him." She spins the glass in her hand, and tilts her head to give me a side-glance. "I love both of you. I want both of you. Don't act like you didn't know."

Her words throw me back in time, to her 17th birthday. When I placed that gold necklace around her neck, the one I'd had made for her. When I'd brushed my fingers down the back of her neck, and she'd shivered.

Happy birthday, baby girl, I'd whispered in her ear. She'd planted a kiss on my lips, soft and sweet and full of a promise of something she could never give me. Our families would never understand, we knew that. But that I could live with. That I could overcome.

But I couldn't hurt Dylan. I couldn't take his girl. And I'd known from the second he'd laid eyes on Stella that he was gone for her. There'd never be anyone else for him.

Until...

I scrape my fingers through my hair with a grunt. "Fuck."

"We're both a mess." Stella laughs, shaking her head. "I'd tell him, but I can't bring myself to destroy what you two have. I can't take everything from him."

I run my hands over my face, slumping in my chair and looking over at her. "What do we do?"

"Do?" She scoffs. "Nothing. We keep our mouths shut, and we do nothing."

"So, you're just going to drop that on me, that you love me, that you want more-"

"I never said I wanted more, we can't have more," she snaps. "Don't talk this into being something that it is not."

"Stella, I can't just know that you want me, and that you love me, and have you expect me to just live with that."

"Yes, I can." She places her glass on the table, and crosses her arms over her chest. "We both just have to live with it."

"You know, I heard you and Dylan."

Her eyes flicker up to mine, and she lets out a low laugh. "Did you now?"

"Yes." I lean on the table, and she lifts an eyebrow. "I liked what I heard."

"You shouldn't."

"But I did." My eyes stray to the neckline of her blouse, which is sitting open just enough for me to see an edge of pink lace. "I jerked off, listening to you moaning, thinking of him, buried inside you."

Her chest lifts as she sucks in a breath, and her eyes widen. She scoops up her wine glass and gulps it down, quickly getting to her feet and crossing the kitchen.

"This is fucked up," she says, leaning heavily on the counter. "This is fucking wrong."

I watch her back, her heaving shoulders, and my nails bite into my palm, the voice in my head telling me stay right the fuck where I am. That I shouldn't touch her, or go anywhere near her because being near Stella Langford means my self-restraint goes out the fucking window.

But I find myself crossing the wooden floor, standing behind her to put my hands on her hips, a gentle touch that has her head shooting up, her breath hitching in her chest.

"What happened in that room, huh?" I move closer to her, so my chest is brushing against her back. "Why'd you send him away?"

"I told you." She turns her head, not quite looking at me over her shoulder. "Because I'm sick. Because I'll break his heart."

I squeeze her hips, and pull her back against me. "Baby girl, you're not sick." I bury my face in her hair, and a small moan leaves her lips. "You're perfect. My perfect fucking chaos."

"We can't do this," she breathes, even as her head falls back against me and her hands find mine on her hips. "You're my brother, for fuck's sake."

"Do I feel like your brother right now?" I press my hard cock against her ass, and her back arches with a gasp.

"Levi, stop." She says the words but her hands guide mine to her breasts, grinding her ass against me. "This is so wrong."

I cup her breasts and she whimpers. I unbutton her blouse a little more, my fingers brushing over her soft skin and into the lace of her bra. I find her pebbled nipples, hard against my fingertips.

"This is wrong," she murmurs again, her hands moving behind her and brushing over the buttons of my jeans.

"Then let it be wrong." I bite her earlobe, and she mewls softly.

The roar of a motorcycle engine has her scrambling away from me. Headlights shine through the kitchen window and illuminate the two of us, like the fucking finger God himself pointing out the sin and debauchery going on in this perfect little house. Stella's pupils are blown and her lips are full as she frantically buttons her blouse, panting and shaking her head.

"Fuck," she breathes, her eyes full of disbelief as she looks at me. "He can't know. Please. Don't tell him."

Stella has no idea just how many secrets I'm keeping. Stella has no idea I'm drowning in deception and lies just as much as she is. Maybe we're all sick. Maybe we're all broken, so broken that our pieces somehow match up perfectly. What would cut someone else and leave them bleeding out makes us the missing pieces of each other's puzzles.

But as Stella wipes away an errant tear and eagerly meets Dylan at the door, as she throws her arms around him and tearfully apologizes, I know it's not meant to be.

I take my heavy heart upstairs, and pull out my phone to look for my own place.

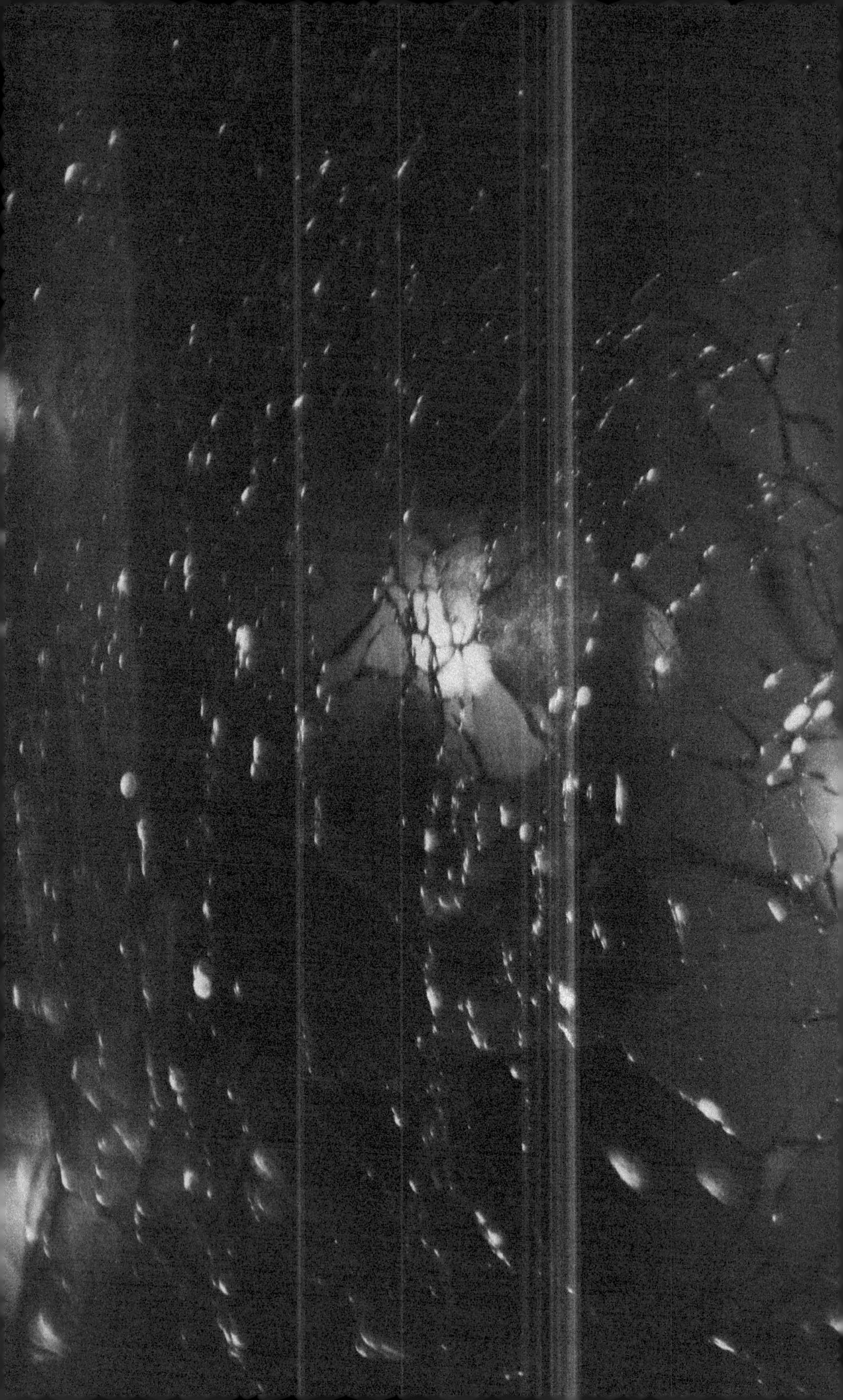

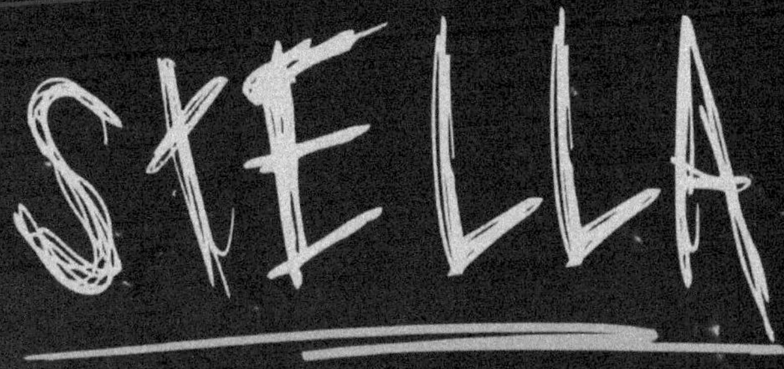

CHAPTER ELEVEN

"I'M A BAD PERSON." Dylan lies in the tub, the whiskey glass dangling from his hand as I massage his scalp.

"No, you're not." I rake my fingers over the rough stubble, which has gotten so much longer since he got out. "You're the best person."

He tilts his head, his eyes shining with tears as he looks at me. "I left him to die alone. What kind of person does that?"

"The kind who'd been abused by him. You didn't owe him anything." I rinse my hands in the water, and cradle Dylan's face. "You are not a bad person. You're incredible, and you're sweet."

"I'm glad he's dead."

"Me too."

Dylan's face screws up as though he's in pain, and he presses the icy glass to his head. "I hated him so much."

"I know, *papi*. I know."

"I wanted him to die in pain, I wanted him to feel everything he'd ever made me feel. And what happened? He just went to sleep." He sucks in a heavy breath, sitting up in the tub and throwing back the rest of his whiskey, sucking on his teeth as the alcohol burns his throat. "I shouldn't wish that on anyone, what kind of person does that?"

"Dylan, stop." I put my arms around him, holding him close as he gasps for air. "Don't do this to yourself. Please."

He lays his head against my shoulder with a heavy sigh. "Everyone's gone now. I don't have any family anymore."

"Yes, you do. You have me, and Levi." I clench my eyes shut, disgust and revulsion burning in my throat like bile. As though to reassure myself, I clutch Dylan closer, not caring that he's soaking my blouse, or that my knees are aching against the hard tiled floor. I deserve to hurt. I deserve flagellation. After I nearly betrayed the man who's now gasping for air and feeling alone. I should tell Dylan to run, to save him from more pain, from more hurt, from all the things he doesn't deserve.

Instead, I hold on to him for dear life, like the selfish bitch I am.

"Will you come with me to the funeral?" He asks after a while.

"Of course I will."

He pulls back from me, seeming to take in my appearance for the first time as he rubs the heel of his hand under his eye. "You look nice. Did you go to work?"

"Yeah, I had to check some cases, and I decided to go back early."

"Oh." Dylan nods, leaning on the edge of the tub. He gazes at me with his dark eyes, and my heart wrenches. "I'm so sorry about the other day. I shouldn't have pushed you. I wanted you, and I wanted to make you feel good. I missed you so bad, and then I pushed you, and I'm so fucking sorry Stella."

"*Papi*, no." I clasp on to his hand, holding it to my cheek. "You didn't. I wanted it. I wanted you, I promise. It was just… intense."

"If you want to wait, I'll wait. I waited ten years for you, I can wait as long as you need."

I have no idea how long I'll need. Not after my confession. I hate myself for telling Levi, for putting this burden on him and straining his relationship with Dylan. Now Dylan needs us, and we have this hanging over us like a black cloud. Shit.

Dylan rises out of the tub, and I get to my feet to hand him a towel.

"When's the funeral?" I ask as he dries himself.

"Next Friday. I'm tempted to have the old bastard cremated, he'd hate that." Dylan's sneer is filled with pain. "But then I think of my dad and I can't bring myself to do it."

"See?" I put my arms around him, holding him close and burying my face in the crook of his neck. "You're a good person. You want to do the right thing by someone who doesn't even deserve it."

He encircles me with his arms, holding me tightly against him, and he's naked and warm and smells amazing. "I'm so glad I have you."

"You do, you have me." More lies.

"Can you… Can you come and lie down with me?" He pulls back, his eyes not meeting mine as he hangs his head. "I'm sorry, I just don't want to be alone, but I'm fucking exhausted."

"Of course."

I follow him to his bedroom, taking my clothes off as he climbs into bed naked. He eyes me uncertainly as he pulls the sheet back.

"I can put clothes on if you want."

I shake my head with a smile. "It's OK. I want to feel your skin."

He lies down with a weak smile, and he shuts off the light as I crawl in beside him. The night is quiet, and crawling in under his arm, smelling his skin and feeling him against me is like coming home. I sigh, putting my hand on his chest over his heart beat, and he trails his fingertips over the back of my hand.

"I was so scared you'd be married when I got out," he says quietly. "I'd have been happy for you. I wanted you to be happy, I wanted you to find someone who'd treat you right, like you deserve. But I spent 10 years praying you'd wait for me."

"I don't think anyone would want to marry me," I whisper, trying to sound light-hearted, but the pain edges my voice all the same.

"Anyone who puts a ring on your finger would be the luckiest person in the world."

I bury my face into his chest, wishing I could somehow slip inside him and let him heal all the broken parts of me. "I waited for you. I did."

He cradles my head against his chest, and kisses my hair. "I'm sorry. I'm sorry I left you that night."

"Don't talk about that now."

He puts a hand around my jaw, forcing me to look up at him. "I should have stayed with you. I would do everything different now, *guera*. I'd stay with you, I'd hold you, til you stopped crying. I'd kiss you, make sure you were safe and then I'd deal with it properly. I'd be a man, not a stupid fucking little boy."

"You did what you thought was right." I wrap my fingers around his wrist, tears welling in my eyes.

"I lost 10 years with you because of what I did. I've made so many mistakes, Stella, so fucking many. But you were never one of them." He pulls me close, his lips brushing against mine. "You're the only thing that's ever made sense."

"You're the only one who makes my head go quiet," I tell him, leaning my forehead against his. "With you everything just stops, and it's just… me."

"Te amo, guera." He kisses me again, harder this time, and I want to let go, I want to wrap myself around him and let him love me in all the ways he needs to. I want to wish myself back to that night, wish that we'd had that first time over, had it the way we deserved to - tenderness and discovery, two young people who loved each other and wanted to find each other.

Instead, just like that night, one of us pulls back tearfully, wrapping their arms around the other and weeping. All the pain spreads over my skin like a bruise, and I hold Dylan as he cries, as he rages against the darkness that surrounds us both.

When he finally falls asleep, I watch his face, and I hate myself again. Because he hoped for me, and I have to let him go. I have to break his heart, I have to take everything from him. I could live a lie. I could. But I can't do that to him.

I hold him all night, unable to sleep, listening to his heartbeat while it remains whole.

I'm broken. And all I do is break everyone around me.

The sun peeks through the curtains of the bedroom, and I look up at Dylan's sleeping face.

I have to let him go. But not yet.

Not just yet.

I leave Dylan to sleep and throw on a t-shirt before I creep downstairs. My head's throbbing and I feel seedy after staying awake all night. I rub my eyes, knowing I'm probably smudging mascara all over my face because I didn't take my makeup off, but I can't find it in myself to care.

A message from Lilly is waiting for me when I pick up my phone from where I left it the night before.

Your mom's in town. She wants to see you.

I groan, and throw the phone back on the table. The last thing I need is to see my mother right now. As if shit wasn't complicated enough. I scoop coffee into the machine and flip it on, hoping the scent is enough to jump-start my system.

I turn and shriek when I see Levi standing in the doorway.

"Jesus, you scared me."

"Sorry." He steps into the kitchen in nothing but boxers, running a hand through his messy blond hair. He eyes me thoughtfully, taking in the t-shirt and the smudged makeup. "Rough night?"

"Dylan's a mess," I reply, raking my fingers through my hair to try and look a little less disheveled. "He was really upset last night. Hates himself for not being there when his grandfather died."

"We should have gone to the hospital." Levi crosses the kitchen to lean on the island, rolling his neck with a groan. "Instead of-"

"Don't." I snap, fixing him with a glare. "I never want to talk about that again."

"Great, Stella, that's great." He advances on me, stopping short and exhaling through gritted teeth. "You know what, you are fucked up. You can't tell someone you love them, and then expect them to just sit with that like everything is fine."

"Well gee, thanks." I resist the urge to slap him. "You can move out, and stay the hell away from me."

"Fine by me." His voice is louder now, and I hiss at him.

"Keep your fucking voice down. This is not the time."

"Oh right, we have to think about Dylan." He narrows his eyes at me, his expression wild and I know he had as bad a night as I did. "Poor Dylan, who you can't hurt. You really don't know anything, do you?"

"What the fuck is that supposed to mean?"

He snaps his mouth shut, biting his lip as his eyes drop from mine. With a shake of his head, he takes a step back from me. "Nothing. I don't mean a thing. I'm tired, and I'm being an ass. I'm sorry." He lifts his gaze to mine, and sighs heavily. "I am. I'm sorry. This is just… hard."

"I know." I want to take him in my arms and say everything I said last night again. Instead, I move towards him and take his hand in mine. "I'm sorry, too. I shouldn't have said anything. I just… I feel like all I do is hurt people."

He notches two fingers under my chin and lifts my face to his. "You don't, baby girl. You're a dream. Just not mine, unfortunately."

I squeeze my eyes shut to stop the tears from falling. "I'm sorry, Levi."

"I found a place, I'll be out of here by next week."

My gaze snaps up to his, and I shake my head. "You don't have to do that."

"I think we both know I do." He sighs, running his fingers through my hair. "You deserve to be happy. I know you tell yourself that you don't. But you do."

"So do you."

"I guess we'll just need to find a way to be that, then." He strokes my cheek gently, a sad smile ghosting over his lips. "My perfect chaos."

I feel like he's slipping away from me. I feel like I'm losing him. And because I'm a bitch, because I'm selfish and awful, because all I can think about is being alone and losing them, because I know one day I will, I do the only thing I can.

I throw my arms around his neck and kiss him.

He reacts instantly, like he was waiting for it, like he could see it coming even when I couldn't. We're caught in a feverish rush, hands frantically pulling at each other, the desire to drag the other person as close as possible so consuming my head spins. His tongue is hot and urgent as it strokes mine, and his hands move under my ass, scooping me up and placing me on the counter. My legs lock around his hips, pulling him close, and his fingers spear into my hair, forcing my head back so he can deepen the kiss.

"It's always been you," he says, panting. "Always, since I saw you in that pink dress, and you smiled at me across the aisle. It's always been you for me, baby girl."

I gasp, looking up at him with wide eyes. "All this time?"

"All this time." His blue eyes meet mine, and he brushes his fingers down my cheek. "I tried so hard to talk myself out of it. I did. But I can't."

"Why didn't you ever tell me?"

He laughs softly, curling a strand of my hair around his finger. "Because you were his girl. I couldn't.. I couldn't take you away from him."

"It's going to kill him," I say softly.

Levi's head drops, putting his hands on the counter either side of me. "Stella, there are things you need to know-"

My phone starts to ring, and I groan loudly. "That fucking phone."

Levi gently pushes my legs away, and steps back to let me climb down off the counter. I slide to the floor, landing on unsteady feet, and take a deep breath before crossing the kitchen to snatch up my phone.

"Hello?"

"Hey cuz!" Lily's voice is bright and cheery and way too fucking jarring for this time of morning and the mood I find myself in. "Did you get my message?"

"I-I did. I just hadn't had a chance to respond yet, it's kind of early, you know?"

"So-rry," she laughs in a sing-song voice. "So, you free to come for breakfast?"

"I, uh, no, we sort of had a, uh…" I realize Lilly and the rest of the family still don't know anything about Levi and Dylan staying here, and I have no desire to have that conversation with her right now. "A friend had a family emergency, so I'm-"

"Oh that's sad." Lilly sounds less than interested. "Your mom really missed you! She's so excited to see you!"

"Yeah, I bet." I shift on my feet, trying to pull the t-shirt down to cover more of my thighs, my cheeks burning. "It's just-"

"The mimosas will be cold! We're over at the Riverwood Cafe, you know, the one by the river?" She laughs lightly, and I hear others joining in around her. "Hurry, sweetie! OK, love you, bye!" The line goes dead and I decide to throw my phone off the next bridge.

"Everything alright?" Levi asks, and I can't even look at him.

"I - my mom's in town, and she really wants to see me."

"Been a while since you saw her, huh?" Levi crosses his arms over his chest.

"She came to visit about four years ago, when she was freshly divorced from husband number 6."

Levi scoffs out a laugh, shaking his head as he retrieves two cups from the glass-fronted cupboard beside him. "Living with her must have been a trip."

My stomach twists, and that bruised feeling returns as I meet Levi's eyes with a level gaze. "I haven't lived with my mother since I was little."

Levi frowns, his head giving a brief shake. "But where did you live when we… After we…"

"With your mother." The past comes crashing down on me, all the things they still don't know, all the things that will keep us apart and they will never understand. I turn away from Levi's confusion, and shrug. "There's a lot you still don't know, and I can't tell you right now. But I think you and Dylan both know by now, that when you pulled that trigger, neither of you were prepared for what that would mean for me."

Levi rushes at me, grabbing my arms with his hands, his wide eyes searching my face. "What do you mean? What happened to you?"

I shrug out his grasp, and take a large step back. "Not now."

"Then when?"

"I don't know, maybe never." I take a few more steps back, and bite my lip. I want to tell him. But it's his mother. "Some things you don't need to know, Levi. And I can't hurt anyone else." I rush up the stairs before he can ask me anything else, before the truth can tumble out of me and spill across the space between us with all the blood and tears those years carried with them.

Up in my bedroom, I have a quick shower, putting on a scant face of makeup and pulling on a sundress. I look for my hairbrush, knocking my book off the night stand as I pull open the drawer. My book flips open, and a black card lands at my feet.

Mallory's card.

I stare at it for a minute, before shoving it back into the book.

There's no point. Who would believe me? The words make bile rise in my throat, as my father's face swims before me. *No one will believe you, sweetness. Who are you? Nobody. Nothing.*

I grab my purse and hurry out of the house, pasting the smile on my face as I go to meet my mother for the first time in years.

CHAPTER TWELVE

STELLA'S GONE when I wake up, and the pain at her absence is visceral. I roll over and clutch the pillow she slept on to my face, drinking in the scent of vanilla that lingers. Her clothes are still draped over the chair in the corner. It could all be so normal, so different, if I wasn't fucked up beyond repair.

She's too good for me.

There's a knock at the door, and before I can respond, Levi's peering around the edge of the door, holding up a blue cup.

"Hey, pretty boy. Brought you a coffee." He smiles warmly, coming to sit on the bed beside me and hand me the cup.

"Thanks." I take a sip, and it soothes my throat that's sore from crying the night before. "Where's Stella?"

"Her mom's back in town, she went for brunch with the family."

"Oh." The pain intensifies, and I chide myself silently for being a selfish fuck. "She probably really wanted to see her mom, huh?"

Levi laughs cynically and raises his eyebrows. "It did not sound like it. But with her family I don't think she has much choice."

"I guess not."

"Did you know she lived with my mom after we were sentenced?"

I take another sip of coffee, and rub my chin. "Yeah, Zee told me. But when I try to talk to Stella about it, she just says that it doesn't matter, and that it's done."

Levi sighs, crawling into the bed beside me and leaning against the headboard. He runs his hands over his face, and lets them drop heavily into his lap. "She said the same thing to me this morning." He gives me a side glance. "So you and her, you made up?"

I shrug, placing the cup on the nightstand, resuming my position beside him simply to feel the warmth of his shoulder against mine. "I guess we did. I didn't think she'd leave me alone like this, but…"

"I'm here," Levi says, and slowly, hesitantly, he lays his hand over mine. I swallow hard, because all the pain and grief, the soreness that lies in every muscle of my body and the ache in my chest, they all dissipate just a little as his strong hand wraps around mine. "I'm sorry for what happened. With your grandpa, I mean."

I scoff bitterly. "I'm not."

"No, I mean-" He breaks off with a sharp breath, frowning at our joined hands. "I should have come to the hospital. I should have been there."

"There's nothing you could have done."

With a strangled laugh he releases my hand and scoots to the edge of the bed, running his fingers through his hair. "God fucking dammit, Kovac, you really make it hard to look after you, you know that?" He looks over his shoulder at me, and there's no swagger, no smirk on his face. Levi Fenton is looking at me with pain and longing, his eyes full of a desire for something neither of us want to admit to.

"I worried about you, all afternoon. All evening." His brow furrows, and he grits his teeth as he sucks in a breath. "I miss you, OK? I miss you, and I'm at work with you, all day, I'm here with you, and I have to watch you and Stella navigate whatever the fuck you two have going on, and I'm just here, wondering who-" He cuts off, his head hanging to his chest. "I don't know how to do this. I don't know what to do with what I feel for you. And it's fucking killing me."

I've never seen him like this. Not over anyone. Levi was always too cool to get caught up on anyone. But now he's sitting here, suffering through a half-mumbled confession of something, I'm not even sure what, and all I can think about is how I just spent a night lying in this bed with Stella, and now I'm sitting here with her brother, wanting nothing more than to kiss him.

"We agreed it was just going to be the one time," I say slowly, and Levi's eyes flash over his shoulder at me as he laughs cynically.

"I think we both know that was a stupid fucking idea." He turns to me, and rubs a hand over his mouth, before reaching out to take my hand again. "If there was a way, for us to be together-"

"There's not." I can't even let that thought take hold. It hurts too much.

"But if there was… I mean…" He lifts his eyes to look at me, and his lip trembles, his brows drawn together. "Would you want to be?"

I pull my hand away with a grunt. "Why the fuck are you doing this to me?" I push the sheet away, climbing out of the bed and clawing my hands against my head. "I - I can't fucking do this right now. I cannot believe you'd fucking ask me this."

He's in front of me in an instant, taking my face in his hands, his eyes almost frantic as they search mine. "I'm sorry! You think I want this? To drive us both half fucking crazy while knowing what it would do to Stella? I'm not doing this because I enjoy it."

"Then why are you doing it?"

His Adam's apple bobs in his throat, and his eyes move to my lips. "Because I need you."

I'm suddenly aware of the fact that I'm naked, and he's

pressing his barely dressed body against me. Everything slips into sharp focus, the heat of his body and the brush of his fingertips against the stubble on my jaw. I know I should push him away. I know this is wrong. But I also know that Levi is right and that sleeping with him just one time opened up the floodgates on all the feelings I'd tried to suppress. It's selfish. It's selfish and wrong, and my better judgment tells me to push Levi out the door and out of my fucking heart and life as fast as possible.

But of course I don't do that. Like the weak, desperate coward I am, I grab him and pull him close, my mouth descending on his and his answering moan making me hard in an instant. I need him too, in a way I never expected to. I'm selfish and greedy, because as I kiss him and taste his mouth and his hands roam over me in a frenzy, I wonder why I shouldn't be able to have them both?

I've lost everyone in my life, don't I deserve more? Why should I have to fucking choose? Why do I have to decide between the two people who own the fucking air in my lungs and every beat of my wrecked and ruined heart? Why can't I have them both? Why can't they both have me?

Levi pushes me on to the bed, and I lie back, letting his mouth and hands explore me.

"Fuck, pretty boy," he says over a rasping breath, wrapping his hand around my cock. His eyes darken as he gazes up at me, and he licks his lips. "I've never done this before."

I stroke a hand through his hair. "I'll tell you what feels good, don't worry."

"Kinda new to me, wanting a dick in my mouth, you know?"

I throw my head back and laugh breathlessly, a hand over my face. "You don't have to do this."

"I want to." When my eyes meet his again, they're soft and desirous. He looks down at my cock, then back at me. "I want to look after you. Even if I'm no good at it, I want to - I want to learn what's good for you." His hand glides up my stomach, and he lowers his mouth to my hip, planting an open-mouthed kiss there, his breath hot as it washes over my skin. "I want to make you feel good."

His touch is gentle, his lips and tongue questioning and hesitant. He runs his tongue up the underside of my cock, from base to tip, circling the head. A small hum vibrates through him as he licks up the precum that's already beading there.

The pace of my breathing picks up, and I try not to buck my hips to meet him. He seems to sense the tension in my body, and his gaze skates up my body.

"Is this how you like it?"

I shake my head. "It's OK, you do it the way that-"

"No. Tell me what you like."

I tip my head back, staring at the ceiling. "You can be rougher. I like… that."

"Rough, huh?" And just like that, the flip switches and Levi's voice is full of swagger and all that fucking confidence. He nips at my thighs, and I hiss in a breath. "My pretty boy likes it to hurt?"

"Y-yeah."

"Good." His mouth descends on my cock, and he sucks hard, the brush of teeth and the pressure of his lips making me clench my molars. He spits on me and strokes his hand up and down, increasing the pressure as he strokes over the tip. He takes me back down his throat, and his mouth is huge and hot, his tongue almost punishing as it lashes up and down my length.

His other hand pushes between my thighs, and his thumb presses against my ass. For someone who said they didn't know what they were doing, he sure as fuck knows something. It shouldn't surprise me that someone like Levi knows what to do no matter who he has in bed, but fuck, the way he sucks and touches, the way he almost seems to answer each of my moans with a chuckle, like he's so pleased with himself - it's not just about him knowing how to suck dick or where to touch me to have my back arching off the bed.

It's fucking heaven. For this moment I'm not alone, and he's showing me just what I mean to him, how much I mean to him. Maybe I'm a fool, because the moment will pass and we'll have to answer for this tangled web we keep on weaving for ourselves.

But right now, there's just Levi, sucking harder and harder until the heat in my spine ignites, and I can't stop myself grabbing the back of his head and jerking my hips to meet every stroke of his hot mouth. And then I explode, pumping my release down his throat as he swallows me down.

I can't hold back the moan that almost crests into a roar, and when he runs his hand over my stomach again, his fingertips slide against the thin sheen of sweat that's broken out over me.

All the tension now gone, my body melts into the bed, and the haze that takes over as Levi crawls over me and kisses me gently - maybe it's some weird post-nut clarity, but I want to tell him I love him and that I want him more than anything, as much as I want Stella. *Yes I want to be with you. If there was a way to be with you, I'd take it. Right now. No questions asked.*

We lie in my bed, the sun washing over us, and my best friend kisses me like there's no one else in the world.

He finally pulls back from me, propping himself up on an elbow, and he grins down at me. "Not bad for my first time, huh?"

"Smug asshole."

He laughs, rolling away from me to get off the bed and head into the bathroom. The faucet comes on, and I hear him washing up. He reappears in the doorway, drying his hands on a towel.

"Come on, pretty boy. Get dressed."

I raise my head from the bed with a frown. "You expect me to walk after that?"

"We have somewhere to be."

"And where is that?"

He crosses the room to lean over me in the bed, and plants a soft kiss on my lips. "We've got to get our girl."

By the time we pull up in the parking lot of the cafe where Stella is meeting her family, I've managed to compartmentalize the shame I felt the entire drive here. Every now and then, Levi's hand strayed over to my leg, and I tried not to think about the fact that he was about to face Stella with my cum inside him.

Levi kills the engine, and turns on me with a wide smile. "Ready?"

"What exactly are we doing here?"

Levi shrugs. "I don't know. Cause some shit. Save Stella from her mother."

"Her family is going to lose it."

Levi's smile turns positively devilish. "Then get ready for the fireworks."

The cafe is brimming with people, all the wealthy Bellford Heights families sipping juice from champagne glasses, tastefully dressed in beige and white. Their diamonds glint in the bright sunshine, and Levi and I look like two serpents slithering amongst the masses in our black t-shirts and arms sleeved in tattoos. Eyes follow us, tables falling silent as we pass, stares and glares meeting us at every turn.

Then, like a ray of sunshine, I spot her. Sitting at the banister, mimosa in hand, her hair swept up on top of her head. Her bright pink sundress stands out amongst the sea of beige.

Our girl.

Is it weird that those words sent an unnamed desire through me? I really am sick. I should be consumed by guilt after what Levi and I just did.

Lilly spots us before Stella does, her mouth falling open with a scoff.

"What are *they* doing here?" She announces loudly enough for the whole cafe to hear, and all eyes at the family table turn to us.

Stella's face is filled with joy and confusion. Her cousins and aunt all stare daggers. Levi laughs jovially, and suddenly I'm filled with the same level of contemptible swagger he is. Fuck these people, all these people who left Stella to Gloria fucking Fenton when she needed them. We might be the criminals - at least we're nothing like these people.

"Morning!" Levi says brightly, leaning over Lilly to drop a kiss on Stella's cheek. She smiles, her cheeks flushing pink as her eyes drop to the table. Levi plucks the mimosa from her hand, downing the rest of it, and casts his smile over the table of glowering faces. "How is everyone today?"

"Fine until you showed up." Lilly throws her napkin on the table, crossing her arms over her chest. "What are you doing here, Levi?"

"Why, I'm here to see my *family*." His lethal grin lands on Stella's mother, who looks like she's already drunk as she holds onto her champagne glass with two hands. "Hey, Molly. How's things?"

Molly's head wobbles on her skinny neck as she turns to look up at Levi. "Who the fuck are you?" She slurs, and all eyes at the table drop.

They might act like they're better than us, but Molly Hartmann is the one embarrassment they can't cover up.

Stella leans over and puts a hand on her mother's arm. "Mom, this is Levi. Gloria's son. Remember?"

Molly narrows her eyes at Levi as he extends a hand to her, taking in his tattooed knuckles. "You look like you just got out of jail."

Levi meets my eyes and we both laugh.

"It's not *funny*," Lilly snaps, and Levi drops down to plant a kiss on her cheek, making her flinch and frantically wipe the kiss away like he's going to give her a disease.

"Lighten up, Lil. Is Colin Bates still hitting that?"

Lilly's cheeks flush bright red as her mother turns to her with a stern look. "Oh my god, will you both just go away?"

"We just got here," I say, rounding the table to stand beside

Stella, who gazes up at me with a soft smile. "Hey, *guera.*" I stroke a finger along her jaw. "You look real pretty."

"Thank you."

"I was sad you weren't there when I woke up."

She stiffens, and gasps go up from the table. I lean down and press a gentle kiss to her lips, and she suppresses a smile.

"Can I borrow you for a minute?" I ask quietly, and she nods.

"Stella, tell me you are not going somewhere with these assholes?" Lilly asks loudly.

"Guess y'all don't know we're living with her, huh?" Levi laughs loudly as horrified eyes turn to him. "Oh yeah, it's a regular little love nest we got ourselves there."

Stella's aunt, whose name I can't remember, rises to her feet. "This is a family function. Neither of you are invited. I'd appreciate it if you'd leave."

Levi snatches a grape from the table, putting it between his teeth and turning from the table with a shrug. "No problem, I'll meet you back at the car, pretty boy."

I pull Stella up from her chair, and we round the table. "Y'all can have her back in just a second."

More eyes follow us as I drag Stella through the cafe, to the building housing the kitchen, down a narrow path and out the back towards the river. Once I know we're alone, I round on her and pull her against me. She squeaks a smothered protest as my mouth claims hers, one hand grabbing her ass hard.

"What are you doing?" She gasps as she frees her mouth from mine. "What the fuck-"

"I wanted to come down here and remind you who you belong to." I grasp her jaw in my hand, forcing her to look up at me. "I wanted to remind you that you're better than all these fucking posers. Even if they think you're slumming it with someone like me."

"That's what you wanted to tell me?" She asks, her body softening against me.

"That's right." I smile down at her.

"So I belong to you?"

"If you do, *guera,* you come home to me and you prove it."

Her eyes flutter, and she sighs softly. "Dylan, I have to tell you someth-"

I cut her off with a hard kiss. I have to tell her something too, too many fucking somethings. But I'm not going to give her a chance to doubt this. I'm not going to give myself a chance to feel guilt over the morning I just spent in bed with her brother. I know this is fucked, I know I'm trying to reel her in harder so she won't walk away when she finds out just what I've been doing behind her back.

I refuse to lose her. My girl. *Our girl.*

When I release her, my hand drops to her throat, and I squeeze lightly. "You come home to me, and you show me who you belong to." I squeeze a little harder, and a small moan leaves her lips. "I told you, I'm a fucking animal for you. And I need you. All of you." I put my mouth to her jaw, nipping her gently. "Now, you go back to that family of yours, and know you're better than all of them."

A shuddering breath leaves her lips, and she nods.

I release her, stepping back and feeling way too fucking smug over the fact that her hair's come loose and her lips are full and red from kissing me. Knowing she's going back to her family all worked up and thinking about what's going to happen when she comes home later.

I head back through the gardens to the car, where Levi is leaning on the hood, smoking a cigarette.

"And?" He asks, grinding the cigarette out under his shoe. "Did we get our girl?"

"I think we're about to find out."

I spend the next few hours back at the house in the garage, working on my bike. Levi leaves for a while, then comes back and disappears into his room. The sun starts to sink low on the horizon, and Stella still isn't back.

I go inside, heading up to the shower to wash off all the grease from the garage. I wonder when Stella's coming back, if my little possessive display scared her off. I'm not much good at this 'taking it slow' thing anymore. The guilt is eating away at me, making me desperate and reckless.

But I need to have her. I need to tell myself that I won't fucking lose her when she finally knows who I really am.

The setting sun hasn't made the temperature drop, and it's hot as fucking Hades when I get out of the shower. I dry off and pull on a pair of shorts, and just as I head downstairs, the front door flies open. Frantic footsteps sound in the hallway and then thump up the stairs.

Stella stares up at me for just a moment before she rushes the rest of the way up the stairs and into my arms. She makes as though she wants to kiss me, pulling back with a brief shake of her head.

"I need you to know that I love you."

When I try to speak, to tell her that I love her too, she claps a hand over my mouth, shaking her head more emphatically.

"I need you to listen. I'm broken, Dylan. I want things I shouldn't. And it's not that you're not enough. It's that I'm not enough. I will never be good enough for you, and I'm sorry."

I wrap my fingers around her wrist, removing her hand from my mouth. I turn her hand, placing a kiss on the back of it.

"*Guera*, whatever it is, we'll get through it."

"I'll hurt you." Her lip trembles, her big amber eyes filling with tears. "I'll hurt you, and you don't deserve it."

"You won't hurt me."

"Yes, I will."

I'm standing on the step above her, so I'm practically towering over her, and when I sink my hands into her hair to yank her head back, her chin rests against my chest, wide eyes gazing up at me as a tear strays down the side of her face.

"Then hurt me, Stella. Fucking destroy me." I brush the tear away with the backs of my fingers, only to have it followed swiftly by another one. "I mean it. Tear me to pieces every single day. I don't give a fuck, as long as I'm with you."

"But-"

I crush her protests with my mouth. No more. Enough. I'm not having this perfect creature weeping in front of me, berating herself for god knows what when the man she's standing in front of is less than perfect. When I'm more broken and damned than she could ever know. But I want to deserve her. Somehow, some way, I want to deserve both of them.

I want to be fucking happy. I want to be brave enough to seize all of this with both hands, to have everything and everyone and be so fucking full of joy that all the dark, all those black spots of pain and damage that blanket my soul are blotted out.

I devour Stella's sobs and tears, drinking in every part of her. Her hands scratch at my stomach, as though fighting a losing battle, too tired to fight this anymore.

"I'm yours," she gasps against my lips.

I tear down the straps of her dress, teeth grazing along her collarbone, the curve of her shoulder, and she pushes a hand into my shorts. Her delicate fingers wrap around me, and she huffs out a breath against my heated skin. One hand braces against my chest, and she pushes me onto the step behind me. She peels off her sundress, then climbs into my lap, straddling me and hesitating for a moment, her shoulders heaving. Her eyes meet mine, her plump lips quivering.

"I waited for you," she murmurs.

"I know."

She takes a deep, shuddering breath, lifting her hips so the head of my cock just caresses her entrance, and her eyes flutter shut.

"*Guera,* I've got you."

Without opening her eyes, she takes my face in hers, and with a small moan she sinks down onto me, enveloping me with all her slick heat. Just that sensation alone has me seeing fucking stars, just her naked warmth around me, her breath washing over my lips.

"You feel so good." I run my hands up her back, into her hair. She's so fucking tight, and with nothing between us, I have to claw on to my restraint not to come. She moves and I hiss in a breath, each circle of her hips taking me closer and closer to fucking heaven. "Fuck, *guera,* fuck. That's it."

The step behind me digs into my back as she rides me, the sensation unpleasant enough that I focus on that instead of the feeling of that sweet pussy working me. She doesn't release my face, keeping me close as she moans, tiny sounds like she's afraid of herself, like the desire is threatening to unleash something bigger than both of us.

"Let go," I tell her. "You let go, it's just us."

"Put your hand around my throat." She says, her eyes meeting mine, danger and need flashing at the same time. "I trust you. I want you to."

I lean back on the step, bracing myself on an elbow as I extend my other hand, bracing it around the smooth column of her neck. Her head tips back slightly, a moan, louder this time, bursting from somewhere deep within her, and her hips start to work me harder.

"That's my girl." I lower my eyes to where our bodies join, and my dick is stretching her almost obscenely, her rosy pink clit rubbing against me. I squeeze her throat a little tighter, and the pulse that jolts through her pussy almost has me come undone right there and then. "*Fuck,*" I murmur over a heavy exhale.

Stella is lost in the moment now, her perfect tits bouncing as she rides me, one hand against my stomach and the other braced against the railing. Her pussy is so tight now, her climax drawing closer and closer. She starts to grind herself against me, and I lift my hips to meet her strokes, to provide that friction that she needs to come on my cock.

I should lift her off me before I spill inside her, I know I should. But she doesn't give me a chance to think or be any semblance of fucking responsible. Her hips buck against me, her head thrown right back, straining against my hand, and as her stomach tenses, I feel that pulse again, followed by another, and another. She moans my name, curling her hand around my wrist, holding on for dear life as my cock twitches and releases deep inside her. I pull her down to me, sliding in and out of her as she lies against my chest, savoring every single clench of her pussy as she rides out her orgasm, as I fill her with mine.

Finally, we're both sprawled on the stairs, her face tipped up into the crook of my neck, panting and sweating. All I can think, the singular thought in my head, is *Finally*. Maybe it's crude to think that way, I don't know. I don't fucking care. Lying here with her in my arms, shuddering and gasping softly, my cum dripping out of her, all I can think is *I finally had her*. It was hurried and frenzied, and my back fucking hurts from these stupid stairs.

But fuck, I've had her, and she's had me.

A door closes softly, and my heart roars.

It wasn't just us. Levi is here too.

Stella doesn't seem to have heard it, her body still lax and soft from her orgasm. I'm overtaken by that greedy feeling again, selfish and consuming, and I know it's wrong.

But I still want them both. And I don't know how to tell her that. This feeling is gutting, and I'm convinced this family is going to fucking kill me.

"Are you OK?" Stella asks softly, lifting her head from my chest to gaze up at me. She looks almost sleepy, drunk and satisfied.

"I just - I didn't mean to come inside you, I shouldn't have done that."

She shrugs, running a finger along my jaw. "I have an IUD. I wanted you to come inside me."

Those words are enough to have me getting hard again. Before I can get too entangled in that feeling, I lift her off me, and she gasps a little.

"You're bigger than I expected," she says with a little laugh.

"Well thanks." I kiss her forehead, and groan as my back connects with the step again. "I need to get up."

Her eyes widen with alarm, and she scrambles off me. "Oh my god, I'm so sorry."

"Don't be. It was worth it."

It's while we're in the shower that I stare down at her, at this woman I love, and the gutting feeling comes back. The realization that I need to tell the truth before she gets in even deeper. I wash her gently, and she sighs.

"Stella, I have to tell you something."

"Mmm?"

Five. Four. Three. I count down to the moment when I know I'll lose her. I count down these precious seconds of her skin being against mine. I'm about to ruin everything, right when I had it all.

But the truth is stinging in my chest, and I need to get it out.

Two. One.

"I slept with Levi."

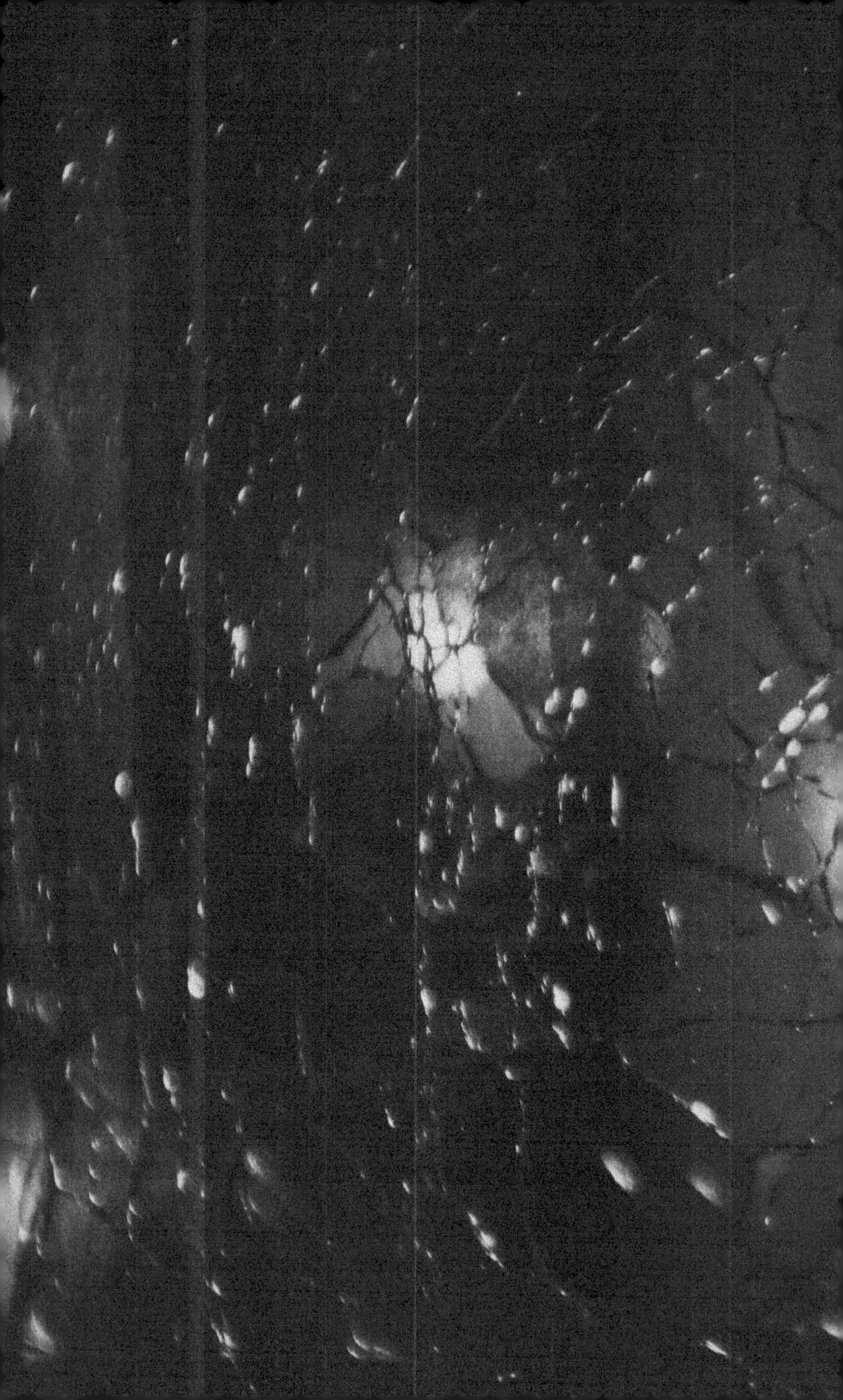

STELLA

CHAPTER THIRTEEN

ZEE'S FACE is frantic as they walk into the restaurant, eyebrows lifting as their eyes land on me and they rush between the tables towards me.

"Girl, what the fuck is going on?" They ask, grabbing me in a hug before they sit down beside me. "Dylan and Levi have been blowing up my phone, they almost called the fucking cops because they didn't know where you were, and now you're calling me and asking me to dinner, and my fucking god, what happened?"

"Nothing, nothing bad, I promise."

Their eyebrows shoot up. "Nothing *bad?* They've had me running around town looking for you because *nothing bad* happened?"

I take a deep breath. "I just had to get out and clear my head, and I needed to talk to you."

"Well, I'm right here." Zee leans their crossed arms on the table, their face still twisted with concern. "Anything you need to tell me, I'm right here."

I take a sip of my water, trying to order my thoughts and figure out where exactly in this whole mess I need to start.

"I had sex with Dylan," I tell them.

They stay silent, watching me with a neutral face. Finally

they nod, and shrug. "OK. Was it… not good?" Their eyes widen, and they reach out to take my hand. "Did he hurt you?"

"No, no, nothing like that. It was… It was really good. Probably the best sex I've had."

Zee's face is instantly a picture of relief, followed by confusion. "Girl, I don't want to push you here, but Dylan was freaking the fuck out, and Levi didn't sound much better. You're telling me you had the best sex of your life and then ran away?"

"Dylan and Levi had sex."

Zee leans back in their chair, eyes wide, jaw dropping. "Levi, as in… No. No way."

"Yes way." I clench my eyes shut. "Oh god, this is so messy."

"Yeah, you can say that again. Why the fuck would Dylan cheat on you? With your stepbrother? With his best friend? I mean…?" Zee trails off, putting a hand to their forehead. "My head hurts, goddamn."

I put my hands to my head. "There's more."

"*More*?"

I drop my hands from my face and grab Zee's hand. "Please, just let me talk. I need to get this out."

"Go ahead. I'm listening."

Before I can stop myself, it all comes tumbling out. Levi's confession that he's always loved me, the kiss we shared in the kitchen, Dylan's tearful admission that he'd slept with Levi and the raging desire that unleashed inside me. I even tell them that I locked eyes with Levi while I fucked Dylan, that I let him watch us, that I could see him getting hard while I rode Dylan right in front of him, and I liked it. *Fuck, I loved it*. Having Levi watch us, his eyes filled with hunger, made me come harder than I ever thought I could.

"I didn't leave because I was angry," I say once all the sordid details have come out. "I left because… I liked it. That's sick, right?"

Zee downs a glass of water, throwing themselves back in

their chair, and staring at the table. "Of all the things you were going to tell me, this was not what I was expecting."

My head drops. "You think I'm disgusting, right?"

Zee's hand is on my arm, and when I look up at them they shake their head emphatically. "No. Never. Oh my god, I'm just… surprised. That's all. But I am not disgusted."

"Levi's my brother, it's just sick."

"Stop saying it's sick." Zee squeezes my arm. "It's not sick. He's your step-brother, and not even one you grew up with."

"Dylan was so upset." I press the heel of my hand to my eye, remembering Dylan's pleas for me to stay and talk to him. "I hurt him."

"Girl, you needed a minute." They cross their arms over their chest, mouth twitching as they watch my face. "So, what you're telling me is they want each other, and you want both of them, and they both want you."

"I suppose so."

"Like, a poly kind of situation?"

I frown at them, considering that term. *Polyamorous.* "I guess?"

"Well, that's not really a big deal."

"How is that not a big deal? People won't understand."

Zee laughs, running a hand over their hair. "Girl, listen to me. I'm the asexual non-binary hairdresser in this conservative little white town, you think I have time to worry about what folks understand or not?"

My cheeks flush, and I nod. "Sorry, I probably sound like a spoiled brat."

"No, you're just confused, and dealing with all the monogamy propaganda we get fed." They lean closer to me, smiling softly. "You're not sick. And the fact Dylan told you openly, even though he knew he might lose you, I mean, maybe this is a good chance for the three of you to talk it out. Really lay out on the table what you all want."

I narrow my eyes at them. "You're taking this way better than I expected you to."

"To be honest, I'm irritated I never picked up on Levi Fenton liking dick."

I grunt out a laugh. "Oh my god."

"I'm serious, girl." They lift their hand and call over the waiter. "My bi-dar is never wrong, and of course Levi fucking Fenton threw it off." Zee gives their order of an iced tea and some sort of fancy salad to the waiter, and I order a martini to try and give myself the courage to go home and face the two men I love.

"What's a threesome like?"

Zee grunts as they pour themselves a glass of water. "One second you're scared of being poly and now you're asking about threesomes?" They lift their eyes to me with a grin. "Bold of you to assume I'd know."

"I don't mean that you'd *know*, but like… have you ever talked to someone who's had one?"

"Yeah. Dylan" They laugh out loud as my face scrunches up, my whole body feeling like it's going to cringe itself into next week. "Girl, listen to me. Whatever it is you think you want, whatever it is you want this situation to be, I think the guys will be more open to it than you think."

I look at them with a heavy sigh, staying silent as the waiter brings us our order. When he leaves, I take a swig of my cocktail.

"I hope you're not going to drive after all this," Zee says as they start on their food. "I'll drive your car home, and you get an Uber."

"What do I tell my family?"

Zee stops chewing, and raises their eyes to me, glaring at me through their eyelashes. "I want you to repeat this mantra to yourself - 'My family sucks. Their opinions mean nothing to me'."

"But-"

"Girl, those people abandoned you to Gloria fucking Fenton. I called your aunt when Gloria landed you in the hospital, remember what she said?"

I swallow hard, and shake my head, even though I do. I can't bring myself to say it.

"Your fucking aunt asked me what you'd done *this time*." Zee throws their fork on the table, and shakes their head, making their locs dance around their shoulders. "You do not need those people, Stella. And if being with Levi and Dylan makes you happy, that's good enough for me. And it will be good enough for anyone who actually gives a fuck about you."

Unexpected tears sting my eyes, and I reach across to take Zee's hand. "Thank you."

"I love you, girl." They pull me close and put a lithe arm around my shoulders. "I don't care whose dick you get where, I just want you to be happy."

I can't help but laugh, and cover my face with my hands again. "Oh my god."

"Now, how about we finish our drinks, you get yourself home, and put these poor fellas out of their misery?"

The house is lit up like a Christmas tree when the Uber pulls into the drive, as though Dylan and Levi were hoping to send up a beacon to light my way home. I tip the driver, and climb out of the car on feet that are still steady despite the two martinis.

I take a deep breath, and walk up the path to the front door as the car pulls away. Before I reach it, Levi tears the front door open, his face crumpling with relief.

"Thank god." He rushes towards me, taking me in his arms. "Jesus Christ, we were so worried."

I look over his shoulder to see Dylan at the door. He shakes his head, leaning against the door frame.

"I'm OK, I just needed a minute."

"Come inside, my god. I thought I was going to lose my damn mind." Levi drapes his arms around my shoulders and guides me into the house, past Dylan's guilt-twisted face, and into the kitchen. He urges me to sit down at the table, fussing over me and bringing me water. But I get to my feet and head out onto the porch, needing fresh air, and something else.

"Do either of you have a cigarette?" I ask, and Dylan rushes forward, pulling an almost empty packet from the pocket of his jeans. I take the next to last cigarette and let him light it for me with a silver lighter, and he hurriedly lights the last one for himself.

"Sit down," I say to them both, gesturing to the seats at the table, and taking a drag of the cigarette that makes my head spin unpleasantly. "I think we need to talk."

They both sit down, backs unnaturally straight as though waiting for me to strike, or scream, or tell them how disgusting they are. I guess I looked exactly like this only an hour or so ago when I sat opposite Zee and confessed all my secret desires to them, braced for judgment and misunderstanding.

"How many times?" I ask, casting my eyes to the table.

"Twice." Dylan says it quickly, a clear confession. "Just twice."

"Just nothing, Dylan." I look over at him, and flick my cigarette into the ashtray. "Don't diminish what happened, that's not fair."

His head drops, and he nods. "You're right. Twice. It happened twice, and I'm sorry."

I look at Levi, taking a long drag of my cigarette. "And did you tell him about us?"

Dylan's head shoots up, and he looks from me to Levi with an expression of pure shock. "Tell me what?"

Levi can't look at him, sighing heavily and reaching for the beer he'd placed on the table. "No, I hadn't told him."

"Looks like we all had secrets, huh?" I stub the half-spent cigarette out in the ashtray, hating the way it tastes and how it's making my head spin, and fix Dylan with a stare. "I kissed him. The day after your grandfather died. And he told me he'd been in love with me for years, but couldn't ever tell me before because he didn't want to hurt you."

Dylan looks over at Levi. whose eyes are still fixed on the table. "Is that true?"

Levi nods slowly, and sighs. "I'm sorry."

"No one is apologizing for anything here tonight."

They both look at me, frowning.

"I mean it. If we sit here pouring out nothing but apologies and regret, we won't get anywhere. Do either of you regret what happened between you?"

"Yes," Dylan replies instantly, and Levi's body language shifts, sitting up straighter.

I shake my head. "No, you regret it because of me. Because you don't want to hurt me. Take me out of it. Do you still regret it?"

Dylan rakes his hands over his head. "It doesn't work like that. I can't take you out of it because you're *in it*."

"OK then, tell me this - did you enjoy it?"

They both stare at me. They were not expecting this, that much is clear. I glance from one to the other and raise my hands when they continue to just gape at me.

"Well?"

"I mean… yeah." Levi finally admits. "I struggled with it, because I was convinced I wasn't gay."

"And you're not," I remind him, and he nods.

"No, I guess I'm not."

Dylan puts his cigarette out and throws up his hands. "What are we doing here? Do you two want to be together? Do you want me to go? I don't understand."

"There isn't any way I would ever want you to go." I drape my arms over my crossed legs and lock eyes with him. "I love you, and I was afraid to lose you because of all this."

"Me too," Levi admits, frowning at the ground. "It... It fucking killed me. Thinking of losing you."

"So what *are* we doing here?" Dylan looks from me to Levi and back again.

"What if we could all be together?" I ask, shrugging. Dylan still looks bewildered, but Levi nods slowly.

"Yeah, what if?" He looks over his shoulder at Dylan. "Maybe we don't have to choose."

Dylan shakes his head, rubbing a hand across his forehead. "I'm still struggling to... You two?" He gestures back and forth between us. "When did you realize this was a thing?"

"Her seventeenth birthday." Levi smiles sadly at me. "Well, before that really. When our parents got married. At least for me. But I didn't think it'd ever.... I don't know."

Dylan fixes me with sad eyes. "So, I'm not enough for you?"

I shake my head. "No, just like it's not that I'm not enough for you." I gesture to Levi. "Was sex with Levi better than sex with me?"

"No," he says quickly. "No, it was..."

"You said it yourself, pretty boy." Levi smiles over at Dylan. "Not better, it just depends on the person, remember?"

Dylan gets to his feet, biting his lip and shaking his head. "I'm gonna need a minute." He looks at me, opening his mouth to speak, then shakes his head again and walks into the house. Levi and I sit in silence as Dylan's footsteps fade into the distance, and then it's just us alone outside on the porch.

"He'll be OK," Levi says to me with a smile. "I don't think this is what any of us was expecting."

"No, I guess not." My head is still spinning from the cigarette and probably the martinis, and I sigh as I look at him. "You watched us on the stairs."

"Yes, I did." He scoffs with a crooked smile. "Never thought I'd be the one who'd be down for this first."

"For *this*?" I want to hear him say it. I want to hear him say he's choosing us both, to live in this relationship together, to tell me that I'm not sick for wanting it.

He nods, sprawling back in his chair, stretching his long legs out in front of him. "The three of us. I don't know what folks call that now, kinda been a little isolated for the last few years."

"Polyamory. That's what they call it."

"Right, right." His mouth twitches into a grin. "Yes, I watched you on the stairs, as you very well know."

"And you weren't jealous?"

He shakes his head slowly. "Not even a bit. I liked it. Seeing you two together, watching him finish inside you. I saw that, and…" He hisses in a breath, and my clit throbs at his words. "I wasn't jealous. I wanted it too."

"Both of us."

He nods, and thanks to his spread legs, I can see the growing bulge in his groin. It feels sick and twisted to have come here to try and talk this whole situation out, to be an adult and work this out so no one gets hurt. Instead, I'm staring at that swelling, feeling myself getting wetter, and wanting Levi to fuck me.

"I love both of you," I admit, meeting his eyes. "I love both of you the same, and totally differently, but I feel like without you, I'm not me. And I won't be happy without you both."

"I feel the same way." He smirks, shaking his head and raking his fingertips along his thighs. "I've never felt the way I do about Dylan, and I never thought I'd like it with a guy. I… I guess I had a lot of things to find out about myself."

"I guess so."

He licks his lips as he gazes back at me. "If you keep looking at me like that, I'm going to have to take you upstairs and fuck you."

My heart takes a leap at his words, my nipples bunching and my throat going dry. "I'm just looking at you."

"You never just look at me, baby girl." He gets to his feet, crossing the porch to stand in front of me, gazing down at me. "You look right through me. Like you know exactly what's in here." He puts a hand to his chest. "And it doesn't scare you off."

"I do know, and it would never scare me." I get out of the chair, standing in front of him, our bodies only an inch apart. "I've never been scared of you, not once. Ever."

"I'm a monster, baby girl." He smiles as I shake my head. "But I'll never hurt you. Not you. Ever. And I'll kill anyone who does." He moves to kiss me, huffing out a laugh as I pull back. I put my hand over his, and he exhales heavily.

"I want things from you, but I don't know if now is the time. Not while Dylan is… adjusting."

"No, you're right." His head dips so our foreheads are touching. His breathing becomes more rapid, and his other hand winds around my waist. "Even though it's going to make me crazy."

"Me too."

"I've dreamed of you, for years. What you look like naked, what you taste like, what you feel like…" He trails off, tilting his head to brush his lips along my cheek.

I look into his eyes, and the urge to touch him, to kiss him and taste all of him, it's overwhelming. "Did you - do you want to come and watch?"

He sucks in a breath. "Watch what?"

"Me, in the shower. It's so hot, I need to cool off." God I'm fucking twisted. Like having Levi watch me is so much better than him fucking me. I try to tell myself that Dylan will be up for it, and that this is fine. He just needs his moment. He just needs some time.

And if he and Levi have taken that time for themselves twice over, maybe me being selfish and claiming him for myself, when he won't even be touching me, isn't that bad.

Maybe I'm just a fucking bitch in heat and I need an ice bath.

But Levi follows me to my room, past Dylan's closed door, his fingers entwined with mine. He closes the door softly behind us as I flip on the lamp. I turn to face him, and he takes off his shirt.

"This is all," he says, dropping the shirt to the floor. "And I won't touch you."

"OK."

"But I want to see."

My breath hitches in my throat. "See?"

"I want you to bend over the bed, and show me your pussy. I want to see it."

I don't move, just stare at him.

"If you want to stop, Stella, you tell me to stop. I'll get the fuck out of here." His eyes skate up and down my body. "But if you don't want to stop, then bend over, spread your legs, and show me just how wet you are for me."

I bite back a moan at his words, and strip out of my shorts and tank top. His eyes stay on my face, and he doesn't move an inch towards me, just watches me. When I'm naked, I turn my back, leaning slowly over the bed.

"Wider," he says in a tone of voice that is the furthest thing from brotherly.

I shuffle my feet along the wood floor, opening wider for him and lifting myself on to my tip toes. It's filthy and carnal, being open like this to him, all of me bared to him. He takes two measured steps closer, and sinks to his knees.

"Fuck, baby girl," he breathes, sounding almost reverent. "This is the prettiest pussy I've ever seen in my life."

The praise has my stomach tied up in a knot, and I moan softly into the bed.

"You like being fucked like this?" His voice is rough, and I swear I can feel his hot breath cross the distance between us. "Bent over the bed?"

I nod against my shoulder. "Yeah."

"Fuck." His voice is full of barely contained restraint, and it makes me tremble. I want to tell him to forget about it all, to

plunge himself into me, to give in to all the longing we've been fighting all these years.

Instead, I push myself up on my hands, sucking in a breath before going to the night stand and opening the drawer. I retrieve my wand vibrator, and turn to face Levi, whose face is dark and desirous in the half light. Wordlessly, I walk into the bathroom, and flip on the light.

I turn on the water, waiting for it to get hot, and Levi follows me, still silent, just watching me. He leans against the counter as I step into the water. I turn on the wand, and hold it to my nipple as Levi gazes at me. His muscles seem to bulge, the tension in his body more than obvious.

"You like to watch?" I ask.

He nods, watching the trail of the wand from my nipple down my stomach. "Your face, when you come, it's fucking beautiful."

"I had a fantasy, the other day." I cough out a gasp as I press the wand between my folds, nudging it against my clit. "I imagined you, in my mouth, while Dylan ate my pussy."

Levi's jaw feathers violently, his knuckles turning white as he grips the edge of the sink.

"Have you ever had a threesome?"

Levi shakes his head.

"Good. I'd like to be your first." I moan, pressing the wand against my clit. "I want both of you. Everywhere."

"In your throat?"

I nod. "Yes."

"You want me to toy with your pussy while you suck Dylans's cock?"

"Oh god, yes." My hand claws against the tiles as my climax begins to rise, growing and tumbling inside me, bringing with it all the knowledge that this is wrong, and that no one will understand. But it all goes away as Levi makes a sound like a growl.

"You want me in your ass, while Dylan fucks your pussy?"

I gasp, because I've never liked anal. It always felt like something that was done to me, not something that was done for me, for me to feel good. But with them… it's different. I want them everywhere, I want to give them every part of myself.

"Yes." It's not a word, but a high-pitched, needy whimper. "I want you, all of you. Everywhere."

"Good girl." He steps closer to the shower, his fists balled at his sides. "I want to watch you come, but next time, know that you'll come with me inside you. It'll be my name you're screaming, mine and his." He puts a hand against the shower screen. "You're ours, baby girl. That sweet pussy belongs to us."

I clench my eyes shut, my stomach tense with desire.

"Eyes on me," he commands.

When I force my eyes open, my mouth sucking in air in small, gasping breaths, he has one hand on the shower screen, the other wrapped around his swollen cock. He's gripping himself, moving in short, hard strokes, his teeth gritted.

"You're going to come for me, baby girl."

"Fuck, *Levi*." I thrust my hips, rubbing my clit against the vibrating tip of the wand, gripping the handle hard and imagining it's Levi's cock in my hand, as though I'm guiding him towards me, inside me, to fuck me and claim me as his.

"I love hearing you say my name," he breathes. "Say it again."

I meet his eyes, and just as my pussy begins to contract, as the pressure of the wand somehow becomes too much and not enough at the same time, I gasp his name. "*Levi.*"

He grunts, his abs contracting violently as his shoulders heave, and he watches me come undone on the other side of the pane of glass. He braces both hands against the glass, his teeth still gritted, and I expect him to come charging in, to lift me up against the wall and have his way with me.

Instead, he watches me come down off my high, and tucks his thick cock away in his jeans. Once I've stopped trembling, he opens the glass door and turns off the water. He wraps me in a towel, drying me off gently, not uttering a word, his eyes full of reverence again. It feels like an act of worship, or gratitude.

When I'm dry, he guides me to my bed, pulling back the covers for me to slide in.

"Are you going to sleep with me?"

He shakes his head and smiles. "Not tonight, baby girl. We've got to work this all out first. I need us all to be together. Otherwise it won't feel right."

I swallow down my disappointment, knowing he's right. "Well, umm... I hope you sleep well."

"I'll be dreaming of that pussy all night. I don't think there'll be much sleeping tonight." His eyes wander over my face, and he reaches out a hand to brush his fingers down my cheek. "You're beautiful."

"Thank you." I grab on to his hand, guiding his fingers to my lips to place a gentle kiss against them. "I'll see you in the morning."

"Yes, you will." He plants a brief kiss on my forehead before leaving the room.

I stare at the ceiling for a long time, trying to make sense of everything that happened today. My heart is a complicated mess, and my head can't keep up at all. But I tell myself that everything that needs to happen, will happen.

As long as I have the two of them, it doesn't matter.

Nothing else matters.

Just us.

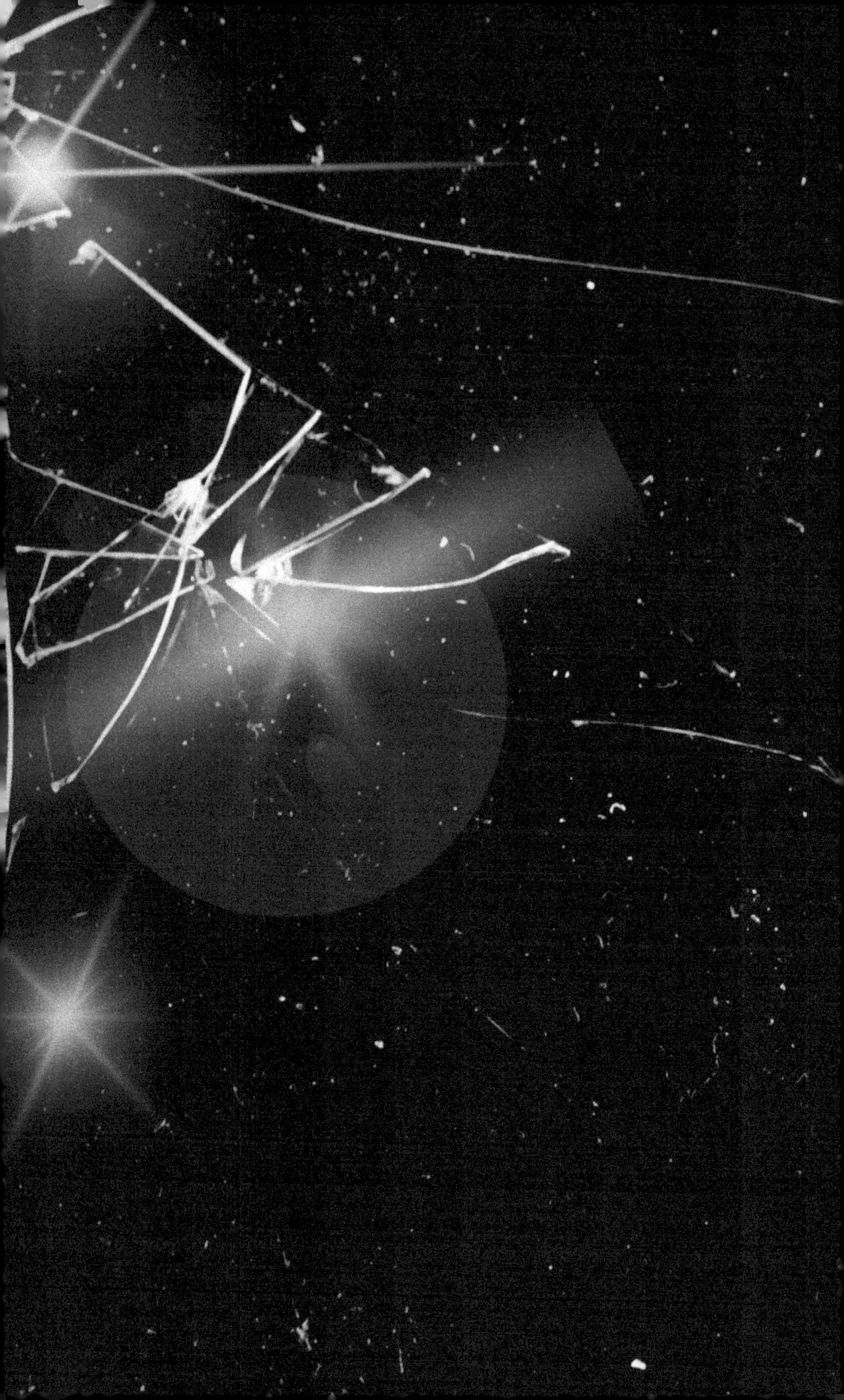

CHAPTER FOURTEEN

MY COCK IS ALMOST PROTESTING by the time dawn begins to filter through the curtains. No amount of lube can soothe the fucking chafe that has formed along my sensitive skin. With a huffed breath, I throw myself back on the bed, feeling sticky and disgusting, needing a shower but unable to bring myself to wash off the feeling of the past night.

Stella, my Stella, *my* perfect girl - fuck, watching her come, watching her split open and unbutton me at the same time, tearing out my heart and mind and my fucking *soul*. It was just sex - well, it wasn't even that. It was just me *watching* her, and it was a fucking religious experience. I can't even imagine what it will feel like when I'm inside her, when I feel that pussy coming on my cock, when I feel that hot, panting mouth wrapped around me.

These thoughts don't do anything to calm my raging erection, and I decide that I really do need that shower.

But before I can move off the bed, the door opens, and Dylan walks in. He's dressed in shorts and a black shirt, drenched in sweat, his chest pounding.

"What happened to you?" I ask, sitting up and pulling a sheet over my obscenely red and swollen cock.

He gestures to the door and nods. "I ran. For a long time. I needed to, uh." He sucks in a breath. "Run."

"Yeah, that was probably a good idea."

He takes in my appearance, and frowns. "So you and Stella, you…"

I shake my head as he trails off. "No. We didn't have sex."

He lifts an eyebrow, shifting on his feet. "No? Why?"

"Because we don't want to hurt you."

Both his eyebrows shoot up, and he scoffs out a laugh. "You're joking, right?"

"No."

"I guess I don't have a right to be mad even if you did." He rubs a hand across his sweaty brow. "I'm a fucking hypocrite, huh?"

"You're just surprised."

"I just always…" He clears his throat, holding out his hands in front of him. "You two, you know, you're… You've always been like brother and sister in my eyes. So this, I mean, this… Yeah, I'm fucking surprised."

"I've never thought of her that way," I admit, and the realization seems to blindside both of us a little. "Our parents wanted it like that, for the cameras, for the press. The perfect blended family. But it wasn't ever that way in my head."

Dylan puts his hands on his hips as he looks at the floor, shifting on his feet again, like he's unsure whether he should go back to running away from his problems, or stay here and face them head on. "So, how do you want this to work?"

"I think we should all talk about this together."

He raises a hand, his eyes meeting mine with fierce determination. "I want to hear it from you first. I want to know how you see this working."

I shrug. "We'll be together, the three of us."

"So you fuck her and I fuck her, and…"

I chuckle, leaning back against the headboard. "I'd kind of like to fuck you, too."

His eyebrows knit together, and suddenly I see all the hesitation and worry, the pain and insecurity that's plagued him and sent him running and running til his body was worn out.

"Dylan, I want you." I rise from the bed, and he watches me with a look of pain in his eyes. "I do. I've never felt this way about anyone before. I didn't think I could. But you make me fucking nervous. I look at you and you're so fucking beautiful, it makes me want to cry and laugh at the same damn time that you'd even look at me."

"How… How long have you felt this way?"

I shrug, trying to pinpoint the moment. "I can't even tell you, it just… It just happened."

"While we were in prison?"

I hesitate for a second, before I nod, and he clenches his eyes shut. "God fucking dammit, Fenton."

I take a step towards him, but he holds up a hand.

"You should have told me." He leans against the door, shaking his head. "I want both of you. I need you, both of you. I can't be without you."

I walk up to him to take his face in my hands, his beautiful brown skin covered in sweat. I draw his face down to mine, so his head rests against mine. "I want you to let me love you, Dylan. In the ways you need me to. I know you need love, so fucking badly. And I can't believe I'm fucking lucky enough to be the man you want to love like that."

His mouth quirks into a painful, cynical smile. "Who knew Levi Fenton was a poet?"

"Who knew Levi Fenton had a heart?" I stroke his jaw with my fingertips. "Who knew it would belong to the both of you?"

Dylan wraps his arms around me, tugging me close and I don't care that he's drenched in sweat. I bury my face in the crook of his neck, peppering kisses over his heated skin and promise myself that I'll love him til all the pain and hurt he's suffered is nothing but a blip, a speck in the distance that he never has to worry about ever again.

"And Stella wants this too?" Dylan asks after a while.

"She does. She feels sick about it, but she does."

"There's nothing sick about this." Dylan tips my head back, his eyes wandering over my face as he sighs. "I was worried too. Last night, this morning, I was all tangled up wondering if it was wrong. Wondering if I was sick. If we all were. But we're not."

"No." I smile at him. "She even asked about threesomes."

"Jesus." Dylan hisses and releases me. He braces his hands against his hips, his body tilting forward as he laughs breathlessly. "Fuck me. Our girl sure is full of surprises."

"That she is."

"She still asleep?" He strips out of his soaked shirt, and the way his abs glisten with sweat in the sunlight does nothing to abate my poor, punished cock.

"I guess so. I was just going for a shower."

He chews the inside of his cheek, tilting his head in a way that makes me want to kiss him hard. "Want company?"

I have to stifle a groan, and between him and Stella I don't know how much more edging I can take. Yes, I want company. I want company that pins me against the wall and lathers me up and fucks me til I can't fucking breathe anymore. I resisted last night, even though watching Stella fuck herself in the shower was torture and all I could think of was how that sweet pussy would taste dripping her release on my tongue. And now Dylan's standing in front of me like some sort of God with his brown skin and those huge dark eyes, and my restraint is about as worn out and chafed as my poor assaulted dick.

"Sure." *You fucking idiot that's the wrong answer.* It feels so normal to follow him to the bathroom, like a regular thing we do. And fuck it if that doesn't make me feel as giddy as a teenage boy with a crush. I want this to feel normal. I want to shower with my… my boyfriend.

I'm sure I'm grinning like a total asshole, and that word shouldn't make me as happy as it does. I shouldn't get too far ahead of myself, because we still need to talk to Stella. We still need to work this out. We still need to make sure this all *works* for us.

But then Dylan drops his shorts to the ground, and his perfect, chiseled ass reminds me that only a few short weeks ago I was buried balls deep in that ass and… My dick practically weeps.

He reaches for my hand without looking, and I find his fingers eagerly, letting him pull me in under the water with him. I'm not used to this. I'm the one in control. Levi Fenton, alpha Dom asshole. But fuck, the feeling I get as Dylan takes my hand and wraps my arm around his waist so his back is pressed to my chest. I turn my head to lay my cheek against the back of his neck, and he makes a sound like a sigh, like he's relieved. Relieved to have me close.

It's the first time I've been naked with another person and have it not be about sex. It's just about *being*. Sure, I'm hard as a fucking steel rod, and I'm leaking precum all over Dylan's ass. But there's no urgency, no need to fuck and get it over with. No desire to just get down to it and walk away like it's meaningless.

I stroke Dylan's stomach, relishing the feeling of his hard muscles under my fingertips. He turns his head, as though to look over his shoulder at me, but his eyes are closed. He looks at peace, and warmth blooms in my stomach at the sight.

"What're you thinking, pretty boy?" I ask softly.

He shakes his head, his eyes still closed. "I'm not thinking. I'm just here, with you."

I take the soap and lather it up between my hands, then set about washing down his back, kneading his tight muscles with my hands, and the groan he lets out has me gritting my teeth to stop myself coming all over his back right here and now.

"That feel good?"

He nods, putting his hands against the wall. "What did you and Stella do last night?"

"I told you, we didn't have sex."

"I know. But you did something." He looks over his shoulder at me with a cocked eyebrow. "You don't wanna tell me?"

I'm about to say that I don't want to make him jealous, that I don't want to rub it in his face that I was ogling Stella's perfect, smooth pussy while he was probably in agony just a few feet away. Then I have to remember that there isn't any jealousy here. Seeing Stella and Dylan fuck on the stairs was hot. I didn't feel a single pang of envy, not once.

Maybe it's the same for Dylan.

"I didn't touch her, but she got herself off for me." I continue rubbing soap over Dylan's back, lowering my hands to his ass and curving around his hips. "First she bent over her bed and showed me her pussy."

"Fucking beautiful, isn't it?" Dylan laughs softly, a sound which turns into a growl as my hands feather closer to his dick.

"Perfect." I breathe against his ear, grazing his earlobe with my teeth. "Bet it feels like heaven."

"It does." His head falls back against my shoulder. "She's so tight and hot, and fuck, her taste."

"Not touching her was torture." I rake my clawed fingers along his hips and he bucks against me. "Her face when she comes, she's like a goddess." I run my soapy hand up his stomach, over his chest to land around his throat. When I brace my fingers around his strong neck, he moans. "Would you like to watch me lick her pussy, make her come for us?"

"Oh *fuck*." His words are hitched, and he laughs. "Why does the idea of you being with her turn me on so much?"

"It's meant to be." I nip at his shoulder, sucking on the skin at the base of his throat, knowing I'm probably leaving a mark but not caring because he melts against me with another delicious moan.

"Tell me it's real." His tone shifts suddenly back to that insecure plea. "Tell me this is real."

"It's real, pretty boy. We're the only thing that ever was."

He turns around, and I almost slip over on the tiles as he

pushes me against the wall. His mouth descends on mine, hungry and furious and full of all the need that he could never give a voice. His hands spear into my hair, and he grinds his hard dick against me, and there's a very strange and unfamiliar flutter in my belly as I think of him being inside me.

Another thing I've never done. The thought is electric and daunting at the same time - Dylan's huge in every possible way.

But I can't give those thoughts too much time. Not now. Not when I tore myself away from Stella promising myself we'd work this all out first. I allow myself a few more moments of Dylan consuming me. Finally I push against his chest, trying to catch my breath and laugh at the same time, and he slumps, puffing out heavy breaths, running a hand over his mouth.

"Sorry."

"Don't apologize, I liked it." I move my hands up his chest to lay around the back of his neck. "But I think we need to call it for now, and go get our girl some breakfast."

"You're right." He gives me a crooked smile.

I think he's going to say something else, and I'm pretty sure I'm going to fucking drown in his dark eyes if he keeps staring at me like this, but then he shuts off the water, sliding back the screen to retrieve a towel for each of us.

By the time we're dry and dressed, Stella's voice is audible through the walls. She's talking loud, in a tight staccato that tells me something isn't right. Dylan frowns at me, and we head out into the hall just as Stella emerges from her room. She's dressed in a black slip dress, her hair loose around her shoulders, her cheeks flushed bright crimson as she rubs her forehead with her index finger and thumb.

"Mallory, I am not going public with this." She sighs heavily. "With *this*. What happened back then. I'm not doing it." She waves a hand angrily through the air as though whoever this Mallory is were right in front of her. "No, enough. I cannot go through that again. I won't. Please don't call this number again."

She swipes her finger over her phone screen, and looks up at us both, eyes wide and shoulders heaving.

"Who was that?" Dylan asks, moving towards her slowly as though she's a deer he'll startle back into the woods.

"A re- reporter." Stella's breath hitches in her throat, and her hands start to tremble violently. "She- she keeps fucking calling me, ab-about…" She cuts off suddenly, her hands shaking so hard she drops her phone, and her pupils blown as she looks at us. "D-Dylan, I-" She gasps, her chest sucking in hard.

I've seen this too many times, when I held Dylan as he tried to stay quiet, so the other inmates wouldn't hear him and think he was weak, an easy target for being a kid scared out of his fucking mind in prison.

Stella's having a panic attack.

Dylan reaches her before me, closing the distance between them and taking her in his arms.

"I'm here, *guera*. You can feel my skin, it's real, and I'm here."

She makes a sound like a sob, strained and catching amongst the breaths that can't escape her throat. Her knuckles are white as she clutches onto Dylan's arms.

"I've got you, *guera*," Dylan murmurs soothingly. "The floor under your feet, can you feel it?"

Stella nods frantically.

"Feel how cool it is," he croons, threading his fingers into the hair at the nape of her neck, rubbing gently. "Feel my hand? That's real, Stella. This is real. You're safe, we're here. Breathe for us, *guera*."

"She… She told me…" Stella's voice is high-pitched, still filled with panic. "She told me, Stanley Iverson, he's… He's sponsoring Gloria's campaign."

Dylan gives me a sideways frown. "Iverson?"

I shake my head, trying to remember the name. Trying to place it amongst all the bloated elites my mother mingled with, the pasty white faces of all those disgusting men who leched over Stella whenever our parents threw a party.

"Baby girl, who's Stanley Iverson?"

Tears run down her cheeks, and her eyes are wide with terror as she looks at me. "Remember m-my s-sixteenth birthday." It's all she says before she covers her face with her hands, and burrows into Dylan's chest.

Dylan's arms crush her against him as she starts to wail, and ice and fire run down my spine at the same time.

Her sixteenth birthday.

As if I could ever forget. When Dylan had bought her all the flowers. When she'd worn that cute white and red polka dot dress, and danced with me under the full moon.

When her father had let her have her first glass of red wine.

And she'd started to sway on her feet. And he'd scooped her up, and told her what a special day it was.

The day after her sixteenth birthday, I found her crying in the bathroom, covered in bite marks and scratches, and unable to sit down.

It would be over a year before I'd understand what had happened. Before she'd finally tell me what caused the screaming nightmares that had me rushing into her room to hold her until she fell asleep again.

I stalk into my bedroom and type out a quick text, before pulling on a t-shirt and jeans, shoving my feet into my sneakers and heading back out to where Dylan is still holding Stella. She's gone eerily silent, just trembling in Dylan's arms every few seconds, as shocks of grief travel through her nerves.

"Stay with her," I tell him. "I need to go see somebody."

Dylan doesn't even need to ask me for what.

He knows.

We've always known this was coming.

I throw my car into reverse and tear down the drive, tires screeching as I speed along Stella's street in the direction of the garage. I catch sight of my eyes in the rear view mirror.

They're going to wish you stayed locked up.

Eric sidles into the office, dressed in a loose purple t-shirt and yellow shorts, the picture of a family father who's just been torn away from breakfast. He lifts his head in greeting when he spots me behind the desk, his hands tucked into his pockets.

"Hey boss."

"Hey." I gesture to the chair opposite. "Sorry to call you in so early on a Saturday morning."

He shrugs as he sits down. "No problem."

"I promise this won't take long." I point to the bottle of water and two glasses on my desk, and he shakes his head. "But I do need to discuss something pretty important with you."

"Sure." He watches me expectantly.

"Mario tells me you've worked for him for a long time."

"Yes sir, 15 years, since I left the service."

I nod, pouring myself a glass of water. "He mentioned you were a veteran. Purple Heart and everything?"

Eric's chest puffs a little. "That's right."

"He assures me you're a good man." I roll the glass back and forth in my hand. "I hope my past doesn't make you uncomfortable."

"Not at all. I know you did what you had to do to protect your buddy. I understand that."

"I'm sure you do, probably better than most." I take a sip of the water, wishing it was something stronger. "You know I'm on parole, right?"

He gives a curt nod. "Of course."

"And I'm sure you know that comes with limitations."

His brow furrows for just a split second before he gives that military nod again. "Sure."

I rub my chin, hoping I've judged Eric accurately and I'm not about to make a big mistake. "Among other things, I'm not allowed to own a firearm."

Eric doesn't nod, just regards me with a deepening frown. "I don't understand what that has to do with me."

I lean on the desk, taking a deep breath before I look him square in the eye. "I need you to get me a gun."

Eric's eyebrows shoot up as he grunts out a laugh. "Excuse me?"

"I need a gun. Something small, easily concealed."

Eric shakes his head, pursing his lips to exhale heavily, rubbing his hands along his thighs. "Sorry, I mean, I'm all for helping a fella out, but, I'm sure you understand that if I get you a gun, I'm committing a felony."

"I know that." I take another sip of the water. "I have something I need to tell you, and I'm going to hope I can trust you with this information."

He sighs heavily, but when my eyes flash to his face he sees something that makes his shoulders go straight, and that quick nod is back. "Of course."

"You said you understood why I did what I did, when I killed my stepfather." I put the glass down, leaning on my elbows and rubbing my hands together. "But the actual story of what happened was never released."

Eric narrows his eyes, shaking his head as he blinks at me. "The actual story? You mean, like a cover-up?"

"Something like that." I rub a hand across my forehead. "I need you to understand this isn't my story to tell, and I can't betray this person's trust. But I understand you're a father?"

"Yes, sir. Two girls. Eldest just started college." The pride in his face at this little statement puts any doubt I had to rest.

"That's amazing, good for her." I give him a smile. "I can imagine that if anyone hurt your girls, you wouldn't hesitate to get revenge, right?"

"Not for a second." His demeanor shifts from proud to lethal in a split second. He may be a jovial family man and wise-cracking mechanic, but underneath he still has the instincts of a soldier.

"I didn't kill my stepfather that night, but I helped. Dylan and I took a plea bargain in exchange for a reduced sentence, because the truth… Well, no one wanted that getting out."

"And what is the truth?"

I look at this man before me, knowing exactly what I'm drawing him into.

No, it's the gun and that's all. He'll get me the gun and then he'll have nothing to do with this.

"My stepfather was helping powerful men in all levels of this country's administration abuse his daughter."

Eric's jaw drops, his eyes almost bulging from his head. "He did what?"

"She broke down one night and told Dylan everything, and then he came to me. We decided that we had to put a stop to it. So we cornered him in his office, and Dylan put a bullet in his skull."

"His *own daughter*?" Eric's shakes his head, his fingers braced against his temples. "He was helping men *rape* his own child? For what purpose?"

Anger claws at the edges of my vision, blank white and simmering with heat. "It would appear he was trying to further his political career, and learned early on what powerful men would give him in exchange for… her."

Eric gets to his feet, leaning heavily on his thighs. "Jesus Christ." He straightens quickly, meeting my eyes. "So this is why you need the gun?"

I nod slowly, pulling open the drawer beside me and taking out my last pack of cigarettes. "A name has come up, and…" I light the cigarette as Eric waits, back tense and brows drawn down. I shrug as I exhale a swirl of white smoke. "You don't need to know any more than that."

"What's the name?" Eric's hands have balled into fists at his sides, and I can see the protector instinct threatening to burst out of him.

"Eric, I'm not drawing you into this any further." I motion for him to sit back down, which he does after a moment's hesitation. "I need a gun, and that's all. Your name never comes up."

"And if the gun gets traced back to me?"

I take a long drag of the cigarette. "I stole it. You'd come into work and showed your new gun to the fellas, so I knew you had it. I obviously know where you live. You smash your basement window, say you didn't even notice it until I was charged."

Eric scoffs, crossing his arms over his chest. "You've got this all figured out."

"I'm not intending on getting caught, but if anything happens to me, there's a sealed letter with my lawyer that has you taking over this place. Your name will be on the deed, the whole works." I wave the cigarette in a circle. "All of this is yours."

Eric's eyes bug out in earnest. "What?"

"And your girl, which college is she going to?" I tap the cigarette on the edge of the ash tray. "I'd like to see that she's not saddled with debts just for getting an education."

Eric runs his hands over his head, his mouth hanging open. "I - I don't know what to say."

"Don't say anything. Just say whether or not you'll get me the gun."

He considers for a moment, weighing up everything I've just dumped on him, his eyes searching the table as though a clean, easy answer will be found in the scratched formica surface. He finally meets my gaze, nodding slowly.

"I'll do it. I'll have it for you by Tuesday."

"Fantastic." I hold out my hand, which he takes with conviction. "I appreciate it. And so we're clear, I'm not buying your silence. I'm rewarding loyalty."

He gives me that curt nod again. "Yes, sir. And you have it."

"Thank you. I'll let you get back to your family." I stamp out the cigarette in the ash tray as he retreats.

Eric stops suddenly in the doorway, and turns back to me.

"Sir, your step-sister." He hesitates, frowning. "I mean… is she alright?"

I swallow hard. Because no, she's not alright. She's at home crying her eyes out and unable to breathe at just the mention of a name. She's so far from alright I'm not sure killing all these ghosts will be enough to soothe her nightmares.

But I don't say any of that. I simply give Eric a smile, and a nod.

"She has us back. She'll be alright."

CHAPTER FIFTEEN

"I'VE ASKED myself so many times what I did to deserve what happened." Stella pulls a leg up onto the chair, resting her chin on her knee as she watches me make orange juice. "I'd sit there and think, why did I deserve a father like that? Why couldn't I have a dad like yours?"

"That's not how life works." I discard one spent orange half into the trash can at my feet and push the next one into the press. "Your father was a fucking monster with the perfect public image." I raise my eyes to her. "You have to know that, *guera*. None of this was your fault. None of it."

"I guess." She rolls her head back and forth, her eyes fixed on my task. She's still pale, but thank fuck she's finally stopped shaking. It felt like forever until she was warm again, until her body stopped quaking as the bad memories clawed their way to the forefront of her mind.

"So, this reporter, where does she come into it?" I pour the juice into a tall frosted glass, and carry it over to where Stella sits at the table. Stella takes the glass from me with a sigh, and shrugs as I sit down beside her.

"She sniffed me out at Zee's salon a couple weeks ago. Told me that Gloria's giving Channel Four an interview, some tell-all thing. She wanted to give me the chance to tell my side of the story."

"And I guess you said no?"

Stella tosses back half the glass of juice, wiping the back of her hand across her mouth as she sniffles. "I sure did. I was hounded by reporters for years after you two went to prison, and I've never spoken to them. Not once."

I want to ask her why, but it feels like a stupid question. What would she have to tell them? Why would they even listen? They'd turn her pain into some fantastical story about the almost-President's daughter, and it would bring her nothing.

"What happened after we went inside?" I ask the question slowly, not sure if I'm ready to hear it or for her to tell it, but with everything that's happening around us, I need to understand.

Stella drinks down the rest of the juice, placing the glass on the table and rolling it back and forth between her fingers as she stares at it intently. "I don't know how much you heard in court, I never knew how aware you two were of what was happening, but… when they read the verdict out and took you both away, I fainted. They called an ambulance, it was on the front page of every newspaper. It started all these dirty rumors, that I was in on it, that I'd secretly married you, that I was pregnant, you name it."

I can't even name the emotion that tears through me hearing this, knowing that while Levi and I were escorted out of that courtroom, my girl was lying helpless on the floor. It's beyond grief, beyond anger and rage, and so much of it is once again directed at me. I left her alone in every way.

"I'm so sorry."

Stella reaches over and takes my hand. "I need you to stop apologizing for that time. Please. I don't need your apologies, I really don't. Please stop giving them to me. It won't change what happened."

"I know, but I let you down."

"Stop it." She leans closer and lays her head against my shoulder. "You're here now, and that's what matters."

"Yeah." I run my hand over her head before she raises it to look out the window at the sunshine.

"After that, it was a weird time. I finally managed to contact my mom, and told her that I wanted to come live with her. She was in France, living with some baron who had an estate in the Loire Valley, husband number 7 I think." She swallows, her lashes fluttering. "She told me that it was a bad time. As though there was ever a good time when it came to my mother." She inhales sharply, and her head drops. "Then my mom told me she'd signed my guardianship over to Gloria. For *stability*. That's the word she used. *Stability*. I needed it, she said. At least she was self-aware enough to know that I'd never find that with her." Her face crumples, her lip trembling as she presses her hands to her face. "It still hurts, to this fucking day. It still breaks my fucking heart that even then, when I had no one else, even then she didn't want me."

I pull Stella into my lap and draw her close to me, wrapping my arms around her and wishing I could make it stop hurting. I wish I had the power to say something, or do something, anything, to take away all the cuts and bruises Stella's parents left behind on her heart. Instead I just hold her silently, not knowing what else to do but just let her know I'm right here, and that I'm not going anywhere.

Finally, she takes a deep breath and wipes her face with her hands.

"I'm alright. Sometimes I just, I don't know, it just comes out." She gazes up at me, her amber eyes still shining with tears. "I trained myself not to cry, you know that? Because it was always worse when I cried."

I swear to god, I'm going to throw up. I clutch her to me tighter, because those words shatter my soul. "You cry all you want with me, I don't care. Flood the house. You don't hold back with us."

"Thank you." She wraps an arm around my neck and buries her face against my shoulder. "You have no idea what that means to me."

We sit like that for a while, until she takes a deep breath and sits up. "I only had 8 months until I turned 18, but I think Gloria had her plan. She wanted a conservatorship put in place so she'd be able to control my father's money. Because the old bastard had never named her in his will." Stella laughs scornfully. "That bitch really thought my dad loved her. You should have seen the look on her face that day."

"The only person who didn't know that marriage was a sham was Gloria." I run my hand down Stella's back. "How was she going to get a conservatorship?"

Stella's eyes meet mine. "By trying to make me go insane."

My lungs contract almost painfully, and the pit of my stomach is icy. "And how was she going to do that?"

She gazes at me pensively, her eyes dropping to my neck. She reaches out and traces a finger along one of the snakes etched into my skin, a sad smile tugging at the corners of her lips.

"I like these. I always wanted a tattoo, I just never knew what to get." She climbs out of my lap and goes to the kitchen counter, pulling open a drawer. She withdraws an orange vial, a pill bottle, and brings it over to me. "I found these. Gloria got careless one afternoon when she went to visit Levi, and they were just perched right there in the kitchen, next to the blender."

"Zyprexa?" I read the name off the vial with Gloria's name printed on the label. "What is this?"

"Olanzapine." Stella's gaze wanders to the ceiling, then back out the window. "It causes hallucinations. Gloria ground that up in my smoothies, I'm guessing with the assistance of the ever-present Valerie." She scoffs. "It didn't have the intended effect, but it fucked me up. Took me years to feel normal again." She looks down at me, her beautiful face twisted with pain, and suddenly she straddles me, taking my face in her hands. "I did things to hurt myself. I did things so I would *feel* something again. I did dangerous, stupid things. I let men…"

She trails off, and my heart stops for a moment. I grip her thighs, pulling her closer to me.

"If anyone hurt you, I will fucking hunt them down."

She shakes her head, dropping her gaze. "Don't say things like that. I let those things happen."

I grip her chin in my hand, forcing her eyes back up to mine. "No. You were used, and no one looked after you. That stops now. Me and Levi, we'll look after you. And anyone who hurt you, their days are numbered."

"Dylan-"

"Tell me about Stanley Iverson."

She inhales sharply, and clenches her eyes shut. I hope to god I haven't lost her again, I hope I haven't pushed her back into that dark place she just escaped from. But she takes several deep breaths, leaning into me and wrapping her arms around my neck, her fingers tracing gently over the back of my head.

"You remember my sixteenth birthday?" Before I can answer, she laughs softly. "Of course you do. You bought me all the flowers. I remembered, after you told me. I don't think I ever even thanked you properly, but that was the most beautiful gift anyone ever gave me. So, thank you."

My nose brushes along her collarbone, her sweet vanilla scent intoxicating. "Any time."

"My dad let me have red wine that night, which was weird. He said it was family tradition. Wasn't one I'd ever heard of." Her fingers continue their slow circles, and she sighs softly. "I hated how it tasted, but I didn't want to disappoint him. I didn't want to be the one to break tradition, and let him down." She shrugs. "So I drank half of it, and then poured the rest into one of the plants, so he didn't see. So he'd think I'd drunk all of it. Within a few minutes, the room was spinning. I could barely hear anything, I couldn't talk properly. My dad, I remember him carrying me out of the room, telling everyone the day had been too much for me."

"He drugged that wine." It's a pointless statement to make. But I'm finally putting it all together, finally asking Stella about everything instead of charging into the night like a raging bull. My anger is so sharp, I can feel its red-hot needles prickling down my spine and at the base of my skull. I close my eyes and remember the look in her father's eyes the second before I pulled the trigger and blew his brains out all over his leather armchair. The fear and disbelief.

And I hate myself because that death was too good for a fucking animal like him. I should have made him suffer.

"Yes, he did." Stella starts talking again, and I focus on her voice, on the slow breaths she takes as she tries to remain calm and not get swallowed up by the pain of her memories. "As he carried me out, he told me that tonight was going to be extra special. Everything we'd been doing til now, led to this moment. Because I was a woman now." Her voice falters into a whisper on the last sentence.

"You don't need to tell me more." I try to pull back from her, but her arms lock around me and hold me in place.

"He put me in a car." Her voice doesn't rise above that whisper, and I hold on to her, my hands splayed on her back, trying to make her know with every part of me that I'm here, *here*. "I don't know how long we drove, but then I was in a room I'd never seen before, some fancy hotel. I remember thinking how soft the sheets were, and then this sort of panic started, because if I could feel the sheets on my back, I wasn't wearing any clothes."

She takes two small, shuddering breaths and her fingers cease their gentle circles on my skin. Now she's just holding on to me. Just anchoring herself. I don't know if she's ever told anyone this before. I still don't know if I'm ready to hear it. But I steel myself for it.

In an eerily hollow voice, Stella goes on. "I knew Stanley

Iverson, he was a good friend of my dad's. I'd seen him before, always in suits and ties. So when he walked in, just in a robe, you know, one of those big fluffy hotel robes, I didn't recognise him at first. Then he said something about Uncle Stanley looking after me, and I realized who he was. Then he took off his robe, and I wanted to get away, I wanted to crawl off the bed and run out of the room, but I couldn't move. He... He asked me if it was my first time, and I couldn't say anything. Then he walked over, and he crawled over me and he smelled so bad, and he was so heavy, this big round gut, pressing me into the bed."

I'm anchoring myself to Stella now too, the two of us just holding each other as she relives what was one of the worst nights of her life and I fight the rage and sorrow and howling grief that won't stop echoing through my skull.

"He hurt me." Her voice drops lower again, so it's barely audible. "It was so... So uncomfortable, it didn't hurt exactly, but... I felt disgusting. He told me he'd paid my father extra to let him do it without a condom. I was lying there, in pain and terrified that he'd get me pregnant. But then he didn't finish. He rolled me over and... There was something cold, between my legs, cold and slippery, and then he... It hurt so bad, and I couldn't even scream."

When she stops talking, neither of us do anything but hold each other. Stella goes limp and soft in my arms, her arms dropping from around my neck so she can curl herself up into a ball on my lap.

I don't tell her that Stanley Iverson is as good as dead. I don't tell her that I'll put a tracker on his phone after I run her a bath. I don't tell her that Levi and I will hunt him down while she has dinner with Zee later this week. I don't tell her that Stanley Iverson will die slowly, and in pain.

I don't tell her any of that.

I simply hold her as the grief and sorrow wash off her, as her breathing normalizes. When she finally stands and stretches her back, I take her upstairs and run her a bath. She kisses me and thanks me, and lowers herself into the water. I tell her I'll be right back, and head into my room just as the front door slams shut and Levi comes up the stairs. He follows me into my room and closes the door behind him.

"Gun's coming." He says, toeing off his shoes.

"Good." I pick up my phone and send off a text. "I'll have the tracker on him by this afternoon."

"How's she doing?"

"I don't even know how she's functioning. Our girl's a fucking fighter." I meet his eyes, and he frowns. "Iverson gets a bad death. Painful, slow as fuck. I want that bastard to suffer til his last breath."

Levi's gaze turns steely as he nods. "She told you what happened?"

"What she remembers. Her dad drugged her."

Levi hisses in a breath, leaning heavily against the door as his head drops to his chest. "Fucking son of a bitch."

I open my mouth to tell him what his mother did, but decide that's a conversation for another time, and one he should have with Stella. But not now, not today. Stella has been through enough for one day.

"This reporter going to be a problem?" Levi asks, crossing his arms over his chest.

"I doubt it, Stella won't talk to anyone."

Levi rubs his neck, hissing in a breath through his clenched teeth. "My goddamn mother, and her fucking interview. What the hell is she thinking?"

The room feels too small, all the hurt and misery and what lies ahead of us weighing down the air and threatening to choke me. This day has been too much already, for all of us.

"Hey." I walk toward Levi, who eyes me warily. "Let it go for today. No more thinking about it."

Levi's mouth quirks into a smile, and his eyes scan me up and down. "You plan on distracting me?"

"I plan on distracting both of you." I put my hands either

side of him against the door, and kiss the corner of his mouth softly. His eyes flutter closed, and his shoulders drop. "Now, no more heavy shit today. You and our girl are going to let me look after you both."

"Sounds good." Levi turns his face to brush a kiss on my lips.

"Dylan?" Stella's voice wafts softly through the air, and Levi moves so I can pull the door open.

"I'm here, *guera*."

I walk into the bathroom to be met with Stella standing on the mat in a towel, her hair up in a messy bun on her head, a soft smile on her face. Her eyes move over my shoulder to Levi, then back to me, and she sighs happily.

"You're both here," she says,

"We sure are, baby girl." Levi moves around me and towards Stella. "We're not going anywhere." He puts his arms around her, and Stella leans into his chest, the smile growing.

This is right. How it'll work, that will come later. For today, it's us, just us. Exactly how it's meant to be.

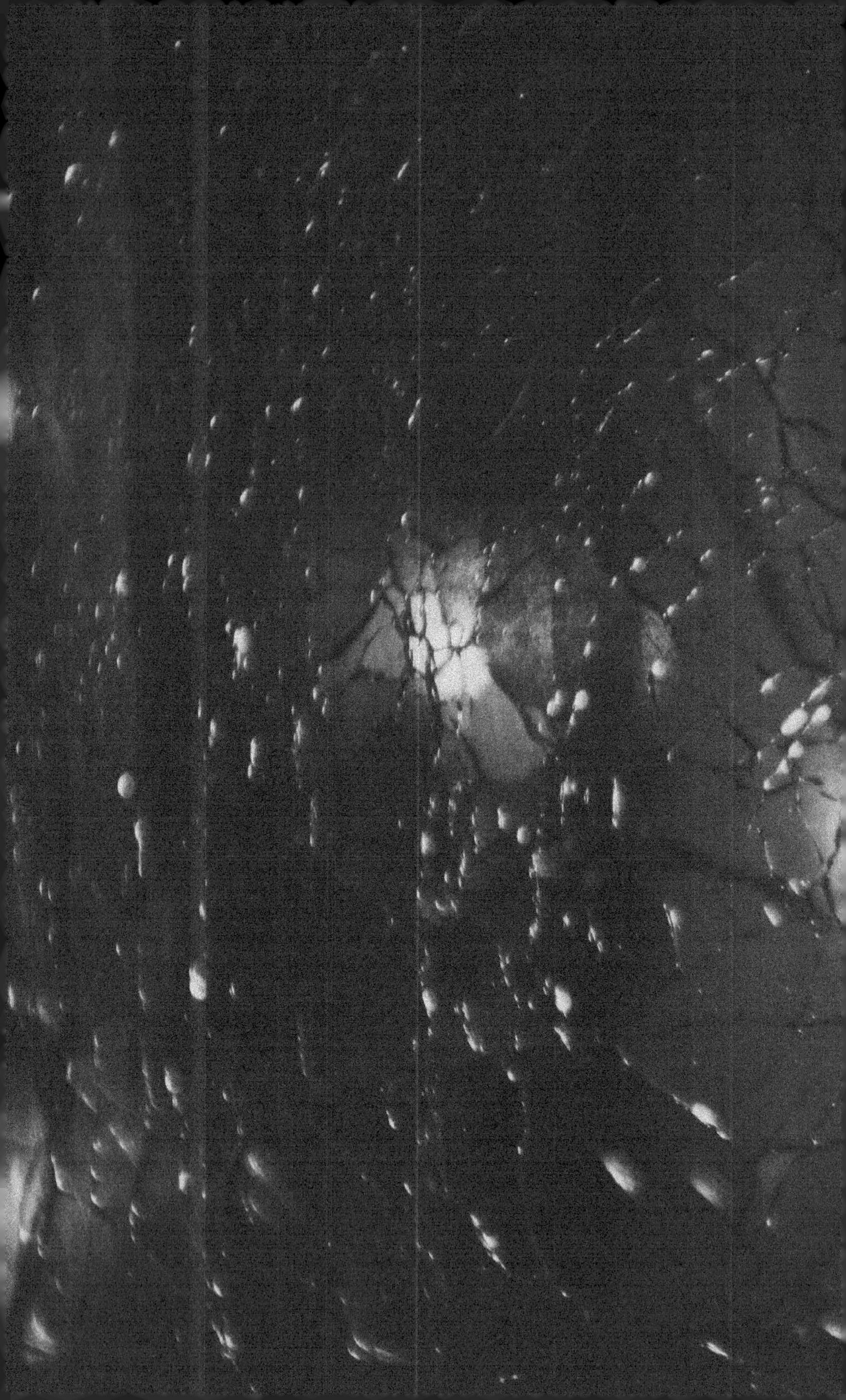

STELLA

CHAPTER SIXTEEN

BY THE TIME the boys have finished pampering and loving on me, I'm a little cloud of happiness. I'm covered in baby oil from the massage Dylan gave me, and Levi somehow conjured up raspberries, and fed them to me while I lay in his lap and Dylan read to us from one of my smutty romance novels. He laughs when I tell him he should get into audiobooks, because his voice makes me want to melt.

The sun is high in the sky when Dylan heads out to get us lunch, and I stay in Levi's lap, wearing nothing but a pair of floaty French knickers. It feels so natural to lie against his chest, to have his arms wrapped around me. He nuzzles into the crook of my neck and kisses me, telling me how beautiful I am, how much he loves me, how much he missed me all those years we were apart.

It's sheer bliss.

"You know, for a man who has a basically naked woman in his arms, you are displaying an amazing level of self-control," I tease, tilting my head so I can look over my shoulder at him.

He smiles softly, tucking a strand of hair behind my ear. "Baby girl, it's not all about sex, you know?"

"I know." I turn so I can cuddle him, wrapping an arm

around his waist. "It took me a long time to figure all that out. That it wasn't OK if a man just wanted sex from me."

"Of course it's not OK."

"And that wanting things because I want them is different to having them done to me. Because that's not about sex, that's about control. Like the choking thing. I like that, I like… I like being overpowered." I gaze up at him. "I like losing control to someone I can trust. Someone I'm safe with, who's doing it for me."

"And that's how it is with us." Levi's fingers stroke over my shoulder, down the divots of my ribs. "With me, and Dylan, it's never about control. It's about you, about making you feel good. And safe."

I sigh, savoring the feeling of his fingers on my back. "I do feel safe with you. And I want things from you that I've never wanted before."

He notches two fingers under my chin, his blue eyes searching my face. "Baby girl, right now, what I want more than anything is to kiss you. But I need to know you're OK first."

I sigh happily and nod. "I'm OK. And I want you to kiss me too."

The kiss is slow and warm, something beyond sexual. It's intimate. I turn so my body is lying against Levi's warm chest, but even with my breasts pressed against his naked skin, he takes his time, and keeps his hands on my back. His tongue traces over mine softly, like he's tasting me and committing that taste to memory.

The fact that he's not pushing me, that he's not trying to become frenzied or touch me anywhere else just turns me on even more. But I don't want to ruin the moment and push for something more, when this is the kiss we've both been waiting years for.

There is a flicker of fear at the back of my mind as I think about how people will react, what they will say. *People won't understand.* I'll just be Stella Langford, eternal victim and unholy mess once again. But I lock that fear away, determined not to spoil this for myself.

The heat of the day has warmed us both, and I'm so slippery from the baby oil that it somehow makes everything feel even more erotic. The smell of jasmine and honeysuckle wafts in through the open window, and that smell will forever remind me of the first time Levi Fenton kissed me because he *could.* My nipples harden, and I can't help but moan a little against Levi's lips. He's allowed to kiss me, and I'm allowed to kiss him.

This is how it was always meant to be.

His hands move gently down my back, and he tentatively cups my ass in his rough palms. It's still not a forceful touch, not urging me to move or try and place me where he wants me. He's hard now, his erection rubbing against my stomach through the fabric of his shorts.

It feels warm and dreamy, and I release his mouth to kiss my way down his neck, over his chest, and my fingers move into the waistband of his shorts. When I start kissing his stomach, he pulls me back up to him and gives me a grin.

"And just where do you think you're going?"

I return that grin, and nip at his chin. "I want to see too. What I saw on the other side of that shower screen wasn't enough."

"Baby girl, you were not just going to look, were you?"

"I happen to like sucking cock."

Levi's head tips back and he groans. "Oh, fuck. You're going to kill me."

I laugh softly, kissing his neck and grinding myself against him. "Can a blowjob be fatal?"

"When it's delivered by a mouth this perfect, I'm going to say that it definitely can be." He pulls me on top of him so I'm straddling him, and his eyes drop to my breasts. "Perfect mouth, perfect tits, perfect ass. How the fuck are we ever going to leave the house again, huh?" His thumb caresses my nipple, and my thighs clench his hips. "I could spend an entire month just exploring this body."

"I'm pretty sure you'd get tired of me at some point." I squeal loudly as Levi locks an arm around my waist and flips me on to my back. He kisses my neck hungrily, his hand moving to my breast to knead and pinch my nipple.

"You make it impossible to take things slow, you know that?" His breathing is heavy against my ear, and my thighs open for him so he can settle between them, grinding himself against me.

"Who said I want to take things slow?"

He stops, raising himself over me, his head dropping between his shoulders. "Stella, I know what you've been through and-"

I grab his face and force him to look at me. "I just told you, that was not about sex. And I'm not just a victim. I'm allowed to want the things I want, and to not be treated like a champagne glass teetering on the edge of a table." I shake my head, brushing my thumbs along his cheeks. "I don't want you to look at me and see fragility."

"I don't, baby girl. You're the strongest person I know. And I would never get tired of you. Ever. Don't think that for one second."

"Good." I pull him down to me and kiss him again, letting his lips consume me as I wrap my legs around his waist. "I waited years for this. I'm not letting you go."

He rises to his knees to slowly peel my panties down my legs, and I'm once again laid bare for him. His eyes trace a pattern over my body, joined by his fingers as they move in slow, delicate circles over my stomach and my hips.

"Open your legs," he says in a low voice, and I spread my thighs so he can see all of me. He hisses in a breath. "Fuck, baby girl." His eyes move to mine, and his mouth lifts into a grin. "Let's try out some more of those toys of yours."

"Toys?" My cheeks flush, because somehow the idea of him using a toy on me rather than just fucking me feels more vulnerable, more exposed and open. "You told me that the next time I came it would be with you inside me."

He grins down at me. "I did say that, didn't I?" He runs the tip of his finger down the lips of my pussy, and just that soft touch has my back arching. "But right now, baby girl, I need to watch you come for me."

"In the - the drawer." I gesture to the night stand, but he's already leaning over the edge of the bed because he knows exactly where my toys are after the other night.

He holds up a pink vibrator as he kneels back between my thighs, and I watch as he clicks open a bottle of lube to drip some on the tip. "Watching you in the shower, it was fucking beautiful. Then with Dylan, my god, Stella. You have no idea what that did to me." He nudges my entrance with the tip of the vibe. "Thinking of licking this pussy after he comes inside you, fuck."

I moan softly as he pushes in just an inch. "What did you two do?"

"I fucked him," he murmurs, and lets out a pleased growl as I gasp, taking more of the dildo. "He felt incredible."

I massage my slick breasts, pinching my nipples as Levi pushes the dildo all the way inside me. "What else?"

"I sucked his cock." He turns the toy on, and the vibration buzzes deep inside me, pressing right against my g-spot.

"Oh, fuck, Levi."

"You know what I'd love to see?"

I shake my head, biting my lip, desperately seeking more, wanting more sensation and more touch and heat, and wishing he'd pull out the vibe and fuck me.

"I want to see you splayed out between us, baby girl, Dylan's dick in your throat, and me buried in this pretty pussy." He's fucking me so slowly with the vibe, winding me up tighter and tighter, as though I'm going to fucking snap. "I want to fuck him while he fucks you."

"Oh shit," I cry, his words sending lust so sharp through my body that my pussy almost aches. "Fuck, Levi, *please*. Please, fuck me."

"Not yet, baby girl. Very soon."

I shake my head, squirming and writhing as the pressure grows in my belly. "I need you to touch me."

I cry out as his hand pushes down on my stomach, applying just enough force that the vibe feels too big and too much. He's fucking me harder now, pressing the vibe upwards with each thrust so the buzzing grazes my clit. My whole body is lit up with electricity, buzzing through each and every cell as I come undone under Levi's hands.

But it's not enough, I want more, I need more. I need all of them, more of them, I need to feel them everywhere. As though he can sense my raw need, Levi lowers his hand so his thumb massages my clit as my climax begins to peak.

"Yeah, oh god, fuck." I arch off the bed, my thighs shaking as I clamp down on the vibe, and Levi presses it against my g-spot as the full force of my orgasm rushes through me. The neighbors can probably hear me, my cries drifting through the open window and out into the sun-soaked air.

But I don't care. Let them hear me, let them know that Levi is mine and I'm his.

Levi withdraws the vibe once my thighs have stopped shaking, and leans down between my thighs to give my dripping pussy one long, slow lick. I suck in a breath, lifting my hips to try and keep his mouth there, so he can make me come again, but with a groan he sits up, grinning at me.

"You taste even better than I thought you would."

I tip my head back on the pillow, covering my eyes with my hands. "Oh my god, you're going to drive me crazy."

He settles over me, kissing my jaw tenderly as he chuckles. "But imagine just how good it'll be when it finally happens."

I wrap myself around him, breathing in his fresh scent. "I love you."

He exhales softly, peppering kisses over my collarbone. "I love you too, baby girl."

The front door opens then slams, and Dylan's voice sounds up the stairs. "You two worked up an appetite yet or what?"

Levi and I giggle, and he plants another kiss on my lips before rising off the bed and pulling me up with him. "Come on, let's see what our man's got."

Our man. My cheeks glow at the words, in the best way possible.

I slip on a blue sundress and follow Levi downstairs. He ambles across the kitchen to where Dylan is unpacking some sandwiches that smell heavenly, along with a fresh green salad. He places a kiss on the back of Dylan's neck, who smiles, turning to kiss Levi on the mouth. He licks his lips and turns to me with a wicked grin.

"Tastes like you, *guera.*"

My cheeks are flaming and my stomach clenches, watching them together and wanting them to just forget about lunch and spread me out on the table instead.

"I like seeing you two kiss," I admit quietly, and Levi chuckles against Dylan's neck.

"Our girl has a voyeur fetish," he murmurs, and Dylan's eyes light up with almost predatory desire. "I just had to tell her all about the things I did to you." He nibbles on Dylan's ear, who sucks in a breath, clutching the countertop with his fingertips. "She fucking loved it."

I swear to god, I'm going to pass out. Because yes, I did fucking love it, the idea of everything Levi just said to me turns me on. I have no idea how we skipped some big conversation about this lifestyle choice and just hurtled head-long into little threesome games. But I don't care. I'm happier than I've been… ever.

Instead of indulging Levi's fantasy, Dylan insists we all sit down and eat. He watches Levi and I with a lovestruck expression, then reaches across the table to take my hand.

"We're going out tonight," he informs us.

"Out?" I ask, taking the pink smoothie he bought for me from the holder on the table. "Where to?"

His mouth quirks pensively. "Somewhere fun, *guera*. You two need to be ready at 8pm, and dressed up."

Levi laughs. "Where are you taking us, *papi*?"

"You'll see."

CHAPTER SEVENTEEN

LEVI COMES down the stairs dressed in jeans and a tight black t-shirt, and I can't help but laugh.

"Jeans, huh? You sure know how to dress up."

He gives me a grin, his eyes raking up and down my body as he takes in my appearance. "Hey, for a mechanic I think I clean up pretty good. You, on the other hand, look amazing."

I tuck my hands into the pockets of my black pants, and lean against the door frame. "Oh yeah?"

"Mmmm, good enough to eat, pretty boy." He puts his hands against my chest, his fingers brushing the skin that's bare between the buttons of my white shirt. "But we might save that for later."

I lean down to run the tip of my nose along his jaw. "You smell too fucking good."

Levi's phone buzzes, and he lets out an exasperated sigh. "Fuck's sake." He snatches the phone from his pocket, and rolls his eyes. "Mom. Of course." He swipes the screen and puts the phone to his ear, turning away from me. "Hi… Yeah, I told you I'd think about it… Well I thought about it, and I have other plans…. Because I do, mother. Enjoy your party." He hangs up, shaking his head.

"What did she want?"

"To know if I was coming to her stupid party tonight." He places his phone down on the side table, chewing his lip. "I'm worried about this interview. I don't know what the fuck she's playing at, what she's going to say. And I don't like that."

"Hey, we said no more heavy shit today." I put my hand on the back of his neck, and he leans into me. "Tonight, you forget about her and everything else. It's just us."

"Yeah, you're right."

The clacking of high heels sounds down the stairs, and we both look up to see Stella looking like a bronzed goddess. She's wearing a tight yellow dress with round cut-outs at the waist, making her tan glow and showing off her perfect body. Her hair hangs loose down her back in soft curls, and big gold hoops dangle from her ears. She pauses on the stairs, twisting into a coquettish pose as she grins at us.

"How do I look?" She giggles as we openly gawp at her and makes her way down to us.

"You look like a fucking dream, baby girl." Levi steps away from me to take her in his arms, and she closes her eyes with a smile. Levi runs his hands over her ample ass, growling and giving her an approving slap. "No panties, just like I said. Good girl."

Praise kink by fucking proxy. Hearing him call her a good girl like that conjures up images in my head that I tuck away safely for later on tonight. This feeling, this need to be with them, and having that need finally fulfilled, it's addictive in the best way.

Stella looks over Levi's shoulder at me, and her smile becomes mischievous. "Well look at you, *papi*." She walks over to me, running her fingers along the gold chain around my neck. "I like you like this."

"I like you with no panties." I drop a kiss on her cheek, and she laughs.

"So, where are we going?" She gazes up at me with her big amber eyes, lined with thick black lashes, and she's so beautiful I want to abandon the plans for tonight and drag them both upstairs with me.

But no, I'm going to take this slow.

"I wanted to take you both somewhere we can just be ourselves."

Stella looks over her shoulder at Levi and claps her hands. "Well that sounds like fun. It's like our first date."

Levi laughs, rubbing his chin. "A threesome first date. I like it."

Stella's gentle laugh joins Levi's and her eyes land back on me. "So, we're really doing this, huh?"

I run my hands through those soft honey curls, brushing them over her shoulder, my fingers tracing down her back to land on the soft skin visible through the cut-outs in her dress. "Is this what you want?"

She nods emphatically, without hesitation. "Yes. Absolutely."

"Good." I kiss her forehead, and she sighs happily. "Because I don't ever want to be without either of you ever again."

A car horn sounds, and I jerk my head in the direction of the door. "That sounds like our ride's here."

Levi heads to the door first, Stella and I following.

"Did you get an Uber?" Stella asks just as Levi bursts out laughing.

I suppress my own grin as Levi casts a grin over his shoulder at me. "Rich boy got us a fucking limo."

Stella instantly flushes red, holding her clutch in front of her face as she steps on to the front porch. "Oh, you did not."

"Hey, let me do the rich kid thing for just one night." I pull the clutch away from her face, and she pouts up at me. "Come on, *guera,* I have something to show you, and I think you'll really like it. Besides." I lean over her, and plant a kiss on her shoulder. "It could have been a stretch hummer. What would the street have to say then?"

She giggles quietly. "True. OK, you get to be rich boy for one night." She sashays down the stairs ahead of me, wiggling her ass in that tight yellow dress. "But next time get an Uber like a normal person!"

I laugh and follow her and Levi to the limo at the end of the drive. The driver gives me a curt wave as I approach, already knowing his destination. I climb in the back, where Levi is sprawled on the opposite seat, his arm draped along the back of the seat and around Stella's shoulders.

"Impressed yet?" I ask as the limo takes off into the growing night.

Stella rolls her eyes. "Limos do not impress me, Kovac. You'll have to try harder."

"Well, I'd like to hope you'll be impressed by the end of the night." Butterflies erupt in my stomach, and I'm consumed with the hope that they actually will be impressed by what I'm about to show them. But maybe they'll think I'm foolish. That it was a dumb decision. I hadn't realized just how much this meant to me until I was bringing the two people I love to see it.

Levi gazes out the window at the passing lights. "We headed to the city?"

"Sure are."

Stella gives me a questioning smile. "Where *are* we going, *papi*?"

I wave her question away. "I told you, somewhere we can be ourselves. In the meantime, I feel like we should… talk. Now I know you said you want this, but I want to be clear-"

"I do want this," she interjects, and Levi strokes a hand along her thigh. "There's nothing clearer than that."

"So, you're completely OK with sharing? Me and Levi?"

She nods. "I want it. I do. I can't explain it. But… knowing you two are together, it… Makes me feel things. I like it. I'm not even jealous. Like, not even a little."

"That's good." I look at Levi, and he smiles at me. "I'm not jealous either. I'm really not. And I know you two have waited a long time to be together, too. So, if you want to be alone, I'm not going to be mad. That's absolutely OK."

Levi shakes his head, pulling Stella close and pressing a kiss to her temple. "I don't need that."

"I've never had a threesome before," Stella says quietly, her eyes moving back to mine. "Like… God I feel stupid asking this. But… What kind of positions are there, and like, I don't want it to be all about me, you know? Like in porn?"

The air in the limo is suddenly charged with electricity, because this is actually going to happen and I need to have a frank, factual discussion about it. Because of course we do. But goddammit, I just want to turn the car around and head back home so I can worship them both til sunrise.

No, no. Take it slow.

"There's lots of positions, *guera.* It's not a stupid question."

"You said you'd had threesomes before," she says shyly, and Levi's eyes flame with the same fire that I'm trying to keep at bay right now. "Like, how did that work?"

They're both gazing at me with a sort of reverence, like the master here to guide his new students. "I'm not an expert, but I mean yeah, I've been with another man and a woman, and with two other men. With the woman, she, uh, took both of us at once, vaginally and anally. And with the men, it was, well, one of them sucked my cock while the other man fucked him."

They're both gazing at me, entranced, desire and curiosity mingling in their eyes.

"You can feel the other guy, when you take a woman like that, right?" Stella is so sweetly naive in this moment, and I smile at her warmly.

"Yes, that's kind of half the fun."

"But how do you fit?" Stella looks from me to Levi and shakes her head. "I don't think I could make that situation work, you're both hung like goddamn stallions."

Levi and I both laugh, and Levi pulls Stella close, peppering kisses over the side of her face as she smiles.

"*Guera,* that's something you ease into. We'd get you all relaxed first, make you come a few times, so you'd be all nice and wet for us. And then it's lots of lube, making sure you feel really good the whole time." My voice dropped way lower than I expected it to, and the way Stella's eyes widen as she looks at me, the way Levi's eyes drop to my crotch, his hand moving across Stella's chest so his pinky grazes her nipple - the air in the limo has suddenly become way heavier, and I know we should be having conversations about this beyond what sex will look like.

But not only do I want to drag the two of them to bed with me for a month, the ten years of celibacy in prison are finally catching up with me. I'm no longer chasing Stella and hoping her self-hatred will abate long enough to steal a moment with me, and I'm no longer sneaking around with Levi like he's some dirty secret.

That's why tonight is so important. That's why where we're going is so important. We can finally be ourselves, we can be together - and we can fuck like rabbits every single night if that's what we want.

I reach across and take Stella's hand. "The important thing is that you know you're safe with us. I know it can be a vulnerable position, being with two men. I never want you to feel you can't say no, or that we won't stop immediately if something hurts, or makes you uncomfortable."

"One hundred percent," Levi agrees emphatically, running his hand down Stella's back. "You say the word, baby girl, and it stops."

"The word? Like a safe word?" She smiles at me, wrinkling her nose playfully. "Oh, I like that. I think my safe word will be… Hmmm. Martini."

"Thought you'd say bikini," Levi says, kissing Stella's neck. "You can just leave it off next time we get in that hot tub, save you throwing it in my face."

I laugh, looking out the window as we start to navigate busy city streets, packed with the Saturday night crowd. We're almost there, the buildings around us industrial brick buildings, all converted into stylish apartments and chic glass-fronted decor stores.

But then between all the sleek fronts, there's a neon sign that says *The Basque,* a Pride flag waving above the double steel doors. The car comes to a stop, and Stella and Levi look out with furrowed brows.

"The Basque?" Stella asks as I open the car door and offer my hand to her to help her out. "Isn't this-"

"You danced here, didn't you?" Levi interjects, climbing out after us and gazing up at the neon sign. "You gonna dance for us, pretty boy?"

I shrug. "I don't think it'd be a good look for the owner to dance in his own club, do you?"

They both regard me with wide eyes, and then Stella squeals and lunges at me, throwing her arms around me.

"Oh my god, *papi,* you bought it? That's amazing!"

Levi puts his hands on his hips, shaking his head, his mouth opening to release a huffed laugh. "Dylan fucking Kovac, night-club owner?"

"The city said it needed a backer, and this place, well…" I shrug, gazing up at the frontage. "It's where I found myself, you know? It means a lot to me."

Levi's mouth quirks into a smile. "I'm proud of you. This is great."

The apprehension I couldn't explain to myself dissipates in an instant, because they don't think it's stupid. They're proud of me. This place was my safe haven, away from the Catholic ramblings of hell and brimstone that my grandfather flung my direction any chance he got. And now I'm here with the two of them, with these two people I love, as our relationship is new and burgeoning and beautiful, and I want it to be a safe place for them too.

"Come on," I say as I take Stella's hand and Levi wraps an arm around her waist. "Let me show you my place."

The bouncers at the door pull the cord aside with a nod and a "Good evening, Mr Kovac."

The floor vibrates under our feet as we walk into the black and steel lobby, music thumping in the club. The tell-tale smell of the smoke machine is carried on the air, a smell that throws me back in time to that summer when I'd come here and dance til the sun came up.

Stella and Levi look around with wide smiles, their gazes meeting every now and then, filled with excitement. I can't stop grinning like a fool.

"Drink?" I ask, gesturing to the shiny black archway that leads to the club.

Stella nods and bites her lip, taking Levi's hand as they follow me to the bar.

The dance floor is already packed even though it's early, and by midnight it'll be a sweaty, heaving mass of bodies. The dancers are up on their podiums, dressed in a variety of lingerie, and Levi leans in to me.

"And what did you wear when you danced here?"

I grin at him. "Usually, only tiny black shorts."

I can hear the growl he lets out reverberate through my shoulder, and he shakes his head with a smile. "I bet you looked real fucking good, pretty boy."

"Best dancer in the club."

He grabs my ass hard. "Might have to give me a show some time, huh?"

My eyes land on Stella, who is watching us with open lust, her face a sweet combination of curiosity and desire.

"Like what you see?" I ask, and she nods eagerly.

We reach the bar, and I lean across to greet the bartender, who's been here since my dancing days. Levi and Stella stand beside me, Stella behind Levi with her arms wrapped around his waist. They look so natural, as she leans up to speak to him, and he laughs, caressing her arm with his fingertips.

"What are we drinking?" I ask them, having to raise my voice over the noise of people and thumping music.

"Ooh, a Cosmo!" Stella exclaims. "I haven't had one of those in years!"

Levi smiles over his shoulder indulgently, and Stella's eyes shine as she gazes up at him. "Just a whiskey for me," he says.

I lean over the bar and half-shout the order to the bartender, when there are hands on my hips. My head snaps to the side, to see Levi and Stella still standing there. Levi's face darkens instantly.

I turn my head to see who is holding me, and look into the face of a young dark-haired man with a lip ring, and tattoos on his forehead.

"Hey," he says, smiling lustfully. "You here alone?"

"No, he isn't." Levi is beside me instantly.

The young man backs away, smiling. "Lucky you." He gives me a nod before disappearing back into the dancing crowd.

Levi turns to me, his mouth twitching into a smile. "Who knew having the best looking guy in the club as my boyfriend would be a problem, huh?"

Boyfriend. Jesus fucking christ, I'm too old for that word to have butterflies erupting in my stomach. But here I am, feeling like a fucking kid.

Levi puts a hand around the back of my neck and draws me to him, and when his lips meet mine, I swear the whole world comes to a stop. It's not the first time we've kissed, it's not the first time I've kissed a man in public. But kissing *him*, kissing this man I love with my entire fucking soul here, with the woman we want to give our lives to watching us - I've never felt more whole, more right, more seen.

When he finally releases me, we both turn to look at Stella, who is leaning against the bar on her elbows. She's biting her lip, and the way her legs are crossed, I can see she's clenching her thighs together. She's fucking loving this.

Our drinks are placed on the bar, and I pluck a hefty tip from my pocket. Stella swoops up her drink, her hips already swaying to the music as she raises it to her lips. I take a sip of my whiskey as she moves in front of me, grinding her ass against my groin.

"I'm told you love dancing," I say, laying a kiss against her shoulder.

"I sure do."

"Shall we?"

She smiles over her shoulder at me, her hair falling against her cheek, and she's the most beautiful thing I've ever seen in my life. She throws back the rest of her Cosmo like it's water, and Levi laughs, taking a hurried gulp of his whiskey before Stella drags us both into the pulsating crowd.

Before long, we're all covered in sweat, grinding on each other as the music thunders around us. Stella's face shines in the flashing blue and purple lights, one arm curled back around my neck, the other draped around Levi's shoulders as she dances between us.

Levi leans in to kiss her, and I curl my hand around her throat to angle her up for him. I can feel her moan, my other hand moving over her breast, shielded by Levi's body so the dancers around us can't see what's going on.

Her hand drops from my arm, snaking its way between our bodies, and she rubs my cock through my pants as she and Levi continue to devour each other right in front of me.

Levi releases her mouth, leaning over Stella's shoulder to kiss me, pinning her between us. He groans into my mouth, and I just know Stella's rubbing him too, getting us both hard in the middle of the fucking dance floor. Deeply unprofessional for the owner of the fucking nightclub, but I don't fucking care.

Levi pulls back from me, grinning widely. "Is there a VIP room here?"

I laugh and look down at Stella as she turns around between us to face me, her face so innocent for a woman who was just rubbing two cocks in a crowded club.

"You wanna see the VIP room?" I ask her, sweeping her hair from her sweaty skin.

She smiles up at me lasciviously, her hips still grinding against me, her voice barely audible over the thumping bass. "Sure, I'd love to see it."

I put an arm around her waist and take Levi's hand, holding them both close as we make our way through the pulsating crowd. The VIP room lies up a winding staircase at the back of the club, its floor to ceiling glass windows giving a perfect view of the sprawling dance floor below.

The bar inside the room isn't staffed when the bouncer at the door lets us in. Blue lights whir and spin on the other side of the glass, casting a glow over the space. Sumptuous couches are set up around the perimeter of the room, and a raised platform with a silver pole extending to the ceiling stands in the middle of the room.

The music is still loud enough to be heard, but not loud enough to stop any conversation.

"Well, this is nice," Stella says, sauntering to the windows and gazing down into the club. "Feels very exclusive."

"Members only," I say, and head to the bar.

"Yeah, and the members are us, huh?" Levi says with a laugh, walking up behind Stella and wrapping his arms around her waist. "Wonder if they can see us up here? Want to flash them and see?" He grabs the top of Stella's dress and pulls it down, pressing her breasts against the glass.

She gasps, her head falling back against his shoulder as she laughs out loud. "Don't you want to save them for yourself? Imagine all those people down there, seeing *your* tits." She turns around, lifting a leg and wrapping it around Levi's waist, grinding herself against him. "But I guess if you want to fuck me right here and give them a show, we could do that." She nips at his chin, and Levi groans as he looks over at me.

"How the fuck does she do this?"

I laugh, shaking my head as I pour us all a tequila shot. "Get your asses over here, we need to celebrate."

"Haven't we been celebrating the whole time?" Stella asks as she and Levi make their way to the bar, still entwined, his arms wrapped around her waist. "Ooh tequila, it's getting serious now."

"Very serious."

The strap of her dress drops from her shoulder as she reaches for her shot glass, and I can't help but notice the sheen on her skin, the fabric of her dress straining over her breasts. *One last drink*. Then, I need to take them both home. The edging is fucking killing me.

We down our shots, and Levi sucks on his teeth. "That taste brings back memories."

"Sure does!" Stella laughs loudly, and heads for the pole in the middle of the room. "Maybe I should dance for the two of you?"

Levi laughs, hauling me to the couch closest to the dais. "Go ahead, baby girl."

Stella steps up on to the dais, taking a hold of the pole. "Can we get the music louder in here?" She asks, swaying her hips slowly as she leans back, her hand firmly wrapped around the shiny chrome.

I pull out my phone, and with a few swipes of my thumb, the speakers in the VIP room are pumping out music at a level nearing the one down on the dance floor. Levi puts his arm around me as Stella begins to dance, his hand on my thigh.

"Fuck she's beautiful," he murmurs against my ear. "Tell me that door's locked."

I turn to him, his sharp, tequila-fresh breath washing over my lips. "It's locked, *guapo*. They won't bother us."

He gestures at the ceiling. "Cameras?"

Another few clicks on my phone, and the security system for the VIP room is blacked out. "No cameras."

Levi pulls me in for a kiss, and he tastes clean and cool from the alcohol, his lips warm and soft against mine. "Good."

He gets to his feet, and ambles over to Stella. She leans down to him with a tipsy smile, and he says something into her ear. Her eyes flash to mine, filling with hunger and lust, and she grabs Levi by the collar to kiss him deeply. His hands run up her dress, pushing it up her thighs, and the resounding *smack* of his hand on her ass is audible even over the music. Her mouth opens against his in a gasp, her mouth quickly twisting into a desirous smile, and I can feel her laugh in my very bones.

My own hand burns with the desire to see her flesh turn pink from my touch, to strike her round ass until she's wet and begging to be taken. Instead, I clench my teeth together, watching as Levi peels down the front of her dress to reveal her breasts. Turning so he's sure I can see, he teases one of Stella's nipples with his tongue, but only for a moment before pulling the dress back up, and saying something to her I cannot hear. She nods, and Levi comes back to my side, sprawling next to me with his hand on my thigh.

"Private show," he says, and he gently pushes my face so I'm not looking at him, but at her. "Eyes on her, pretty boy. Watch our girl dance for you."

I groan lightly as his hand brushes over my groin, and Stella begins to dance around the chrome pole like she's been doing this for years. "Dance for us, you mean?"

"This is all for you," Levi breathes against my ear, unzipping my pants and taking a hold of my hardening cock. "A reward, to show you how proud we are of you." He bites my earlobe as he starts to pump me, growling against my skin as I gasp. "Such a fucking good boy, aren't you?"

The praise has me harder than steel, and I slouch back against the warming black leather of the sofa. I keep my eyes on Stella as Levi spits into his palm and fucks me with his hand.

Stella drops low to the floor, balancing expertly on her six inch heels like a trained dancer, and her dress rides up as she spreads her knees. Her cunt is glistening, a bright ruby red in the blue light of the club, the memory of that taste tracing over my tongue. My cock leaks pre-cum all over Levi's hand at the thought, and the sudden slickness has me sucking a breath.

Levi drops to his knees on the floor in front of me, pushing my thighs apart. My chest pounds as I breathe, looking down at him and running my hand through his hair.

"Watch her, pretty boy." He drags his tongue along the underside of my cock, and my head falls back against the couch, my eyes on Stella as she rises back to her feet, turning her back to me. At the moment that Levi takes me in his mouth, sucking me deep into his throat, Stella peels her dress from her body, pushing it over her ass, letting it drop down her long legs, and kicking it off the dais.

My brain short-circuits as Levi sucks me hard, Stella dancing right in front of me in nothing but a pair of high heels. Right here in my own club. Thank fuck that door is locked. Thank fuck no one can see in through those windows and see our girl bend over, exposing that perfect, smooth pussy.

Stella flicks her hair over her shoulder as she straightens, half-turning towards me, her hands on her breasts. She circles her hips, her round ass moving in a way that has me envisioning her on top of me, her hot cunt enveloping me as she screams and moans.

I need to touch her, I can't handle this. I need to be touching them both. The pressure in my spine and my stomach builds as Levi's mouth works me, and I raise my hand, gesturing to Stella with two fingers to come to me now.

She obediently steps down from the dais, sauntering towards me, swinging her hips. Our girl, totally fucking naked in a nighclub.

She looks down at Levi's head bobbing in my lap with open hunger, then kneels on the couch beside me. I grab the back of her head and pull her in to me, kissing her and suddenly aware of her features in a way I never was before, the taste of her tongue and the heat of her lips, the way her body feels against my exposed chest.

Her delicate fingers stroke down the side of my throat, and I break the kiss to turn into her touch, her fingertips pressed to the seam of my lips. Fuck, I love her hands. I take her fingers into my mouth, sucking on them as she kisses my neck, my collarbone, her mouth traveling further, further, until her teeth close around my nipple and bite. Not hard enough to hurt but enough to have me moaning around her fingers, my hips bucking to shove my cock to the back of Levi's throat. His hands spread on my thighs, holding me in place.

I hold Stella's hand to my mouth, biting and sucking on her as my other hand moves between her thighs, finding that slick heat it was seeking out. Her moan echoes across my chest as I slide two fingers over her clit, sweet and engorged, begging to be devoured.

Pleasure, like iron, like silk, runs down the length of my shaft, my balls drawing up tight as Levi continues the relentless movements of his tongue, his teeth raking along my sensitive skin. Stella whimpers and mewls against my chest as I massage her clit, and it's heaven, perfection fucking incarnate to have them both here, my best friend sucking me harder and harder, and the first woman I ever loved moaning and scratching at my chest as I drive her closer to her climax.

Or maybe it's sin, and I'm so far gone that I don't care that my grandfather was right. If this is sin, if this is an abomination and an insult to God, then so fucking be it. I'll let those flames consume me forever, if this is what that is. If this is how I spend eternal damnation, I do not give a single fuck.

Stella comes quietly, and I can feel she needs more, I can feel it in the way she tries to guide my fingers inside her, the way her hips roll greedily, completely involuntarily. She needs, just like I need.

And then I throw my head back, Stella's lips against my throat as I groan, one hot stream after another pumping down

Levi's throat, the pressure of each swallow wrenching out every last drop of my release. It's so much, so fucking much, I can feel it escaping his lips and running all over me, coating his chin and my thighs. He pulls back, lips full and eyes wild with need, when Stella descends on him, kissing him hungrily, and my fucking god, watching her lick and suck at his lips, tasting me, *me* on his tongue, I know I need to get them both out of here right now.

As though she can sense my thoughts, Stella turns to me, her hands raking up my stomach. "Take me home," she says, and though I can't hear the words over the music, I don't need to. Her perfect mouth huffs a hot breath against my skin, still vibrating with what Levi's tongue just did to me, and they both gaze up at me, bright and dark all at once, lit up with what else this night is going to bring us.

Somehow Stella is back in her dress, and Levi cleans me up suitably to go back out in my own goddamn club. We're grabbing at each other, stumbling drunkenly though our desire has made us all stone-cold sober, or drunk on something else entirely. I can taste the saltiness of my release on Levi's lips, and I can't help but push him against a wall and kiss him, drink him down as he presses his rock-hard dick against my hip.

"Come on, pretty boy," he says with a groan, ice blue eyes flashing in the whirring club lights as he gazes up at me. "I need you both in my bed, right now."

Stella is at my back, her hands around my waist, and I look down to watch her rub Levi through his jeans. Levi clenches his eyes shut, hissing out a breath. Her heat seeps through that flimsy dress, through my shirt to my skin, and here between them, deafening music around us, I feel whole and *right.*

We make it back to the car through a blur of bodies and lights, and Levi swipes shut the window to the driver. In an instant, before the car's even pulled away from the curb, he has Stella on the floor. They're a tangle of limbs, her legs wrapping around his waist as their lips meet feverishly. Her dress rides up around her hips, baring her ass to me as I lean back against the seat and watch.

I forgot how much I like to watch. Maybe it's the fact that my climax is still burning through my body, spent and sated and fulfilled enough to just sit back and watch, enjoy the sounds and smells of their arousal from here. Stella whimpers and moans into Levi's mouth as he ruts against her. It's filthy and desperate, their need for each other, not caring that we're in a car driving through the city, lights and people rushing past the windows as the driver takes us home. It doesn't matter to them, and it sure as fuck doesn't matter to me.

"Oh god," Stella breathes, her back arching as Levi pulls down her dress, his mouth covering one of her plump nipples, a hand bracing under her hip to hitch her up higher, giving me a perfect view of her dripping pussy. "Levi, I need you. Please. Please." She fists his shirt, twisting and arching, fighting to get as much of him exposed as she can.

Levi pulls back from her, and grins over his shoulder at me. He pulls Stella up to her knees, and she leans against him, eyes closed, lips seeking his.

"Bend over, baby girl," he commands, directing her towards me.

Without hesitation, she lays over me, and I wrap my arms around her, her greedy mouth consuming mine. Sweat lines her lips, and she's trembling ever so slightly. Her dress is pushed up to meet my arms, and Levi's fingers brush my forearms as he caresses her back.

She cries out as she kisses me, the sounds muffled by my tongue. She breaks the kiss, her eyes closed and her mouth parted as she moans. "Oh fuck," she murmurs. She looks over her shoulder, and my gaze follows hers, to where Levi is kneeling behind her. His hand is between her thighs, I can hear how wet she is as his fingers move.

He looks down at her, at where his hand is fucking her slowly, and growls low in his chest. "Such a pretty pussy." He shoves her forward against me, aided by the movement of the car as it takes a curve in the road, and he buries his face between her legs.

Stella moans against my neck, her fingers clawing at my skin.

"Does his tongue feel good?" I ask her, tipping her flushed face up with my fingers, so her hooded eyes are gazing up at me. She nods, panting, licking her lips.

"Oh fuck, it feels too good."

"Good girl." I cup her breasts in my hands, catching her nipples between my fingers, earning me a sweet, needy moan. "I told you, *guera,* we're going to get you wet and ready, make that pussy come for us so you can take us both."

Her brow furrows, her head falling against my chest, her heartbeat thumping through her ribcage. Her movements are smaller now, her moans high-pitched.

"That's it, nice and quiet." I pull her up to meet me, so her desperate breaths are caught between us. "Don't scream now, this is just for us. Be quiet for us, *guera,* we don't want to share this with anyone else." She bites her lips together, her body shivering, her nipples so hard they could almost graze open the skin on my chest.

Levi is still kneeling between her legs like a man praying, worshiping, drawing her climax out slowly with every stroke of his tongue against her needy flesh.

The car begins to slow, telling me we're off the highway and winding our way through the suburbs. Almost home.

Stella muffles her open-mouthed cry against my skin, hands desperately clinging to the back of my neck as she tries to hold on, to not be lost in this moment and scream out her climax. She bucks against Levi's mouth, and he groans into her cunt. Just like in the club, I can sense her need, her urgency to have more, more of us, all of us, just like she said.

Levi kisses his way up her back, leaning over her, wrapping a hand around her throat. "Fuck, baby girl." He kisses her neck, rubbing himself against her bare ass. "I need to be inside this pussy."

The minutes tick by agonizingly slowly as the car winds its way through the streets of Bellford Heights. Levi pulls Stella's dress into place, and he kisses me so I can taste her on his lips, and Stella lies against my chest, watching us with wide eyes.

Finally, the car comes to a stop, and Levi guides a weak-kneed Stella across the lawn, her legs wobbling atop her high heels. I fling an over-generous tip to the driver and thank him. He probably heard what went on in the back of the car, and I don't much care.

Under the light of the moon I head for the house, and once I'm inside I hear footsteps on the stairs, Levi and Stella going up ahead of me. I close the door behind me, and follow them.

Soft light spills from Stella's bedroom, and when I walk in, she's already naked, on all fours on the bed, watching as Levi sheds his clothes. Her eyes move to me as I walk in, and as I set about stripping off, her gaze moves from me to him and back again, taking us both in, her expression soft and wanting.

"How do we do this?" She asks.

I move to the bed, and she sits back on her folded legs as she gazes up at me. I stroke the hair from her face.

"Where do you want us?" I'm letting her take the lead, letting her decide how this goes.

Her brow furrows for a moment, and then she looks over her shoulder at Levi. "I want you in my pussy." She turns back to me, looking up at me with trust and love. "And I want you…" She trails off, her cheeks flushing red.

I lean over her, taking her face in my hands and kissing her deeply. "Whatever you say, *guera*." I look over at Levi, and gesture to the bed. "Come here, *guapo*, and lie down."

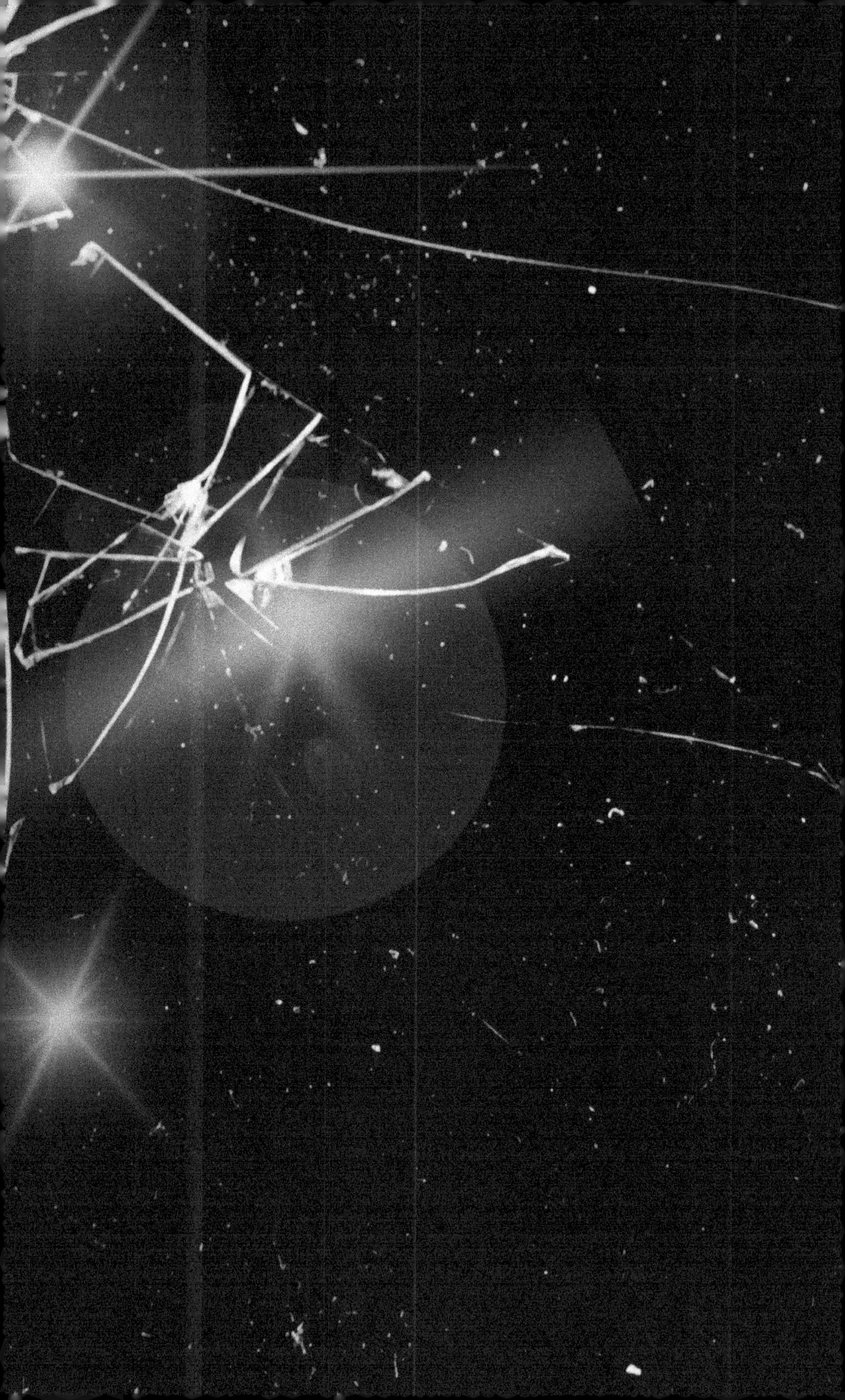

CHAPTER EIGHTEEN

STELLA POSITIONS HERSELF OVER ME, and I want this moment to slow down so I can memorize how she looks, hovering over me like a disheveled angel. Her make-up is smudged, blackening her eyes, and it makes her look even more beautiful, more imperfect, more undone, more *mine*. I can still taste her, and the memory of that pulsating cunt against my mouth, the fucking triumph of knowing I made them both come with my mouth - my cock is fucking aching for release.

I worry for a moment that I won't last long enough to please her. I'm sure she feels like heaven, and since she's already sitting on top of me I know we're dispensing with the idea of a condom. I'm going to be inside her, raw and naked and aching with the need to fuck, to come, but I'm going to have to take this slow for her.

Goddammit, I hope I can.

She leans down over me, her heated skin pressed to mine, and I run my fingers through her hair. Her big eyes gaze down at me, and her full lips are trembling ever so slightly now. My dick is pressed to her hot pussy, and I groan as she shifts her hips. She lowers her cheek to mine, her eyelashes tickling my skin as she blinks. With a soft moan, she grinds herself against me.

"You know how many years I dreamed of this moment?" I say softly against her throat, and she sighs.

Dylan stands over us, a bottle of lube in hand, his dark eyes watching us with unfettered lust. He doesn't speak, doesn't rush us, doesn't even move towards us, just lets us take our time.

Stella runs a hand down my side, over my stomach, and lifts her hips as she wraps her hand around my cock. She raises her head to look into my face, and then the tip of my cock is nudging at her entrance. She releases me, her hands resting on my chest, and with a small puffed breath, she lowers herself onto me.

The sharp volt of pleasure that shoots up my stomach empties my lungs of air and my mind of all reason. There's just her, my hands on her ass and holding her still because my god, if she moves now before I can think or breathe again, I'm going to spill inside her sweet pussy immediately.

"Fuck, baby girl." My fingers dig into her ass, and she makes a small circle with her hips, moaning.

She takes my face in her hand, her amber eyes hooded, her lips parted and quivering.

"Are you OK?"

I nod, stroking my fingers down her spine, memorizing every single divot, the feeling of her silky skin beneath my fingertips. "I just... *Fuck*. I just need a second. You feel too fucking good."

She lowers her head to the crook of my neck, rolling her hips in that way that has me gasping, biting my lip with a whimper.

"I like that I feel so good for you." She kisses my neck. "I like hearing you make these sounds because of me."

I try to regulate my breathing, focus on the tickle of her hair against my chin as she lies against me, barely moving. Sweat has broken out over my body, and I dare to lift my hips, just a little, just enough to slide deeper inside her. My movement is answered with the sweetest whimper, and Stella's nails dig into my shoulders.

"Levi," she breathes, and I never want to stop hearing her

saying my name like this. A sigh, a scream, it doesn't matter. It's the most beautiful sound in the world.

The bed dips slightly with Dylan's weight as he kneels behind Stella. "You look so beautiful, *guera*." He runs a hand down her back. "If it hurts, or you want to stop, you say the word, remember?"

She nods, a tiny laugh bubbling from her lips. "Martini."

"That's right." There's a click of a lid being opened, and Stella's shoulders tense for a moment. "I'm going to get you nice and wet, all slippery for me. It'll feel very full, but I'll take it slow."

His voice is so deep, so even and reassuring, and it makes me shiver, goosebumps erupting down my arms.

"Hold her open for me, *guapo*," he says, and I spread Stella's ass wider with my hands.

She's trembling now, and Dylan leans over her, kissing her shoulder.

"Are you ready for me?" He murmurs, and Stella nods.

He rises back to his knees, and I can feel the lube dripping down through Stella's slit, coating the exposed base of my cock, my balls and my thighs. I kiss her gently, along her jaw, her cheeks, and her body is soft and pliant against me.

I'm not prepared for how it feels for me when Dylan slowly starts to push inside her. I'm focused on her, at least I should be, reading the movements of her body, her sharp intake of breath, the way her fingers cling to my collarbone. But *fuck*, feeling Dylan pushing in further and further, pressing against my own engorged cock, I gasp for air, scrambling to hold off and hold on and just not fucking lose it in this moment.

Stella makes a sound between a cry and moan, lifting her head from my chest, and Dylan's hand is on her back again, stroking and soothing.

"Breathe, just breathe." He brushes his fingers along her jaw. "Do you want me to keep going?"

Her brow furrows, and she grits her teeth, nodding. "Yes, keep going."

Dylan pushes in further, and Stella coughs out a gasp.

"Oh *fuck,*" she murmurs. "More, that's... Fuck, that's better. Oh *god.*"

Dylan finally sits flush against her, and he closes his eyes for a second, his hand stroking up Stella's stomach between her breasts, his mouth against her cheek.

"My fucking god, *guera,*" he croons, looking down at where we're joined, both of us filling her completely. "You're doing so fucking well. You're a goddess."

"You feel so good," I murmur, lifting my hand to stroke her throat, which is shuddering and bobbing as she breathes. "Does that feel good for you?"

She nods, eyes hooded. "I want to move."

"You move." Dylan's hand keeps stroking her back, and his voice stays steady even though I can feel that's trembling too, his sweat-soaked thighs pressed against mine. "You move, and I'll move when you're ready."

Stella rolls her hips, and the same moan breaks from all of us, somewhere between ecstasy and relief, because my god, this has to be what Heaven feels like. The heat of her pussy and the sheer size of Dylan's cock choking my own - there is no way this is going to take long. Stella raises herself slowly, hands pressed to my chest, and then she starts that rhythm of her hips, over and over.

Dylan's jaw is set, and he groans, his head dropping back a little. As Stella settles back against me, he pulls out just a fraction, as though his restraint has torn, and with a grunt he pushes back inside her.

"Oh *fuck,*" Stella cries, her stomach contracting. "Fuck, yes, do that again."

Dylan withdraws a little more, dragging down the length of my cock, and when he bottoms out against Stella's ass again, she tosses her head and mewls.

"Fuck. Harder. Please, don't stop."

Immediately, Dylan begins to fuck her, fucking both of us, as Stella remains still because she doesn't need to move at all. Each roll of Dylan's hips against her sends her slamming down on me, and I swear I can't fucking breathe.

"Her clit," he says to me, panting, and I let go of Stella's round ass to curve my hands around her hips, obeying his command because this dark-eyed god above us both is completely in control. Holy fuck, he's the most beautiful thing I've ever seen.

I massage Stella's clit with my thumb, and she's soaked in her arousal and lube, her hips bucking against me with every thrust of Dylan's cock. Her long nails dig into my skin, leaving welts behind, and I want her to fucking mark me. I want to wear these scars for days and days, I want her tattooed on my goddamned bones for eternity.

"Levi," she pleads, her head tipping back, Dylan's hand gently cupping her throat with his enormous hand. "Oh my god. Oh my god. Dylan, please, please."

"We've got you," he murmurs. "We've got you. Let go, *guera*."

I can't deny the white-hot stabbing in my balls. At the moment that my release begins to erupt inside her, more and more heat filling that impossibly tight pussy, she screams, contracting on my cock, grabbing and pulling and drawing out every drop until I'm drained and shivering beneath her. Stella collapses onto my chest, whimpering and moaning as Dylan's thrusts turn into short, hard ruts.

I gaze over her shoulder at him, breathless and aching, the feeling of his hard cock too much against me. Her body is almost fighting the intrusion with each pulse of her pussy, until he groans, pulling out of her, gritting his teeth as he presses his cock to the cleft of her ass, and hot jets of cum spurt across Stella's back.

Stella lays on my chest, her breath cooling the sweat on my skin. I kiss her forehead, stroking her hair from her neck.

"You did so well, baby girl."

She smiles sleepily, and shifts against me. "I cannot believe how good that felt."

Dylan leans down to kiss her cheek, his own chest still heaving. "You took us so well, *guera*." He drops another kiss to her shoulder, then climbs off the bed. "Stay here, I'll be right back."

He disappears into Stella's bathroom, and water runs for a few minutes, and then he comes out with a washcloth and a towel.

He kneels behind Stella, gently cleaning the cum and sweat from her skin. When she's clean and he's dried her down, she lifts herself off me, and rolls onto her back beside me. Dylan's eyes land on my cock, covered in my release, and his eyes flame. I brace myself for another round, my cock twitching in anticipation, but Dylan simply washes away the traces of what we just did from my thighs.

Stella rolls on to her side, watching as Dylan takes care of me, and she sighs. "I didn't know it could be like that," she says softly.

Dylan's mouth quirks into a crooked smile. "You might be a little sore tomorrow, I'll run you a bath to help."

She giggles, rolling on her back and throwing her arms over her head. "You're the sweetest, *papi*. Give me the railing of my life and then offer to run me a bath."

Dylan drops the towel and the washcloth to the floor and crawls over her, grinning down at her, kissing her softly. "I'm very, *very* good at looking after people."

"Mmm, yes you are."

Dylan's gaze shifts over to me, and he smiles. "You OK, *guapo*?"

I nod, even though I don't think that's an accurate way to describe what I'm feeling now. My heart's still threatening to beat its way out of my chest, and looking at these two people, who I love more than anything I've ever loved in my whole life, I'm so much more than OK.

Dylan leans over me, notching a finger under my chin and turning my face to his. He kisses me slowly, softly, and my determination to be the alpha male, the big man, it melts away.

"I love you," I whisper against his mouth, and I mean it, I do. With every part of me, I love him and I love Stella, and I know that I'm going to set this all right.

His mouth curves into a smile against mine, and he strokes the hair from my forehead. "I love you too, *guapo*."

Stella curls up beside us, sighing happily. She doesn't speak, just lets Dylan and I lie down either side of her, kissing her neck and her shoulders, stroking her hair until she falls asleep between us.

Dylan's eyes become heavy too, and after a while, his shallow breaths wash over Stella's shoulder. I lie awake for a long time, listening to the beat of my heart and feeling the heat of Stella's body as she lies under my arm.

This is the beginning of us, of this life together. But first, Dylan and I have work to do. And as I look down at Stella's peaceful face, I know that what's coming could break her heart all over again. It could tear us away from her for good.

But I spent ten years in prison hungry for revenge, hungry for the justice she was denied.

I roll on to my side, breathing her in as I fall asleep.

They're going to pay, baby girl. Every nightmare that haunts you, they're going to pay in blood.

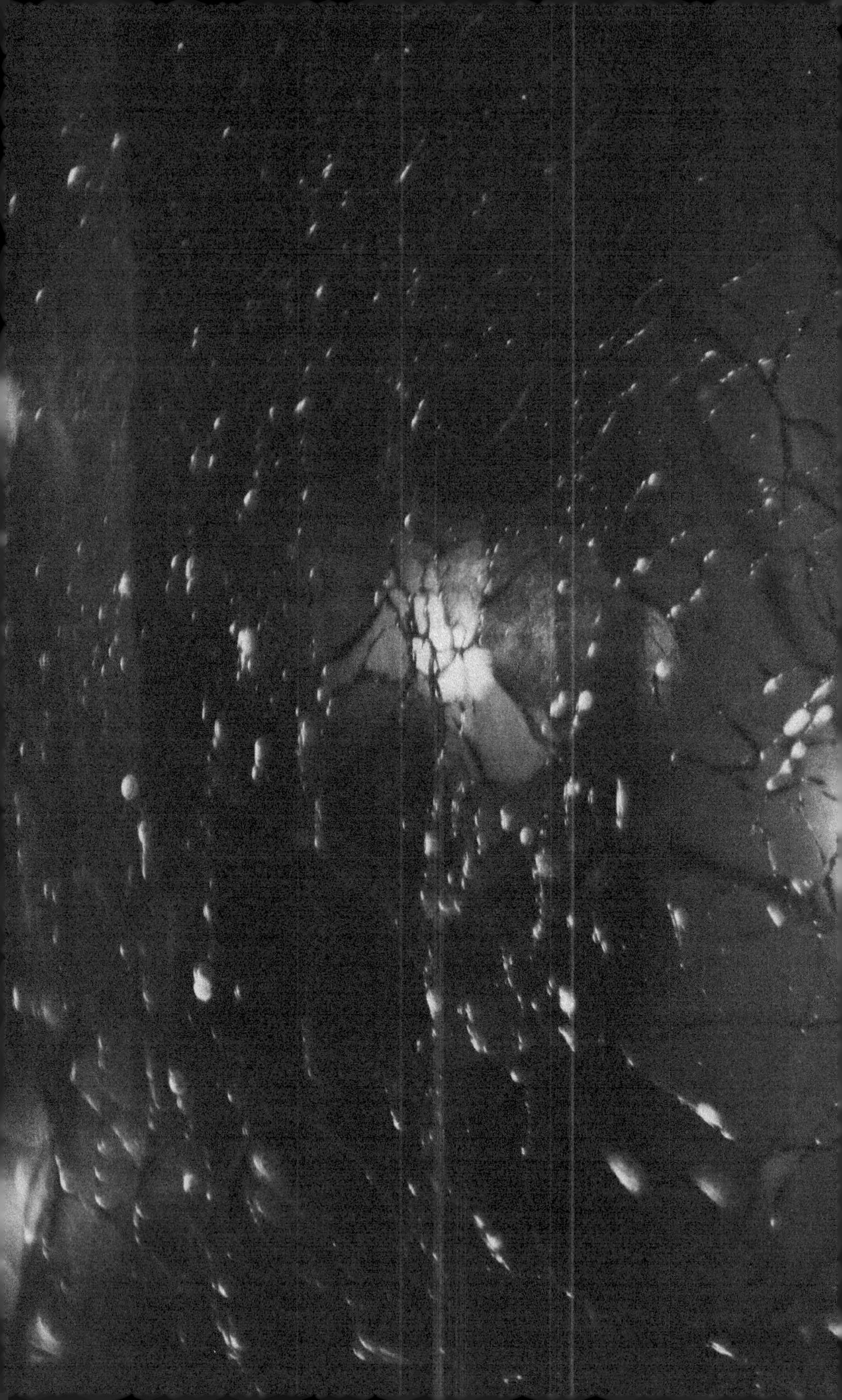

STELLA

CHAPTER NINETEEN

I WAKE up to the heat of the men lying either side of me, and a dull ache between my legs. I test my body carefully, moving my hips side to side, and while I'm sore, it's not terrible. When Dylan first entered me, I was sure I was going to burst, like he was going to split me straight up the middle. But the pain had quickly given way to pleasure, and when I think of how it felt when Dylan moved, how it felt to take both of them, hearing their moans and heavy breaths as they were both inside my body, it's enough to have me squirming and feeling hotter and hotter between them.

An arm drapes around my waist, and a hard cock is pressed to my ass as Dylan exhales heavily against my neck.

"Good morning, *guera*," he murmurs.

I roll over carefully, trying not to wake Levi, and Dylan smiles down at me sleepily.

"Are you sore?" He asks, and I shake my head. He cocks an eyebrow. "No?"

I squeeze my thighs together, clawing at his neck to draw him down to me, suddenly filled with need. "Just a little."

"More than a little, I think."

"I don't care." I grab at his shoulders, trying to haul him on top of me which is about as easy as lifting a truck. He chuckles softly, which quickly dissolves into a groan as I wrap my hand around his cock. "Please, I need more."

"Mmm, say that again."

"Please?" My voice is strained, and I wriggle underneath him, trying to open my legs for him but he holds me in place. "I need you inside me."

"Beg for it, *guera*." He raises himself over me, wrapping a hand around my throat, pinning me to the bed.

"Please," I squeak out, trying to speak under the pressure of his hand. "Please, fuck me."

His dark eyes gaze down at me, and he squeezes my throat harder. "Say it again."

"Please, please, please."

He lowers his face, drawing my bottom lip into his mouth and biting down on it before commanding, "Again."

"Please fuck me."

"Three slaps against my ribs to stop," he murmurs, and I can't cough or gasp as he thrusts into me hard.

Even though I'm still slick from Levi's cum, there's a stinging heat as Dylan works his cock inside me. But it doesn't hurt, not really. It feels right. The ache heightens my pleasure, and I'm light-headed from the pressure of Dylan's hand on my throat.

"So pretty for me, aren't you? Begging to be fucked right next to Levi while he's sleeping." Dylan laughs almost cruelly, and seeing his face twist like that, being at his mercy and surrendering control to him makes my pussy pulse around him, and he groans. "This pussy is heaven. Fuck, so fucking tight for me."

My back arches off the bed, and I'm aware of movement beside me. Levi lifts his head, but I can't move, still pinned to the bed by my throat. Even so, I can feel the heat and desire rolling off Levi as he watches Dylan fuck me.

Having Levi's eyes on us just turns me on even more, makes me more desperate to come and have him too, and how was I ever going to leave this bed again?

"Can you take more?" Levi asks against my ear, and I panic

for a second, because there's no way I can take him as well after I just had them both inside me a few hours ago. Desperation for them both wars inside me, but I shake my head as much as I can under the grip of Dylan's hand.

Levi looks up at Dylan, his face darkening with lust. "Let her up. On her knees."

Dylan has me flipped over on my stomach, then hitched up to meet his hips in a split second. Before my hands have found their grip on the bed, he's shoved back inside me, and I cry out as Levi grabs my jaw, forcing my mouth open. He looks down at me, panting as Dylan fucks me relentlessly. He's hesitating, waiting for me to say yes.

Which I do by taking his swollen cock into my throat with a loud moan. He tastes sweet and salty, my lips burning as he stretches me. His blunt head hits the back of my throat as Dylan drives into me, forcing me down on to Levi's thick length until I'm choking and tears are running down the side of my face.

I can barely breathe, but I don't care, because I'm about to come, moaning and tensing between the two of them as they fuck my throat and my pussy, just like I dreamed. Levi's fingers tangle in my hair, his hips jerking as he says my name, muttering out praise and curses.

I choke on my cries as I clench around Dylan's cock, and his fingers dig into my hips with enough pressure to leave bruises as he swells and twitches and begins to spill inside me. Levi fucks my mouth harder, driving more and more tears down my face, and then a hot stream pulses down my throat, so deep I barely taste him. I swallow hard, eliciting another groan from him, then another, as I take all of him down, fighting to breathe through my nose and blinking away the tears that flood my eyes.

"*Fuck*, baby girl," he breathes, stroking my hair. "Fuck. This mouth of yours..." He pulls out of my mouth, stroking my jaw and running his thumb over my lips as I pant and moan, Dylan still buried inside me. "Do you know what it does to me to see you like this? Completely fucking ruined by us?"

I mewl and stretch, wanting more, and more, but Dylan pulls out of me, his cum dripping down my legs, and he gathers me down onto the bed with him, his arms around me as he showers kisses over my shoulders.

Levi collapses down beside us, and strokes my cheek tenderly. "So beautiful," he murmurs, and my eyes flutter closed. "So fucking perfect, and beautiful. My perfect chaos."

I lie between them like that for a long time, drifting in and out of sleep, and it's only when my stomach begins to protest loudly at the lack of food and the too-many burned calories that we finally leave our little love nest. The guys head downstairs to make breakfast while I have a quick shower, admiring the scratches and love bites all over my back and neck.

I'll have to get some industrial strength concealer on that for work tomorrow.

My phone is flashing when I get out of the bathroom, and I'm tempted to ignore it, and just head downstairs. But for some reason, I pick it up, and check my messages.

One is from Mallory, dated late last night. I roll my eyes, because this bitch just won't let up. I open it, and nearly drop the phone.

> Someone has emailed a set of photos to me. Stanley Iverson is visible in one of them. I'm keeping this between us for now. But please call me.

A set of photos. I'm going to throw up. How the fuck did they find my father's photos? Where had they been hiding all this time? My head spins, and I bring up Mallory's number to call her immediately, but then swipe it away again, sweat breaking out over my face.

Shit. Shit. Fucking goddammit. If someone has those photos, who else has seen them? Who else knows?

I nearly swipe the screen away, until I remember there was a second message. It's probably Mallory again, and I wonder if I should just block her.

But the message isn't from Mallory.

> Sender Unknown: Bang Bang, girlie pop. Keep your mouth shut.

There's a photo attached to the message, blurry and dark, taken from behind what appears to be a car window. A woman with a blonde bob is lifting groceries out of the back of her car, a toddler perched on her hip.

My stomach drops, and cold sweat breaks out over the back of my neck.

I'm almost 100% sure it's Mallory. Mallory, and her baby.

"Oh shit." I clutch the phone to my chest and hurry down the stairs to the kitchen.

The guys both look up with warm smiles which quickly turn into frowns. Dylan rushes towards me, grabbing on to my forearms.

"What's wrong?"

"The reporter, that's - Oh my god, I think that's her, and her baby, and-" I shake my head, handing him my phone and covering my mouth with my hand. I can't speak. I can't say out loud what I think is happening, because it's too terrifying and awful to even consider.

Dylan's eyes flicker over the message, then to the photo, narrowing for a second before realization breaks over his face. He looks over his shoulder into Levi's concerned face.

"Someone has eyes on the reporter and her family."

Levi's jaw feathers, and he leans on the counter. "Fuck."

"What does this mean?" I look from one to the other, looking for an explanation, for shock. But they both look like they expected this. Like they know something I don't. "Why are you both so calm? You don't even seem surprised."

Levi rounds the counter to put his hands on my shoulders.

"Baby girl, listen to me."

I shrug him off, backing away from him. "No, there's something going on here and I want to know what it is." I look over at Dylan and shake my head. "The way you were talking the other day, and then you." My gaze moves back to Levi. "You charging off the second I mentioned Stanley Iverson. There's something going on here and I want to know what it is."

"*Guera,* there's nothing going on." Dylan moves towards me slowly, his big dark eyes fixed on my face. "I need you to know that."

"You're a bad liar, Kovac, you always were." My words are laced with venom, and he winces. "Now, you both listen to me. If there's something going on here, if you two have some stupid little plan for revenge, I'm telling you both right now to stop."

"That's not an option."

Levi's voice is steely and low, and filled with a threat that has Dylan and I both turning to look at him. His eyes move from Dylan to me.

"Baby girl, I need you to understand something."

"I understand everything." I snatch my phone from Dylan's hands and back away towards the door. "I understand that once again revenge is more important than me."

"That's not how it is at all." Dylan holds his hands up, matching my steps as I back away from them and furious tears begin to well in my eyes. "You didn't get justice, and that's on us. This is how we make it right."

"No, this is how you both become vigilantes!" I scoff out a disbelieving laugh. "How can you do this? How can you risk all of this, *this*?" I gesture between the three of us desperately. "After everything I did, after everything I gave up for you, to have you back to have you *here*-" I break off, scrubbing my face with the back of my hands furiously.

"What do you mean?" Dylan is right in front of me, hands gripping my upper arms and staring me down. "What do you mean, what you gave up?"

"The fucking plea bargain, Dylan." I push him away, my chest pounding and my hands shaking. "The plea bargain. The one you two agreed to. I had to agree to it too."

Levi and Dylan glance at each other, confusion furrowing their brows.

"What do you-"

I cut Dylan off with a wave of my hand. "You really think I wouldn't have come to see you? You really think all I wanted to send you was those stupid nothing letters? Neither of you ever stopped to think that maybe, just maybe, something else was going on?"

Dylan's face crumples, and he cradles my jaw in his hands. "Stella, what did they do?"

I've gone too far. I shouldn't have said anything. This is going to make it worse. This is going to fuel the vengeance I can feel simmering within them both just beneath the surface. But it's too late. A scalding hot tear runs down my cheek, and I shake my head, wishing I could rewind time and be back in bed with the both of them, love-drunk and warm, and miles away from the reality that's just going to tear us apart again.

"Gloria made me do it." I whisper, trying to shield Levi from more pain, from more distance from his family. "Her, and Oswald. They came to me and said if I cared about the two of you, I'd agree to it. I wasn't allowed to come and see you, and I had to let them read all my letters first. It wasn't until... Until I fought it, and got to you when your parole was announced, that I was able to... To..."

"But why?" Levi's voice is drenched with pain, and when I gaze over Dylan's shoulder at him, his face is dark and filled with grief, shoulders sagging. "Why would they do that?"

"Your grandfather said it would help us all forget." I want to run away, but instead I sag into Dylan's arms, and he holds me to his chest, hands threading into my hair. "As if I could ever forget. As if I could ever stop loving you."

"*Guera,* I'm so sorry." Dylan's lips caress my forehead, and Levi is at my back, fingers running down my bare arms.

"Baby girl, we're not going back to prison." Levi's voice is warm against my ear. "You hear me? We're not going back to prison. Ever."

"Levi, please."

"No." Levi presses me between them. "Baby girl, no matter what happens, we're not going back there."

"If you do this, I'll lose you again." I gesture to the phone. "And they're watching us. They're threatening some innocent woman and her fucking *child*. You have to stop. We have to warn her."

Dylan shakes his head, dark eyes gazing down at me. "No, that will place her in more danger. I'll have eyes on her, make sure she's safe, I promise."

"Dylan, you cannot burn the world down for this."

"Yes, we can." Levi's voice is heavy, and he strokes a hand down my arm. "And those men will pay."

I feel weak between them, weak and helpless and part of a plan that I once again have no control over, one I can only stand by and watch play out in front of me. My head falls against Dylan's chest, and I sigh heavily, trying not to cry, because that won't make anything better.

"I need you both to promise me you won't do anything stupid," I murmur, knowing full well my pleas are falling on unhearing ears.

"Everything's going to be just fine," Dylan assures me, kissing my forehead again and again.

His words don't make me feel any better.

Going back to work is the last thing I want to do.

I procrastinate way too long on getting dressed and ready, the house quiet since Dylan and Levi have already left for the garage early in the morning. We didn't talk any more about their plans for revenge, because there isn't any point.

And maybe, just maybe, deep down I want the men who hurt me to pay.

I hate admitting it to myself, struggling to meet my own eyes in the mirror as I apply make-up. But maybe some small part of me wishes the woman looking back at me could take that gun in hand herself. I don't think I could ever kill somebody, but the thought of getting revenge, hearing someone beg for their own life while I'm completely in control of it, someone who hurt me and left me with trauma so deep it almost drowned me for years…

My phone rings, jerking me from my thoughts. My heart leaps into my throat when I see it's the office, and I panic for a second that I mooched around for *way* too long, and am, in fact, now late for my first day back. I surely didn't lose track of time that badly?

My eyes flash to the time on the screen. It's only 8.10AM. I'm nowhere near late.

"Hello?" I say, pressing the phone to my ear. "This is Stella."

"Hi Stella, it's Clark here." My boss's voice is stern, and I instantly feel as though I'm in trouble. My boss calling me this early on a Monday? Something is definitely wrong.

"Hi there, you're calling early," I reply, trying to keep my voice bright and not let it waver.

"Yes, I'm sorry about that. But, um, listen… Stella, are you alright? Are you safe right now?"

I blink at my reflection. "I'm still at home, do you need me at the office right now?"

"No, that's the last thing we need right now."

"Sir, I don't understand what you're telling me."

"Stella, I need you to get somewhere safe right now, I've called the police and they're on the way to your house." He takes a deep breath, and panic sends a cold sweat prickling across my top lip. "The office received a threat this morning, an envelope and a phone call. Someone threatened to shoot everyone in the office if you entered the premises. There was a bullet with your name engraved on it in the envelope."

My knees threaten to buckle, and I catch myself on the counter. "Oh my god. Clark, I - I'm so sorry, is everyone safe?"

"They're fine, honey, I promise you, we're all fine." The fact that my stoic boss is calling me honey, his voice full of almost paternal concern, tells me just how fucking spooked he is. "I called the police immediately, and they're on their way to you, like I said. I just want you to be safe."

"OK, I'll - I'll let them in. I just… I don't know what could have caused this."

"This isn't your fault, I promise." Clark's voice wavers a little, and I can hear commotion in the background. "I need to go, but I'll be in touch. The office is closed for now, and until you talk to the police, I think you should just take some time off."

"Of course, I'll take unpaid leave, I'm so sorry for all this, sir." My palm is sweating, my phone slipping from my grasp so I have to readjust, my stomach threatening to empty the three cups of coffee I drank straight down the sink. "I'm so, so sorry."

"Don't apologize, please, just… Be safe. I need to go, the FBI just arrived. If you need anything, anything at all, don't hesitate. We're all here for you."

I hang up without saying another word, because I don't think I can. *The FBI*. Everything feels like it's careening out of control, and fast.

As quickly as I bring up Mallory's number, I swipe it away again. What if her phone's being monitored? Maybe Dylan and Levi are right, and I'll just put her in more danger if I call her. And since someone left my name on a bullet…

My coffee comes up. I wretch into the bathroom sink until I'm sweating and shaking.

I hadn't understood it when Oswald had put a plea bargain in front of me. I'd been confused by me having to agree to anything. I'd told him to go fuck himself. But then he'd told me there were people who had an interest in keeping me quiet, and only he could protect me. The powerful senator, who only had his grandson's best interests at heart.

I look at my pale reflection, and it all starts to make sense.

Gloria and Oswald have something to do with this, I'm sure of it. Whatever protection they were offering me, they've withdrawn it now.

I jump at the sound of my doorbell, inhaling deeply through my nose to calm myself.

The man and woman at the door are dressed in suits, their badges on display. Detectives. They nod through the glass, the woman smiling reassuringly. I open the door slowly, hoping I don't look like an absolute mess.

"Hi, Stella Langford?" The woman asks, and I nod slowly. "I'm Detective Hawkins, and this is my partner Detective Fallon."

"Hi, my boss said he'd sent you over."

"That's right. We have reason to believe a threat has been made against you, and wanted to ask you a few questions if that's alright?" Her reassuring smile is back.

"Sure." I step back, letting them into the house, and as I close the door, I see my neighbors standing on their front lawn, watching intently as these two cops walk into my house. The rumor mill is going to be running wild, I'm sure. They probably suspect the two tattooed men living with me are up to no good.

And they wouldn't be entirely wrong.

I clench my eyes shut, feeling more and more tangled with every passing second.

"Miss Langford?" Detective Fallon's voice sounds behind me. "Are you alright?"

I inhale sharply and push the door closed before turning to face them. "I'm fine, thank you." I gesture to the kitchen, and they walk in ahead of me. "Just a little shaken up, I guess."

"Completely understandable," Detective Hawkins says. "Is it alright if we sit down? You look a little pale."

I nod, wordlessly sitting down at the kitchen table as the detectives take a seat opposite me.

Detective Fallon clasps his hands on the table, eyeing me with concern. "Miss Langford, is there anyone who'd want to see you get hurt?"

I run a hand through my hair and try not to laugh. These detectives have no idea just how many people want to see me get hurt, how many people have tried to hurt me. But I can't tell them any of that. Instead, I just shake my head, trying to look surprised, innocent, shocked. All the expressions I've rehearsed over the years, pushing away everything that ever happened to me.

"Not that I can think of," I lie, shrugging. "I'm shocked. I don't have any enemies, not like that."

"Did your boss tell you what was sent to the office this morning?"

I nod, and watch as she pulls out her phone, and brings up a picture of a shotgun shell. 'Stella' is scratched into the side of it. I swallow hard, and meet the detective's eyes as I shake my head.

"I can't imagine why anyone would want to hurt me. I'm… just me."

"We understand your brother and his friend are living with you," Detective Hawkins says. "Is it possible that someone is trying to get to them through you?"

My stomach churns at the word *brother*, and it feels like one more crack in this already broken situation.

"No, they don't have any enemies." More lies. More and more fucking lies fracturing my life.

Detective Fallon lifts an eyebrow for a split second, betraying his disbelief. "No enemies at all? I find that hard to believe."

I fix him with a cold stare. "And why is that?"

Detective Hawkins quickly lifts her hands. "We're just trying to find an answer to all of this. A serious threat like this, we'll be looking into it heavily."

"Well, you do that then." I flick my hair over my shoulder,

not sure what else to say, what else they could want from me. "I don't know what you expect to find."

"All we want to find is an answer to all of this, so that you're safe, and whoever is making these threats can't follow through on them."

"I'll be fine, it's probably some kid pulling a prank." I get to my feet, screaming at myself internally to not waver for a second, to not wobble on my feet and betray just how fucking terrified I am right now. "Now, if you'll excuse me, I have some work to see to."

"Of course." Detective Hawkins pulls out a card as she rises out of her chair, and places it on the table. "This is my number, if anything else happens please call me immediately."

"We can have someone watch the house," Detective Fallon says. "If that would make you feel safer."

I shake my head and laugh lightly. "My housemates will keep me perfectly safe, don't worry about me. I'll hire private security if I feel like I need it."

The detectives exchange a glance, and my throat feels tight. I hate using the Rich Girl card, I hate feeling like I'm bragging about being wealthy. But I also want these fucking cops out of my house.

I walk past them to the door, opening it for them and giving them a wide smile as they pass me. "Have a great day!" I call out after them, before slamming the door shut and scurrying back to the kitchen and snatching up my phone.

I type out a frantic text to Dylan, before stopping myself. No. I can't tell them. They're already hell-bent on revenge, and this will just accelerate any plan they have. If I tell them someone is threatening me like this, they'll never let me leave the damn house again.

I slowly delete the text, letter by letter, retreating into yet more lies, more secrecy. As the message disappears completely, I wonder if my life will ever be anything but.

CHAPTER TWENTY

I'M NOT ENTIRELY sure why I'm here. Maybe I'm looking for assurance that what I'm about to do is justified. Maybe I just need to be sure.

And the target of my curiosity doesn't take long at all to appear.

Molly stumbles out onto the back porch of Stella's family home, the requisite glass of wine clasped in her hand. She's barefoot, her hair loose down her back, and at a distance it's almost possible to see the young Molly Hartmann, the woman Harold Langford fell for all those years ago. Her hair is darker than Stella's, graying at the temples now, and the alcohol has worn her skin to an unhealthy pallor.

But when she tips her face up to the dusky pink sky, there's a glimpse of her - not the alcoholic, not the neglectful mother. Just Molly. As she should have been if she wasn't an addict.

I wait at the tree line, knowing she'll find her way over here soon, and I don't have to wait long. Voices waft from the house, and Molly's head snaps to look over her shoulder, a sigh lifting her chest. She makes her away across the soft green lawn, coming closer and closer to where I stand in the shadows.

I don't speak until she's 10 feet from me, stepping out into the dimming light.

"Hello, Molly," I say quietly, and she jumps, spilling dark red drops of wine at her feet.

"Jesus, Dylan!" She brushes her hair from her face, eyes wide. "You scared the shit out of me."

"You remembered my name, Molly. Good for you."

She narrows her eyes, and takes a steadying gulp of wine. "I'm not completely useless, you know." She tilts her head, gaze straying to the house before returning to me. "What the hell are you doing out here? What do you want?"

"You know, I wasn't even sure what I wanted when I came up here," I reply, tucking my hands into my pockets. "But now, I think I know that what I really wanted was to have a little talk with you."

"A talk?" Molly raises an eyebrow. "Sure you don't want to drag me off into the woods and take off my head? Hiding out here in the dark like a serial killer?"

I laugh softly, shaking my head. "I don't have any interest in killing an old drunk like you, Molly." She winces slightly at my words, but I ignore it. I'm not here to make her feel better. I'm not going to assuage her guilt. "But I do want some answers."

"Answers?" She laughs into her wine glass, before draining the last of its contents. "Answers about what?"

"Did you know?"

Her eyes flash to mine, her mouth pulling into a firm line. She exhales heavily through her nose, and turns away from me to gaze up at the last of the sunset. Crickets sing in the woods around us, and she brushes a bare foot along the grass. It's an inappropriately idyllic scene for Molly Hartmann to admit to knowing her daughter was being abused. But admit it she will.

"You know, I always wanted to be a mother," she says softly, eyes fixed on the green ground beneath her. "You probably don't believe me, but I did. I'd play dollies all damn day as a girl, I carried my babies around with me everywhere. I'd cry if someone dropped them, if they weren't dressed for the weather, because they'd be cold." A small laugh bubbles from her lips, and she pressed the back of her hand to her mouth with a gasp. "Crazy, right? To want to be something so badly, and then completely fail at it."

"I'm not going to feel sorry for you, if that's what you want." I lean against the tree behind me, regarding the woman before me coolly. "Your failure to be a good mother was a choice."

She shakes her head, still looking at the ground. "You're right, and I don't expect you to pity me, Dylan. I don't deserve that." She nudges a twig with her toe, the wine glass clasped in her fingers. "I'd love to tell you I didn't know. That it blindsided me as much as it blindsided you." She lifts her eyes to mine, and gives me a weak smile. "But that would be a lie."

I grunt out a harsh laugh, and run a hand over my mouth. "Jesus Christ, Molly. How could you?"

"I didn't *know*." She emphasizes the last word with an outstretched hand, but that determination quickly drops from her face. "But there were signs. So many signs, and I ignored them all."

"Why?"

She shrugs, lifting the wine glass to her mouth, and quickly remembering it's empty. Without her emotional support wine in hand, she eyes me helplessly, and shrugs again.

"It all started innocently enough. You marry a man with hopes of being the president, you know he's going to use everything he can to make himself look good. I was considered a trophy wife once, can you imagine?" The laugh she lets out almost makes me feel sorry for her. "And then I gave him a picture perfect baby, I mean, I'm sure you've seen pictures of her. She was beautiful. And her eyes, that orange color, like an exotic cat." She sighs, her hand brushing over her stomach for a brief second, as though remembering a time when she could shield Stella from all the evils of the world. "Stella has been turning heads since she was born."

The words twist my stomach, just as much as Molly's tone. Her meaning is more than obvious.

"So, what was this innocent start?" I ask, crossing my arms over my chest, suddenly feeling a chill despite the warm evening.

Molly reaches out to stroke her fingers down the trunk of a tree, smiling softly. "Baby pictures make great Christmas cards, that's what Harold said. So we had a photographer take pictures of Stella in her red and white Christmas outfit, and sent those out. And Harold's office was flooded with thank you cards." Another sad sigh. "And then it was every holiday, pictures of Stella waving a flag for Fourth of July, dressed in a little camo dress for Memorial Day. Her chubby little hand held up in a salute." Molly runs a hand over her face, pushing a stray whisp of dark blonde hair back over her head. "I could never have guessed…" She trails off, looking at me with big, sad eyes.

"When did you start to suspect something was wrong?"

Her eyes become a little unfocused, and I'm unsure if I'm about to lose her. She sways on her feet, gazing up into the trees.

"Just after her third birthday."

The words threaten to knock me off my feet, and send a searing rage through my veins that's so violent, I have to hold my arms against my body to stop myself laying into the fucking tree behind me. *Her third birthday.*

"When she was still a little baby?" My tone threatens to reveal the maelstrom of emotions within me, but Molly doesn't seem to notice, still swaying and gazing up at the evening breeze snatching at the bright green leaves waving overhead.

"I asked him, isn't it weird to send out pictures of a little girl in her swimsuit? In her little star-spangled banner gym suit? I didn't like it, but he told me it was normal. That these men had kids themselves, and wouldn't think anything of it."

"Easy to objectify another man's kid, I guess."

Molly laughs bitterly, flexing her toes into the ground. "I was so stupid, Dylan. I was so, so stupid." She sighs, her gaze dropping back to the gardens around us. "That was about the time things went south between me and Harold, and the divorce happened pretty quick after that. I told him I wanted Stella, but he said I wasn't fit to be a mother. Which, well…" She trails off, leaning her shoulder against the tree next to me. "I failed her, Dylan, and nothing I say will make that right."

"No I guess not." I push away from the tree, the smell of alcohol rolling off her making my already churning stomach threaten to empty its contents all over the damn ground. "You know it didn't stop at pictures, right?"

I pray to see horror in her face. I hope and pray that she didn't know. *Please, you can't have known.* No mother could know that was happening to their little girl, and do nothing. *Please, please, tell me you didn't know.*

But Molly's sagging shoulders and shining eyes, the down-turned corners of her mouth, confirm my very worst fears.

"I'm so sorry, Dylan."

"Save it," I snap, my hands trembling against my body. "I don't need your fucking apologies." I take a deep breath, gritting my teeth, trying to get a handle on my fury. "When did she tell you?"

"When she had the abortion."

My heart fucking stops. *Abortion.* I try to kickstart my brain, to absorb what that word means, to make sure I actually understand it. *Stella had an abortion.*

"What abortion?" I ask, watching as Molly continues to sway on her unsteady legs. "Molly, when did Stella have an abortion?"

She rubs her forehead, closing her eyes. "Her first year of college. She was a mess when you both went inside. She slept with everyone, anyone who'd look at her. She was throwing it around like a little wh-"

I lunge at Molly, baring my teeth like I'm a fucking wild animal, and cage her in against the tree. Her eyes widen, and she hiccups loudly, covering her mouth with her hands.

"You call your daughter a whore and I will fucking end you, you disgusting old drunk. Now tell me what happened."

"I-I don't know, some guy she slept with got her pregnant, so she had an abortion." Molly sounds almost indignant, shaking her shoulders and looking up at me. "You think you were the only man for her? That she'd wait for you? I told her to forget about you and move on, but then she rang me crying, saying she'd had an abortion. I was berating her for it, telling her she should take responsibility for herself and not just erase her problems."

She jumps when a growl echoes through my chest, and her eyes widen a little.

"I was wrong to say that, I know that, OK? I… I was in shock. And then…" She sweeps a hand through the air. "Then it all just came out. She told me everything, what her father forced her to do, what she'd been subjected to."

"And then what?"

"She asked me to come home," Molly says, her hands jerking upwards in a little helpless gesture. "She was upset, said she wanted me there."

"And?" I lean closer into Molly's face, even though her breath is heavy with wine and liquor and makes me want to gag. "Did you come home to your daughter when she needed you?"

"No," she spits back, and instantly her face is overcome with shame. Her eyes drop from mine, her shoulders sagging. "No," she says again, softly this time, her voice full of defeat. "No, I did not. I told her I'd call her aunt, and have her come to her."

"And how'd that work out?"

Molly sighs, shrugging heavily and pushing me away. "What do you want from me, Dylan? I fucked up, OK? I was a terrible mother, and I fucked up. I let her down." She lifts a finger. "But I am here to tell you that Stella is no saint."

"You fucking disgust me." I turn away from her, sure I'm going to beat the shit out of this woman if I have to look at her any longer. "You all really just abandoned her, and then blamed her for the fallout."

"Stella is an adult now, she has to make her own choices."

I round on this stupid old woman, clutching her pathetic

empty wine glass, and she suppresses a shriek. "Have you seen what she's made of herself? Have you even fucking opened your eyes and seen how brilliant she is? How far has she come, and all on her own? Do you even see how amazing your own daughter is?"

Molly nods briefly, her face full of indignation. "Yes, of course."

"Good. Then know you had absolutely nothing to do with that."

Her face drops back into that expression of helpless shame, her brow furrowing, lifting the wine glass to her lips like it will somehow magically refill and she'll be able to drink away all her guilt.

"I'm sorry," she whispers.

I spit at her feet, and she recoils, taking a step back.

"Brudny." Filth. "Fuck you, Molly. I told you, I don't need your fucking apologies." I jab a finger in her direction. "You come near my girl with your poison again, and I will be a fucking problem for you, you understand?"

Molly blinks slowly at me, her mouth gaping. "Are you telling me to stay away from my own daughter?"

"You lost the privilege to be near her when you left her with a fucking predator. You are not welcome around her anymore. And I will enforce that. Trust me."

I don't wait for a response. I turn and storm through the forest, back to the edge of the property where my bike waits. My whole body is lit up with rage, the injustice of everything that happened to Stella shifting further and further into focus. Everyone let her down, not one person was there for her.

And that includes me.

While I was sitting in prison, raging over Stella's letters that meant nothing, not for one second thinking what she was going through, she was out hurting herself. I hate that the thought of another man getting her pregnant has me seeing red. As the engine of the bike roars underneath me, as the growing night whips past me and I weave my way through evening traffic to head back to her house, I loathe the insane part of me that cannot get that thought out of my head - another man came inside *my girl.* Another man got her pregnant.

This shouldn't matter, not after what I now know. Not after what Molly just admitted to me. But I'm an animal. I'm completely crazed by the time my phone pings, the tracker showing Iverson's location.

I pull off to the side of the road, getting a handle on my possessive rage, and send Levi a text.

Iverson's family is gone, he's on his way home.

The little dots circle as Levi types out his reply.

Stella just left to meet Zee. I'll see you soon.

I take a deep breath, steadying myself, focusing on the task ahead. I know Stella had a life after me, I know she had one since me, the years in between that didn't belong to me. But the thought of her lying in a hospital bed, crying and alone while going through something like that... Even if she wanted the abortion, even if that was entirely her choice, I wasn't *fucking there for her.*

Not now.

I tip my head back, gazing up at the darkening sky and the rising moon. I need to be ready for this.

I rev the engine of my bike, heading along the winding street, past the huge sprawling estates in the rich part of Bellford Heights. It's a Friday night, the houses all dark as their occupants escape to one of their weekend getaways, up in the mountains or out at the beach.

An alarm beeps, letting me know Iverson is only a mile from his house. I rev my engine, tearing down the road at a speed that is definitely not legal, until I spot Levi's blue Alfa parked by some trees.

I pull up beside him, and he gets out of his car, tucking the handgun Eric obtained for us into the waistband of his jeans.

"Fucker is almost home," I tell him.

"Good." He hands me a black mask, and rolls one down over his own face. "Let's go take our friend Stanley for a little trip out into the woods."

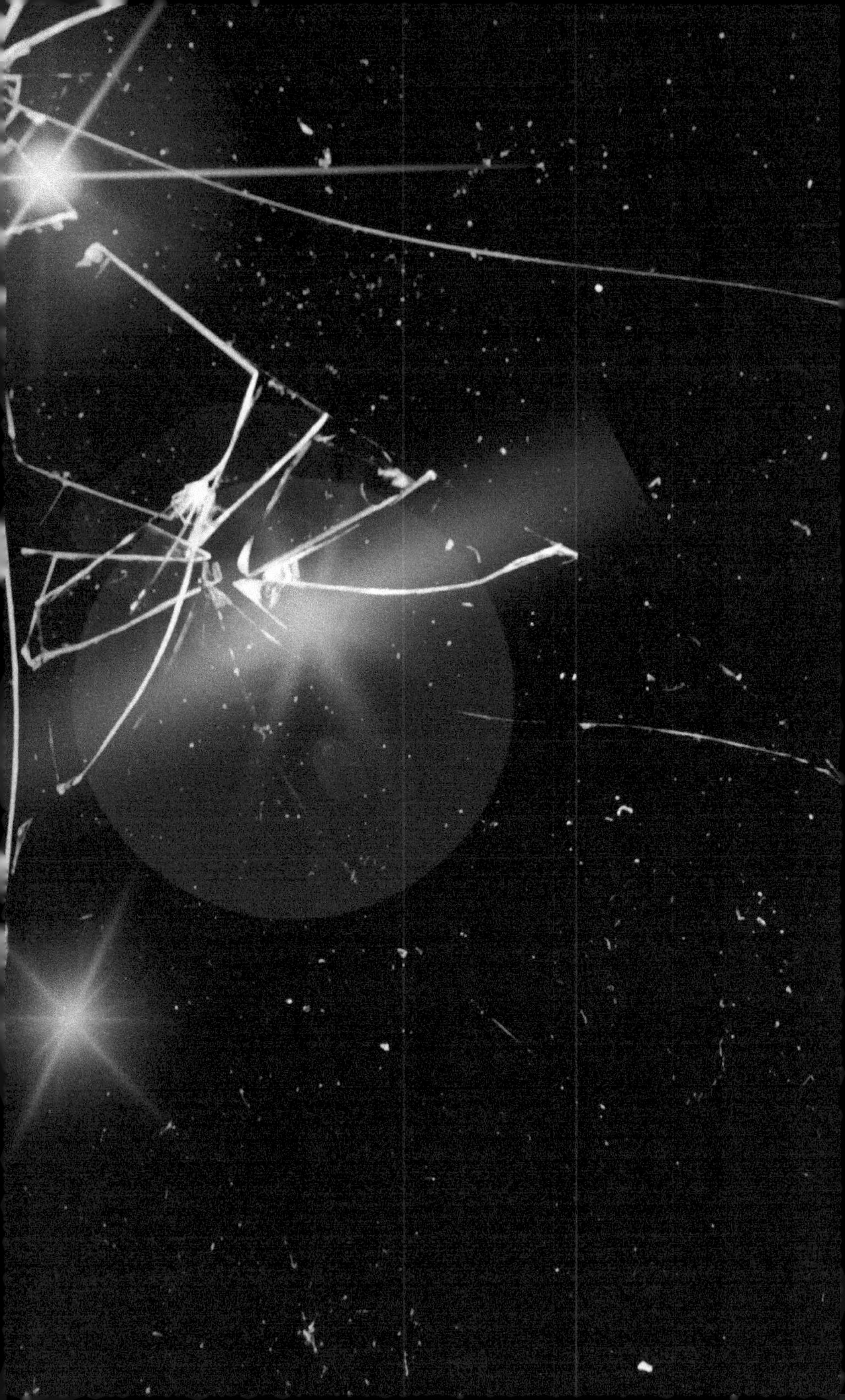

CHAPTER TWENTY-ONE

STANLEY IVERSON LOOKS as pathetic tied up naked in a barn as I thought he would. His bald head shines in the harsh fluorescent light, white hair scattered around the periphery of his scalp. His body is slack and worn, a round gut protruding over his thighs, and several liver spots adorning his arms and hands. Hair coils from his ears, and his fingernails are almost purple.

"He looks like shit," Dylan mutters, his voice muffled behind the mask covering his face.

"I'm surprised he survived the taser."

Dylan laughs cruelly, scooping water out of the trough beside us and dousing the inert man tied to the chair with it. Iverson startles, sputtering and writhing against his bonds.

"Morning, sunshine," Dylan drawls, brandishing the knife and flipping it in his hands. "We were just saying we're surprised you made it. That taser must have hurt like shit."

"Help!" Iverson throws the plea over his shoulder. "Help me!"

"Save it, old man." I flex my fists, itching to beat the shit out of this guy right now. "No one can hear you out here."

"Who the fuck are you?" Iverson's eyes are wild, flashing from me back to Dylan, taking in our features, memorizing our tattoos, as though he has a hope of telling the cops anything about the two masked men who attacked him in his driveway. "Who are you?" He demands again.

Dylan leans on his knees. "You look nervous, Stan. Do you have a reason to be nervous?"

"Who the fuck are you?" He strains and writhes, the rope biting into his withered, pale flesh. "Do you have any idea who I am?"

I cross my arms over my chest and laugh out loud. "We know exactly who you are, Stan."

"Then you know exactly how much shit you punks are getting yourselves into." He spits at our feet, eyes blazing with fury. "I'm going to have you both locked up in a pit so deep, not even the devil is going to be able to find you."

Dylan laughs, tossing the knife into the air and catching it by the hilt. "You got a lot of fire for an old man in your position."

"What do you want?" Spittle foams at the corner of Iverson's lips.

Dylan rolls his shoulders, tilting his covered head in my direction. "What do we want, *guapo*?"

I suck on my teeth, rubbing my chin through the mask. "Man, you know what I really want? I really want to know how that little girl in the pictures on your mantelpiece is, Stanley." I drop into a crouch in front of Iverson, whose eyes are widening. "She's real sweet. You must be proud of her. Your granddaughter?"

He bucks and roars, the chair shifting beneath him and the ropes binding him leaving red grazes behind. "You sick fuckers, if you touch her-"

"I don't touch little girls, Stan." I lean closer to him, close enough to smell the sweat and fear dripping from his pores. "I'm not like you."

Iverson freezes, he even stops breathing for a second. His eyes widen even further, his pupils blowing out. He starts to splutter, shaking his head, his eyes darting around the room as though his salvation could be found in the corners of this abandoned old barn.

"I-I don't know what you're talking about." His voice doesn't carry a hint of conviction, but is laced with fear. "You sick bastards leave my family alone."

Dylan nods slowly, turning the knife in his hand, over and over. "It's a horrid thought, isn't it? To think of someone taking your granddaughter, and hurting her. Must make you sick to your stomach."

"I mean, what kind of monster would do that?" I ask Iverson, holding my hands up. "Who would take a little girl, one who's been drugged, into a hotel room?"

Iverson's eyeballs are going to roll out of his skull. His head swivels from Dylan to me and back again, his mouth flapping uselessly. He begins to shake his head, sweat beading on his forehead.

"Imagine how scared she'd be," I say softly, retrieving the gun from my waistband, and holding it loosely in my hand. "Lying there helplessly, while a sick old man leered over her. While he told her he'd paid extra to violate her without a condom."

"Know what we're talking about yet?" Dylan's voice drips ice.

Iverson's head isn't so much shaking as it is quivering. Thick lines form in his forehead as his eyebrows lift. "I have no idea what you-"

His words are cut off with a howl as Dylan plunges the knife into Iverson's meaty thigh. Blood sprays across my chest, and I rise to my feet, backing away a few steps as Dylan yanks the knife from Iverson's flesh.

"Are we remembering yet?" Dylan's voice thunders over Iverson's screams and blubbered pleas. "I'm not hearing any recollection, maybe we need to do the other one to help you out, huh?"

"No, please, please," Iverson sobs, drool dripping from his lips. "Please, don't hurt me."

Dylan presses the flat of the bloody blade to Iverson's throat, forcing his head back. "Then maybe you should start talking, old man."

"I didn't want to hurt her," Iverson whimpers.

"Who?" I cock the gun and press it to his temple, and Iverson begins to cry in earnest. A pool forms in the dirt below his chair as the pathetic old man pisses himself. "You never wanted to hurt who, you disgusting old fuck? I want to hear you say her fucking name."

He's shaking so hard now, I'm sure his heart is about to give out. His blue lips quiver, his eyes clenched shut, sweat pouring down the back of his neck.

"S-Stella." He barely gets the name out. "Stella Langford."

Dylan's dark eyes burn into mine, and I can see the violent feathering of his jaw through the mask over his face.

"And what did you do to her, huh?" Dylan presses the blade harder against Iverson's chin, drawing a thin line of blood.

The man snaps for air, his chest sucking in hard against his ribs. "Her father said, he said, he said it was fine, he assured me. It was fine!"

Dylan slams the blade into Iverson's other leg, and his screams echo around us, out into the night. He waits until Iverson runs out of steam, nothing coming out of his mouth but pathetic, high-pitched gasps, his head slumped against his shoulder.

"I'm sorry," he whispers. "I never meant to hurt her."

"You raped her." I use the barrel of the gun to force his head back up. His eyes are glassy as they open slowly. "You lay on top of that girl, and you raped her."

"It wasn't just me," he says. "There were more. Please, don't kill me."

"Who else, huh? We want names." Dylan fires up the taser. "Otherwise, you're useless to us."

"Please don't kill me. Please. Please. Please." He starts to retch, as though he's going to throw up or fucking give up and die on us, so I move the gun away from him and take a step back.

"Names. Now." I tell him.

Iverson shakes his head desperately. "No, I don't know."

"Then what good are you?" Dylan points the taser at him, and Iverson shrieks.

"Gloria, she can tell you!"

Dylan's head snaps to look over at me, and suddenly my mask is suffocating me.

"What name did you just say?" I ask slowly, feeling the floor beneath my feet shift and tilt.

"Gloria," he says again.

"Gloria who?" Dylan asks slowly, and Iverson whimpers.

"Glor-Gloria Fenton," he murmurs, his head rocking back and forth against his shoulder. "She knew about everything, she planned it for god's sake. Had a goddamn red ledger, called it her date book. She and Valerie, they'd write all the dates down when they were planned." He blubbers and sobs, drool running down his chest and mingling with sweat. "We were promised that Stella wouldn't remember a thing. She was meant to be drugged, so she'd never know. Like she'd just gone to sleep, like it was nothing."

Nothing. Like it was nothing.

Dylan sucks in a sharp breath, practically glowing with rage. I can't breathe at all. My chest is heaving, almost as much as Iverson's is.

Like it was nothing.

I remember holding Stella on the floor of her shower as she screamed, as she cried and told me she couldn't tell me what had happened. I remember Dylan's face when he came to me and told me what Harold had been doing, everything Stella had been subjected to.

Like it was nothing.

I tear my mask off, suddenly caged in and suffocating, unable to stand it any more. I cast it to the ground, running a hand over my sweaty face. The second Iverson's eyes land on me, they light up with recognition.

"I know you! I know you!" Buoyed by hope, he tries to shuffle the chair towards me. "Please, don't kill me. I won't tell anyone, I'll just go home, and it'll be over."

"Gloria planned these dates?" I ask, disbelief pooling in my stomach, so heavy I'm sure I'm going to be sick.

Iverson nods enthusiastically. "It was her idea. She told Harold that pictures weren't good enough anymore. That we all wanted the real thing."

Dylan lunges at the man and smashes his fist into his cheek. Iverson topples over with a cry, landing flat on his back in the dirt. "You disgust me."

"I'm sorry," Iverson says. "I'm only a man, you know? A pretty girl like that-"

Dylan kicks him in the side before hauling him upright again. Blood trickles from Iverson's temple, and he starts to cry loudly again, as though all hope has left him now.

"I'm sorry, I'm sorry." His shoulders shake, tears running down his face, running tracks through the blood and dirt on his cheeks. "I'm so sorry."

"No you're not." Dylan looks over at me. "I think we give this fucker a taste of his own medicine." He lifts the mask to reveal his face, and he looks like Dylan, but not at the same time, his features twisted with cool and detached vengeance.

"Wh-what do you mean?" Iverson looks up at Dylan, fear etched into every line on his face. "What are you going to do to me?"

Dylan leans down and leers at him menacingly. "Stella told me what you did. Everything you did to her. You ever had someone fuck you in the ass when you didn't want it?"

Iverson writhes and cries. "You sick bastard, don't you touch me!"

"Oh not me, you sack of lard." Dylan traces the knife along Iverson's belly, and the man's eyes bug out. "I had something a little sharper in mind for you."

I'm still frozen with shock as Dylan kicks the chair to splinters, and kneels on Iverson's back. Iverson only screams until the knife is lodged between the pock-marked cheeks of his ass. Once the blade is firmly pushed inside him, he goes limp, cheek pressed to the ground, eyes wide. The little puffs of dust his breath kicks up tell me he's still alive. But just barely.

His body is shutting down. Dylan pulls the knife out, and plunges it in again. A weak sound comes from Iverson's throat, high-pitched and grating.

"Dylan," I say gently, and his dark eyes move to my face. "Kill him."

Dylan tilts his head, and pulls the blade from Iverson's body. He spins on his back, grabbing the tufts of hair at the base of the man's neck and yanking his head from the dust. The bloody blade flies across Iverson's throat, and there's a violent spray of blood across the ground.

Dylan drops his head to the ground, and the man's body twitches for half a minute as he bleeds out all over the dirt floor. And then it's over.

Dylan stands, his hands covered in blood, and he flings the knife to the ground. He pushes the mask from his forehead with the back of his hand, and turns to me with dark eyes filled with concern.

"Levi?" He takes a step towards me, lifting a hand then seeing all the blood and letting it drop. "Levi, it's alright. It's over."

I back away, shaking my head, holding up my hands. "She knew. She fucking knew." I meet his eyes, rage and revulsion turning to acid in my stomach. "My mother. My own fucking mother."

"I know."

"She helped… She helped them… Do that to Stella." My eyes

land on Iverson's bloody body, my hands flexing as I realize I'm still clutching the gun. "She helped them." I storm past Dylan, who stands back and lets me take out every emotion searing through my veins. I empty the clip into Iverson's inert frame, his body rocking back and forth in the dust with every steely impact. The trigger clicks and clicks when the gun is empty, and my eyes sting with furious tears, and the sweat that's running down my brow.

Then there's a warm hand on mine, curling around the gun and lowering it.

"It's over," Dylan murmurs again, taking the gun from me. "It's done, *guapo*."

I look into his eyes, and shake my head. "It's only just fucking begun."

His jaw feathers, and he takes my face in his hands. His skin is tacky from blood, but it doesn't disgust me. It's fucking appropriate, two monsters covered in blood, their kill dead on the ground at their feet.

"I'll do it," Dylan says softly, leaning his forehead against mine. "I don't want you to have to do this."

"I'll kill her." I brace my hands against the sides of his neck, not a tender touch like his, but one of urgency, of rage, the need to feel and fuck and hurt overwhelming. "My mother dies by my fucking hand."

"Levi-"

The kiss isn't soft and sweet, it's fire and fury, and it catches Dylan off guard for a split second, sending him stumbling long enough to have me forcing him against the edge of the rickety wooden bench behind him. It creaks in protest against his weight, his bloody hands against my chest, heavy with all the darkness we can't escape.

It's not me anymore, something else has taken over, like I'm standing in the corner of the room, watching this other man force Dylan to his knees. I watch as this other me takes out his cock and shoves it down Dylan's throat. A mouth that isn't mine curls into a cruel grin, a hand that doesn't belong to me braces against the back of Dylan's head.

"You sure look good choking on my cock, pretty boy." The laugh echoes around the barn, punctuated by the sounds of Dylan's frantic mouth, matched by moans that escape a throat that isn't mine.

I'm a monster.

I'm nothing but a dark shadow, dimming the light in every room. I'm fucking my best friend's mouth next to the bloody body of the rapist we just murdered.

I'm broken. I'm not normal.

And I don't fucking care.

I look down at Dylan, my blood-soaked god, on his knees for me, sucking me down and groaning as I hit the back of his throat over and over again. He's as monstrous as I am, the perfect match to the darkness inside me.

And Stella is the one thing that can save us from that brink, the anchor that stops our complete descent into hell.

I groan loudly as the pleasure courses down my spine, and I pump my release down Dylan's throat. I shudder as sweat beads and rolls down my bare chest, my head tipped back, my hand caressing Dylan's head.

He releases me with a soft pop, and traces kisses along my hips. "Better?"

Oh, that fucking voice. It's enough to have me needing him again.

"Much better." I gaze down at him, stroking my fingertips along his jaw. "Tell me you're mine, pretty boy."

"I'm yours." He rises to his feet, brushing a kiss against my lips. "For fucking eternity."

When he kisses me deeply, I can taste the salt of my release on his tongue.

But I can't get lost in him right now. Now we need to clean up the mess surrounding us.

Dylan opens the hatch to the crawl space, where the tub of

hydrofluoric acid is waiting to eat away Iverson's body. We roll his dead weight across the floor, and drop him into the tub beneath us, where he lands heavily with a wet thud. Dylan kicks the hatch shut, and walks to the trough, scrubbing off as much blood as he can.

"What do we tell Stella?" I ask.

Dylan shakes his head. "We head back home separately, you clean the gun and the knife at the shop. I'll go shower all this shit off in the garage. She'll never know. She's probably still out with Zee." He shakes the water from his hands, then turns to look at me. "We're going to kill them all. Every single name in that book."

"You really think my mother would keep something that would incriminate her?" Even as the words leave my mouth, I realize what I'm saying. Dylan cocks an eyebrow, and I know he's right. I huff out a cynical laugh. "Leverage. Of course she still has it."

"It's in that house," Dylan says with steely certainty. "And when we find it, we kill every single one of them."

"There's some powerful names on that list."

He shrugs, the snake tattoos on his shoulders shifting with the movement. "I don't care."

There's no point saying we could get ourselves killed doing this. Going after all the most powerful names in the country? It's a death sentence.

But we spent 10 years aching for revenge, and we're not giving up now.

Dylan pulls the mask down again, before throwing on his leather jacket and gloves to cover the rusty stain of blood on his skin. He straps up his helmet, and with a nod, guns his engine and takes off into the night.

I watch the moon hanging over the forest for a minute, before stowing the knife and the gun in the trunk, and heading back along the bumpy dirt road out of the forest. The summer night passes by my windows, the trees illuminated in the headlights.

I'm going to kill my own mother.

But first, I need to look her in the eye and hear her tell me she helped these men rape my step-sister. I need to hear those words from her mouth. I need to hear her admit to hurting the woman I love.

The night whips past me, the forest giving way to street lights, and a paved road.

I'm going to kill my own mother. And I feel nothing but unadulterated rage.

CHAPTER TWENTY-TWO

THE HOUSE IS dark as I roll my bike down the drive to the garage. Stella's car is in the drive, but she must be asleep. Thank god. I don't want her to see me like this, bloody and frenzied, the feeling of Levi's hands and cock still blazing through my body.

What kind of person gets turned on by death?

I catch my reflection in a dark window, and I know exactly what kind of person does. That sick fucker looking back at me right now.

The garage door closes with a soft thud, and I pull off my helmet and gloves, before flipping on the light switch.

"Rough night?"

The sweet voice sends a chill down my spine, and I turn to meet Stella's critical gaze. A tumbler of whiskey and ice dangles from her perfectly manicured hand, her hair pulled up on top of her head. She rises to her feet, her body encased in a floaty white slip dress.

She's an angel, the sun to my night.

She crosses the garage to stand in front of me, her eyes wandering over the mask still pulled down over my face. I don't know what to say, I don't know how to explain to her what just happened.

She tilts her head, raising an eyebrow as she takes another sip of whiskey. Her eyes drop to my hands, then she lifts her fingers to my jacket, pulling the zip down to expose my blood-splattered chest.

"You know, if you want to lie to me, you need to make sure Zee isn't going to blow your cover instantly." She runs a finger down my chest, over my tattoos, over the blood staining my skin. "They were very confused to hear that they'd insisted on dinner tonight when it had, in fact, been the two of you insisting they take me out." Her mouth quirks, and she sips her whiskey, the ice clinking against the crystal. "Needed me out of the way, huh?"

"Stella, I can explain."

"Was it Iverson?" Her voice doesn't waver as she asks, her eyes still fixed on my chest.

I swallow hard, and nod. "Yes." I lift my hand to remove the mask, but Stella stops me with a slow shake of her head.

"How did you kill him?" Her amber eyes move over the black mask. "I want to know what you did."

I shift on my feet, and shrug the jacket off my shoulders. "We took him from his house, from his driveway, and drove him out on my grandfather's property, out into the woods to an old barn." I take a deep breath, sweating under the mask. "I cut his throat."

Stella watches me with detached neutrality, not a hint of shock to be seen in her face. "Is that all?"

"Stella, I don't want to burden you with this."

Her hand traces up my chest, the touch of her fingers setting me on edge. I want to seize her in my arms and throw her down on the ground right now. I want to bury myself in her sweetness and promise her with my body and my soul that I won't stop until they're all dead, and all gone.

"I was burdened with all this for eleven years, Dylan." Her eyes meet mine again, burning into me. "Just tell me he suffered. Tell me he begged for mercy. Tell me he died in pain, afraid." The cool tone in her voice sends a jolt of lust into my stomach.

"He did." I lean over her, brushing my mouth against her skin through the fabric of the mask. "I killed him for you, *guera*. Just like he deserved."

She shivers, and leans against me. "Thank you." She exhales softly against me. "Where's Levi?"

"Cleaning up."

"Mmm." Her voice hums in her throat, and her arms wrap around my waist, drawing me close. She doesn't even care that I'm covered in blood and sweat, that I'm staining her pristine white dress. And suddenly I'm overcome with the need to stain every part of her, to sully all this perfection, this mask she's been forced to wear her whole life. I want to tear it down and smash it to pieces.

I pick her up, my hands moving up her thighs as they wrap around my waist. "Such a good girl," I purr against her neck. "Never wearing panties, so I can toy this pussy whenever I want."

Her head falls back on a moan, my fingers digging into her perfect ass as I carry her to the pool table. I lay her down, and she lies back, watching as I push her dress up around her hips. I hitch one of her legs up over my shoulder, pressing my face against her ankle, her scent wafting through the mask.

I gaze down at her, at perfect, accomplished Stella Langford, her white dress stained with the blood of the man who violated her, who took what wasn't his to take, who took what she wanted to give *me*. I meet her eyes and see the same desire that's clawing its way through my bloodstream right now, the same need and urgency.

My life, my heaven, laid out before me with her dress around her waist and her pussy on display for me, pink and swollen and aching to be fucked. It's so fucked up, and so wrong, and yet so incredibly right to take my cock in my blood-stained hand, running the blunt head through her slickness, hearing her pant and moan and beg.

"Fuck, I love it when you beg for me, *guera*," I say, pressing just the tip of me into her heat. "You have no idea what it does to me."

Her back bows, her arms flung above her head. "Please, Dylan, please. I need more."

"My needy girl." I push in a little further, gritting my teeth as I try to maintain my restraint, letting her take me in slowly. "You need *papi* to take care of this greedy pussy? Fill it up with my cum?"

She bites her lip and nods, her eyes squeezed shut.

I withdraw my cock and slap her pussy, her eyes flying open instantly, her hips bucking against the table as she cries out. I should remind her of her safe word, but the fluttering of her lashes and the moan that reverberates deep in her throat as I lower my mouth to her pussy and kiss her smooth skin are so fucking sweet.

"I need those eyes on me, *guera,*" I murmur against her skin. "Do you understand?"

"Yes, *papi*."

"Such a good girl." I straighten back up, lifting both her legs so her feet are locked behind my neck. "What's your safe word?"

Her lips curl into a smile as her eyes meet mine. "Martini." Her mouth opens in a short gasp as I press the tip of my cock inside her, and she's even hotter than she was a moment ago. Her legs tense against my body as I sink right into her.

"So tight for me like this," I murmur, raising a hand to the mask, but Stella shakes her head again.

"No, leave the mask on." Her eyes flash with shy desire. "I like it."

I growl against her leg, running a hand down to her smooth thigh as I thrust into her. It seems fitting, that this masked face was the last thing Iverson saw before he died like the pig that he was, and now I'm fucking the woman he violated. It's sick that I even think of it, it's a whole other level of fucked up, but the satisfaction I feel knowing his body is being eaten away by acid while Stella is here and alive, skin flushed and sweet, needy moans escaping her lips - it's twisted but it feels like justice. A small chunk of it, but one that means everything to me.

She's mine. She's ours.

Her eyes obediently stay on me, her lashes fluttering gently as I continue to slide in and out of her. She's so hot, getting wetter with every thrust of my cock. Her back arches, lifting her off the table and pressing her hips down so she's even tighter around me.

"Dylan," she mewls, her hand reaching out to find mine, guiding me down to her. I brace my other hand against the table, and she directs me to hold her throat. "Please."

My hand that extinguished a life not even an hour ago is now curled around the throat of the woman I love, eliciting nothing but pleasure. Her breaths come in short, sharp gasps, her pussy clamping down on me.

"Come for me, *guera*," I command. "Let me know this is mine."

Covered in sweat and blood, my perfect girl's mask fractures, and she claws her nails into my shoulders. She screams my name, her body shuddering, and I slam into her, my release meeting hers. My hand relaxes around her neck, and she sighs, her head turning to the side as her body slumps against the table.

I raise myself off her and finally peel off the mask, running a hand over my sweat-soaked skin. Stella smiles, her eyes closing gently, and I run a hand down her body.

"Do you know how beautiful you look right now?"

She giggles, pushing the hair from her face. "I bet I look like a dream."

"You do. You are a dream, my dream."

She turns her face to look up at me, and her expression shifts. "You're done now, right?"

I pull out of her gently, and my eyes drop from hers. "We should go inside."

She sits up suddenly, and seizes my face in her hands, gazing up at me desperately. "Dylan, I'm glad he's dead, but please, you can't go on some crazy hunt to try and find everyone who ever hurt me. How would you even find them?"

I consider for a moment not telling her, keeping what I know secret. But I'm sick of the secrecy. She's in this now. She always was, we were just too stupid to see it. I'm not keeping her in the dark anymore.

"Gloria has a diary."

Stella's brow furrows, and she shakes her head. "A what? I don't understand."

"Gloria knew. Gloria planned it. With your dad." I stroke her cheeks, the hair from her forehead. "She had a diary, and she wrote all those names down."

She shakes her head, her brow furrowing. "No, she- she… I mean, she wouldn't have kept that. I mean…"

"Yes, she would have." I kiss her forehead, wishing I could make this all stop, make all this darkness go away. "Gloria would have kept it for leverage. I promise you that." I cradle her head against my chest. "And now we're going to find them all."

"No!" She pushes me away with both hands, sending me stumbling just as the headlights of Levi's car light up the driveway.

I look over my shoulder to watch him enter the garage, his brows drawn together as he takes in the scene before him.

"I told her," I say, and Levi's jaw feathers.

"You shouldn't have."

"Yes, you fucking should have." Stella slides down off the pool table, raking her fingers through her hair. "Oh my god. Oh my fucking god."

Levi gestures to Stella with an open hand, regarding me with a thunderous expression. "You see this? This is why we can't have her in this."

"We're in this together," I counter. "I'm done lying to her, that got us nowhere but prison last time."

Levi exhales through gritted teeth, shaking his head. "It's not fucking lying, Dylan, it's protecting her."

"Protecting me?" Stella stands beside me with her fists balled at her sides. "I am so tired of you using that as an excuse."

"I cannot have you getting hurt again, Stella." Levi takes a step closer to her, and Stella waves him off.

"Stop treating me like a victim, Levi. Stop acting like I'm some pure delicate flower. I'm *not*."

"I do not treat you like a victim." Levi moves closer to her, and takes her hand. "Baby girl, it's not like that. But you've been through enough, I don't want you going through more."

"You don't get it." Stella yanks her hand away. "You just don't fucking get it, Levi. You are putting me through more by doing all this." She gestures to the mask on the ground. "I told you I didn't want you doing it, and you did it anyway. So now I know, and I'm in it, OK? That was your decision. You caused this, both of you."

"You think I wanted this?" Levi's face twists between helplessness and anger. "You think any of us wanted this fucking life? Do you know what it was like being in prison?"

"I never asked you to do any of this!"

"But we did it because we're fucking animals!" Levi leans over her, his eyes dark and deep and filled with pain. "You want to love us? You want to be with us? Then this is what you get. You get two damaged and broken fucked up psychos who'd murder anyone who breathed near you." He grabs her hand, and she struggles, but he doesn't let her go as he presses her palm to his chest. "Here, right in here. You told me you'd never be afraid of what was in here. You told me you'd never be afraid of *me*. Is that still true?"

Stella twists her arm, trying to fight Levi's grasp. "Stop it!"

Levi yanks her closer. "Well? Do I scare you? Are you afraid of me?"

"No!"

"Do you love me for everything I am, even if it's wrong?"

Stella gasps, pushing against him with her free hand, casting a glance over her shoulder at me. "I - I don't..."

Levi grabs her jaw to force her to look at him, staring her down. "Do you love me?"

Stella nods. "Yes."

"Are you scared of me?"

"N-no."

Levi cocks an eyebrow. "No?"

"No. Never. I just... I don't want to lose you."

Levi strokes her hair, pressing her against him. "You won't, baby girl. Ever. I swear it. But this is who I am, who we are. And we're not going to stop until they're all dead." He smothers Stella's protests with his mouth, kissing her ferociously, a mark of ownership. Stella stops fighting him, and wraps her arms around his neck.

"I will never hurt you, Stella," he murmurs against her cheek, running a hand down her back. "Never. Not you."

"I know." She gazes up at him, steely determination etched into her face. "But you have to stop acting like I'm some pure little angel. I'm not."

Levi's eyes move to me, taking me in, before looking down at Stella. "Did it turn you on, knowing we'd killed for you?"

Stella's throat bobs as she swallows, and she nods slowly. "Yes. I liked it."

"So fucking twisted." He buries his face in the crook of her neck, and her body arches against him, her hands moving under his shirt. "I love it."

I leave them alone in the garage, entranced and entwined with each other, to have their moment just like Stella and I did. Desire twists my insides as I head to the bathroom and wash off all the blood, all the filth of what I just did. I know this won't be the last time I return home to Stella, covered in darkness and sin, trying to convince myself I was smart enough not to get caught.

I collapse into bed, and after a while, I hear Stella and Levi's footsteps on the stairs. They head for the shower, the falling of the water punctuated by their cries and moans. They don't come and join me, instead heading for Stella's room, where the sounds of their fucking continue, until my eyes get heavy and I fall asleep.

Iverson is dead.

And Gloria's fucking next.

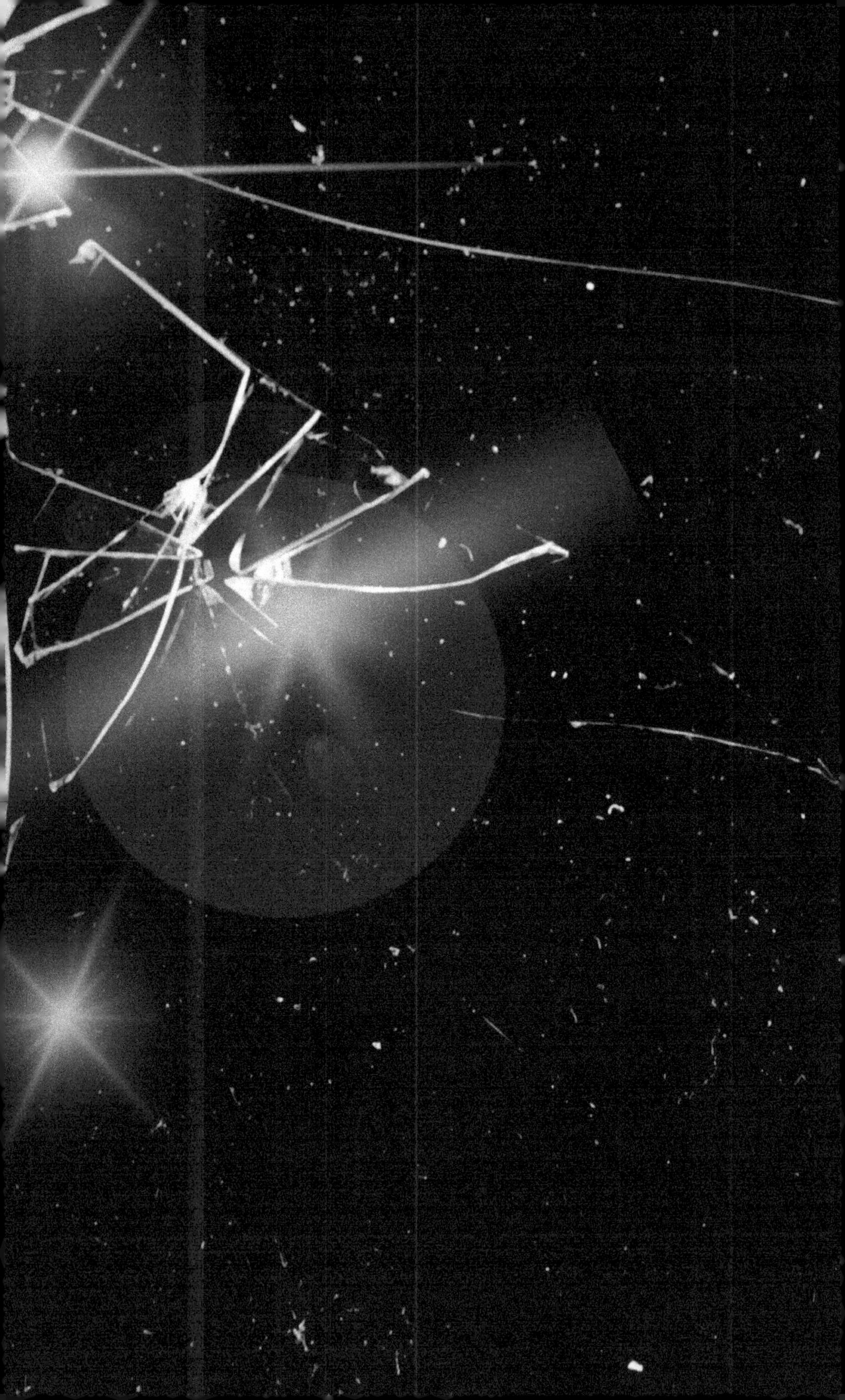

CHAPTER TWENTY-THREE

"YOU'VE MANAGED to find gainful employment?" My parole officer, a man with round glasses and thinning grey hair called Dave, looks over the form in front of him, his voice betraying just how bored he is by his job.

"Sure have." I stretch my legs out in front of me, hot sun spilling in through the window of the stifling office. "I'm my own boss, as a matter of fact. I bought a garage."

Dave's eyes widen as he pulls a face at the form. "How great for you."

"Thanks." I suppress a laugh. This guy has no time for a rich kid like me.

"And you're keeping out of trouble?" He looks at me over the rims of his round glasses.

I smirk and shrug. "Sure am." *Except for that guy I helped murder a few weeks ago, I'm clean as a fucking whistle.*

Dave holds my gaze for a few beats, before looking back down at his form with a sigh. "I don't think we have anything else to discuss. Unless you need access to some programs or something."

"I'm good, man. But thanks."

"No problem." Dave could not be any less interested if he

tried. He looks up at me with a wan smile. "That's all for today then."

"Great, thanks for your time." I get to my feet, and my phone buzzes in my pocket as I leave Dave's cramped office and head down the dilapidated hallway of the parole office. I pull my phone out to see a message from Dylan.

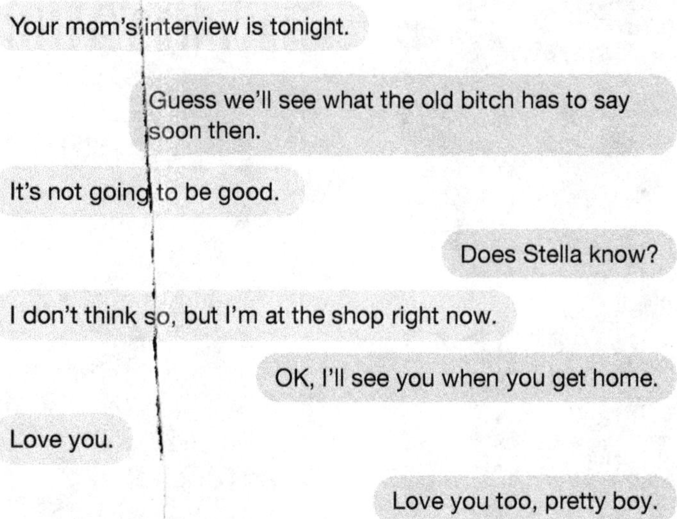

I'd gone back and forth on when to kill my mother. The thought itself didn't bother me - she had to die for what she did. What bothered me was the When. I'd wanted to run out into the night and do it immediately after Iverson had sputtered out his confession. But Dylan had insisted we needed to bide our time, or it would look too suspicious.

Iverson's disappearance had made headlines, and his family were on social media daily, begging for someone to give them some idea on what had happened to their beloved father and grandfather. That is, until his office was searched and child porn was found on his computer. Then they'd gone real, *real* quiet.

No one would miss him.

But my mother... That was a whole other matter.

My phone buzzes again, and I can't help but break into a grin when I see it's a photo of Stella, naked in the hot tub, her breasts wet and glistening and on display for me.

I'm so lonely.

You better be like that when I get home.

Better hurry, I might have to get myself off soon.

Don't you fucking dare touch that pussy.

Another picture pops up, and I grit my teeth at the sight of Stella's fingers between the lips of her cunt. *Fucking tease.*

These past few weeks have been like heaven. While Dylan and I are busy at the garage most days, the time we have at home together, the three of us, I never thought life could be this good. And it's not just the fucking. I mean, OK, the fucking is spectacular. I'm still amazed that we've all fallen into this easy rhythm with each other, no jealousy, no animosity. Sometimes we're all together, sometimes it's just two of us.

I love it all.

I dare to imagine a future together, a life where we have everything we ever wanted.

I dare to imagine being a father for the first time in my life. And I wouldn't even care if it was me or Dylan who got Stella pregnant. It would be *our* baby. The thought heals a small part of me, the idea of surrounding a child with all this love.

But I'm not brave enough to bring that up yet, and I honestly just want to savor this time alone with the two of them.

Even with demons chasing us down every day.

I'm not going to think about my mother and her interview today though. That bitch's grave is already dug out and waiting. I'm going to pick my moment. And she'll suffer for everything she did.

But right now, I want to get home to my girl. Those pictures have driven me to the fucking brink. The whole drive home from downtown to Stella's pretty tree-lined street is torture. When I pull up, I head straight for the back porch, to find her still in the hot tub, waiting for me.

Her eyes light up as I appear and start stripping off.

"You took forever," she purrs, giggling as I get in and gather her in my arms.

"It took forever to get here, thinking of this pussy at home, just waiting for me." I lift her on to the edge of the tub, slippery and naked, and run my cock through the slickness between her thighs. "You got yourself off, didn't you?"

A smile curves her lips. "I just wanted to be ready for you."

We both look down to watch me sink into her slowly, and she gasps, pressing her forehead against my cheek.

"Oh god," she murmurs. She moans as I fill her completely, her head falling back, her fingers digging into my shoulders. "The neighbors might see."

"I don't fucking care." I settle back into the water with her on my lap, and she rides me slowly, her perfect tits in my face. "Fuck, baby girl, this pussy is going to drive me insane."

"Oh my god, you feel so good." She hisses as I grab her hair, angling her head back so I can suck on the delicate skin of her throat. Her cunt clenches around my cock, and I groan against her skin.

"What the hell is this?" My mother's voice rings across the yard, and Stella scrambles off me immediately.

I turn to look over the edge of the tub, to see my mother's wide eyes and gaping mouth as she stands in the drive.

"What is going on here?" My mother demands, clutching her purse in shaking hands, moving closer to the porch.

"Why are you here?" Stella clambers out of the hot tub and throws on a blue robe, pushing her hair from her face. "You're not welcome here, get out of my yard."

My mother fixes her with a venomous gaze as she steps up onto the decking. "I'd appreciate you being quiet while I talk to my *son*."

I rise out of the water, my hard cock very much on display, and my mother's face goes beet red as she averts her eyes. "Why are you here, Mother?"

"For god's sake, Levi, put some clothes on," she snaps, her eyes fixed on the ground. "Have some dignity."

"Dignity? Interesting choice of word." I get out of the tub and wrap a towel around my waist. "Does dignity bring you here today?"

She fixes her furious eyes on me, shaking her head. "How could you? How could you sleep with… With *her*? It's disgusting! It's obscene!"

"Well, you'd know all about obscenity, wouldn't you?" I move to Stella's side and kiss her temple. "Go inside, baby girl."

Stella's gaze snaps up to meet my eyes, and she shakes her head. "I don't want her here."

"I know, let me take care of it." I kiss her lips gently, and my mother makes a choking sound. "Go inside, and wait for me there."

Stella's gaze slips from mine over to my mother, and her eyes darken. Her lips twitch, but she doesn't say anything, heading into the house and slamming the French door behind her so hard that the windows shake.

My mother is still glaring at me, her lips a tight white line. "Explain yourself."

"Explain what?" I pick up my jeans and retrieve my cigarettes from the pocket, lighting one for myself and exhaling a plume of smoke in my mother's direction. "What are you even doing here?"

"I hadn't heard from you in weeks, you haven't answered any of my calls. I assumed you were still living here."

"Congratulations, you assumed correctly."

She exhales heavily through her nose. "I stopped by the garage and your charming Mexican friend told me in no uncertain terms that I was not welcome."

I make a mental note to give Dylan a blowjob tonight. "He has a fucking name, Mother. And he'd be right."

"And then I come here and find you… You doing… *that* with your step-sister. And in broad daylight?" She gestures at the neighboring houses with a diamond-encrusted hand. "You want everyone to know you're committing incest?"

"It's hardly incest, mother." I take a long drag on the cigarette, eyeing her furious expression. "Besides, there are worse things you can do than commit incest."

My mother crosses her arms over her chest, tapping her foot against the decking. "And what would those be?"

"I don't know." I flick the ash from my cigarette. "Like, imagine if you helped someone commit a crime? You know, imagine someone made it possible for a person to do that, to hurt an innocent person?" When I meet her gaze, I see a flicker of uncertainty. "I mean, that'd make someone a piece of shit, right? *That* would be really bad."

Her face settles back into an expression of disgust, and she gives her shoulders a shake. "Don't try and change the subject. I forbid this, Levi. I will never accept this relationship."

"Well, since I don't answer to you, I guess all I can say is too fucking bad." I suck on my cigarette with a chuckle. "I'm fucking Dylan, too, if that makes you feel any better."

My mother's eyes almost roll straight out of her skull. "That's not funny."

"What's wrong? I thought you were all about progress." I laugh at her expression as I take another drag of my cigarette, sidling towards her. "Imagine what it could do for your image, telling everyone you have a bisexual son in a polyamorous relationship? What a fucking campaign slogan for the next governor."

My mother slaps me hard. "You're disgusting."

I rub my jaw, laughing again. "Not so progressive after all, I guess."

"You will pack up your things and move out of this house,

immediately," my mother snaps, jabbing her finger in my face. "I will not accept any son of mine living in this sort of depravity. And if you refuse, I'll make sure your grandfather makes Stella and Dylan's lives extremely difficult."

I lunge at her, grabbing a hold of the strap of her bag that's slung over her shoulder. Her expression is one of a startled deer, her eyes wide and filled with fear.

"I'm telling you this very plainly, Gloria." I ignore the flinch at the use of her name. "You are not coming into this house and threatening the people I love."

"Let go of me."

"You think you can do what you like, and no one's ever going to know?" I lower my face, staring into the cold and heartless face of the woman who gave birth to me. "There are consequences, Mother. And don't think for one fucking second you can outrun them."

My mother jerks out of my grasp, the strap of her purse giving way with a loud snap. She clutches it to her chest, smoothing down those imaginary misplaced hairs, wobbling on her Louboutins.

"Do not threaten me, Levi. You may be my son, but I won't protect you if you continue to be disloyal."

"Fuck your loyalty." I flick the cigarette in her direction, and she stumbles backwards before the glowing stub can singe her overpriced skirt suit. "Fuck you, and the family, and your loyalty. Now get the fuck off Stella's property."

"You'll regret this," she spits at me, before turning on her heel and hurrying down the drive to the waiting town car.

"Don't fucking come back!" I bellow after her. I exhale heavily as her car pulls away, rolling my head on my shoulders. My mother threatening the two people I love, that just won't fucking fly. If I wasn't going to kill her before, I sure as fuck would be now.

And my grandfather might need taking care of, too.

In prison, someone had told me how he'd killed his grandmother for her life insurance money. An air shot, between her toes. Everyone thought it was a heart attack. He'd almost gotten away with it. Until he'd gotten high as balls and told their cousin all about it, the day before the check was meant to clear. On video tape.

Fucking idiot.

But it does give me an idea on what good old Oswald will have happen to him while he has his nightly brandy in his study.

I head into the house to find Stella in the living room, legs curled up under herself, staring out the window.

"Is she gone?"

I cross the room and sit beside her on the window seat. "She's gone, and she's not coming back."

Stella laughs bitterly, twirling a strand of hair around her finger. "That's what you think." She looks over at me. "Her interview is tonight, did you know?"

"Yeah, Dylan told me."

"Yeah." Her gaze wanders back out the window, fixed on the trees swaying gently in the sunshine. "Is it weak of me to say I'm scared of what she's going to say?"

"No." I reach across and take her hand, stroking her fingers with mine. "My mother's like a fucking landmine, you never know where to step."

"That's for damn sure. Guess we all lucked out in the mothering department." Her hand curls around mine. "Except Dylan. His mom sounds like she was great."

"She was."

"It's why I never wanted to have kids. What the fuck would I know about being a good mother?"

"I think you'd be a great mother."

Her eyes meet mine, and her shoulders slump a little. "You want kids, don't you?"

I sigh and shrug, looking down at our hands. "It's… I don't know. It's complicated. But I guess yeah, it's something I could see myself doing. Especially… Now. I mean, can you imagine being a kid and having *three* parents around you, who adore you? Who just... love you? Imagine being surrounded by all that."

When I look back up at Stella, her eyes are shining with tears.

"And what if it wasn't yours?" She asks quietly.

I shuffle closer to her, so our legs are touching and her warmth seeps against my skin. "That baby would be *ours*."

Her eyes flutter closed, and I lean in to brush a kiss against one of her eyelids. A single tear runs down her cheek, and I kiss it away.

"We don't have to do anything you don't want to do, baby girl." I tip her head back, and she opens her eyes to gaze into mine. "A life with you and Dylan, that's enough for me, *more* than enough. But never let *them* stop you from living. Never let their decisions make you think you're anything like them. You're not."

"Do you believe Iverson?" She shifts closer to me, and I lean back so she can lie against me between my legs. "I mean, what if he was bluffing?"

"A man in his position wouldn't be bluffing, trust me."

Her big amber eyes gaze up at me, and she winces a little. "I'm afraid to ask."

"Don't. You don't need to know."

She lays her head back against my chest with a sigh. "You know, I've always wondered what it would be like to kill someone. To have that power in your hands, to take a life." She laughs softly, stroking my bare skin with her fingertips. "It's twisted, I know that, but... I've thought about it, more times than I'd like to admit. I've... I've wondered what went through my father's head, when..." She trails off, and it hangs in the air between us.

"It's fucked up." I run a hand over her hair, threading my fingers through it and holding her close to me. "It's a power trip. One that breaks a part of you."

I feel her flinch, but she doesn't move away from me.

"When... When your father died," I go on slowly, "he was

angry. He didn't show an ounce of remorse. Not even a bit. Not even when Dylan had that gun pointed in his face and was screaming for him to admit what a bastard he was. He was just… angry. That he'd lost control. That now two teenagers were deciding his fate."

"He hated Dylan."

"I know. He hated both of us."

Stella sits up and tilts her head, her brows knitting together. "What was the last thing he said?"

I don't want to tell her this. I don't want to repeat those words, because it was fucked up in the worst way. The words that had Dylan's eyes widen and his jaw clench before he pulled that trigger and blew Harold Langford's brains out. *If you think she'll ever stop being a whore, you're wrong.*

So I lie.

"He kept saying we were bastards, and that we'd pay." The lie sits heavy in my mouth, lie after lie about what happened that night. But Stella doesn't need to know.

She scoffs, gazing back out the window. "And pay you did."

"I'm sorry."

She looks back at me with a pained expression. "If your mother knew, if she planned it…"

"She did. I'm sure she did. Iverson wasn't lying. He was desperate, thought we'd show him mercy in exchange for information. There's no doubt in my mind that he knew."

"You're going to kill her." It's not a question. Stella's eyes drop to her lap. "I know you're going to. I know it."

I reach across and take her hand, pulling her closer to me again, desperate to feel her warmth and not lose her in this darkness. "Hey, listen to me, we're going to make this right."

"Does this all make it right, though?" She shakes her head, urgency filling her eyes. "Levi, we could just go. The three of us, just leave. Go somewhere, and forget about all of this."

"You think those bullets in the letterboxes are going to stop if we just leave?"

Her eyes widen. "How do you know about that?"

"I find out what I need to in order to keep you safe."

"This is insane, Levi." She jerks her hand out of my grasp. "This isn't right. You have to stop."

I set my jaw, shaking my head. "Not gonna happen."

"You think they'll stop if you go around killing everyone?" She gets to her feet, bracing her fingers against her temples. "These people are powerful. You think they're not going to know it's you and Dylan? You think they won't take it out on me when they can?"

I rise and yank her against me. "Do not say that. I will not let them hurt you."

"You can't watch me every second of every day." She reaches up and strokes my cheek. "Levi, you just talked about having a family. Imagine that? Imagine them finding out where we live? Where our kids go to school? Imagine them seeing our daughter at the park?" Fresh tears well in her eyes, and my stomach drops at the very thought of a little girl with Stella's big amber eyes and Dylan's brown skin, *our daughter*, being hurt like Stella was.

"I'm not going to let that happen. We're sending a message to these people." I clutch her face in my hands. "They will know not to fuck with us. They will know that. And they will never hurt you, or Dylan, or me, or anyone else we care about. And if they do, I will rain fucking hell down on them."

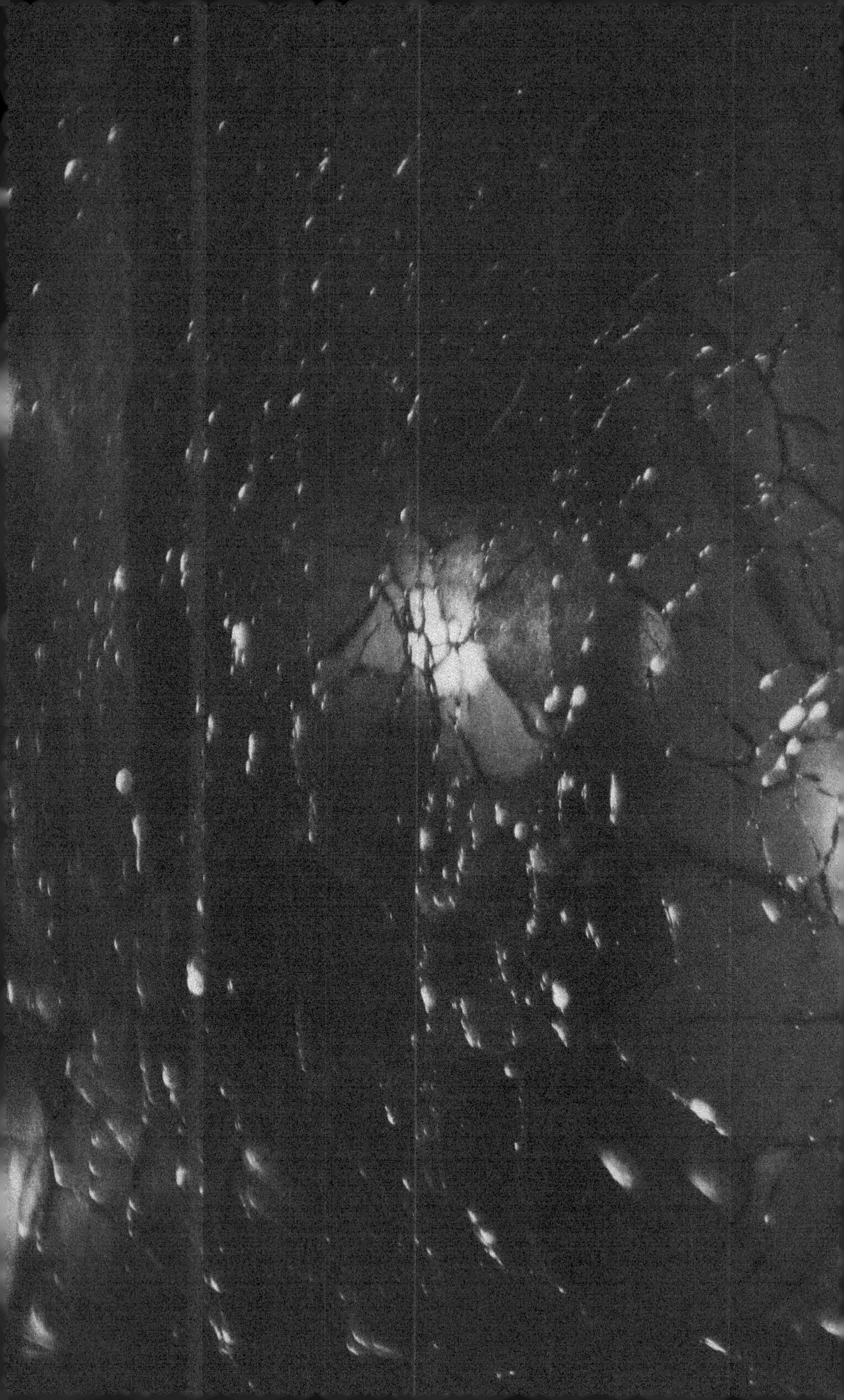

STELLA

CHAPTER TWENTY-FOUR

THE BOOKSTORE IS BUSIER than usual, and the banter of the groups around me does nothing to soothe the headache that I've been nursing all morning. Dylan and Levi left for the garage just after dawn, and my leave has continued on now for over a month.

I'm bored out of my brain, and have spent way too much time wandering around downtown Bellford Heights buying books and drinking enough coffee to give me the jitters.

I miss my fucking job.

The FBI gave the office the all-clear to reopen a week after the threat had been called in. Clark kindly told me that I should stay away a little longer, and so now I find myself with an armful of books, a thumping headache and a cramping belly because my stupid period is due. And Gloria Fenton-Langford's interview airs this weekend.

Happy fucking Thursday to me.

I round the towering shelves to head to the counter, and almost drop my books.

Oswald Perlman is standing by the door, dressed in the three piece suit he seems to live in. The chain of a pocket watch dangles from his waistcoat, and he looks so out of place in the bright and cheery bookstore, looming in the doorway like a bad dream.

His thin lips lift into a smile as I edge closer to him.

"Hello, dear." He gestures to the counter. "I told them to charge whatever you buy to me. I'm sure I've missed enough birthdays to owe you a gift by now."

"I don't need a gift from you."

The young woman at the register looks from Oswald to me and back again. "Is everything alright here?"

Oswald smiles at her sweetly, running a hand over his thinning white hair. "It certainly is. My granddaughter and I haven't seen each other in far too long, I think she's just surprised."

"That's one way of putting it." I place the books on the counter and try to give the young woman a reassuring smile. "I'm sorry, I changed my mind, can I leave these with you?"

"Uh, sure I guess, I mean-"

"Thanks!" I stride past Oswald and out onto the sunny street, desperate to get as much distance between me and him as I can.

"Stella, could you give me a moment?"

How the fuck is an old man this fast?

"No, I can't." I snap over my shoulder, heading for my car.

"This will only take a few minutes."

"I don't c-" I stop short when I see a man in a suit standing by my car, dark sunglasses on, and the wire of an earpiece snaking down his neck into the back of his crisp white shirt. I turn to face Oswald, who still has that indulgent smile on his face. I jerk my head in the direction of my car. "Your employee I suppose?"

"Yes, he is as a matter of fact. Just looking out for your safety."

"Sure you are." I cross my arms over my chest. "I'm not interested in talking to you."

"Stella, I am not here to cause you harm." He ambles closer, infuriatingly calm, his hands pressed into his pockets. "I am here simply as a father, concerned for his daughter. And for his granddaughter."

"I am not your granddaughter."

Oswald sighs, bouncing on the balls of his feet as he gazes up at the swaying trees. "You know, I always liked you. You were a good kid. I never liked your father much, but then again, my daughter has always had extremely questionable taste in men." He sucks on his teeth and shakes his head. "*Levi*. What a name to pick for your kid. I told Gloria that biker was no good. Posing as a poor man when he was rolling in money, trying to be *cool.*" He jerks his fingers to sign out quotation marks, and scoffs. "And then he goes and gets himself killed on that stupid bike, and leaves my daughter a widow, and my grandson fatherless."

"I don't care about any of this. Leave me alone." I turn to head to my car, and I swear to god I'll punch this idiot standing by it square in the face if I need to.

"I know you're in love with my grandson."

I stop short, and take a deep breath. When I turn back, Oswald is still looking up into the bright green foliage, squinting lightly in the sunlight.

"And because you were always a good kid, I'd like to look out for you in a way I should have looked out for my own daughter."

"I don't need you to look out for me."

"Oh, I think you do." His gaze drops from the trees to land back on me, and he ambles closer, totally relaxed, in no hurry at all, as though he's completely assured that I'll stay right here and listen to what he has to say. "The fact is, Stella, I can make all of this go away. Everything. It will all stop."

"What do you mean?" Dread snakes its way up my throat.

He holds out an open hand in the direction of the French cafe we're standing in front of. "Please, come and join me. Let me buy you a coffee." His demeanor is more terrifying than if he was outright menacing. This portly old man smiling at me, eyes crinkling, only the beard missing to transform him into a friendly Santa Claus - it's enough to have ice running down my neck and goosebumps breaking out over my arms.

Every instinct in me screams *danger, danger* as I take leaden footsteps into the cafe.

It's busy inside as well, wait staff rushing around and serving *croque monsieur* and cafe au lait to the chatting patrons. Oswald and I take a seat at the back, and I'm sitting ramrod straight, eyeing him uncertainly as he leans back in his chair and gives an order I don't even hear to the smiling waitress.

Why am I here? I should run. I should get out of this cafe and run home and start packing my shit. I should insist that Levi, Dylan and I get the fuck out of this town right now.

Instead, I stay where I am, staring at the old man who takes out his phone, then pats his pockets looking for his glasses. He withdraws them from the pocket of his jacket, and places them on his nose, looking down at his phone and swiping his fingers across the screen.

"Technology is truly incredible," he says with a dry laugh. "My god, when I remember how excited my brothers and I were when we got a phone installed in the house. We used to sit on the floor and just stare at it. And if it rang, we all ran like it was going to eat us alive." He eyes me over the rims of his glasses. "Your generation has no idea, growing up with all this stuff at your fingertips."

"Lucky us." My knuckles are probably white under the table, digging into my purse in my lap, but I refuse to let him see how nervous I am. "So, what did you want to talk to me about?"

"Ah, yes." He puts his phone down on the table and leans back in his chair. "My grandson. My daughter informs me you and he are, well… To put it delicately, Gloria says she caught the two of you in a compromising position?"

"You could say that." I raise my eyebrows at him. "That's what you wanted to talk about? You want details or something?"

Oswald's lips twitch into a smirk. "You don't mince words, do you?"

"No point mincing anything besides my opponent, first rule of law school."

He raises an eyebrow. "You see me as an opponent, Stella?"

"I don't know, are you?"

I keep my eyes locked on his as the waitress comes and sets down two coffees and two almond croissants. Oswald only breaks his gaze to smile up at the waitress and thank her, before turning back to me.

"You know, I was there for my daughter's interview, the one that's airing Saturday." He reaches for the sugar dispenser and pours a generous amount into his cup, stirring it slowly with the silver spoon. "I sat in that studio, and had to listen to my child recount just what she had gone through in that marriage. All the terrible things her husband had done to hurt her. The humiliating things he subjected her to. Things a father should never have to hear."

"They're all lies."

Oswald withdraws the spoon from his coffee, tapping it gently against the porcelain cup three times, before placing it down on the saucer. "You seem very sure of that."

"Because I am. I lived in that house. I saw them together. My father didn't care enough about Gloria to do anything remotely humiliating to her."

Oswald lifts the cup to his lips, taking a small sip. "Your father was incapable of love, I think. Though I'm told that before your mother became a raging alcoholic, he was obsessed with her. That is…" He lifts his eyes back to mine. "Until he had a new object of his obsession."

I feel sick. I'm going to faint or throw up, I can't decide which.

"How old were you when he started asking you to pose naked for photographs?"

How does he know this? I suck in a breath, unable to hide my trepidation, and Oswald's face betrays his silent triumph.

"Well? How old were you?"

I swallow hard, my eyes stinging, and I blink rapidly, desperate not to cry right now. "I was ten."

Oswald sucks on his teeth, tearing his almond croissant in half. "Ten years old. Still a baby."

"He said it was lucky I developed early. I never knew what that meant."

Oswald shakes his head, taking a bite of his food and chewing slowly. "Terrible. Just terrible. I'm sorry, Stella."

"How long have you known?"

"Since a colleague of mine showed me the pictures."

My blood runs cold, and I grip the edge of the table to steady myself. "When?"

"Ohh, now let me see." He taps his fingers against the tabletop. "I'd say it would have been around thirteen years ago."

"Wh-what?" I choke out. "No, that was… That was when… You mean, you knew? When Gloria married him, you knew?"

"I've always known." His level gaze makes my heart drop into my feet. "Like I said, I never liked your father. But I did see the value in what he could offer my daughter."

"And what's that?"

"What she should have had, all along. A place in the White House, the first lady of this country. Her pathetic biker boyfriend was never going to offer her that." He shakes his head, the feathering of his jaw the only sign of his contained rage. "That man was a menace. But one that was… Easily dealt with."

His meaning dawns on me slowly, and goosebumps break out over my skin again. "What do you mean?"

"I have a way of dealing with people I need dealt with, Stella." He swipes the screen of his phone, and pushes it towards me.

I look down at it, at the grainy video playing on the screen. I swear I stop breathing. The room caves in on me, and I'm hot and cold at the same time, watching the video loop and play again and again.

"Where did you get this?"

"I have my ways."

I can't tear my eyes from the screen. From the woman, flopping between three men, who take turns to shove her head down into their laps. To push their dicks into her while another man holds her down. Her eyes roll back in her head, and she's clearly drunk, and high. One man ejaculates on her face. Another holds up her legs so one of them can fuck her ass. Her mouth opens in a silent scream, but the man claps his hand over her mouth.

I look so different. I barely recognise myself. Gaunt and hollow. A shadow of who I am now.

But I remember waking up after that night. I remember waking up sticky with cum and shame, on the floor of a seedy motel that I had no memory of stepping foot into. The three men at the club had offered me one drink after another, had fingered me roughly on the dance floor, and I hadn't cared at all.

Then I'd let one of them take me to the bathroom, and he'd fucked me without a condom. I'd lain back on the counter, and let him press into me, staring at the speckled ceiling of the nightclub bathroom, watching it turn into a haze as I dreamed of Dylan, as tears stung my eyes wishing he was there with me.

That was the last thing I remember clearly. After that, it's nothing but flashes of rough carpet against my ass, of choking on sweaty flesh and tasting salt, gagging on the smell of body odor. I'm not even sure I said stop, or no. I'd begged them to not hurt me, but that had probably been in my own head.

They'd drugged me, just like my father had, and I'd let them use me.

Just like my father had.

My lip trembles, and Oswald reaches across the table to take the phone back.

"I'm so sorry to upset you, dear." He puts the phone back in the pocket of his waistcoat, his eyebrows drawn down. "That footage, it was hard to watch."

"How did you find that? I didn't… I didn't even know they filmed it."

"No, I suppose you didn't." He exhales through his nose, clasping his hands over his rounded belly. "I know you made some terrible choices, Stella. And I would hate for those choices to be visited back on you."

"Are you threatening me?"

"No, not at all." He holds his hands up. "I'm merely saying that no one's past should ruin their future. And that it would be a shame if this, and the other records of your transgressions, were to become public."

"A video of a woman being raped doesn't ruin her reputation anymore, Oswald, this isn't 1950."

Oswald laughs indulgently, and shakes his head. "Oh my dear, you are so sweetly naive. Have you seen what happens to women like you when these things become public? What people will believe about you? It's no secret you were a mess after the boys went to prison, and this, along with the fact that you're taking two men to your bed, and one of them being your stepbrother, well..." He raises his cup back to his lips, taking a sip and shrugging lightly. "It wouldn't be a stretch to imagine what sort of damage all of this could do to your reputation."

"What do you want, Oswald?" My throat is threatening to swell shut and stop any words coming out at all.

"I want you to break it off with Levi and Dylan."

"No."

He ignores me, breaking off another piece of his croissant. "I want you to publicly announce that Gloria was nothing but supportive, that she was an exemplary stepmother, and that any accusations against her made by the media are nothing but lies."

"No."

"You will do all of this, and then you can have your life back."

"I don't think so."

The old man shrugs, taking off his glasses to clean them with the white tablecloth. "You will do as you're told, and I won't have any arguments over it."

"And what if I'm pregnant?"

Oswald wasn't expecting that. His eyes flash to mine, narrowing dangerously. "I beg your pardon?"

I smirk, leaning on the table. "What? You know where babies come from, Oswald. And Levi, Dylan and I have been doing a whole lot of that."

"You have an IUD in place, I know that from your medical records."

I adopt the ruse, and shake my head, mirroring his own laugh from just a moment ago. "Oh Oswald, you old men really know nothing about anatomy, do you?" I lean on my elbows on the table. "It fell out with my period, a while ago, and I just didn't bother replacing it. And those two men, well, they've left enough cum inside me to populate all of Europe."

"Don't be vile." Oswald's face is anything but friendly now.

I'm startled at how easily I'm lying to him, and I'm not even sure why this is the lie I chose. But I can see I've gotten right under his skin.

"So, Oswald, you might be a great-grandfather soon."

"You filthy whore," he snarls, his face menacing under the overhead lights. "Get rid of it."

"No." I rise to my feet, taking my purse with me. "And if you ever threaten me again, I will make sure everyone knows exactly how involved your family was with what happened to me. Do not test me again. Do you understand?"

Oswald says nothing, just regards me with a lethal gaze.

"Thanks for the coffee," I say, before heading out of the cafe and into the sunshine. The man by my car is gone, and I panic for just a split second that he's planted a bomb or something in my car. My reason takes over, and I give myself a shake as I start the engine. He can't have done that in broad daylight.

Every car that drives behind me is a tail. I'm convinced of it. I take the term defensive driving to a whole new level, weaving in and out of traffic to avoid anyone following me for too long. By the time I get home, I'm sweating and shaking, and desperate to wash this feeling off me.

I pull out my phone and type out a text to Dylan.

Please come home asap. But don't tell Levi.

Three little circles whirs almost immediately as Dylan types back a response.

Why? Is something wrong?

Please just hurry.

I'll be right there. Are you OK?

I just need you.

I need to tell Dylan, and I don't know how to tell Levi. I know this is going to draw us all in deeper. I head up to the bathroom, and throw on the shower. While the water heats up, I stare at my face in the mirror.

And I realize I can't tell them what just happened.

They'll just kill more people. I can't be responsible for that. I can't have them getting into a rage and getting themselves caught. I'll lose them. I can't lose them again.

Oswald was goading me. He's going to try and trap them. Gloria is going to go on the air and say how awful my father was, how abusive he was, and paint herself as the victim. My stomach drops as it all starts to fall into place. As all the messy pieces start to knit themselves together.

Gloria is going to tell the world they killed him for her.

I clutch a hand to my mouth. I have to be wrong. I have to be.

But whatever she has planned, I can't tell Dylan and Levi. If they head out into the night and kill Oswald, and Gloria, it's going to destroy everything. I can't do that. I just can't.

I strip off my clothes and get into the shower, pressing my trembling hands against the tiles. *Breathe. Breathe, and remember this is real.* I stave off the panic attack, letting the warm water rush over my head. I press my hand to my stomach as another cramp tenses my muscles, and blood starts to trickle down my legs.

I stay there for a long time, letting the water wash away all the blood, until there's a soft knock on the door and Dylan walks in. He looks alarmed for a minute, then raises his eyes to me.

"*Guera*?" He steps towards the shower. "What happened? You worried me."

"I was being stupid. My… My period was late, and I freaked out."

Dylan's eyebrows shoot up. "You thought you were pregnant?"

"Mhmm." I nod and smile. "I did. But I'm not. My period just came."

Dylan perches his hands on his hips and exhales heavily. "Jesus Christ."

"Sorry to scare you."

"I mean, I'm fine, I just…" He huffs out a nervous laugh. "Sorry, it's just kind of caught me off guard. I didn't think it was possible for you to get pregnant right now."

"I mean, IUDs can fail, Kovac." My voice shakes slightly, and I hope my smile isn't wavering. "And you two have been doing a pretty good job of shaking things up in there."

He laughs out loud, running a hand over his head. "I guess we have."

"Would it bother you if I was?"

"No." He says quickly, his eyes locked on mine. "Not at all. If it happens, it happens."

"Do you want to come join me? It's lonely in here."

He cocks an eyebrow. "You're on your period, you sure you want me in there with you?"

"Orgasms are great for cramps."

Dylan smiles and shakes his head, but immediately starts stripping off his clothes. "What the lady wants, the lady gets."

I know I'm reverting back to old coping mechanisms. I know this probably isn't healthy. I know I shouldn't lie to them, and I waver back and forth on whether or not I'm placing us all in more danger than if I just told them what the fuck was going on.

But as Dylan lifts me up against the wall and fucks me hard, as my body reacts to him and he murmurs dirty words in my ear, I can't even consider what the future looks like for us right now.

"I love you," I gasp, my arms wrapped around his neck.

"Fuck, I love you." He hooks one of my legs over his arm, groaning as he sinks deeper inside me.

I press my head back against the tiles, clenching my eyes shut, tensing my body with everything I've got and forcing myself to release to him. My orgasm doesn't bring sweet relief though, it shatters through me as I gasp Dylan's name and tears bite at my eyes.

Dylan presses his mouth against my throat and moans loudly, shuddering as he comes inside me. I wrap myself around him, biting my lip to stop it trembling, and wonder what the fuck we've gotten ourselves into. What ticking time bomb Gloria and Oswald have placed right underneath us.

I can't think about it. Not again. But as Dylan dries me off and gets me comfortable, wrapping me up in bed and getting me tea and a hot water bottle, I can't help but feel like my pretty little life I've built for myself is all about to come crashing down around me.

CHAPTER TWENTY-FIVE

THE CROWD of reporters outside the garage catches me off guard. My head is swimming slightly, a lack of sleep and an unhealthy excess of fucking all night leaving me with the worst sort of hangover. I just want to be back in bed with Stella and Levi, but one of us needed to head in to meet with the accountant, and I volunteered.

Now I wish I'd just rescheduled the meeting and stayed in bed.

The throng rushes at me as I take off my helmet, cameras flashing and phones outstretched.

"Dylan, do you have any comments on Gloria's statements?" Is one of the questions I hear amongst the hyper chatter they throw my way.

"I don't know what you're talking about." I run a hand over my head and attempt to make my way to the garage, bumping into the bodies blocking my way. "Can you all please move? I don't have time for this right now."

"Dylan, how long were you aware of Harold Langford's abuse?" Another displaced voice, a question thrown over the heads of the reporters around me.

"No comment." I shove against the crushing bodies. "Now get out of my way."

"How long had you and Gloria been involved?"

That one has me stopping short. I turn to try and find the voice who just threw the question my way, the question I must have misheard,

"What did you say?" I ask, my eyes trying to find the person. All the reporters follow my gaze, and a man with cropped brown hair in a blue shirt raises his hand.

"Yes, Dylan, here, Larry Jones, Sonoma County Informer. Gloria Langford and you, how long had that relationship been going on?"

My eyebrows shoot up. "Are you fucking kidding me?"

"Gloria's interview, last night, she revealed-"

"She didn't reveal shit," I interject, and wave a hand. "I don't know what the fuck you're talking about."

"Dylan, is that why you killed Harold Langford?"

"I-I didn't…" I shake my head and turn to the garage. "Get the fuck off my property."

"Dylan! Dylan!" The voices all rise as I start to push my way back to the garage.

"Fuck off or I'll call the cops!"

I make it to the garage and slam the door behind me. It's quiet and dark inside, being a Sunday morning. I wish someone else was here, noise and light and the banter of the mechanics to lift my mood, just a little.

What the fuck has Gloria done now?

I head for the office and look up the number for our lawyer. Her bright voice sounds when I reach her voicemail, and I leave a message for her to call me as soon as possible.

I hesitate, looking down at my phone, and take a deep breath. Then I search Gloria's interview.

There she is, perched on a blue armchair, legs folded demurely. Her hands are clasped on her lap, and she's not wearing as much make-up as she usually does. Her hair is swept back in the signature chignon, and she's dressed in a black skirt suit. Pearls lie around her throat. She's every bit the picture of the grieving widow, her eyes sad, her lips downturned and quivering slightly as she gazes at the pleasant looking older woman opposite her.

Gloria Fenton-Langford is a fucking good actress.

"So, Gloria," the woman says, smiling warmly, "You said when you agreed to this interview with us, that the world deserved to know exactly what kind of man Harold Langford was. What did you mean by that?"

Gloria's throat bobs as she swallows, and she sniffles lightly. "I needed everyone to understand things about him, about the way he was, and why the things that happened, happened."

The woman frowns and nods. "You mean the night he died?"

"Yes, but also… Before that." The dramatic pause is so perfectly put that I can't help but roll my eyes.

If I didn't want to fucking kill her, I'd almost be impressed.

I lean against the edge of the desk, bouncing my foot while Gloria talks endlessly about how Harold scared her, how he was a powerful man, how he'd transformed from the sweet, doting husband to a monster who barely let her leave the house.

Lie after lie spills out of the mouth of this privileged bitch, and the interviewer eats it all up, nodding with maternal understanding, reaching across to offer Gloria a bright white handkerchief and to pat her knee a few times.

It's sickening, a display so well-rehearsed it's practically scripted.

"Gloria, you also told us that someone very close to you saved you, and that the truth of your husband's death had never been revealed, to protect this young man." The interviewer raises her eyebrows as Gloria sniffles and presses the handkerchief to her dry and tearless eye.

Gloria nods. "It's been so hard to keep this secret, but no one would have understood."

My blood starts to chill, and I straighten up from the desk. What in the fuck is she talking about?

"What would no one have understood, Gloria?"

"He was so young, he was my son's best friend." She eyes the interviewer shyly. "Who would have understood that we were in love."

The floor drops out from under me. She can't be talking about me. There's no way she's talking about me. There was never a single moment I was alone in a room with Gloria, let alone any fucking indication that she even *liked* me. I was the dirty immigrant kid, the freak, the corrupting force in her son's life. She hated me, glaring at me over the edge of her martini glass at any party the Fenton-Langfords ever held.

But now, the interviewer expresses perfectly timed surprise, a lift of her eyebrows and a parting of her perfectly made up lips, and Gloria nods when the camera lands back on her.

"Is that why Harold attacked Dylan that night?" The interviewer's voice sounds as the camera remains fixed on Gloria's face, and she keeps nodding.

"Yes." She says after a while, her voice a hoarse whisper.

"You know this for sure?"

"I believe it to be so." A single tear strays down Gloria's cheek, and where she squeezed that from, I have no idea. "That night, Dylan and I had… Well, we'd…"

The bitch fucking *blushes.*

I feel sick. I swear to fuck I'm going to throw up on my damn feet.

"You'd made love?" The interviewer asks, and Gloria's gaze drops to her lap as she nods.

I nearly hurl my phone across the room. "Fucking *bitch,*" I hiss at the screen. "You fucking lying *bitch.*"

"Was that the first time?" The interviewer asks, and Gloria nods again, lifting her chin, her eyes sparkling.

"It was… It probably sounds terrible, but he made me feel… My goodness, I'm sorry." Her gaze flashes off camera, and she puts a hand to her forehead. "I'm so embarrassed to admit this, but having a young man like that worship a woman like me, made me feel so special and like I was beautiful, and not just someone's mother or an old woman."

The room starts to spin. I throw the phone down on the desk and lean heavily on my hands, staring down at the screen that holds Gloria's fucking face. She seems to come to life as she recounts this relationship that had bloomed between us, this sick twisted fantasy that she's dreamed up.

"Now Gloria, we'd been led to believe that Dylan was in a relationship with your stepdaughter, Stella. Is that not true?"

"No, it is true." Gloria's smile drops at the mention of Stella's name, in a way that can't hide her disdain. "At least, that's what he let her believe, because there was no way we could be open about it, admit to it. He wanted to protect my integrity."

"So, he was lying to Stella?"

Gloria swallows hard, and her eyes flash uncertainly off camera for just a split second. She has to reel this back in somehow, to make her look like the wounded party and not some greedy cougar who stole her stepdaughter's boyfriend.

"Dylan cared for Stella, like a sister," Gloria lilts softly. "He didn't know how to let her down gently. The last thing either of us wanted to do was hurt Stella. She'd been through enough, being abandoned by her mother at such a young age."

My rage is incandescent. I can practically taste it, searing acid at the back of my throat. This fucking, dirty ass bitch. My hands curl into fists, imagining snapping that privileged ivory neck. She's going to fucking pay for this shit.

The interviewer leans back and clasps her hands over her knee. "So, when you said that you believe your relationship with Dylan was what led to the altercation resulting in your husband's death, what do you believe happened?"

Gloria takes a shaky breath, her eyes fluttering briefly to her knees as she smooths her skirt over them. "That night, after Dylan and I had… After we'd been together, Harold came home early from a meeting. Dylan's bike was still parked in the drive."

"He caught the two of you?"

Gloria lifts her chin. "No, I think Dylan was doing the honorable thing, and telling Harold the truth. That we wanted to be together."

The video stops playing, the bar at the bottom showing that this part is done, and I search through the list to find part 2. It's not there.

Fuck, fuck, what else did she say?

Then I see Part Two airs tonight. I slam my fist into the table.

God fucking dammit. What is this bitch playing at?

I pull up a number on my phone, and it rings twice before a groggy male voice answers.

"What?"

"I need a trace, Flea."

"On who?" The tapping of a keyboard sounds in the background.

"Gloria Fenton-Langford."

More tapping, and the man clears his throat. "This bitch is going to be expensive."

"I didn't expect anything less," I say with a cynical laugh. "Name your price."

"Twenty-thousand."

"What's a hacker living in his mom's basement going to do with twenty k?" I'm teasing him, he knows I'm good for it. I'm going to pay this kid who just got out of prison, and do it gladly. But irritating him is kind of fun.

Flea sighs audibly. "My parole says I have to be here, so the least I can do is make this shit hole comfortable. Now, we on?"

"Sure." I chew my lip, a strange feeling settling into my gut. "And one more, too."

"Who else you need to follow around, huh?"

"Oswald Perlmann."

Flea makes a choking sound. "The senator?"

"Yeah, that one."

Flea puffs out a breath, and there's more clicking in the background as he types furiously. "You know that one's gonna be extra."

"I'll give you fifty thousand."

Flea laughs out loud, a gravelly sound that echoes down the line. "For that much, I'll tap his phone and send you everything on it."

"Do that. I want it all by tonight."

"Consider it done, amigo. Anything else I can help you with?"

"No, that's it."

"Good." The line goes dead as Flea hangs up.

I spin the phone on the table for a moment. I don't know why I asked for Flea to trace Oswald, and I sure as fuck can't explain what would be on his phone. But the way Gloria's eyes kept flickering off camera, as though someone was standing there…

Maybe I'm being paranoid.

But then I remember that Stella had told me that Oswald and Gloria had come to her with that plea bargain, the agreement that she wouldn't come and see us, and that her letters would be monitored.

Oswald has something to do with this, and while my sleep-deprived brain can't sort through it all right now, there's more at play than anyone is letting on.

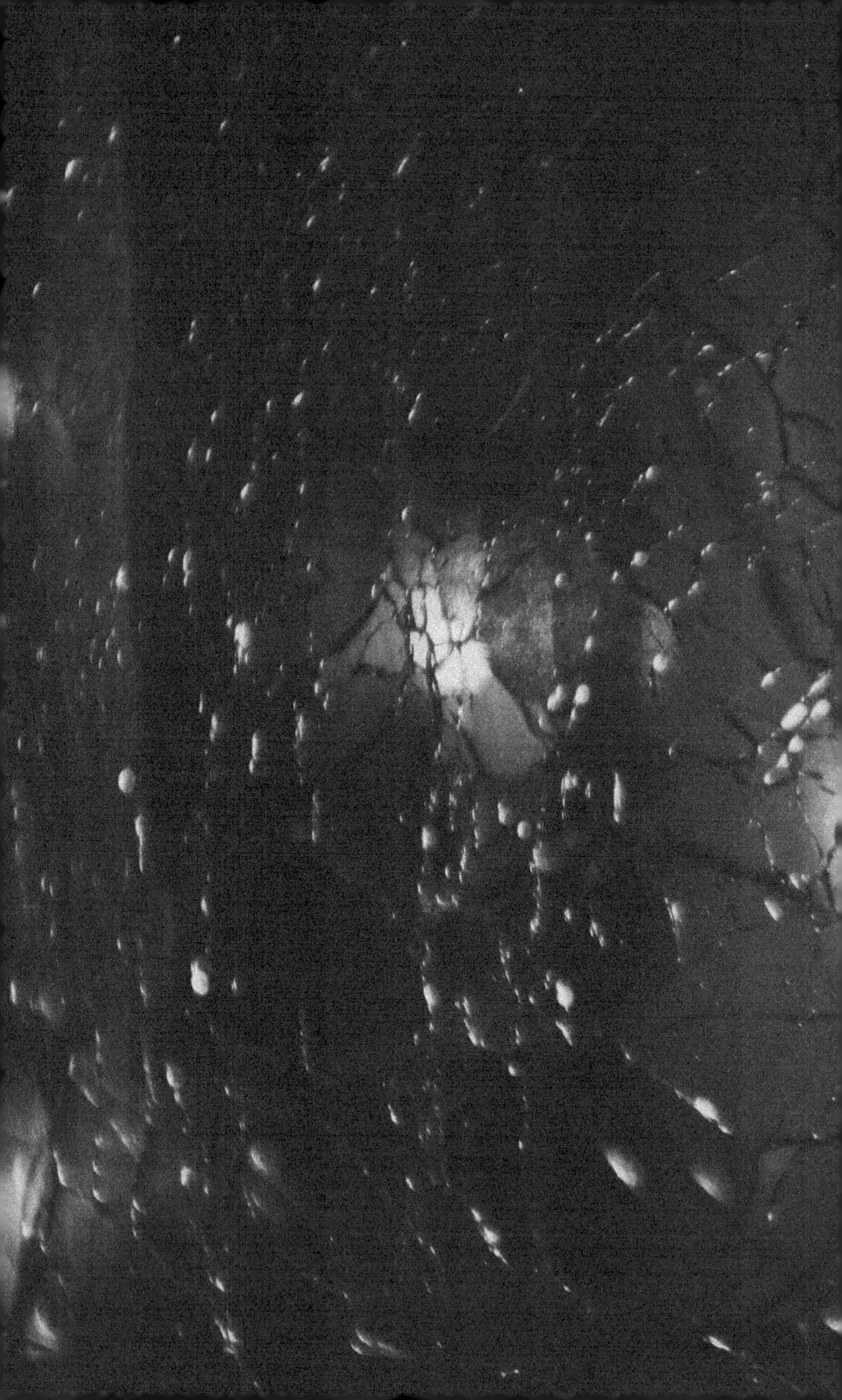

STELLA

CHAPTER TWENTY-SIX

"SHE'S FULL OF SHIT, RIGHT?" Zee's eyes are wide as I click off the television.

Dylan's leg is bouncing as he taps his foot against the ground, alternately rubbing his forehead then his mouth, then running his hands over his head in a loop of frustration, before he springs from the armchair and crosses the room to the window.

"Fucking bitch," he hisses. "Sick fucking bitch. As if I'd ever fucking touch her." He lets out a growl and throws the drapes closed. "And now there's reporters outside the damn house."

"Were you ever even alone with her?" I ask, disbelief still running through me.

Dylan laughs bitterly. "No, not fucking once. She hated me, you know that. I was nothing but a filthy Polack or a fucking beaner, depending on what day it was and how many martinis she'd had." He paces the lounge room like a caged animal. "What the fuck is she playing at? What the fuck is she hoping to get out of this?"

"Victim status?" Zee offers. "I mean, she's not above using anyone for her own means."

"Yeah, but this? *This?*" Dylan's hands curl into fists, and he exhales through gritted teeth. "Fuck this, I need to breathe." He storms out of the room, and the porch door slams loudly.

Zee lets out a low whistle, and throws themselves back in their chair. "Well, this sure as hell is messy."

"Levi's going to kill her," I say without thinking, and then that icy feeling drops back into the pit of my stomach. I hope my face isn't pale, and that Zee doesn't see the change in my expression. But I know it's possible. I know every time the guys leave the house that they could come back covered in the blood of yet another person they've put in the ground.

But I can't tell Zee that, and they simply shrug and take a sip of their water, thinking I'm joking.

"She's sure as hell cruising for some bad karma," Zee says, placing the glass back on the coffee table before eyeing me warily. "You doing alright?"

"Yeah I'm fine, just been a crazy couple of days. I - well…" I want to tell Zee about Oswald, about the video and his threats. But I glance over my shoulder, knowing that if Dylan catches the slightest hint of anyone threatening me, we're just going to topple deeper into this whole awful situation. Instead, I turn back to Zee and give them a wan smile. "I guess I thought I was pregnant for a minute, so Dylan's a little on edge."

"You thought you were *what*?" Zee starts forward in their chair. "Oh my god, seriously?"

"I'm not, I'm not, my period was just late so I freaked out. The IUD messes with my cycle sometimes."

Zee puffs out a breath. "I swear to god, y'all are going to give me a heart attack one of these days." They tilt their head. "I mean, would you have been alright if you were? I don't even know if you want kids."

"I don't," I say quietly, looking down at my hands. "I mean, I never did, because I always thought I'd be a bad mother, you know, history repeats itself, right?"

"Hey, no, that's not how that works." They toss their locs as they shake their head. "I think you'd make a great mother, *because* of what happened to you. You'd never want a kid to go through what you went through, are you kidding me?" They shift to the edge of their seat and reach out to take my hand. "Only if that's what you wanted, of course."

I shrug, shifting to tuck my legs underneath me on the armchair. "I don't know. If it happened, I guess I'd be OK with it." I lift my eyes to meet theirs. "But with all this insanity around us right now, I'm glad I'm not."

"Yeah, can't say I blame you there, it's all just crazy to me." They gesture with an open hand to the tv, opening their mouth then letting their hand drop and shrugging. "I don't even know what to say. I can't believe she's saying Dylan killed Harold for *her*. I mean, how can anyone believe that baloney?"

"I guess people will believe anything that's sensational enough." I rake a hand through my hair, chewing my lip as I cast a glance to the back door. "Dylan doesn't deserve this."

"No, he sure as fuck doesn't." They rub their chin and sigh. "I mean, can she even say stuff like this? Isn't this, like, defamation or something? Can't he sue her?"

I can't help but scoff bitterly, because of course those very words had been thrown at me by both Levi and Dylan since Dylan came tearing back into the driveway yesterday.

"No, there's nothing Dylan can do," I say with a shrug. "He can go on the record and deny it, but you can't sue someone just for lying, not like this. She's not causing any harm or defamation with her lies, so it wouldn't hold up in court."

Zee's eyebrows rise so high I swear they're going to disappear into their hair, before their face drops back into a scowl. "I don't even know why it shocks me that a white woman can say whatever she wants and get away with it. I mean…" They gesture vaguely around the room, and collapse into their chair with a huff. "Goddamn stupid bratty bitch." They eye me apologetically. "Are you gonna be OK?"

I sigh, smoothing my hands over my bare thighs. "I don't know. I just wish… I wish we could just run away from all of this. But I know that's not an answer."

"Hey, it could be." Zee gives me a crooked smile, and laughs when I roll my eyes. "I'm serious. The three of you, pack up and move, why not?"

"And where exactly would we go?"

"I don't know, Boston, New York?" Zee chuckles. "Come on, girl, there's a whole world out there, you don't need to stay here forever. In fact, you probably shouldn't."

I don't know why Zee's idea is hitting me like this, when I just had this same conversation with Levi. I gaze out the window, at the pretty, tree-lined street, and for the first time I don't see the little dream I'd built for myself. I see the facades everyone in this town has built up around themselves to survive. To fit in. To make sure no one knows just what goes on behind closed doors.

"I don't know if I could convince them to leave," I say quietly, and suddenly I want to tell Zee everything. I want to confide in someone about Oswald, about the video he has of me. But I know they'd be worried, and for no other reason than that, they'd tell Dylan and Levi. I pull my knees up to my chest, and let my head drop, wrapping my arms around my legs. "Oh, my god. This is all a fucking mess."

"Hey, hey, it's alright." Zee is at my side, kneeling on the ground beside me. "Girl, it's going to be OK. I promise. This will all blow over, and then you can all move on."

I lift my head and gaze at their hopeful face. "I'm tired of feeling this way."

"Then we need to get you all some relief for a while." They reach for their bag, and pull a silver cigarette case from the front pocket. "Here, you smoke these with your men, and all of you just take a load off."

I snort lightly, taking the case from their hand. "I hope this is the good stuff."

"Only the best for my girl." Zee grins up at me, taking my hand and hugging it to their chest. "I love you. And I love Dylan. And Levi's fine too, I guess."

"Yeah, he's alright," I say with a giggle.

"I just want you all to be happy." Zee rises to their knees and plants a kiss on my cheek. "Now, go out there, get naked in that hot tub, and enjoy the finest herb Sonoma county has to offer. Then let those men bang you into oblivion."

I laugh out loud, and Zee smiles widely.

"There she is." They get to their feet and plant another kiss on the top of my head. "Take it easy, call me if you need me."

"Will do."

I sit there, holding the cigarette case in my hands and watch as Zee gets up to leave, casting back a last smile and wave from the door, before heading out into the warm afternoon. I wait a few minutes, letting the thoughts careen around my head, wondering where Levi is and hating that I worry about it. If they ever find out about Oswald, I know bad things will happen. I don't even want to know what would happen if they ever got a hold of those guys.

I focus on a knot in the wood floor, for too long, as I try to remember that night, which club I'd been in. But then the old familiar icy feeling runs down my back, and nausea sends bile up my throat. I don't want to think about it. I hate that it's even been brought back up.

They can never know. They can just never know about that.

I go to the kitchen and gulp down a glass of water before heading out onto the porch. Dylan is pacing the lawn, hands curled into half-fists as he stalks back and forth.

"You're going to wear out my nice green grass if you keep doing that," I call out, trying to be lighthearted.

Dylan stops, head still dropped, chest heaving. But he doesn't move towards the porch.

"*Papi,* come up here." I put the cigarette case down on the table, and shuffle my shorts down my legs. "Come and join me."

I pull the t-shirt off over my head, and then he lifts his eyes, taking in my naked body.

His eyes are dark, almost black, and his jaw is set as tight as a steel trap.

"I know you're mad," I say, lifting up the case, opening it to take out a spliff. I light it with his silver lighter, and inhale deeply. The sweetish smell envelops me, and I puff out the smoke in Dylan's direction. "But right now, we can't change it. So just come here."

Dylan moves slowly up the stairs, and removes his clothes on the way, flopping them over the banister before standing right in front of me. He reaches out to take the spliff from my hand, and lifts it to his own lips, taking a long, crackling drag.

"You ever fucked when you're high?" I ask, and he nods slowly.

"You?"

I shrug, taking it back from him and sucking down another breath as I climb into the hot tub. "Yeah, but they were bad lays, so I never got to enjoy it." I settle in the warm water, and turn to watch Dylan climb in after me, the water catching the light on his muscles, and this pot must be really good, because my head is already a little floaty.

I hold the spliff out to Dylan, who takes a drag and leans his head back against the edge of the tub, puffing the smoke out into the sky.

"Remember when I took you out on the bike, to that lake, up in the mountains?" He asks, his head still tipped back.

"Yes, I remember that day." I smile, stroking my hands through the water. "You said it was a secret, and no one else knew where it was."

"That's right. Our secret place." He lifts his head, and gazes at me with those inky dark eyes. "You held on to me while we rode up there, into this totally isolated place, and you just… trusted me. You never thought for a second I'd hurt you."

"Because I know you'd never hurt me, *papi*." I move around

the tub to his side, and he places the spliff against my lips, holding it for me as I inhale and his eyes wander over my face. "I've always trusted you. Always."

"I remember laying you down on the grass," he says quietly. "I lay you out underneath me, and god I wanted to fuck you, but I didn't want to make you do something you weren't ready for."

"See?" I lean in and place a kiss against his neck. "I trust you. Completely. And besides." I pull back with a smile."You did sort of get me off after all."

He chuckles, taking another deep drag. "Good old teenage dry-humping for the win." He puts an arm around me and draws me close, groaning softly as my hand moves over his stomach. "Seeing your cheeks go all rosy, hearing you moan in my ear, fuck, *guera*, you have no idea…" He groans again, louder now, as my hand wraps around his hard cock. "It was you. It was always you. I never wanted anyone like I wanted you."

I lean closer and nip at his earlobe, delighting in the goosebumps that erupt over his skin. "And what about Levi?"

Dylan laughs, exhaling heavily as I pump him slowly. "Him, too. I mean, not back then. I don't know. Maybe?"

"Have you fucked him yet?" I ask, squeezing my thighs together as the image of Dylan buried inside Levi swims in my mind's eye.

Dylan shakes his head. "No, he's nervous."

"Hey, I took you just fine, what's he got to be nervous about?"

Dylan is up in an instant, and has me bent over the edge of the tub. I can't help but yelp as he shoves inside me, surprised at the sudden intrusion. He doesn't move, just leans over me, filling me as he kisses my shoulders, pushing aside my hair to nip at my neck.

"You like having me in your ass?"

I nod, trying to wriggle my hips to get the friction I so desperately want, but Dylan has me pinned in place.

"I love you fucking my ass," I murmur.

"You want to see me fuck Levi?" He bites my shoulder, and I gasp. "You want to watch while I claim that pretty rich boy?"

I giggle over a moan, taking another drag of the spliff as Dylan presses it to my lips. "Yes, I want to see that."

He thrusts into me a few times, before stopping and chuckling darkly as I protest. "I'm not going to let you come, *guera.* I want you all worked up for our man. I want you desperate to come."

"You're so mean." I moan loudly as he thrusts into me again, his fingers circling my clit, coming again to a stop, and offering the spliff. I don't know how long we do this, but it feels like hours. Hours of him fucking me hard for a few seconds, my body clawing and scrambling for release, then him simply staying inside me, stroking every inch of me with his fingertips, teasing my nipples with wet hands.

Hands clutch my face, and I open my eyes to find Levi gazing at me.

"You look so pretty when you're getting fucked," he murmurs, kissing me softly. "Does he feel good?"

"He does. You should have him, too." I nip at his lips, and Levi chuckles.

"Maybe we should take this inside then," Levi says, looking over my shoulder at Dylan, his eyes filled with need.

I'm higher than I realize, because I'm in my bed now, spread out on the soft white sheets, Dylan gently licking my clit as he spreads lube over a jeweled plug, teasing my ass with it before pushing it inside me. I shudder, sinking into the delicious feeling as Levi sucks one of my nipples into his mouth.

"So pretty like this," Dylan murmurs, stroking my clit with his fingers, lifting his eyes to Levi. "Come and taste her, *guapo.*"

Levi moves down to bend over the edge of the bed, lowering his mouth to my soaked pussy. He groans as he licks my clit, and my back arches off the bed. He presses two fingers inside me, making me feel even fuller with the plug, and my brain is short-circuiting at the sensation.

"You ready for me, *guapo*?" Dylan's voice is low and commanding, and I lift my head to watch him position himself behind Levi.

Levi huffs out a breath against my skin, and nods. "Yes."

"Keep making our girl feel good," Dylan says, coating his thick cock in lube, his eyes meeting mine as I raise myself up on my elbows.

I watch with open fascination as Dylan sinks slowly, so slowly, into Levi. Levi moans and shakes between my thighs, his hands digging into my skin hard enough to leave bruises. I don't mind. I stroke his head, my body tensing as his tongue continues in slow, shaky strokes.

Dylan's eyes damn near roll back in his head, his huge hands holding Levi steady. "Oh fuck, *guapo*," he breathes, his head falling back. "Oh my fucking god. Fuck, you feel so good."

Levi's ragged breaths wash over my skin as he keeps licking and sucking, and my teeth dig into my lip as I try to hold off, not wanting to come yet, because I want to keep watching Dylan fucking him, keep feeling every quiver of Levi's body as he takes him.

Every muscle tenses, and I hold my hand over my mouth, as though suppressing the moans that want to tear free from my throat will somehow stop the orgasm that's clawing at me. But it's no use, and I fall back on the bed, screaming as I pulse against Levi's mouth. I'm still shaking and moaning as I'm dragged down the bed, and Levi impales me on his hard cock in one swift move.

My quivering pussy clamps down on him, the fullness from the plug and his thick length threatening to topple me over the edge again. I look up to see Dylan at Levi's back, his hand wrapped around Levi's neck. Levi's eyes are closed as Dylan continues to fuck him, brow furrowed.

"You going to fill up that pretty pussy while I fuck this ass, *guapo*?" Dylan's thrusts are punishing, and Levi strokes in and out of me with each move.

"Fuck, fuck *oh fuck*." Levi shudders, his shaking hands gripping my thighs, and his stomach tenses.

"That's it." Dylan wraps his other arm around Levi's waist, and he grits his teeth. "So fucking good for me, fuck."

Levi's head falls back against Dylan's shoulder as he moans loudly, his hips jerking as he seeks more of me, reaching down to stroke my swollen clit, and I thrash on the bed. I can't move away, his hand still holding me firmly, and as Dylan picks up the pace, clenching his teeth as he chases his own climax, I swear I'm going to pass out.

I press my hips down, seeking the pressure of the plug and instantly heat shoots up my spine, flooding my head with sweetness as my second orgasm shatters through me. Levi cries out, and with two sharp thrusts, I feel him pulsate inside me, spilling and spilling as Dylan moans his name.

Hot cum drips out of me, and spurts across my legs as Dylan pulls out of Levi and releases all over us. My whole body is shuddering and shivering, my nipples almost painfully hard. Levi slumps over me, catching himself on his hands, and his shaky breaths wash over my lips.

"Fuck," he murmurs, and I lift a hand to stroke it through his sweaty hair.

"You did so good," Dylan praises, running a hand down Levi's back. "You're fucking perfect."

"That felt incredible," Levi says, meeting my eyes with a smile. "That just… That felt so fucking good."

"Told you," I say with a giggle, and kiss his warm lips.

Dylan leans down over us, and kisses Levi's neck, who hums appreciatively against my mouth. "So fucking good. You took me so well, *guapo*."

The buzz lasts long enough for us all to shower together, and Dylan gets to his knees to taste Levi's cum between my legs while Levi lazily massages my breasts. I come again, my shaking legs hooked over Dylan's shoulders, Levi's mouth on mine.

I'm theirs. I'm theirs forever, and they're mine. That thought is enough to have the buzz wearing off. Because I know I need to get them out of this town.

Or all of this is just going to go away, and I'll be alone again.

CHAPTER TWENTY-SEVEN

"I HAVE to head to the club for a meeting."

Levi's head pops up from behind the bike he's working on. "Oh, yeah?"

"Yeah, just some administration thing." I hate lying to him. "I'll see you at home later."

"No problem." He smiles at me warmly, before dipping his head to go back to his work. "See you there."

I shrug on my jacket and pull on my helmet, before climbing onto my bike. I check the location for the millionth time. The little red dot shows my target hasn't moved. He's still right where he was two hours ago, when Flea sent me the pin.

I gun the engine, and the bike roars as I head out of the parking lot and out onto the open road.

The past week has been hell. And it wasn't just dodging reporters, avoiding all the drama Gloria had rained down on us with her lies.

No, it was much more than that.

I can't think about it too much. I didn't know what I was expecting when Flea sent me the access to Oswald's phone, with a warning that there was stuff on there that would be extremely hard to watch. I thought I was prepared. I'd seen terrible things before.

Nothing could have prepared me for a video of Stella, *my* Stella, my beautiful girl, being raped and defiled by three filthy fucks in a dingy motel room. My stomach curdles at the memory. Her dead eyes, her screams, all silent on the video, but loud enough to rattle my soul to its very core. I heard everything, felt everything, smelled everything, as though I was in the room with her.

And when I saw her mouth the word that broke me, when I saw tears slip down her cheeks and her lips move as she pleaded, *"Papi, papi, please"*, I knew what had to happen. This was a matter for me to settle. She'd lain on that floor, pleading for me to come and rescue her while she was drugged and assaulted…

I'd said nothing to Stella or Levi. I'd just asked Flea to find out where the video had come from, who'd filmed it. A feat that should have been impossible.

But then this morning, a location was shared to my phone, for an apartment an hour away, in Bakersfield. The shitty side of town. The loser who'd filmed himself and his buddies assaulting Stella lived there alone. Flea was still working on identifying the other two.

One name is enough for me right now. The late afternoon sun beats down as I coast down the interstate, and after a half hour, I take the Bakersfield exit. A text from Flea pops up on my phone.

> The guy owns a gun, just thought you should know.

I expected nothing less. Which is why I stowed the gun Eric procured for us under my seat. Risky? Sure. A cop pulls me over and searches me, I'm done. And a brown man like me, I know he'd sure as fuck search me immediately. But I send a prayer up to my parents, to have those angels looking after me, so I can make this right.

Revenge might be a sin, but since I'm damned anyway, who gives a fuck? Maybe God can give me a pass on all of this. An eye for an eye, right?

I pull up outside a run-down apartment block. Craig Ellis lives in the apartment at the end, facing the dumpsters. Fitting.

The apartments are quiet, their occupants all obviously at work. A beat up Camry is parked outside Ellis's door, a Confederate flag sticker on the bumper. I park my bike down the side, out of sight, and tuck the gun into my waistband, under my jacket.

Something clicks beside me as I walk towards Ellis's door, and I know I've activated someone's ring camera. I keep my head down, pulling out my phone to text Flea.

Apartment 221 has a camera. Deal with it.

That'll cost you.

Just get it done.

Flea sends me a thumbs up, and I move to Ellis's door. A tv can be heard inside, and I test the door handle. This idiot has his door unlocked. It's almost too easy.

I let myself into the apartment, and withdraw the gun. The lounge room is empty, and the sound of water running drifts down the hallway. While Craig Ellis washes his hands or his ass, whichever, I settle myself down in the arm chair, the gun resting on my knee, and wait for this fucker to emerge.

After a couple of minutes, he walks out of the bathroom, running a hand through messy dark hair, shirtless in a pair of basketball shorts. He doesn't spot me at first, moving towards the kitchen and opening the fridge to retrieve a beer. He turns towards me just as he opens the bottle, and it drops to his feet as he yelps.

"Who the fuck are you?"

I raise the gun and gesture to the couch with it.

"Shut up and sit down."

"Get the fuck out of my place!"

I cock the gun, and he goes pale. "I said, sit down, Craig."

He lunges for the pantry, presumably where his gun is kept, but slips in the spilled beer on the floor, tumbling down hard. I'm over him before he can flip over, and his eyes widen as he stares down the barrel of my gun.

"Try that again, and I'll put a bullet in your fucking eye."

He raises his hands, shaking visibly. "What the fuck do you want? I don't have any money."

"I don't need your money. Now get your ass up and sit on the fucking couch."

I keep the gun trained on him as he staggers to his feet, and moves over to the couch. He stinks of cheap beer, and he's visibly sweating. Once he's down, I take my place in the arm chair.

"What do you want, man?" His voice cracks as he eyes the weapon in my hand. "I don't even know you."

"Six years ago, you filmed yourself and your buddies raping a woman you picked up in a club."

Ellis blinks slowly, his brow furrowing. "I what?"

"You heard me. Pretty blonde, you picked her up in a nightclub and drugged her." I pull out my phone and bring up the video, holding it up so Ellis can see the grainy clip play.

He squints, then realization lights up his eyes. "Oh my god, that chick? Seriously?" His confused gaze moves back to me. "So, what? You her boyfriend or something?"

"Where are your buddies?"

He scoffs, shaking his head. "I haven't spoken to them in forever, Joey moved to Texas and Kyle, I mean, he's in prison as far as I know." He throws up his hands. "You seriously tracked me down over this? That's ancient history, man!"

"Do you know who she is?"

Ellis's breath catches in his throat, and he shakes his head. "Listen, whatever is going on in that family, I had no part of it."

I frown at him, leaning on my knees. "What do you mean?"

"Her grandfather, man." He says it like I'm an idiot and should know what he's talking about. "Some hotshot senator, Oswald somebody, I don't fuckin' know. He told me she'd be at the club and paid me to get footage of her doing freaky shit. I know it was wrong, OK? I get it. But I was broke and he offered me 20k."

My blood runs hot with rage. I curl my fist around the gun, gritting my teeth. "How the fuck do you even know him?"

"Joey, he was friends with Oswald's driver. He gave him a job when Joey got out of prison."

"So, he just knew you'd be up for messing with some innocent girl, huh?"

Ellis hacks out a laugh. "Innocent?" He jabs a finger at my pocket. "You've seen the video, she look innocent to you? That girl was the easiest piece of ass I ever scored. Straight up whore."

Ellis doesn't even have time to be startled or throw up his hands in self-defence as I charge at him and smash the gun into the side of his face. His head snaps to the side, bright red blood spraying from his mouth, and he spits out two teeth.

"You fucking asshole!" Blood and spittle drip from his lips as he clutches a hand to his jaw. "What the fuck is wrong with you?"

"Why did Oswald Perlman want you to mess with her? Huh?" I shove the barrel of the gun against his temple, and Ellis whimpers.

"Don't kill me, man. Please." He blinks up at me, tears welling in his eyes. "Please, don't kill me. Look at me. I'm pathetic. I'm nobody."

"You got that right." I press the gun harder against his head. "She asked you to stop, didn't she?"

Ellis coughs out a sob. "I'm sorry, OK?"

"No, you're not."

"She dragged me into the bathroom! She opened her fucking

legs and let me hit that without a fucking rubber, she fucking wanted it!"

I squeeze my eyes shut, trying to contain my fury. "Why did Oswald want you to mess with her?"

"I don't fuckin' know!" Ellis drops to his knees, holding his hands up. "Please, he just said he wanted a video that'd show her being a freak, it was fucked up, OK? But I was desperate. You got any idea how much money that is to someone like me?"

"Did she ask you to stop?" I grit my teeth as my gaze locks on him. "Did she plead for you not to hurt her?"

"She just kept begging for someone to come get her," Ellis says, his eyes pleading. "She kept saying *papi*, over and over. I didn't know who the fuck that was. But she never asked me to stop! I swear!"

I double over, leaning heavily on my knees. "Fuck. *Fuck*."

Ellis cowers, his whole body trembling now. "Please, she wanted it, OK? She was just some slut in a club, I never meant to-"

The gunshot rings out, and Ellis is flung flat on his back. His right eye is blown out, the optic nerve hanging from his skull, his mouth wide. A stain spreads across the front of his shorts as he loses control of his bladder.

Craig Ellis dies on the floor of his shitty apartment in a pool of blood and piss. A death that this son of a bitch deserves.

My shoulders are heaving and my mind is racing as I head out of the apartment back to my bike. The cops won't be far away if someone heard that gunshot. I stow the gun in my bike, and roar out of the parking lot, taking the backroads away from Bakersfield to avoid the interstate.

Oswald fucking Perlmann paid three men to film themselves raping Stella, that I know for sure. Which means Gloria probably had some part in it. They wanted as much dirt on Stella as they could get. But why hold on to this for so long?

My phone buzzes, and I answer it, heavy breathing sounding in my ear over my AirPods.

"Dylan?" Stella's voice is barely audible.

"*Guera?* What's wrong?"

"Someone's in the house."

I gun the engine, speeding down the open road. "Where are you?"

"I'm in the closet," she whispers. "I can hear them."

"Baby, stay there, Stay right where you are, I'm on my way."

"I'm scared."

"I'm coming, Stella. I'm coming." *Fuck, I'm too far away.* "*Guera,* listen to me, stay on the phone to me and text Levi."

"His phone is off," she breathes. "I… Oh my god, Dylan, they're coming up the stairs."

Fuck fuck fuck. "I'm coming, fuck, baby just stay there. I'm coming. I'm coming."

"I love you." She sobs softly. "I love you so much."

"Don't you fucking do that." The bike tops out at its maximum speed as I tear down the road but I'm still too far away. "Don't you fucking say goodbye to me right now, baby. You're OK. I'm coming. I'm coming right now."

Suddenly she screams, and my blood runs cold.

"Stella!" Helplessness unlike any other runs through my veins, as I hear her scramble and scream. "Stella!"

"Two men!" Her voice sounds in the distance, like she's dropped the phone. "Six foot! White! I can't-" Her voice is cut off with a heavy exhale as though someone's struck her. "I can't see their faces!"

"Stella! I'm coming!"

I get closer and closer as I listen to her being beaten, as I hear her scream and beg them to stop. Then the phone goes quiet, and I swear to fuck, if they've killed her, I'm about to unleash a hell on this world that will make the devil himself not want me.

Please be alive. Please be fucking alive.

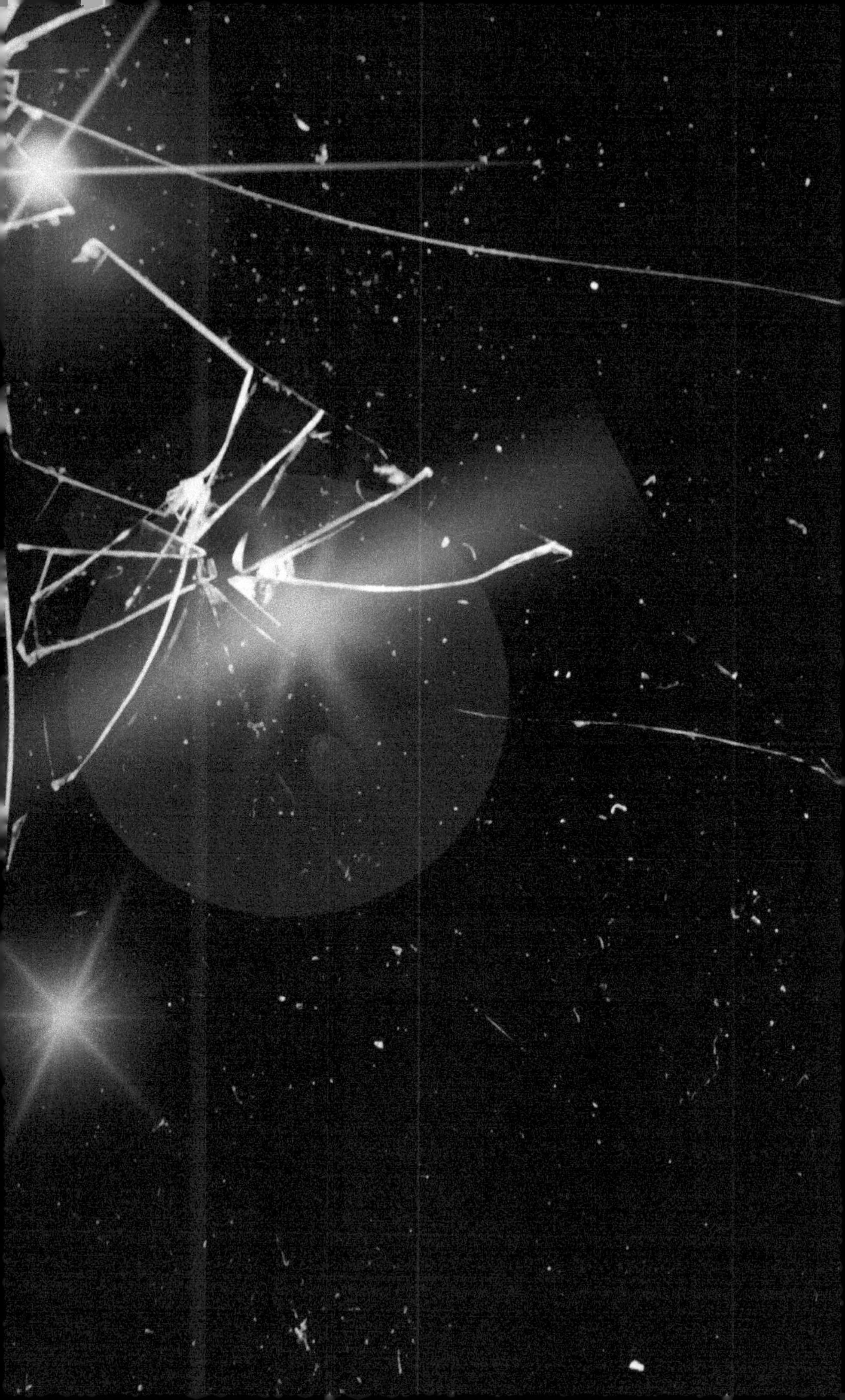

CHAPTER TWENTY-EIGHT

I CAN'T STOP PACING the hallway. Dylan is pale as he stares straight ahead, Zee clutching his hand as they sit beside him. But my restless feet won't let me sit down.

"This is my fault," I say, running a hand through my hair. "My fucking phone died, I forgot my goddamn charger." I pound a fist into the wall, the shitty fucking beige walls of the hospital corridor. "I was so close, if I'd made it…"

"Levi, you couldn't have known," Zee says gently, gazing up at me with bloodshot eyes. They've been crying quietly, trying to stay strong for the two of us. "No one could have seen this coming."

"Where were you?" I look down at Dylan, who won't meet my gaze.

"I was… I was dealing with something. I… I should have been…"

"You told me you were at the club!" I lean over him, and his gaze flashes up to me. "You told me you were at a meeting! Where the fuck were you?"

"Levi, enough," Zee says gently, rising to their feet. "This isn't going to help."

"I'm sorry." Dylan murmurs, his head dropping to his chest.

"I… She called me, and all I could do was listen…" His shoulders start to shake. "I'm sorry. I'm so sorry."

I exhale heavily and drop to my knees, wrapping my arms around him. He slumps against me as he cries.

"I'm sorry," I murmur, pressing a kiss to his neck as he grabs me tightly. "I'm sorry, baby. It's not your fault."

"I had to listen," he murmurs, his voice strained. "I heard all of it, heard them beating her and heard her screaming, it was… I'm… I'm so sorry."

"Hey, it's not your fault." I draw back and cup his face in my hands. "It's not. You couldn't have known this was going to happen."

"There was so much blood," he gasps, fingertips digging into my arms. "I was so fucking scared she was dead. They'd-"

"She's going to be fine." I interject, clutching him close again and meeting Zee's alarmed eyes over his shoulder. I want to believe it. Stella has to be alright. There's just no other option. I won't accept anything else other than her walking right on out of this hospital with us.

But I know it was bad.

Zee's face when they came to find me at the garage - I never want to see that look on someone's face again. I feel sick just thinking about it. And then that horrific drive here, hearing how Dylan had found our girl on the floor of her bedroom, barely breathing and beaten to within an inch of her life…

"Mr Fenton?"

I spin to face the doctor behind me, a middle-aged man with dark hair and glasses perched on his nose.

"Yes, that's me."

"Hi, I'm Dr LeRoy, I'm looking after Stella right now. I understand you're her brother?" He says, and Zee and Dylan rise to their feet.

"Is she OK?" Dylan asks.

The doctor looks back and forth between us, his brows knitting together lightly. "Are you all family?"

"We all live together," I snap. "Please, is Stella alright?"

"She's suffered from internal bleeding, and her spleen did rupture."

Dylan collapses, resting his hands on his knees, shoulders heaving as Zee rubs his back, their eyes filling with tears.

"She's going to be fine," the doctor goes on quickly, raising his hands. "We managed to stop the bleeding, and she's recovering now. The injuries were focused on the abdomen, so she's got some fractured ribs, but nothing that she won't come out of."

I run a hand over my mouth, fury and anguish pooling in my stomach. "Oh my fucking god."

"The police are on their way." Dr LeRoy looks from Dylan back to me. "This is obviously a serious crime, they're very concerned with what happened here."

"Yeah, so are we." Zee helps Dylan back into his chair, shaking their head and glaring at the doctor. "When can we see her?"

"She's sleeping right now, but I'll keep you informed." He gives me a reassuring smile. "Your sister is going to be just fine."

I don't even tell him she's not my sister, I'm too wound up in grief and anger to even reply. I simply nod and watch him retreat down the corridor back to Stella's room.

"Something's not right here," I mutter, shaking my head as I look down at Dylan. "Something is very, very fucking wrong."

"Oswald had dirt on her," Dylan says, tipping his head back to rest against the wall behind him. He runs a hand over his tear-streaked face and sighs. "He had a video of her on his phone, he was blackmailing her, I'm sure of it."

Zee's eyebrows shoot up, and they look back and forth between us. "What is going on here? What the hell have you two gotten yourselves into?"

I raise my hands. "Zee, you don't understand."

"Damn right, I don't." They spring to their feet, jabbing a finger in my face. "Whatever the fuck is going on here, my best friend is lying in a hospital bed because of it right now."

"I fucking love that woman," I snarl in response. "I wouldn't do anything to endanger her."

"Then what is going on here?" They put their hands on their hips, and look back down at Dylan. "Hmm? I'm waiting."

"We're not going to tell you that." Dylan's tone is soft and measured, and he rises to his feet. He looks down at Zee with brotherly tenderness, and puts a hand on their shoulder. "We can't involve you in this, Zee. It's just not going to happen. I care about you too much for this to come crashing down on you, too."

"Stella could have *died.*" Zee shoves a hand against Dylan's chest. "She could be in a fucking morgue right now."

"I won't let that happen." Dylan takes Zee's hand, the one that just pushed him, and curls both of his around them. "I need you to go home and be safe. We'll call you if we need you. But you need to leave this to us now."

"Dylan-"

"Zee, go home." Dylan's eyes are positively black as he gazes at them. "I need you to go home, and if we need you, we'll tell you. But this is bigger than you can even guess right now, so I need you to be out of it. Please."

Zee's face crumples, and they wrap their arms around Dylan's waist. "What the fuck have you done?" They murmur, dashing a hand over their eye.

"What needs to be done," Dylan says, planting a kiss on the top of their head. "Now, go on home. I'll call you when she wakes up."

Dylan is the picture of calm determination, and Zee finally relents when they realize there's no point fighting anymore. They hug us both, and hurry down the hospital corridor, arms wrapped around themselves.

"What dirt does Oswald have on Stella?" I ask quietly, and Dylan turns to fix his eyes on me.

"Not here," he says in a low voice. "I'll tell you later. But we need to move soon. This is only going to get worse."

"Is that where you were?"

He nods slowly. "Partly. But I'll tell you later." His eyes shift over my shoulder, and his body language changes, squaring up as his jaw sets.

I glance over my shoulder to see two cops moving down the hallway, flanked by two detectives. I turn back to Dylan with a heavy sigh.

"Fucking great."

"They're not going to help us," Dylan growls. "Fucking useless cops."

"No, they won't, but we just play along for now, OK? Fuck them. We deal with this ourselves."

We both face the approaching cops, who eye us warily.

"Levi Fenton?" The female detective looks up at me, showing me her badge. "Detective Hawkins. We spoke to your stepsister when the threat was called into her place of work."

I cross my arms over my chest and look her up and down. "Good for you. I see you really followed up on that."

She raises a hand with a small sigh. "Mr Fenton, I understand that you're upset, but-"

"Upset?" I scoff. "Upset? Upset is when someone scrapes my car and doesn't leave a fucking note. This?" I gesture in the direction of Stella's room. "This has me more than a little *upset*."

"We understand that," the male cop says in a patronising tone of voice that makes me want to put his head through the fucking wall. "But your sister refused police protection, otherwise we could have prevented this."

"Oh, I *know* you're not blaming her for what just happened," Dylan says, moving around me smoothly to get in the male cop's face.

"He never said that." Detective Hawkins lifts a hand as though to ward Dylan off, never actually touching him. "Now, you both need to calm down. I know this is hard, and you're worried. But getting mad at us won't help Stella."

Dylan adjusts his gaze to land on Detective Hawkins, rolling his shoulders as he tries to contain his rage. "Help Stella? Hmm? So, what have you done to help Stella? Found out who sent those bullets yet?"

Detective Hawkins sighs, clasping her fist in her hand. "We're still investigating. We have some leads, but-"

"Just say you got nothing," I interject, scoffing out a laugh as I run a hand over my mouth. "Man, you all are really great at your jobs."

"Good enough to catch two punks and have them put in prison for murder," the male detective counters.

"Cal, enough," Detective Hawkins snaps, and the smug asshole rolls his shoulders, meeting my eyes with a satisfied smirk.

"Yeah, Cal, how about you shut that mouth of yours?" Dylan snarls, and I put out a hand to pull him back to me.

"Come on, he's not worth it." I look back at Detective Hawkins. "So, what do you want? Why are you here?"

"We wanted to take a statement from you about the phone call, what you heard, anything Stella might have told you about her attackers."

"Two men, six feet tall, wearing masks, I guess? She couldn't see their faces." Dylan huffs out a breath and shakes his head. "Nothing useful."

"The hospital said the attack was brutal, focused on her abdomen?" Detective Hawkins raises her eyebrows as she looks at Dylan. "Mr Kovac, was your girlfriend pregnant?"

My head snaps to look at Dylan, and something like realization seems to dawn over his face. His brow furrows as he stares at the floor, and I can practically hear the cogs turning in his head.

"No, I mean…" He shakes his head, still not meeting her eyes. "No, she's not."

My stomach drops, because something isn't right here. But this isn't the time or the place. Instead, I pull my cocky rich asshole mask back into place, and stare down the cops.

"Look, we're both tired, and this has been a hard day. Dylan can come down and give you a statement tomorrow, but for now, we'd appreciate it if you left us alone." I look from Detective Hawkins to her colleague, both of whom seem to have lost their willingness to fight rather quickly. But they know who I am, who my family is, and just how hard I can make their lives if they push me. "So, if that's all, we'll let you get back to work."

Detective Hawkins plucks a card from her pocket and hands it to me. "Call me if you need to, and come down to the station tomorrow. Someone will help you."

"Great. Thanks."

Detective Hawkins sighs, then looks at her partner, jerking her head over her shoulder to indicate they should leave. Wordlessly, they head down the hallway and out of sight around the nurse's desk.

"What the fuck?" I murmur to Dylan without looking at him. "Pregnant?"

"She… she had a scare," he replies quietly. "She told me, last week. But it was just a scare."

"But someone thought she was." I turn and look up at him, that sick, sneaking feeling of dread washing over me. "Someone thought she was, and they wanted her to lose it."

"Levi…" Dylan raises his hands and puts them on my shoulders. "Levi, listen to me-"

"Is this my mother?"

"I don't know."

"*Where were you*?" I hiss, and his eyes drop from mine. "Dylan, what do you know that you aren't telling me?"

He puts a hand around the back of my neck, holding me firmly but tenderly. "*Guapo,* listen to me. I can't tell you here."

"Is it my mother?" I hiss, and his eyes snap back up to meet mine. He nods slowly.

"And your grandfather."

"Are you asleep?"

Dylan's voice sounds in the darkness beside me, and he rolls over to move closer to me.

"No." I haven't been able to put my mind at rest since the doctors sent us home. I keep waiting for the phone to ring, to tell us that Stella is waking up so we can run back to the hospital and be there when those beautiful amber eyes open up.

But the phone stays quiet, and I've been staring at the ceiling for an hour.

"I thought not." Dylan puts a hand on my chest. "I'm sorry, baby."

The word *baby* makes my heart hurt. Because he didn't want to hurt me when he told me about my family, about the video of Stella my grandfather had on his phone. But he could see it in my face when he told me what that piece of shit rapist had told him.

I'd already known my family was an endless mire of filth, debauched and ruined, beyond anything good. But to hear that, to know my grandfather paid someone to rape my girl, and then paid someone to beat her within an inch of her life to kill the baby they thought she was carrying - I swear to god, it's like I don't even have a soul anymore. I just want to kill, and hurt, and make every single last one of them bleed.

"Why didn't you tell me?"

Dylan sighs, rolling on to his back and throwing an arm over his head. "I don't know."

"Yes, you do."

Another sigh. "I felt guilty."

I roll on to my side, barely able to make out his silhouette in the dark. "Guilty?"

"In... In the video. She was calling out for me." He runs a hand over his face, letting it thud back on to the bed. "She was calling for me, and I wasn't there. I wasn't there for her, when she needed me. She was a mess, she was so lost, and it was all my fault."

"It wasn't your fault, it was *our* fault."

Dylan swings his legs over the side of the bed and sits up, leaning heavily on his knees. "No, you still don't get it. I left her that night, I left her after she had cried and begged me to never tell anyone what happened. I betrayed her, and I left her, and I pulled you into it, and this whole fucking mess is my fault." He sucks in a heavy breath, cradling his head in his hands. "I had to fix it, OK? Me. Just me."

"No, not just you." I move to put a hand against his back, leaning closer when he doesn't move away. "Listen to me, this isn't your fault. This is Harold's fault, and my mother's fault, and fucking Oswald's fault. All of it. We're just the pawns, stuck in their sick and twisted little games."

Dylan's shoulders slump further, as though the hopelessness within him has taken a physical form and is weighing down on him. "I left her alone again, to go and kill some nothing asshole. She could have died because of me."

"Stop!" I grip his shoulders and force him to look at me, cupping his jaw in my hand when he refuses. My eyes have adjusted enough in the darkness to see his face, heavy and sad, brows drawn together. "Listen to me, this was not you. You did what you had to do, and now we know, we fucking *know* what they all did, and how far they went. They deserve everything they're about to get, and none of that is your fault. None of it, do you understand?"

"Levi-"

"Do you understand?" I grip his face harder, pulling him closer so our foreheads rest against each other. "I love you, and I love her, and we're going to get through this, and we're going to be happy. I am not letting you bring this guilt with you."

"I'm the one who kills Oswald."

I nod, and he lets out a sigh. "He's yours. I'll watch, gladly."

"Thank you." He lifts his mouth to meet mine, kissing me slowly at first, the slightest quiver of his lips betraying the emotion coursing through him.

My phone vibrates on the nightstand, and we break the kiss instantly. I snatch the phone up and press it to my ear.

"Hello?"

"Mr Fenton?" A woman's voice sounds down the line.

"Yes, that's me."

"This is Dr Gable, from Mercy General. I'm calling to let you know that your sister's awake, and she's asking for you."

CHAPTER TWENTY-NINE

STELLA'S HAND is so small in mine. I gently stroke her fingers, over her cracked and broken nails. My girl's a fighter. She fought them with everything she had.

"I'm going to take you to get these nails done as soon as they let you out," I tell her with a smile.

She scoffs out a laugh, gazing at me with swollen eyes. Her lip is split, and bruises line the left side of her face.

"I think I might need a facial, too," she whispers, her voice rough and cracking.

I lean over her and brush her hair gently from her forehead. "Whatever you want. Anything, you name it. Smutty books, facials, a fucking week in the Bahamas. Whatever you want, *guera*. It's yours."

"How about a new home?" Her amber eyes are bloodshot, rimmed with purple and yellow, and they begin to shine with tears. "Somewhere far away. Just you, and me, and Levi."

I sigh heavily and press her hand to my mouth. "That sounds good."

"Maybe we could live in a big city, huh?" Her fingers stroke my cheek, and tears start to fill my eyes at the touch. "I think I'd like that."

"I think I would, too." I raise my eyes back to hers, and shake my head. "I'm so sorry."

"What for?"

"Not being there."

"Oh, Dylan." She sighs heavily. "This isn't your fault."

"This was Oswald, wasn't it?"

She blinks rapidly, her brow furrowing. "Why would you say that?"

"The video he had on his phone, of you." I hate that I say these words as soon as her mouth drops open in a startled gasp, and she shifts her head on the pillow, avoiding my eyes. "*Guera*, please don't turn away from me."

"How did you know?" A sob snatches away her voice, and her shoulders shake against the bed.

"Did you tell him you were pregnant?"

She shakes her head, still refusing to look back at me. "I wasn't, I promise. I wasn't."

"But he thought you were?"

"He told me to leave you." She puts a hand to her face and whimpers. "He told me I had to leave you both, so I goaded him. I was so stupid. I don't even know why I said it." She turns back to me, wincing as she does. "It was the dumbest thing I could have done, and I don't know why that was the first thing that came to mind. But I… I wanted them to know there was no way I was letting you both go. It was the only thing I could say, and I'm so stupid." She presses a hand to her face as she starts to cry, and I gently gather her in my arms.

She feels so fragile, like broken glass, and I don't want to hurt her. She shakes gently in my arms, tears soaking my shirt.

"I'm so sorry, *guera*. I'm so fucking sorry I wasn't there to protect you."

"I was so scared."

"I know, I know." I kiss her hair, holding her close and wishing I could protect her from the world and all the hatred and anger that's pursued her for all this time.

Suddenly, her head snaps up and she looks at me with wild eyes.

"Those men, in the video, Dylan, you have to know, I was so drunk, and I was high, and they… I don't even remember it really."

"Hey, no, none of that." I stroke her cheek, swiping away the tears that won't stop falling. "Don't even say anything about that. None of that was your fault."

"I just wanted you." Her face crumples and her head falls back against my shoulder. "The whole time, I just wanted you. You were all I could think of. I wanted you so badly."

The image of Stella's mouth torn open in a silent plea on that grainy video swims through my mind, and I clench my eyes shut.

"I'm going to make this right. I promise."

She goes still in my arms, and exhales heavily. "I just want to go. Please, can we just go?"

I stroke her hair as she nestles against my chest, and I know I'm going to lie to her. I'm going to tell her that everything's going to be just fine, and we're going to leave. We're going to find a beautiful apartment in Boston or New York, just the three of us, and live out our days. We're going to be happy. We're not going to be pursued by someone's vengeful family, and Levi and I are not going to have hands stained with blood. We're not damned. We're not tainted souls driven by revenge and thirsty for the dying light in the eyes of everyone who ever wronged her.

I know it's a lie. But I'll say it anyway. Because for once, I know the truth isn't going to help. It's never helped me before.

"*Guera,* you're going to get better, and we're going to take you home."

"And then we'll leave?" Her voice is small and hopeful. It shatters my heart.

"Yes. We'll get out of here."

The door swings open, and Levi steps into the room. The

scowl on his face is instantly replaced by a smile as his eyes land on Stella and me.

"Hey, baby girl," he says, perching on the other side of the bed. "How're you feeling?"

"Better." She lifts her head and turns in my arms to look at Levi, reaching out a hand to him. "A little sore."

"The doctors said you're a real fighter." Levi takes her hand in his, raising it to his lips. "Like I didn't already know that."

Stella sniffles and laughs softly. "Yeah well, I've dealt with worse."

Levi's eyes flash to mine for a split second, and he sighs.

"Dylan said we can leave," Stella goes on, shuffling a little closer to Levi as he puts an arm around her shoulders. "We're going to go, the three of us. Right?" She looks at me, her eyes brightening a little.

I smile and nod. "That's right. We're going to get the fuck out of here, and we're going to be so happy."

"Sounds good to me." Levi kisses Stella's temple. "Anywhere you want to go, you name it."

"Hmmm, good." She nuzzles into the crook of his neck, eyes fluttering closed. "We can start looking at places soon, then."

"Yes, we can." Levi's jaw feathers slightly, and I'm relieved Stella can't see it.

My phone buzzes in my pocket, and I excuse myself to the hallway to answer it.

"Thanks to you, my shitty basement got a full upgrade," Flea says down the line, hacking out a laugh.

"Glad you're happy, man."

"You wanted a schedule, I got you one." Keys tap in the background, and Flea coughs loudly so I jerk the phone away from my ear. "Sorry, I got a cold."

"No problem, those summer colds are vicious."

"OK, so, Perlmann-Langford schedule shows they're having dinner tomorrow night." Flea's chair creaks audibly, and he sniffles. "They will be convening at the Fenton family home, 7pm sharp."

"Great, I appreciate it."

"Yeah, no problem."

I move the phone from my ear to hang up, but hear Flea's "Aht-aht-aht" over the line, and raise the phone back.

"What?"

"You OK, man? You seem stressed."

"I-I'm in the hospital, with someone I care about."

Flea sucks on his teeth. "Sorry to hear that. I just wanted you to know that Oswald has been in touch with someone. A Michael Gray, ex-Marine. It would appear he's hired muscle."

"Of course he has." I grunt out a laugh. "Thanks for letting me know."

"Listen, I don't usually give a fuck, whatever you do, you do. " Flea's voice changes tenor, and it's unsettling to hear anything like concern coming from him. "This guy, this Michael Gray, he got a dishonorable discharge for war crimes. He didn't go to prison because Oswald stepped in and pulled some senatorial bullshit."

"War crimes?"

"This guy is a psycho." Flea's voice drops to an almost whisper. "He killed women and kids, man. With zero remorse. Just opened up on 'em. This guy doesn't have a conscience. Just… Be careful, OK?"

Goosebumps break out over my arms. Flea doesn't care about anything or anyone, except his mother. To hear this cynical, nonchalant man warn me makes my stomach drop.

"Thanks for the heads-up."

"Anytime."

The line goes dead as Flea hangs up.The chilled feeling doesn't go away. I watch Levi holding Stella through the glass window, watch those small slivers of hope fill Stella's eyes as she talks to him about moving away and leaving all this behind us.

My resolve almost falters. Maybe Stella's right. Maybe we

can leave all this behind us and just run away. But then my hand tightens around my phone. *No*. They'll never leave us alone. The fact that Oswald hired this war criminal tells me in no uncertain terms that it won't be over til we make sure it's over.

We can't stop, not now. Not until every last one of them is dead.

Days ago, I was praying that Stella was alive, that she'd live through the carnage I heard over the phone. Now, I send up another prayer. Or perhaps it's a bargain? A threat?

You owe me. After everything you've done, everything you've taken from us, you owe me. You owe me this. So turn the fuck away and let me make this right. And if I come out alive, I might just forgive you. But you fucking owe me.

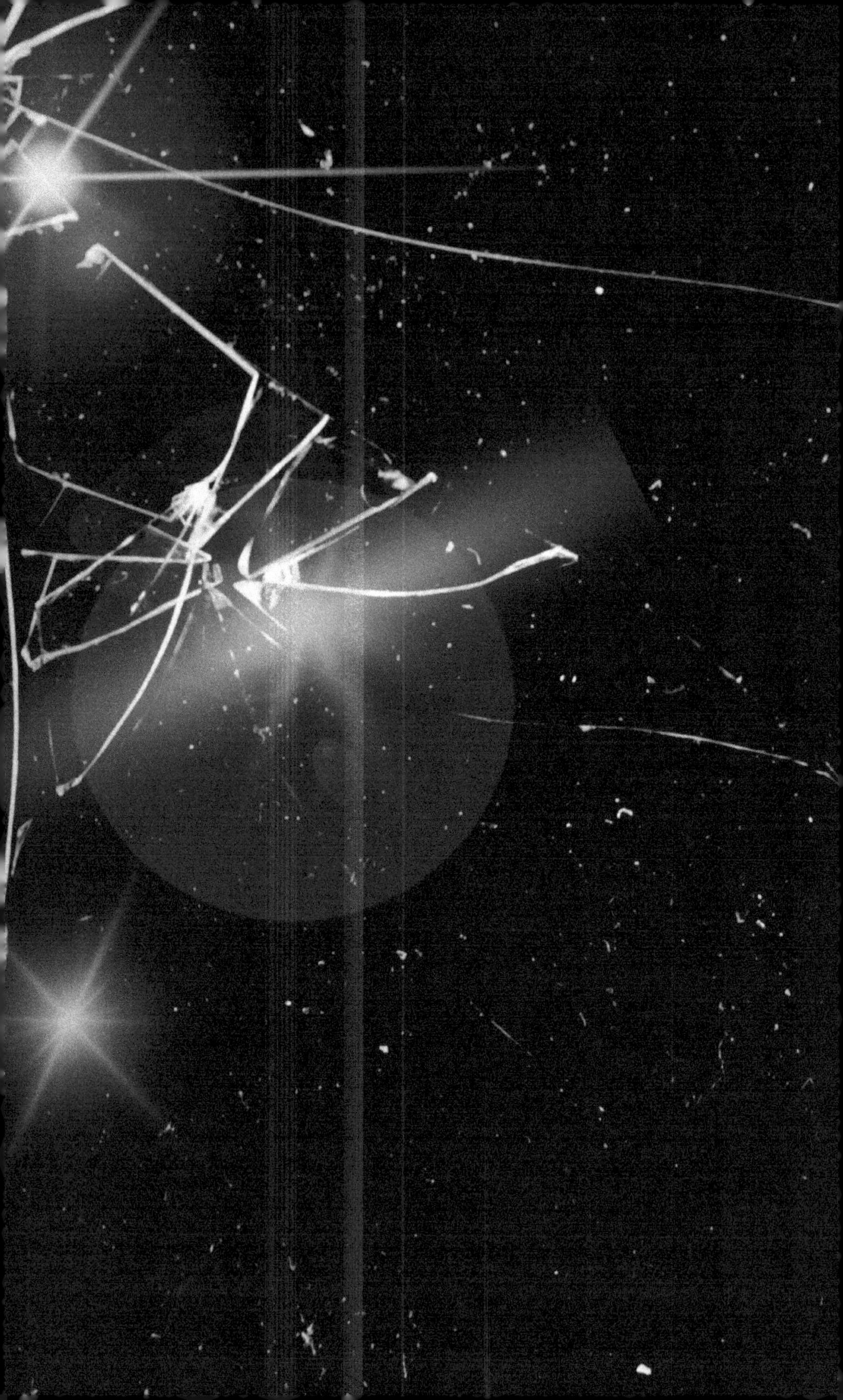

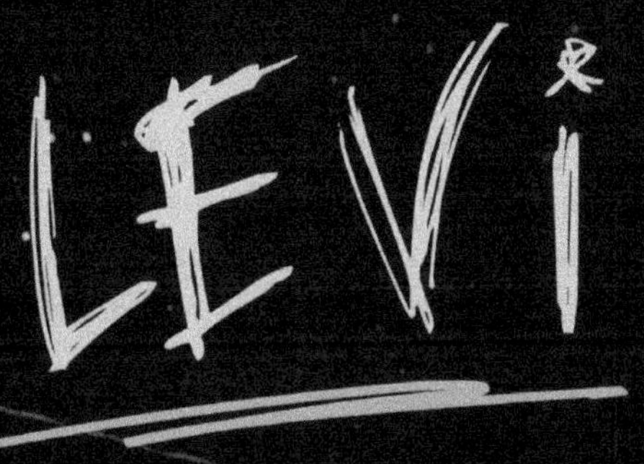

CHAPTER THIRTY

I'VE NEVER BEEN afraid of dying.

Inevitable things don't scare me.

My father died when I was almost too young to remember him. I have flashes of recollection - the glint of sunlight off his visor as he pulled into the drive, his laugh as I ran towards him, the feel of his leather jacket when he scooped me up in his arms - but other than that, there's nothing.

I'm still sad he died, but death is a part of life. I'd have lost him sooner or later.

So yeah, I've never been afraid of dying.

Until now.

It's not even that I'm afraid, not really. Not for myself, anyway. But as I stare at Dylan's back, watching him brush away droplets of water from his back, his muscles flexing as he stretches his arms over his head to pull on a black shirt, I'm suddenly fucking terrified of death.

I don't want him to die. I can't bear the thought. A life without Dylan is a life I can't even fathom, something I don't even want to imagine for a second.

So I stare, and stare, watching him move and breathe, knowing he's alive and that we're walking into a situation that

I'm desperate to finish but am fucking scared to my soul will end him.

Dylan turns around to catch my gaze, and stops short.

"Something on your mind?"

I swallow hard and nod, realizing I've bunched my t-shirt hard in my sweaty hands. I drop my eyes and clear my throat, yanking the shirt on over my head.

"Just thinking. Strategy, you know?"

"Sure." Dylan pulls on his pants, his eyes still on me as he does up his belt. "Strategy."

"Mhmm." My hands are fucking shaking, and Dylan crosses the room to stand in front of me. I can't look at him. If I look into those dark eyes, I'm going to fucking tell him all my fears. But he doesn't give me that choice, notching a hand under my chin and forcing me to look up at him.

"Hey." His eyes search my face for a moment, and the corner of his mouth lifts into a crooked grin. "It's going to be alright."

"I know."

"You know, I never told you…" I trail off, and Dylan lifts an eyebrow.

"Tell me what?"

"There was a night, in prison, when you'd had a bad time, and I'd… I'd helped you."

He smiles and nods, taking my hand. "You helped me a lot back then."

"Yeah well, on this night, you fell asleep, with your head in my lap." My eyes sting at the memory, and I clench them shut for a second to try and get a handle on my emotions. "I remember sitting there, and you were… I mean, you were just lying there, trusting me, letting me take care of you. I think… I think that was the moment I knew…" I look up at him, his dark eyes boring into mine. "There's never been anyone else for me. It was you and Stella, always. All those girls at school, I was just talking myself into something."

He huffs out a small laugh. "Sure did a whole lot of talking to yourself there."

"Yeah, what can I say?" I shrug lightly, and raise my hand to cradle his jaw. "I'm an idiot."

"Yeah you are." Dylan lowers his head and brushes a kiss against my lips. "I love you anyway, though."

"I love you, too."

"You scared?"

I shake my head. "No." *Not in the way you think.* "I'm angry. I want it done. I want them to pay."

"Me too." He presses another hard kiss against my lips, pulling back to speak, but I smother his words as I grab him and pull him down to me. I kiss him furiously, nipping and biting at his lips. He yanks me against him, his hands on my ass, and grinds against me in a way that has me groaning into his mouth.

But we finally do have to pull back, and get ready to go. And that feeling of dread sinks back into my stomach.

I hate this.

There's a cool breeze springing up as we get on our bikes. The sun sinks behind the horizon, giving way to a slowly darkening sky. I pull on my helmet and look over at Dylan, the picture of calm as he zips up his leather jacket.

Don't take him from me. Please.

I don't believe in God. I don't believe in anything, but Dylan and Stella. But just in case some mystical old man with a beard is looking down, I beg anyway.

Don't take him from me. Let us finish this.

I push down the dread and the fear, and instead conjure up the image of Stella crying in her bathroom. My sweet Stella, covered in bite marks and scratches. Unable to sit down. Clawing into me and sobbing. Refusing to tell me what happened.

My dread is replaced by rage, blinding and souring rage, sending acid through my veins. The bike roars under me as I tail Dylan to my mother's house, headlights of passing cars streaking by us until the night becomes quiet, and we navigate the empty streets of uptown.

The perimeter wall of my mother's house is lit up, and the gate guard waves us in as we approach. Idiot, doing a great fucking job. The fucking irony that he could have waved in anyone dangerous, but waved in Gloria's son, who's going to kill her tonight. It's almost enough to make me laugh.

My grandfather's car is parked outside the house, his driver sitting in the front seat with headphones in, engrossed in some show on his phone. As long as he stays there, he'll be fine.

Dylan and I pull up, the engines of our bikes falling silent. Dylan pulls off his helmet, and looks over at me with a grin.

"You ready?"

I nod, reaching under my seat to pull out the gun and tuck it into my waistband. Dylan is already armed with a knife, and I know this isn't going to be a good death for any of the fuckers in this house. It's all going to look like a tragic accident, everything that happens here tonight will be covered by ash and flames.

I can't wait to watch it burn.

Dylan follows me down the side of the house to the kitchen door, and soft music plays in the distance. The kitchen is quiet, the food already served and the staff dismissed for now. Dylan pulls out his phone, swiping through a few screens.

"Zee's still with Stella," he tells me, swiping again. "And this Michael Gray isn't in the house, he's downtown."

"Good." The hired muscle has no reason to be here tonight, they don't suspect a thing. The thought has me grinning.

They don't see this coming at all.

My mother's laughter meets us as we enter the hall, and I head to the dining room, following the sound. High heels clack on the floor, and I turn to see Valerie heading for us. Perfect.

"Hi, Levi!" She says brightly, her smile instantly dropping as Dylan grabs her, covering her mouth and holding the knife to her throat.

"The ledger, where is it?" He hisses into her ear.

Valerie shakes her head, eyes wide as she stares at me. There's a muffled protest, and Dylan presses the tip of the knife harder into her skin, drawing a tiny drop of blood. Valerie squeaks and goes still. I withdraw the gun, holding it loosely in my hand, and Valerie's eyes almost pop out of her skull as they land on it.

"The ledger, Valerie," I say softly. "The one where you planned out the schedule to have Stella raped. We'd like to know where it is."

Valerie shakes her head again, tears beginning to fall from her eyes.

Dylan traces the knife over her stomach. "I will gut you like a fucking fish, do you understand me? Now, tell me where that fucking ledger is."

Valerie lifts a hand and frantically jerks it in the direction of the study. Dylan shoves her forward with his body, keeping his hand firmly over her mouth. I follow them as he pushes her into the door, and she scrambles at the handle, opening it and stumbling on her heels as Dylan forces her to move. I close the door behind us, putting the gun back in my waistband.

"Now, you sick bitch," Dylan growls, "where is it?"

Valerie mumbles something against his hand, and Dylan sniggers darkly.

"Want to talk, do we?"

Valerie nods, her nostrils flaring as she breathes.

"If you scream or try to run, I will slice your throat, do you understand?" Dylan's voice is menacing and sends goosebumps down my arms. He moves his hand slowly, keeping a firm grip across Valerie's shoulders, the knife pressed to her skin.

Valerie gasps for air, her chest jerking in and out, sweat beading on her forehead. "Th-the safe," she stutters, pointing at a painting behind the desk. "It's a r-red diary, it's in there."

Dylan's dark eyes land on me and he gives me a nod. "You know the combination?"

Valerie shakes her head. "I-I don't, she never told me."

"Liar," Dylan snarls, and Valerie whimpers.

"I swear, I don't, please, please don't kill me."

Dylan claps his hand back over Valerie's mouth and grits his teeth as he looks at me.

"Any ideas?" he asks me.

I'm about to say that I don't know, because my mother sure as fuck never told me that sort of information, and if she didn't even tell Valerie, I can't even begin to imagine what that safe holds. And then my eyes land on her desk, on the picture of my father, his wide smile and blue eyes, just like mine.

"Yeah, I know it." It's my father's birthday. The one tiny remnant of my mother's humanity, the love she had for the only good person who ever graced the halls of this fucking house.

I pull the painting from the wall, some useless old ancestor who's long dead and doesn't matter anymore. I throw it to the ground, revealing the steel door of the safe in the wall. I punch in the combination, and the light on the door switches from red to green. There's a mechanic clunk as the steel bars roll back, and the door heaves open an inch.

I feel a pang for just a split second, thinking of how much my father loved my mother. Then I imagine his horror at what she turned into. A woman who scheduled a teenager to be raped like she scheduled her fucking salon appointments. My dad would be horrified.

At least he'll never have to see her again. Because tonight she'll be headed into the deepest pits of hell.

The red ledger is at the very bottom of the pile of papers and wads of cash. Its cover is faded, the leather corners worn.

I pull it out, spilling the contents of the safe all over the floor, and throw it on the desk. I open it up, to find my mother's handwriting, neatly laying out names and dates, times and hotel rooms. One senator after another, even the names and numbers of their fucking PAs. All laid out neatly.

I feel sick, rage gnawing at my ribcage.

Page after page of names and dates. Plans and requests.

The senator requests a full wax, prefers smooth. Requests S be dressed in a sundress with hair in pig tails.

I lift my gaze to Valerie, who's still crying softly with Dylan's hand over her mouth.

"You knew about this?" I jab my finger against the open page. "There's two people writing in this. I know my mother's handwriting. The other person is you, right?"

Valarie's face crumples, and Dylan jostles her roughly.

"Answer the fucking question." He commands, and Valerie shrieks behind his hand as the knife slices into her skin.

She nods, and Dylan moves his hand to release her pleas.

"Yes, I did, I knew, I'm so sorry, I'm so sorry, Levi, I swear, I didn't-"

"Don't you fucking dare say you didn't know what they were doing." Dylan growls into her ear, and Valerie cowers, her eyes darting to the side as she freezes. "Don't you stand here and say you didn't really know, that you had no choice."

"Please," she whimpers, tears pouring down her face. "Please, I'm so sorry. I never wanted anyone to get hurt."

Dylan's eyes lift to mine. "Is it all there?"

I nod. "It's all here. Names, dates, even special requests."

Dylan's jaw feathers violently, and the knife glints in the light as he lifts it from Valerie's throat and plunges it into her stomach. Valerie's body jerks back and forth as Dylan stabs her repeatedly, blood pouring down her legs. Her mouth opens in shock, no sounds coming out.

Dylan shoves her away from him, and she crumples to the floor, face down. She claws weakly at the carpet, whispered pleas falling from her lips.

"It takes a while to die from a stab wound to the stomach," Dylan says, crouching down beside her to wipe the knife clean on the fabric of her skirt. "Anywhere from 3 minutes, up to 20. It depends. But it gives you time to try and make your peace with God before you meet him." He rises to his feet and spits on her body. "*Zgnic w piekle.*"

He steps around Valerie's bloody body and moves to my side at the desk. He casts a glance down at the ledger, and shakes his head. There's nothing else to say. We have the proof now, and all the names.

I scoop the ledger up from the desk, and we leave Valerie bleeding out in the study to go to the dining room, where my family awaits us.

"Valerie?" My mother calls lightly as we approach, the smile on her face instantly dissolving as we enter the room. "Levi? *Dylan*?"

My grandfather turns in his chair, brow furrowing as he takes us in. His eyes land on the blood on Dylan's hands, and his hand darts to his coat pocket.

"I wouldn't do that, old man." The gun is in my hands and trained on him, and he freezes, holding his hands up. "Everyone's going to stay nice and quiet, OK?"

My mother's eyes are wide, and she doesn't move as Dylan approaches her.

"Hey, Gloria," he says with a smile, crouching down beside her. "So, I hear you and me got it on, is that right? How was I? Did I treat this dried up cunt good?"

My mother scoffs out a laugh, pulling her face into a haughty mask as she clasps her hands in her lap.

"Get out of my house," she says, her voice wavering ever so slightly.

Dylan laughs, his mouth twisting in a cruel smile. "I thought we could rekindle our love. You really want me to go?" He rises to his feet and grabs her throat in a bloody hand, shoving her back against her chair.

"Do not touch her!" Oswald bellows, jerking as I cock the gun and take a step closer to him.

"You keep your mouth shut, old man," I say, throwing the ledger on the table. "I know you knew about this?"

"You hire low-class thugs to do your dirty work, they're

going to talk." Dylan grins across the table at Oswald. "Your man squealed on you immediately."

"You killed him, didn't you?"

"Right around the time your men beat the shit out of our woman, yeah." Dylan's face darkens. "How much do you have to pay for men to assault an innocent woman, huh? What's the going rate for a man like you to have people do his dirty work?"

My mother raises a hand and slaps at Dylan's arm. "Let me go!"

Dylan rounds on her, clawing his hand around her throat, jerking her head forward and slamming it back against the chair. "Listen here, *puta,* you shut your fucking mouth before I make you suck on my fucking blade, you understand me?"

"Don't you dare touch her!" Oswald rises to his feet, and I step forward to slam the gun into the back of his skull, sending him sprawling across the table, hacking coughs breaking from his mouth.

"You move again, old man, and I'll put a bullet in your ear." I stand over him as he groans and slumps back into his chair, blood trickling from the back of his head and staining the white collar of his shirt.

"What do you want?" Gloria asks, and I'm shocked to see tears welling in her eyes. She looks at me and shakes her head. "You're not going to kill your own family, are you?"

"You think you're my family?" I chuckle, shaking my head. "When have you ever acted like my family, huh?"

"I was a good mother," she insists, fighting against Dylan's hand. "I lost my way after your father died, that's all. I loved him so much. Losing him destroyed me, Levi. You have to understand that."

"Don't you dare bring my father into this." I train the gun on her. "Don't you fucking take his name in your mouth. He'd be standing right here next to me if he was still alive."

She clenches her eyes shut, her lips quivering. "Don't say that."

"He'd be fucking disgusted by you, by what you've become." I jerk the gun at the ledger as she opens her eyes. "These names, that's all of them?"

She nods, Dylan's hand around her throat impeding her movement. "That's all of them, every single one."

"Was it your idea?" Dylan asks.

Her eyes flash up to him, and her lashes flutter, the column of her throat shifting in his hand as she tries to swallow.

"I-I just… I mean, Harold had been doing it for-"

Dylan yanks her head forward again and smashes it back against the wooden frame of her chair, and Gloria lets out a strangled cry. Oswald's hands ball into fists on the table, but he doesn't try to move, his eyes flickering to me and the gun for a moment.

"I asked if it was your fucking idea, you sick fucking hag." Dylan snarls into Gloria's face, his expression a mask of sheer rage.

"I-I knew what he'd been doing to Stella," she stammers, trying to push away Dylan's arm weakly. "He'd been taking pictures of her for years, her mother knew about it for Pete's sake."

"I'm going to ask you one last time." Dylan withdraws the knife from the holster at his waist, and drags the tip of the blade along Gloria's cheek. She whimpers and squeezes her eyes shut. "And if you don't answer me, I'm going to do what I just did to your fucking secretary, and spill your insides all over your fucking filet mignon. Now, *answer me*."

"It was my idea!" Gloria cries, her voice strained by horror as Dylan digs the knife into her cheek, drawing a stream of blood that mingles with the tears pouring from her eyes. "It was my idea! I know it was wrong, but Harold, he was power hungry, he wanted more, always more, and what I gave him wasn't enough. He told me that. Do you have any idea how humiliating it was to be married to someone more obsessed with his daughter than his wife?"

"You sick bitch," I say, revulsion curdling at the back of my throat. "So this was just a grudge for you because you married a fucking pedophile? Instead of helping Stella, you punished her?"

"You have no idea what it's like to get older!" My mother screeches at me, slapping hard at Dylan's arm. "You have no idea what it's like to become invisible! Stella was so beautiful, and everyone loved her. You think I didn't see your face at my wedding?" She sneers at me, writhing in Dylan's grip. "I knew you were in love with her for years, I could see it. Sneaking into her room to sleep with her, don't think I didn't know!"

"I never touched her like that, not once." The gun is shaking in my hands, my rage barely contained. "I held her through her nightmares, the nightmares *you caused,* you twisted fucking monster."

"She was *drugged*, she had no idea it was even happening!"

At these words, Dylan's eyes widen, pools of black and white rage, and he slams a fist into my mother's stomach. She lets out a hollow howl, sucking in a breath as her eyes bug out of her head. Oswald cries out in protest, trying to dart out of his chair, but I slam the gun into his temple. He sags against the edge of the chair, putting a hand to the blood running down the side of his face, losing his balance and crashing to the floor.

Gloria starts crying in earnest now, her panic seeming to peak as Dylan releases her and steps back from her. She watches me approach slowly, the gun gripped in my hand, and she shakes her head.

"Levi, please," she murmurs, hands gripping the chair. "Please, baby boy, I'm your mama. I love you."

"I don't need your kind of love." I raise the gun to point it at her face. "I don't need anyone like you anywhere near me. You're evil."

"Levi, please, please."

"Levi, get down!" Dylan's voice tears me out of the moment and I drop into a crouch, turning to see Dylan charging across

the room at the man who's appeared in the doorway with a gun in his hand, pointing directly at me.

The man aims at Dylan, and fires, the shot flying past Dylan as he tackles the man around his middle and sends them both tumbling to the ground. Dylan's fists rain down on the man, who lifts his arms in defense, twisting his arm to smash the gun into the side of Dylan's face.

Dylan recoils for a moment, but it's long enough for the man to land a strike to Dylan's side and get the drop on him, rolling Dylan onto his back and straddling him. He raises his weapon, but stops when I cock the gun against the back of his skull.

"Drop it, fucker."

The man lifts his hands slowly, dropping the gun to the floor with a clatter.

"Now, get up slowly." I keep the gun trained on him as he climbs off Dylan and rises to his feet. "Turn around."

The man faces me, his face locked in a sneer as he looks me up and down.

"Mr Michael Gray, I assume?" I ask, my eyes flickering down to Dylan as he snatches up the gun before getting to his feet. "Looks like you picked the wrong family to work for, my friend."

The bastard smirks at me, hands still raised. "You're quick, I'll give you that. But I was warned about that. Thugs like you, you're good at fighting, but you're dumb."

"Dumb?" I snort. "You're the one with two guns pointed at you right now."

He laughs, a fucking chilling sound. "And if it had been me, I'd have used one by now."

He moves so quickly I don't even see it coming. One second, the gun is in my hands, the next, I'm disarmed, a fist slamming into my face, the gun gone from my hands, and a shot ringing in my ears.

DYLAN

CHAPTER THIRTY-ONE

THIS ASSHOLE'S speed catches me by surprise.

I fire on sheer instinct, aiming for his shoulder because I don't want to hit Levi. At this range, the bullet could go straight through this fucker.

Blood spurts from Levi's nose, and he goes down as my bullet tears into Michael Gray's shoulder.

But this fucker barely flinches, instead turning tail on me with a roar. I don't have time to fire again as he lunges at me, throwing me to the ground. The gun goes off, but the bullet strikes the ceiling uselessly.

He's on top of me, the gun pointed straight at my face, but before he can fire, he's torn backwards as Levi locks his hands around his neck. He slams him down to the ground, landing two hard punches in the guy's throat.

"Fucking fucker!" Levi bellows, grabbing him by the collar and slamming him into the ground, then striking him in the jaw two, three, four times. "Who's the fucking thug now?"

A bloody Oswald seems to rise from nowhere, charging at Levi, armed pathetically with a steak knife, and I fire at him over Levi's head. The bullet lands square in the old man's forehead, and he hits the ground immediately.

Gloria starts screaming, launching from her chair and trying to run from the room.

"Oh, no you don't." I get to my feet and give chase, gaining on her easily. I grab the bitch's hair and drag her backwards as she shrieks and flails blindly at my arm. I slam her down on to the table, holding the gun to the base of her skull. "Stay the fuck down."

"No, no please," she whimpers, hands shaking against the gleaming tabletop. "Dylan, oh my god, please, please don't kill me."

"I'm not going to kill you." I look over at Levi, who is still holding Michael down against the floor. His shoulders are heaving, blood trickling from his nose, over his lips. "Your son wants that honor."

Gloria begins to cry again, holding her hands out beside her head. "Please, please don't kill me. I'm sorry. I'll admit to everything. I'll say anything. I'll do anything. Just please, please don't kill me."

"You think that's good enough for us?" I press the barrel of the gun into her flesh. "You think we'll be happy with that? You're fucking wrong." I lower my head and she flinches as my breath washes over her hair. "I don't negotiate with psychopaths."

"You're the psychopath!" She bucks underneath me, casting a venomous glance over her shoulder and crying out as I slam her head into the table.

Levi rises to his feet, eyes on mine as he wipes the blood from his face. He grits his teeth and looks down at Michael, before landing a kick in the side of the man's head that has him going still instantly. Out cold.

"Fucking asshole," he snarls, before looking back at me and sidling slowly across the room. "Well, mother, looks like this is it, huh?"

Gloria wails, hands shaking, legs threatening to give out underneath her at any moment.

"Levi, no, baby boy, no, you can't do this!" She collapses on the table, sobbing and clawing at her face. "You can't, you can't, please! *Please!*"

Levi moves to my side, holding out his hand. I hand the gun to him, and he holds it for a moment before putting it down to his mother's head. She's blubbering now, pleading and whimpering as she realizes that she's taking her last few breaths.

"You drugged Stella?" He asks, his voice cold and calm.

Gloria doesn't respond, just continues to plead and cry.

"You drugged her? You put her in the hospital? You did everything you could to hurt her?" Levi shakes his head, running his tongue over his bloody teeth. "And now you lie here, begging not to die?"

His finger moves to the trigger, and he tilts his head.

"You know, mother, I actually want to see you die. I want to watch the light fade from those fucking eyes."

He reaches out and grabs her by the back of the head, yanking her upwards. He's half-spun her towards us when a bullet tears through the side of her head, sending bone fragments and brain matter up in a cloud of red.

It takes me a second to even place the shot, to recognise what's happening. My eyes move to the other side of the room, over Oswald's inert frame, to where Michael was lying just seconds before. But he's not lying unconscious on his back anymore.

Michael is on his knees, a gun aimed at us. Levi realizes too late as his mother's dead body slumps against him, and dropping her is losing him time. Michael swings the gun in his direction, and Levi isn't raising his weapon fast enough to fire first. Michael has a clean shot.

I shove myself against Levi just as the gun goes off, pushing him to the ground with Gloria's dead body wedged between us. Michael curses, and I see from underneath the table that he's getting to his feet.

I snatch the gun from Levi's hand and rise back up over the

edge of the table, dipping back down as Michael fires off another shot.

"Dylan!" Levi pushes Gloria off him, but I put out a hand.

"Stay down!"

Michael is stalking towards us, and I don't have much time. I drop underneath the edge of the table, and take aim at his knees. I squeeze the trigger, the shot landing in Michael's thigh.

He cries out, crashing to his knees, his hand flying to the wound. He looks up, in time to see me getting to my feet, and raises his gun.

But this time, I'm faster.

The gunshot rings through the dining room, and Michael's eyes go wide. His gun clatters to the floor, and he lifts shaking hands to his neck. The wound is enormous, blood pulsing from his arteries in violent crimson streaks that splatter the floor around him.

He looks at me, eyes clouding as death takes him, and his mouth moves but no words come out. He tries to snatch a breath, but there's nothing but more blood, coating his tongue and lips in a thick film.

He crumples to the floor, face down, arms spread beside him. His body convulses a few times, and then he goes still.

I put the gun down on the table, my chest pounding. It's over. It's finally over.

"Dylan?"

I look down at him, and smile. "I'm here, *guapo*." And then I remember the pain in my side.

I put a hand to where blood is pouring from between my ribs, and Levi is on his feet instantly.

"Fuck, Dylan, oh my god." He presses his hands to the wound, shaking his head, his big blue eyes wide and wild as they meet mine. "I'm sorry, oh my god, I'm sorry. I wasn't fast enough. I should have been faster, I'm sorry, I'm so sorry, baby."

I give him a weak smile, feeling the blood bubbling from the wound as the air is sapped from my lung. "You did great, *guapo*. It's alright. I'll be alright."

But I can feel that I'm not going to be alright. My breath catches in my throat, and I falter as Levi cries out and tries to hold me up.

"Baby, no, no, not like this, not here, please." He growls as he tries to keep me upright, buckling under my weight as my vision begins to grey. "Dylan, no, come on, get up, please, *please*."

"I'm sorry," I murmur against his neck, tracing my fingertips along his jaw. "I'm sorry. I love you."

"*No*."

I'm on the ground, my head cradled in Levi's lap, his desperate, bloody face gazing down at me.

"Don't you die on me, Kovac." He shakes his head, dashing away a tear. "Don't you dare fucking die on me."

"You look after our girl," I tell him, and sirens begin to wail in the distance. "You hear me? You go, and look after our girl."

"I'm not leaving you!"

"Yes, you are." I smile up at him. "You blame this all on me. You didn't know anything. You blame this all on me, and you go look after our girl."

"Dylan, stop! I'm not leaving."

The sirens get louder, and black spots begin to dance in my vision.

"Levi, go. Please go."

He's staying there, not moving, not leaving me. They'll find him. They'll put him away. Stella will be all alone. I try to tell him that Stella needs him, that he has to think of her, but words aren't coming out when I try to speak. Just gasping breaths. The wound doesn't really hurt anymore. Everything feels strange, and warm. My limbs won't obey me.

Levi is still looking down at me, shaking his head, his pleas sounding as though they're coming from another room. Suddenly, his head shoots up, and he bellows. There's movement out of the corner of my eye, and there's a black flash, followed by the muffled shot of a gun.

Levi is thrown backwards, and I reach for him blindly.

Levi.

Levi.

Levi.

But my hands don't work anymore. Nothing works.

The sirens wail, louder and louder. There are shouts, and more gunshots. Then there's no more light, and no more sound.

There's just nothing.

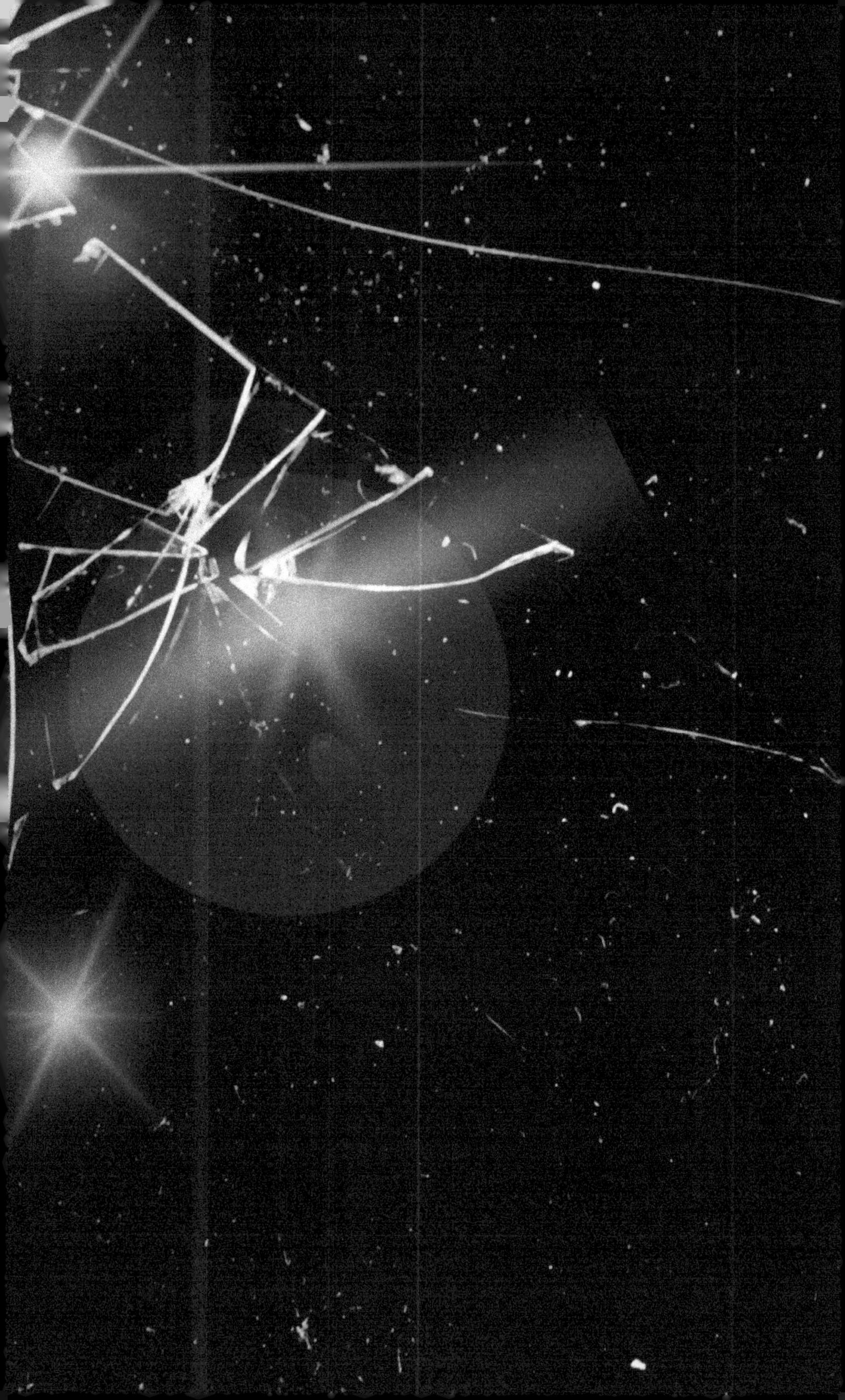

CHAPTER THIRTY-TWO

"STOP FUCKING TOUCHING ME!" There's hands all over my face, and a hot liquid running into my eye. My head is pounding, and everything is blurry. "Get the fuck off me! Where's Dylan?"

"Sir, you need to calm down, you've been shot." The man's voice is stern, hovering over me as the room sways back and forth.

No, not the room, the ambulance. The ambulance they bundled me into, while I was screaming and lashing out. They took Dylan from me, after that rat bastard Michael Gray got back up like a fucking horror movie serial killer, and fired off one last shot at me. The cops shot him, I'm pretty sure of that, but he managed to hit me with his last bullet.

Now my head is pounding and I don't know where Dylan is, I don't even know if he's alive.

"Where's Dylan?" I ask again. "Is he alive?"

"I'm just worried about you right now." There's pressure on the wound on the side of my head, a sharp sting as some liquid washes over it.

"Please, is he alive?" My voice cracks, my hands balled into fists.

"I need you to calm down so I can control this bleeding."

It's useless.

I lie on that stretcher and pray, I pray so fucking hard. I beg God and the world and the universe and whatever other mythical creatures that might exist in that vastness above me to just *let him live.* To let him be alive for both of us. We can't do this without him. He doesn't deserve this. Not after everything he's been through.

Let him live. Let him be happy with us. Please. I'll do anything.

The hospital is blurs of white and blue, nurses and doctors in scrubs racing past me as they wheel me through the corridors. Lights pass overhead, one after the other in quick succession, filtering through the blurry haze of my one good eye.

I've lost too much blood. I feel lightheaded, too weak to fight and too dizzy to get up.

"Is he here?" My voice is barely a whisper. My hand shoots out to grab the arm of the person beside me. "Is he here?"

"Who?" A soft voice responds, and a warm hand is over mine. "Is who here?"

"Dylan. Dylan. Is he here?"

There's no answer, just a pat on my hand that's meant to be comforting, and more shouted commands. No one tells me anything. They just put needles in my arm, and a mask over my face, and call for a surgeon.

Even as thick black starts to pull me under, I ask them where Dylan is. I ask them over and over, until I go to sleep.

The warm hand is still there.

But it's quiet now. So quiet.

The hand squeezes mine gently, and there's a small sound, like a sob.

I try to open my eyes. Slowly, slowly, my left eye opens.

"Levi?"

I know that voice. I squeeze the hand holding mine, hoping to god it belongs to that voice.

The hand squeezes back, and there's another, louder sob.

"Levi?"

I try to focus on the figure sitting beside me, on the honey-coloured hair that's backlit by a dim lamp. I try to turn my head towards her, but there's wires and masks in the way.

"Don't move," she says softly. "Baby, don't move. Just stay there. I'm here. It's OK."

"Stella?"

"I'm here, Levi. I'm here."

The relief that washes over me is fleeting, and my hand tightens around hers.

"Where's Dylan?"

Stella doesn't answer, just starts to sniffle, her other hand curling around mine. Panic grips me.

"Stella," I plead, my voice like gravel. "Stella, please, where is he? Please, please…"

"He's still in surgery." Zee's calm voice sounds from my other side, and their hand rests on my arm. "We don't know anything yet."

Surgery. That means he's not dead. That means he could still make it. Surgery is good. It has to be good. He's strong, he'll make it. He won't die. He can't.

"I'll go see if there's any news," Zee says softly, giving my arm a squeeze, and their footsteps pad out of the room.

I can see better now, I can focus on Stella, sitting beside my bed. She's still in a hospital gown, her face peppered with fading bruises. She's in a wheelchair.

"What are you doing out of bed?"

She smiles softly, tears glistening on her cheeks. "You think they'd keep me away from you?"

"You should be resting."

"I'm fine," she assures me, reaching out to stroke my cheek. "I promise, I'm fine." Her smile fades just a little, and her eyes flicker to the door. "Don't say anything," she murmurs. "The cops are sitting outside. If they ask you anything, you don't say a word."

Of course, the cops.

Even if Dylan makes it, this whole shit show is going to come raining down on us. There's no ashes or flames to cover what we did in that house. I close my eye, and take a deep breath.

"I'm sorry, Stella."

She shuffles onto the bed beside me, burying her face in the crook of my neck. My arms are too heavy to lift, so I can't pull her close. But she lies against me, holding my hand and crying softly.

"It's going to be alright," she murmurs. "I promise. We'll make it alright."

"All I ever wanted was to make things right."

"Don't talk about that now."

"I need to, pretty girl." I kiss her head, stroking her fingers with mine. "All I ever wanted to do was protect you. And I let you down."

She wraps her arm around me gently, tears soaking my shoulder as she cries.

"I want a life with you, and Dylan," I tell her quietly, her body shaking. "I want to wake up next to you every day and know I have you to come home to at the end of it. That's all I ever wanted, Stella. You, and him. Us. Together. And I fucked it up." I entwine my fingers with hers, and she looks up at me, tears continuing to pour down her face. "I love you so much, and I'm so, so sorry."

"I'm not." She shakes her head, biting her lip. "I'm not. I'm going to make this right. I promise."

Stella looks over at the door, and I gingerly move my head to watch Zee walk into the room. Their face is drawn, their eyes filled with sorrow. Stella's sharp intake of breath sets my heart racing.

"No," Stella gasps, her hand flying to her mouth.

Zee quickly raises their hands. "He's out of surgery, but he's in the ICU."

"Is he going to be OK?" Stella asks, gripping my hand harder.

Zee exhales heavily and shrugs. "They don't know. They said he's in pretty bad shape." They dash a hand against their face. "They said all we can do is wait." They slump into the chair beside my bed, running their hands over their face.

We all lapse into silence. There's nothing else to say right now. Nothing else happens in that room, but tears and prayers, and the hope that, just this once, someone is fucking listening.

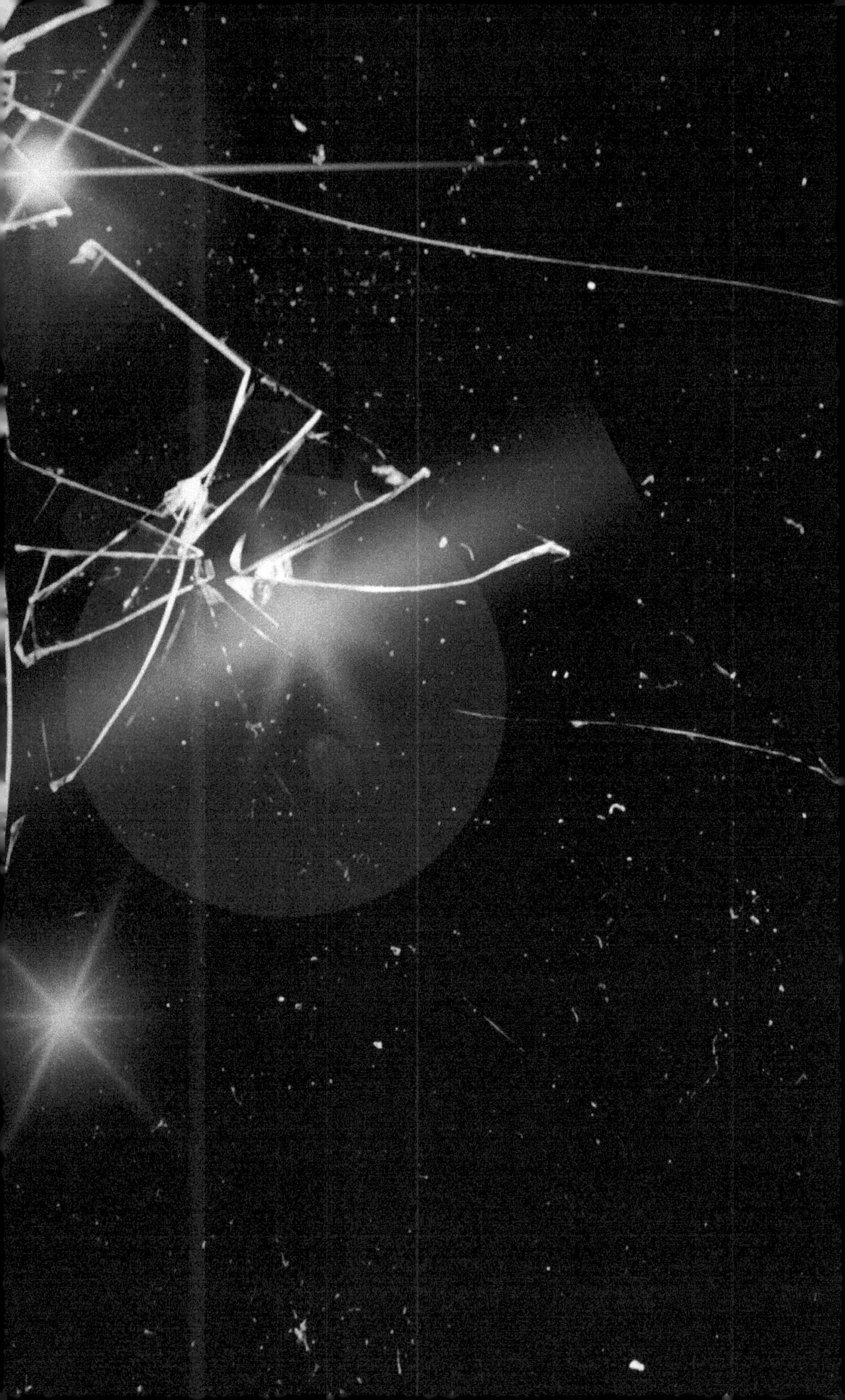

CHAPTER THIRTY-THREE

THE DOCTORS MANAGE to keep the cops away from me for two days, insisting I need to recover before they're allowed to talk to me.

My right eye is fucked.

The doctors do test after test with lights of different colors, and I can't see any of them, just a dull haze, like a lighthouse through the fog. They keep saying it could still improve. They keep telling me not to lose hope.

I don't even care about my eye. Because the news coming back from the ICU is that Dylan is improving. There were 6 awful hours last night when his patched-up lung collapsed and he was rushed back to surgery. Stella shivered beside me that whole time, sleeping fitfully while we waited for news.

But he made it. Dylan made it back to us. He held on. They took him back to the ICU and said he was improving rapidly. Stella was allowed to go and sit with him for a while.

I'm still under guard in the hospital room.

And now, the doctors can't keep the cops away anymore.

"I'm not leaving," Stella says as the two detectives enter the room. "I'm here as his lawyer."

Detective Hawkins nods, and pulls up a chair beside my bed. "How are you feeling, Mr Fenton?"

"Like I got shot in the head."

Hawkins suppresses a smirk and shakes her head. "Glad to see you're still with us."

"Thanks."

"He's not making a statement right now," Stella interjects. "You can ask what you want, but I've advised my client to say nothing."

"Understood." Hawkins casts a glance over her shoulder at her partner, who's leaning against the window behind her, arms crossed over his chest, then turns back to me. "Now, your lawyer is correct, you don't have to answer anything today. But I did want to let you know what happened in your family home."

Here we fucking go.

Hawkins takes a deep breath, clutching her hands in her lap. "It would appear Michael Gray had been planning this attack for some time."

I stare at her for a beat, before blinking and shaking my head. "He'd… I'm sorry, *what*?"

"I know it's a shock," Hawkins says, giving me a sad smile. "Your grandfather trusted him, I know he went in to vouch for Gray when he was court-martialed. I'm very sorry for your loss, Mr Fenton."

"I don't.. I mean, I'm sorry-" I break off, putting a hand to my head that's started to throb.

"My client is still recovering," Stella says, her tone tight and professional. "I'd appreciate you not overloading him right now."

"I'm very sorry, Miss Langford, I don't mean to cause any distress."

"What do you mean he was planning it?" My brain is jumping through hoops trying to figure out what the detective is telling me. The shock at not being cuffed to the bed and being read my rights has thrown me so violently, all I can do is sputter and stare at the detective who's regarding me with sympathy and understanding.

"We found some very complex documents on Gray's computer, detailing the blueprints of the house, location pins, extensive files on you and your family." Hawkins sighs, and raises her hands. "It had been planned for a long time. I can't give you too many details right now, but I did want you to know that we'll do everything we can to investigate, and to give you closure over the deaths of your mother and your grandfather." She leans forward, putting a hand on the bed and smiling at Stella and I in turn. "Anything you need, you let us know. You have my number."

My face no doubt betrays a suitable amount of shock, because the detectives leave the room without another word. I stare at the door, several beats passing before I turn back to look at Stella.

"They think it was him," I breathe, and she nods, her own eyes wide with shock.

"It was." She says it quickly, gripping my hand. "It was him. He did it all. He planned it. Right? That's what the detective said. It was Michael Gray."

I nod slowly. "Yeah. It was him."

"You were there having dinner, and you tried to save everyone. But he got you." Stella nods slowly. "But you don't have to say anything more. That's all. Because you don't remember it all. He shot you, and your memory is foggy. You don't remember. That's all you need to say."

My devious, pretty girl has it all planned out, while my stupid ass is still trying to piece together how this happened. But maybe it doesn't matter. Maybe this is a miracle. Maybe this one time, God was listening.

"Hey, pretty boy."

Dylan smiles weakly at me, curling his fingers around mine. "Hey, *guapo*. What took you so long?"

I laugh softly, shaking my head. "You were the one who was down here sleeping the whole time, lazy ass."

"*Pierdol sie,*" he murmurs with a laugh. *Fuck you.*

"I understood that." I lean over and brush a kiss against his cheek, still terrified any touch will hurt him. "I love it when you talk dirty to me."

"I'll keep that in mind." He turns his head slightly, gazing up at me with his big dark eyes, and winces a little as he looks at the patch over my right eye. "Is it bad?"

I shake my head. "No, they just want to keep it covered for now, hoping I get some vision back."

"I'm so sorry."

"Hey now, absolutely not." I lean my forehead against his, and bite back tears that threaten to spill over at any second. "I was so fucking scared you weren't going to make it. I'm just… I'm so happy you're alive."

"I'm here, *guapo.* I'm here. God doesn't fucking want me, lucky you do, huh?" He nudges my cheek with his nose, the plastic tubing hissing as it funnels air into his body. "I'm not going anywhere." He sighs heavily. "Except maybe prison."

"They know about Michael Gray," I say quickly, pulling back and clutching on to his hand, praying he can read my meaning. "They said they found the plans on his computer. He'd been planning it the whole time, killing the family. We just got in the way."

Dylan blinks slowly, absorbing one word at a time, the monitor beside him beating rhythmically in time with his heart rate.

"He did, huh?"

I nod. "He did."

"Dirty son of a bitch," Dylan says, scoffing lightly. "Good thing the cops found all that on his computer."

"Absolutely." The way he says it makes me think he knows something I don't, but now is not the time.

"Hey, *papi*." The sweet voice sounds behind me, and Dylan's eyes light up.

"*Guera*," he breathes, watching as Stella moves around the bed to his other side. "You're here."

"Of course I am." She sits beside him and reaches out to take his hand. "Doctors gave me the all-clear, I can go home."

"That's fantastic!" Dylan smiles widely at her. "And you're alright, really?"

"Yeah, I am. He did say no vigorous sex for six weeks, but I think we'll be able to hold off, huh?" She leans over and plants a soft kiss on Dylan's lips. "Have to wait for you two knuckleheads to get out of here anyway."

Dylan huffs out a laugh, then winces as he sucks in a sharp breath.

"Easy now," I say, getting to my feet and stroking his forehead. "Does it hurt? Do you need anything?"

"No, I'm fine." He exhales through gritted teeth, and gives me a strained smile. "I promise, I'm fine. It just aches."

"I'm not surprised, considering they had to reconstruct your whole lung," Stella says with a shake of her head. She looks over at me, and bites her lip, collapsing down into her chair and putting a hand to her mouth. "I'm sorry, I-" She breaks off and covers her face with her hands, and her shoulders start to shake.

Dylan looks at me with helpless alarm, before I scramble to my feet and round the bed to put my arm around Stella's shoulders.

"Hey, baby girl, come on, it's over. It's over now."

"I was so scared." She sobs into her hands. "I was so scared that I was going to lose both of you." Her hands drop from her face, and she scowls up at me. "Don't you ever do that again. When you say it's over, you better fucking mean it."

My eyes flash to Dylan's, before I smile down at Stella and cup her jaw gently with my hand. "I mean it, baby girl. It's all over now."

I should let this go. I know I should. But the words Gloria

scrawled in that fucking ledger won't let me go. Reading what those men did to Stella, their sick requests... I don't know if I can let it all be over.

The police have that ledger for now. And I hate myself that I can't promise Stella with my entire heart and soul that it's truly over. Because if I ever find a way to get my fucking hands on that list, I don't think I can let it be over.

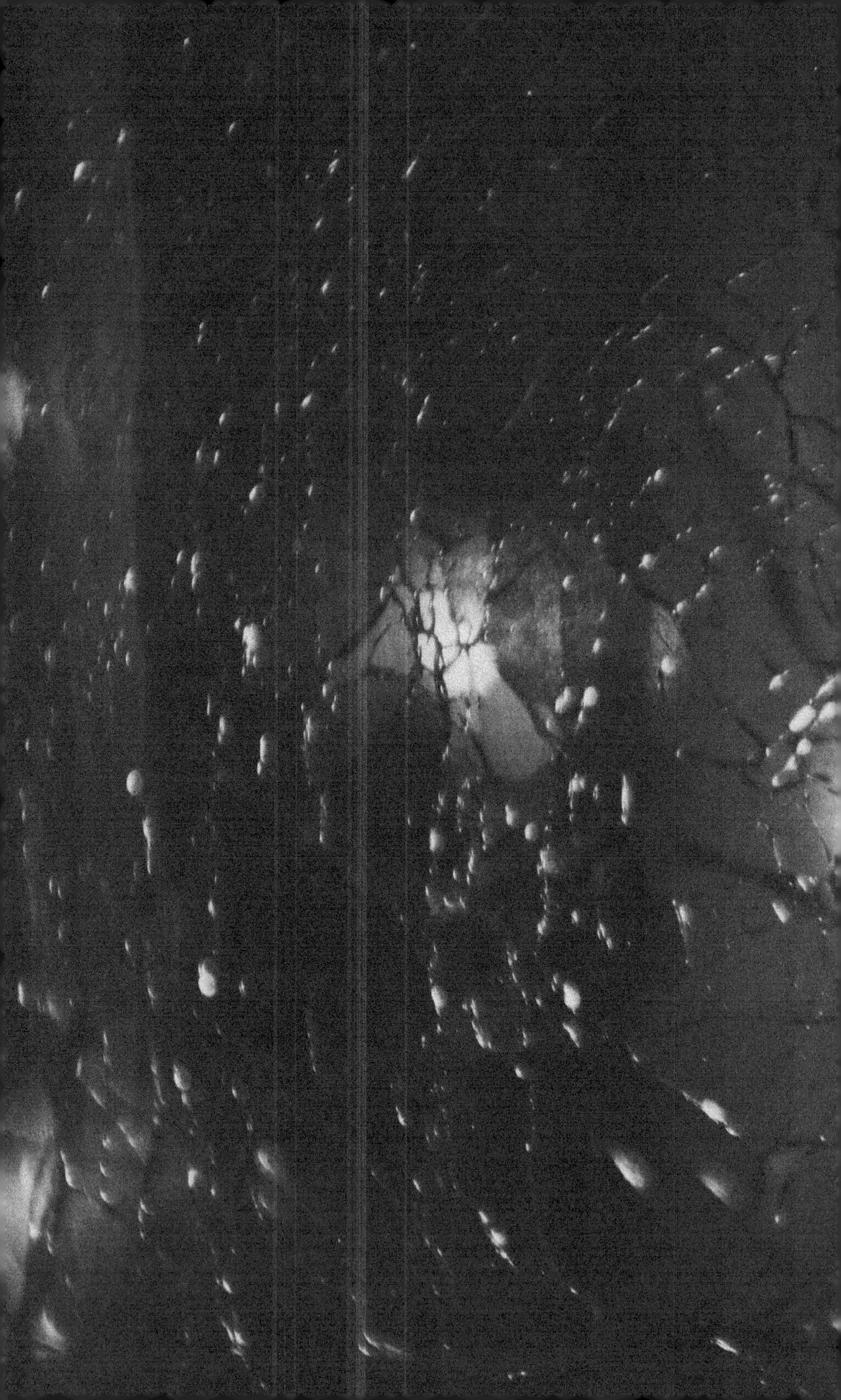

STELLA

CHAPTER THIRTY-FOUR

A COOL BREEZE blows through the golden leaves as I walk the path down the side of the modest white house. Six steps lead down to a door with a giant biohazard sign on it, and I knock three times. I wait for a moment, hearing movement inside, which then stops. After 30 seconds or so, the door remains closed, so I knock again, louder this time.

"I'm not here!" The man's voice is tight with irritation.

"Well, maybe you can be here for just a minute, this won't take long!"

There's shuffling, and suddenly the door flies open to reveal a skinny young man with scruffy dark hair, lip rings, and a thick spider tattoo around his neck. He gazes at me curiously with his dark brown eyes, tonguing one of the lip rings before his mouth lifts in a smile.

"I'd say I'm happy a pretty girl finally made it down here, but I don't think you're here for me, are you?"

I shrug, lightly. "Sorry, Flea, not today."

"Damn." He steps to the side and gestures into his apartment. "Would the lady like to come in? Excuse the mess, I wasn't expecting company. Though I am impressed you managed to find me."

"Hmm, I have my ways."

I step over the threshold, into a dimly lit room. It's hardly messy, everything neatly lined and orderly, the only sign of any mess is some diet coke cans lined up on the window sill beside the desk. The desk that holds three enormous computer screens, where lines of code flip wildly and location pins move on maps.

"I hope I haven't interrupted, you seem busy," I say as I turn to face Flea, who closes the apartment door and leans back against it.

"It's fine. For you, I'll make time."

"Well, thanks." I sigh, shifting on my feet. "It's sort of strange, you know so much about me and I know nothing about you."

"That's kind of the point of a hacker," Flea replies with a crooked grin. "Don't worry, your secrets are safe with me."

"That's kind of what I'm banking on."

Flea lifts an eyebrow and folds his arms over his chest. "Oh yeah?"

"Have you been watching the news? Kept up with the case?"

"Your case?" His face remains neutral, and his shoulders jerk in a little shrug. "I guess so. A few details keep filtering through."

"And are there any details you think are missing?"

Flea's poker face is award-worthy. His expression doesn't shift an inch. He simply gazes at me, the corners of his mouth turning down for a split second before another nonchalant shrug twitches at his skinny shoulders.

"I have no idea. You tell me."

"In the seizure of Levi's family property, the police recovered a diary, with appointments in it." I look out the window at the late afternoon sunshine, illuminating the slowly changing leaves. "Those appointments pertain to some abuse I was forced to endure."

"Well, you're right, that hasn't been mentioned at all."

I look back at him with a bitter smile. "That's right. But you and I both know they have it." I take a step closer to him, hugging my arms around my waist. "You've seen it, right?"

Flea scoffs. "What makes you think I've seen it?"

"My stepmother wasn't stupid. She would have never kept only a physical copy of that book. She had those details elsewhere, and since you've most certainly hacked every bit of technology this family possesses, I know you've seen it."

I keep my eyes locked on him, as though I can draw the truth out of him if I just look at him long enough. But it doesn't even take that long. Flea's shoulders slump, his hands falling from his chest to be tucked into the pockets of his ripped jeans, his gaze dropping from mine as he sighs.

"I'm so sorry," he murmurs, shaking his head. "I'm so fucking sorry that all happened to you. It's was so… so wrong."

"Thank you. It was." I take another step towards him, dipping my head a little to try and meet his eyes. "I need that list, Flea."

His head lifts and he gives me a side glance. "What are you going to do with it?"

"What I should have done years ago, but I was always too scared to do." I shrug and shake my head. "I know that Dylan and Levi won't let this go, and I think you knew that, too. Which is why you never handed that list over, right?"

Now I have surprised him, and the poker face is gone. His eyebrows shoot up, underneath the tousle of dark hair covering his forehead.

"I just… I didn't want…" He breaks off, lifting a hand to rub the back of his neck.

"You didn't want Dylan getting hurt." I finish for him, and give him a warm smile. "And you knew he would, if he went after all those powerful men. That's why you framed Michael Gray, for what happened at the house that night."

"Hey, now…" Flea pushes off the door, putting one hand on his hip and gesturing to the air with the other. "I mean, I'm not admitting anything, and you're a lawyer you know-"

"I'm not here to get you in trouble, Flea, that's the last thing I want."

He puffs out a heavy breath. "Dylan's, you know, he's alright. I was a kid in prison, I was barely 18. He looked after me, you know? I mean, look at me." He gestures to his lithe torso, and hacks out a laugh. "I was an easy target, but he made sure no one bothered me. He's a good man." Flea's voice is heavy with admiration. "And good men make mistakes. I didn't want him to make another one."

"So you kept that list to yourself, huh?"

"I guess so." He tucks his hands back in his pockets, nodding his head slowly. "I don't feel right keeping it from you, and I think you're tired of all of this. If you really want to end it, do this the right way, then I'll give it to you."

"That's exactly what I intend to do."

"Good." Flea moves to his bed, crouching down to pull out what looks like a military footlocker. He spins the dial on the padlock until it flips open, then reaches into the brown metal box. He withdraws a CD and a thumb drive, getting to his feet to hand them both to me.

"Don't laugh," he says as he waves the CD in my face. "These might be outdated technology but I like to be careful and back things up every way I can."

I hold my hands up with a smile. "No laughing here, promise. I appreciate this." I take the thumb drive and the CD from him. "I just want this all to be over."

Flea sighs heavily, and squints at me. "You think it will be? I mean, if you name these men, don't you think it'll make things worse for you?"

"You know, I don't know." I put the items in my purse and turn back to face him. "But I'm done living my life like this. These men deserve to be punished, and if the police won't do it, I'll force their hand."

"Good for you." Flea nods, crossing his arms back across his chest. "I… I really am sorry all that happened to you. You seem nice, and you have good taste in books. I'm glad you're, you know, you're OK."

"Thanks, Flea. I am." I want to reach out and touch his arm, to maybe hug him, but I don't think that kind of contact would be welcomed. It feels so hollow to just say thank you, but it's all I can offer him. I fish my card out of my purse, and hand it to him. "If you ever need anything, call me."

"Like, legal advice?" He asks cynically.

I can't help but laugh. "Well, I hope you never need that again, but if you do, sure. But anything else - a place to stay, a job, maybe a date with a pretty girl?"

He eyes me with a smirk. "Oh yeah?"

"Sure. I know people."

Flea laughs softly, rolling his shoulders. "Thanks, I'll keep that in mind."

"You do that. Take care, Flea." I give him one last warm smile, before I head out of his basement apartment and into the Fall sunshine. Back in my car, I take out my phone, pulling up the number and knowing it will be answered quickly.

"Stella?" Mallory's voice is bright down the line. "How's everything going?"

"Everything's great, thanks."

"Do you have the list?"

I swallow hard, putting my hand on my purse. "Yes, I do."

"Good, that's good."

"Mallory, I'm not going to lie. I'm a little scared."

"That's totally normal," she replies, and I can practically hear her smiling down the phone. "I am so proud of you. And you're doing the right thing. I'll see you soon?"

"Yeah. I'm on my way."

We hang up, and I dial Dylan's number.

"Hey, *guera*," he drawls down the line. "Where are you?"

"I have a meeting. I just wanted you to know I'll be home late."

"No problem, we'll be here."

"Good." I stay on the line, not saying anything, just staring at my purse.

"Stella?" Dylan's voice is warm in my ear. "Is something wrong?"

"No, no. Everything's great. I promise. I'll explain when I get home."

"OK." He doesn't sound too certain, but doesn't press me for more details. "I love you."

"I love you, too. Give Levi a kiss for me."

"I can do that."

"Bye." I hang up before he can respond, and start my car. The engine hums, and I stare out the windshield. *This ends now. Under my terms.*

The studio lights are brighter than I was expecting. My leg bounces against the soft velvet of the armchair, my fingers ticking restlessly in my lap. I don't want to break out in sweat and look nervous on camera, so I take a few deep breaths.

You can do this. It's going to be fine.

Mallory is talking to some colleagues, the final touches being applied to her makeup. She flips through a folder, nodding as the man beside her points to several pages. She closes the folder and waves off the makeup person, before striding across the studio to me.

She sits down in the armchair opposite, and says something quickly to the cameraman, something I don't catch, because blood is roaring in my ears. When her gaze lands on me, her expression softens, and she reaches across to pat my knee.

"You're doing great, Stella."

"I feel like I'm going to throw up."

She smiles and shakes her head. "You won't. You're safe here, it's just us."

I suck in a breath and nod. "Just us. Yeah."

"Ready?"

I nod again, clutching my hands together to stop them shaking. Mallory turns to gesture to a cameraman, and panic wells in my stomach.

"Mallory?" My voice wavers, and she turns back to face me instantly. "What if they don't believe me?"

Mallory tilts her head, her eyes filled with compassion. She extends a hand to lay on top of mine. "They will. I believe you. Everyone here believes you. They will, too."

I nod slowly, and puff out a breath. "Then let's do it."

Mallory settles back in her armchair, and dips her head to the cameraman. "Ready when you are."

"Rolling," he replies, and the studio falls completely silent.

Mallory's gaze lands on me. "Just for the camera, I'd like you to say who you are, and why you're here."

I blink under the harsh lights, focusing on Mallory's eyes. "My name," I start slowly, "is Stella Langford. I'm the daughter of Harold Langford. I'm here because for years, my father sold me to powerful men for his own gain. And I want those men brought to justice."

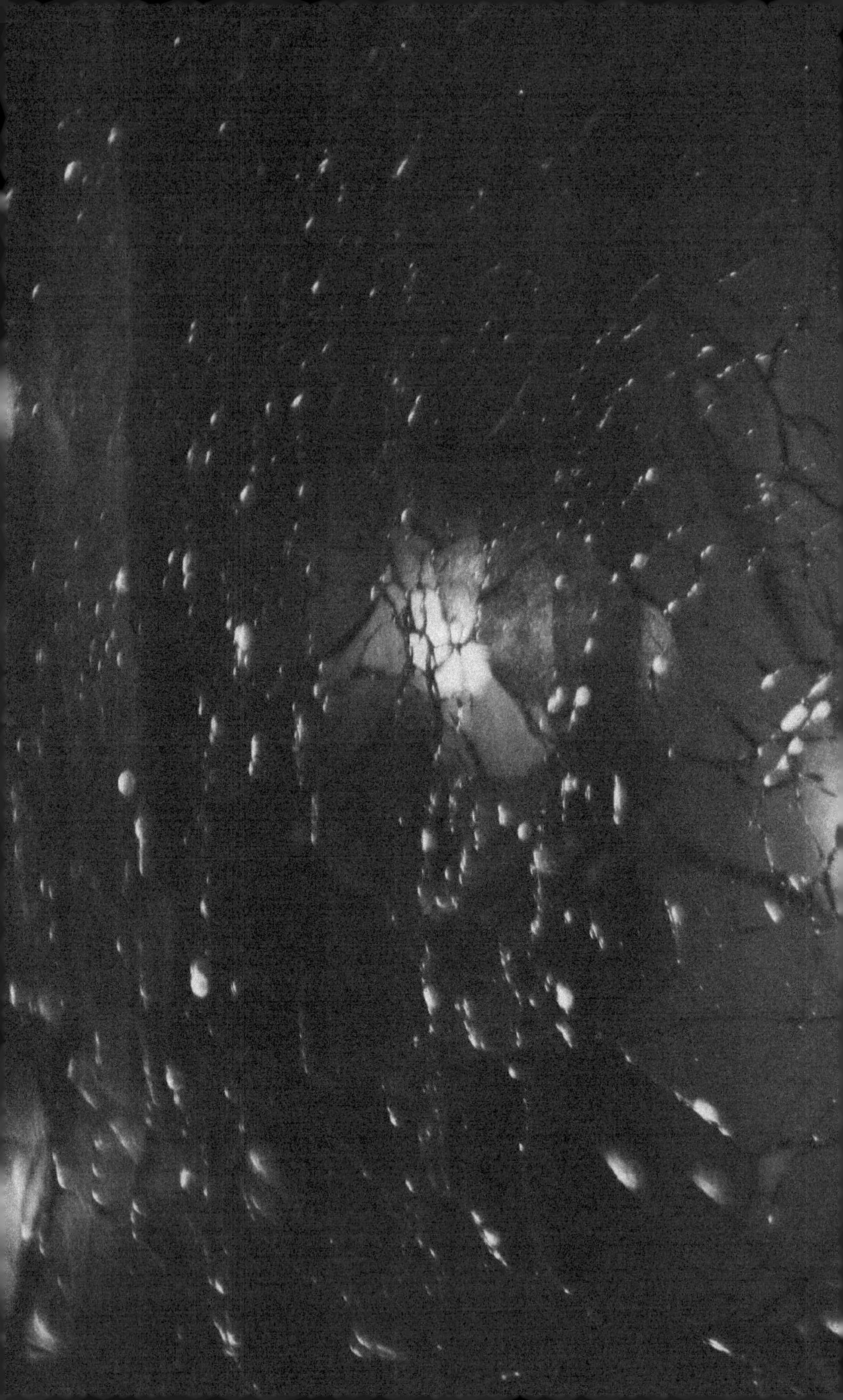

STELLA

CHAPTER THIRTY-FIVE

"THE MOVING truck will be here in half an hour!" Levi calls from downstairs, and Dylan groans.

"Finally!" He carries the last box from my bedroom out onto the landing, dusting his hands once he's set it down. "They're late."

"We could have given someone the keys and had this all done for us, you know." I tease him, wrapping my arms around his neck and smiling.

"I have trust issues," he replies with a grin. "Besides, once it's on the truck, we get a whole week in a hotel in Boston, to fuck." He kisses my jaw. "To explore." He nibbles on my earlobe, making me shiver. "And to maybe fuck some more."

"Well, it is snowing there right now, guess it makes sense to stay indoors and keep warm, right?"

Dylan growls against my throat, his hands running down my back. "Yes, it does."

"Zee's here!" Levi calls, and I pull back from Dylan with a grin.

"Come on, you can keep devouring me in the hotel tonight."

"Why wait?" He asks, his eyes dropping to my mouth. "You never had sex on a plane before?"

I grunt out a laugh and swat at this chest. "Yeah sure, big

guy, like you could even fit into one of those plane bathrooms." I grab his hand and drag him down the stairs, to find Levi and Zee standing outside on the front porch.

"Hey girl!" Zee throws their arms around me, hugging me tightly. "You all good to go?"

"Sure am," I reply, wrapping my arms around myself and leaning my head against Levi's shoulder. "You?"

"Almost, truck's coming tomorrow."

"I can't believe you're moving to Boston, too," Dylan says, leaning against the door frame.

"I know, right." Zee sighs, gazing at us all contentedly. "Look at us, who would have thought we'd all finally leave Bellford?"

"Yeah, crazy thought." Levi kisses the top of my head. "I think it's about time, though."

"And everything else, that's been OK?" Zee asks gently.

I sigh heavily and shrug, shuffling my foot against the wooden planks of the porch. "Well, it's been a little wild, I guess. One of the supreme court judges, he, uh, well you probably heard they found him hanging in his garage."

Levi tenses beside me, and Dylan moves to my other side to take my hand.

"I did hear about that last night." Zee shifts on their feet. "Sorry, I shouldn't have brought it up."

"No, it's alright. It's happening, right?" I puff out a breath and squeeze Dylan's hand.

"Are they going to make you fly back for the court case?"

I shake my head and meet Zee's eyes with a smile. "No, they said due to the nature of the crimes, I don't need to appear. I submit my victim impact statements and that's it. No more."

"Good, that's good." Zee exhales heavily, and returns my smile. "I heard Lily and Jared got engaged."

Dylan laughs cynically. "Match made in heaven there." He and Levi grin at each other over my head. "Can't wait for that wedding."

"I doubt we'll be invited," I tell him, swatting them both in the stomach. "It's not like they talk to me anymore anyway." The mood becomes heavy again, because we all know my family stopped talking to me only because my mother died just before Christmas. Now that connection is gone, I'm not a part of it anymore. I'm not a part of anything anymore. "It's fine, I don't care anyway."

Everyone is silent, unsure of what to say, and mercifully at that moment, the truck pulls up and Zee remembers they'd brought us all coffee. We sit on the porch together, watching the movers pack our lives up in the big blue and white truck, and reminisce on the times we had in this town.

It wasn't all bad, I guess. Good things happened here, too. But my mom's death was the final straw, coming in amongst all the TV reports and interviews, since my interview with Mallory aired five months ago.

Dylan and Levi were furious when it happened. Not with me, but with themselves, I think. They slunk around, guilty and raging, for weeks, jumping at every shadow, convinced someone was going to leap out of the darkness and take me from them.

It's not like the thought didn't cross my mind, too. Too many times, I'd check my rear view mirror, convinced the car behind me had been following me for too long. I had trouble sleeping some nights. I was afraid of showering when the house was empty, because I wouldn't hear anyone approaching. And then awful self-doubt began to take over, making me wonder if maybe I'd made a mistake.

But then the letters started pouring in. Endless letters, bags of them, filled channel four's studio. One victim after another, coming forward, some of them now well into their 40s or 50s. Detailing the abuse the men who'd abused me, who'd been powerful and connected enough not to be afraid, had subjected them to.

All my fears of not being believed, my self-doubt, dissipated. I'd finally spoken out, and had given these other people the strength to speak out, too. The uproar was huge. Senators had to resign, judges stepped back. Some denied it all, and were ridiculed on social media. Others, like the Supreme Court judge, took themselves out, consumed by guilt or the fear of consequences.

Mallory was relentless, hunting down every lead and confirming stories, working tirelessly to do exactly what she had promised to do - give the victims a voice.

Finally, my fears gave way to something else. Pride.

My mother had tearfully begged me for forgiveness, admitting she'd known everything. When I didn't give it to her, she drank herself into a coma, and her heart gave out. I'd felt a terrible combination of relief and guilt, and Christmas was a hard time.

But Dylan and Levi were there for me every step of the way, loving me and talking me through it all, unwavering in their support. They told me constantly how strong I was, how brave, and how proud they were of me.

And then, right after Christmas, I surprised them by buying a house in Boston, a gorgeous old place in Beacon Hill. I was done with Bellford Heights. I was ready for a fresh start, and they were, too.

They signed the garage over to Eric, rewarding him for his testimony against Michael Gray. The police had discovered that Gray had broken into Eric's house and stolen one of his weapons to try and link the murders of Stanley Iverson and Craig Ellis to Dylan and Levi. Yet another part of his despicable plan.

The truth remained unspoken between us, and Dylan still had no idea that Flea (whose name was actually Bentley) had given me the list. It was one of those things that he just didn't need to know. Just another thing I wanted to leave buried here, in our hometown, and forget about.

"Hey." Dylan's voice and smiling face tear me from my thoughts, and he reaches over to stroke a finger under my chin. "You zoned out there for a second."

I smile and shrug, taking a sip of my latte. "I'm fine, just thinking about all the things to buy to fill that huge house with."

"It is huge," Levi says with a laugh, stretching his legs out in front of him. He meets my gaze and winks. "Our girl likes 'em big."

Zee bursts out laughing and throws a napkin at him. "Yeah OK, TMI, bitch!"

Levi's beautiful face is almost bursting from smiling, and I don't even see the scar anymore. It's angry and gnarled, stretching from under his eye, up his forehead and into his hairline. His right eye is lighter than his left now, his vision still poor, but it doesn't bother him, and it sure as fuck doesn't bother me and Dylan.

He's here, and he's alive, and he's beautiful.

I lean back against Dylan with a sigh as the last of the boxes get loaded into the truck.

"Well, that's the end of an era then, huh?"

Dylan kisses my temple, stroking his fingers down my arm. "Yeah, but the start of something even better, *guera*."

I gaze up at him, and he kisses the tip of my nose. I look over at Levi, who gives me a warm smile, and Zee, who is huddled up beside him and grinning like a fool at the three of us.

Yes, the start of something even better.

I am a part of something. I'm a part of this, right here.

And I couldn't ask for anything more.

EPILOGUE

THREE YEARS LATER

"I WANT TO TOUCH YOU," she breathes against my mouth, sucking in a breath as I tighten the scarf securing her hands to the headboard.

"Not now, *guera,*" I murmur, brushing my lips along her cheek, down to her jawline, drinking in that sweet vanilla scent. "Now, you're going to lie here, and you're going to watch." I grind my cock against her needy pussy, and she whimpers, squeezing her thighs together to try and keep me close. "You like to watch, don't you?"

"Y-yes." Her eyelashes flutter. "I do."

"What's your safe word?"

She opens her eyes and grins at me, snapping her teeth at my lip. "Martini."

"Good girl." I move down the bed to wrap another length of white silk around one ankle, tying her down completely, legs wide and fully on display for us. I step back to admire my handiwork, and Levi wraps his arms around my waist, nipping at my shoulder.

"You look so beautiful, baby girl," he says reverently. "But there's something missing."

"And what's that?" Stella asks in that sexy, bratty voice that makes my cock even harder. She licks her lips as Levi raises his hand to show a bright purple vibrator. She laughs lecherously, stretching her limbs and testing the strength of the scarves. "And how exactly am I going to use that when you have me all tied up, hmm?"

It's my turn to raise my hand, and I show her the remote. "Who said you'd be in control?"

Her eyes sparkle with devious delight. "Well, merry fucking Christmas to me."

Levi drips lube onto the tip of the vibe, and crawls over Stella on the bed, kissing her hips, her stomach, her breasts. When he kisses her mouth, and her lips open for him, he presses the vibe to her pussy, gently at first, teasing her entrance.

"Edging me already?" She murmurs, biting his lower lip.

With a hard thrust, Levi pushes it inside her, and her back arches off the bed.

"Brats get fucked," he says with a laugh, and Stella leans up into his face with a grin.

"You think this thing is fucking me? I take both of you at the same time, this is nothing compared to that." She bites his chin with a chuckle. "You need to try harder, baby."

"Fucking brat," Levi says with a shake of his head. He lowers his head and sucks one of her nipples hard, eliciting a pleasing little squeak from our girl, before climbing off her and moving back towards me. He looks me up and down with a grin, wrapping his hand around my cock, and pumping me gently. "Fuck, you look good, pretty boy."

"I'd look even better on my knees, don't you think?" I smile as his eyes flare with desire, and slowly sink down before him. "For now, you're in charge." I hand him the remote, turning him so we can both see Stella splayed out on the bed. Keeping my eyes on her, I slowly move my mouth down Levi's length. He groans softly, and there's a click. Stella's thighs flinch ever so slightly, her mouth dropping open a little.

"You like watching him suck my cock?" Levi asks her, and there's another click.

"Mmm, yes." She rolls her hips a little, trying to draw her knees together, but the scarves limit her movement. "I love watching you fuck his mouth."

I moan at her words, the sound vibrating around Levi's cock, and he hisses in a breath. His fingers rake over my head, and his hips jerk a little. I release him with a pop, grinning up at him.

"Don't get too excited, *guapo*." I lick his tip, and he shudders. "The night's just getting started."

I draw him back down my throat, inch by fucking glorious inch, until I'm almost gagging on him. His abs ripple as he breathes, his teeth gritted, and he clicks the remote again. Stella lets out a loud moan, and I look over to see her head fallen back, her breasts so mouthwateringly on display. Her thighs shake lightly, and Levi clicks the remote again.

She goes limp, panting on the bed, and looks over at us with hooded eyes.

"I hate being edged," she says with a very well-acted pout.

Levi chuckles, jerking his hips against my face. "Liar." He presses the remote several times, and Stella cries out. "You fucking love it."

"Shit, Levi, oh my god!" She arches and writhes, and the sight is almost enough to have me spilling down here on the floor.

Levi turns the vibe off again, leaving her gasping for air and shaking on the bed.

"Where are we, baby girl?" He asks in a low voice, and Stella laughs breathlessly, rolling her eyes.

"Jesus, fuck, Fenton, you worry too much," she chides, giving him a smile. "I'm just fine."

"Hmmm, that sounds like a challenge."

"Some challenge, this tiny little vibe." Her eyes slam shut, a loud moan leaving her lips as Levi turns the toy on all the way. "Oh *fuck*."

"Still tiny?" He runs a hand over my head as I continue to suck him slowly, running my tongue along his shaft.

Stella strains against the scarves, trying desperately to jerk her legs together. "F-fucking pathetic," she gasps, a strained laugh leaving her lips. But her body is betraying her, her brow furrowing as she bites her lip, the moans catching in her throat becoming more high-pitched.

With an almost cruel laugh, Levi turns the toy off, at the same time that I release his cock. He groans, reaching down to seize my chin between his fingers.

"Looks like we're both getting edged, baby girl."

I nip at his fingers, and look over at Stella. "Look at the mess she's made on the bed, *guapo*."

Levi follows my gaze and growls low in his chest. "Fuck, she's dripping."

"I thought I was meant to be *watching*," she says breathily, her lips lifting into a grin. "If I'm just going to be watching you two stand here, I want a refund."

I laugh, grabbing the back of Levi's neck and pulling him in to kiss me. His tongue strokes mine, his hands wandering over my body. I break the kiss and spin him around, forcing him down at the edge of the bed.

"You want to watch, *guera*?" I retrieve the bottle of lube from the floor, clicking it open and coating my hard cock. "You want to see me fuck your pretty boyfriend?"

"Yes." Her eyes are wide and wanting, biting her lip as she watches me coat Levi's ass in lube, and press the aching tip of my cock to his heated flesh.

I lean over him, kissing and licking at his mouth, and pluck the remote from his hand. I meet Stella's gaze as I press the first button, at the same time that I begin to ease myself into Levi. He gasps, tensing for just a second before he relaxes into me, a shuddering groan echoing in his throat.

Stella whimpers softly, her skin flushing sweet red.

"Feeling hot, baby girl?"

She nods. "So hot."

"You need to come?" I flick the vibe up to the next setting, and she coughs out a gasp. I roll my hips against Levi, whose body is gripping me so hard, I need to take it slow, or I'm going to spill inside him immediately.

Stella shakes her head, her eyes locked on us. "No, I want - Oh *fuck* - I want to watch you two first."

I wrap my hand around Levi's throat and pull his body up against mine. He whimpers, his neck shifting under my grip. "You hear that, *guapo*?" I breathe against his ear. "Your pretty baby girl wants to watch you get fucked." I rock against him, and he moans. "You like that, huh? You like having this tight little hole fucked while she watches?" I stroke his cock with my other hand, and his fingers dig into the sheets hanging off the edge of the bed.

"Fuck, yes." He turns his head to kiss me, breath pounding in his chest.

"You're not allowed to come, though," I tell him, and he tenses as I keep stroking him. "You're going to come inside our girl, when she can't take anymore, understand?"

Levi nods, his back arching, and fuck that just has me buried even deeper inside him. I want to fuck him hard, see my cum lash his back and feel that sweet release, but I continue to take my time, stroking him and Stella both to sweet frustration. Levi's hands are almost shredding the sheets by the time Stella cries out, no more sassiness or brattiness, just pure need.

"Fuck, Dylan, please, oh my god. *Please,* I can't take it anymore." She's almost sobbing, her mouth torn open as moan after moan pours from her lips, her legs straining hard against the silk scarves.

Her desperation unlocks something inside me, and I pull out of Levi, pressing my throbbing cock to his back. My release spills and spills out of me, dripping and running down his skin as I pant against his neck.

"Go and fuck her til she's screaming," I command, biting his earlobe.

Levi charges onto the mattress, shaking with his own need

now, and kneels between Stella's thighs. He lifts her hips, withdrawing the vibe from her pussy and replacing it with his cock. She cries out as he punches his hips into her, his head falling back as he fucks her hard, fingertips digging into her thighs.

She gasps his name, her back bowing and lifting her from the bed, and I crawl up the bed beside her. She turns to look at me, her mouth trembling. Her pleas are incoherent now, and her eyes roll back in her head as her orgasm starts to course through her. Her arms pull the scarves so taut that she's lifted off the bed, suspending between the headboard and Levi's hips, crying out and cursing.

Levi's thrusts are punishing, and as Stella screams out his name, he collapses onto his hands, jerking his hips before tensing. He moans loudly as he releases inside her, leaning his head against her chest as he shudders.

Stella collapses against her bindings, utterly spent. Levi slumps over her, kissing her collarbone and her throat.

"Fuck, you're perfect," he murmurs, and she smiles, her hair sticking to the sweat that's beaded on her face. "You're so fucking perfect for us."

Levi rises off her to allow me to untie her, and I gently rub her wrists and ankles. She doesn't even seem to mind the redness, just watching me with a satisfied smirk.

"You better do that to me too," she says, and I shake my head.

"You're insatiable, you know that?"

Levi laughs and heads into the bathroom, turning on the shower. "You only just figured that out?"

I scoop Stella off the bed, and she wraps her arms around my neck, head falling against my chest.

"I love you, *papi*."

I kiss the top of her head, carrying her into the bathroom. "I love you, too."

We spend way too long in the shower, until the whole room

is steamy and we're all panting and exhausted yet again. This really has to be heaven. This life is perfection.

Finally, we stop fucking and lie down in our enormous bed together, Stella and Levi either side of me. They eye each other with open excitement, then look at me.

"What?" I ask them both, looking back and forth between them. "What is going on with you two?"

"We have one last present for you." Levi kisses my cheek softly. "Something we wanted to wait until today to give you."

"Why?"

"Because today is your dad's birthday." Stella smiles widely at me.

"My *dad*?" I cover my face with my hands. "Jesus, you two, what a time to bring up my father."

When I drop my hands, they're both holding a piece of paper each. They hand them to me at the same time, practically giddy with excitement, kneeling in front of me.

I eye them with confusion, and take them both, unfolding Levi's first.

It's an official letter from the state of Massachusetts, complete with a fancy signature and a stamp at the bottom.

A legal name change.

Previous Legal Name: Levi Oswald Fenton
Current Legal Name: Levi Kovac

I blink at the paper, then unfold Stella's.

Previous Legal Name: Stella Marie Langford
New Legal Name: Stella Marie Kovac

• • •

My mind whirs, trying to absorb it all.

"You-you changed your names?" I look at them both, then back down at the papers. "You both changed your names? To my name?"

"We agreed that we wouldn't get married, because, well, obviously." Stella shrugs, and reaches out to take my hand. "But we want to belong together, to each other. And this way, well…"

"We're yours, pretty boy." Levi's mouth twitches into a grin. "Yours, forever."

I blink back down at the papers. "Mine. You're… mine. My family."

"Yes, we are." Stella shuffles next to me, snuggling under my arm and stroking my jaw with her fingertips. "For always, *papi*."

"Why me?" I ask incredulously. "Why my name?"

Levi leans in to press a kiss to my shoulder. "Because he was a good father, and he loved you. He wanted you to be happy."

"So, this is like our birthday present to him." Stella smiles up at me. "The family he always wanted his son to have."

I press a hand to my eyes as they start to sting. "God fucking dammit, you two."

"We're not even sorry." Levi moves beside me and lets my head fall against his shoulder, brushing his fingers over my head. "This is how it was meant to be. Always."

I lean into him, trying not to cry but feeling so fucking happy I could burst. Stella's arms wrap around my waist and she sighs contentedly. I let them wrap me up and hold me, and yes, this is how it was meant to be, always.

I found them, Dad. Just like you always told me to. I found them, and I'll always be happy. Just like you said.

ACKNOWLEDGMENTS

The road to this book was a wild one, and it would not have been possible without the love and input of so many wonderful people.

Mark, my amazing husband, without you none of this would be possible. My biggest cheerleader, forever and always. I love you.

My Mum, who herds babies and cooks dinners and is always celebrating my wins - you told me when I was 7 years old that you'd shout it from the rooftops when I was a bestselling author. And now look where we are.

My children, who believe in me and cheer me on every day. I am so blessed to be your mum.

Deana, my wonderful PA who picks me up whenever my imposter syndrome kicks in - I could not imagine having a better person by my side. You're amazing.

Allie Shante, my author bestie, I love you bby. You're the best.

Alla and Marty, the art you have created for this book is phenomenal. Thank you!

My wonderful Street Team, who hype and shout and spread the word every which way they can. I am so lucky to have this amazing group in my life, and I am grateful for you all.

My ARC readers - thank you for your time, your passion and your dedication.

Makenna, for once again taking my ramblings and making a blurb out of them. You're an angel.

And of course, you, dear reader. Without you, none of this is possible. You are truly making my dreams come true.

Thank you

Thank you

Thank you

ABOUT THE AUTHOR

RD Baker blames her love of all things dark and twisted on too much unsupervised reading in the 90s, and VC Andrews. She lives in the Blue Mountains, Australia, on Darug/Gundungurra Land, with her family.

Want to stay up to date? Head to rdbakerwrites.com to sign up for RD's newsletter!

www.ingramcontent.com/pod-product-compliance
Lightning Source LLC
Chambersburg PA
CBHW070551310726
48982CB00011B/1538/J

* 9 7 8 0 9 7 5 6 6 1 0 8 6 *